The Almost Forgotten Wife

by Gus Leodas

ISBN: 1494935945

ISBN 13: 9781494935948

Library of Congress Control Number: 2014900430

CreateSpace Independent Publishing Platform

North Charleston, South Carolina

The Almost Forgotten Wife

by Gus Leodas *

Member of International Thriller Writers, Inc., and
Mystery Writers of America and
Directors Guild of America

Madge's husband and daughter share secrets that exclude her. Exempt from the family mystery she is an outcast, ignored, and treated as nothing more than a household item, a part of the furniture, and a houseplant thirsty for water.

Madge Kiley's daughter is on trial for killing her rapist in self-defense. Madge's husband is a United States senator. The daughter's truth will destroy the senator's career and send the daughter to prison. Her lawyer abandons her trial.

The daughter's new attorney asks Investigator Mitchell Pappas to help with a case filled with obsessive love and hate that surge the plot to its unexpected conclusion.

*Best Seller author

DEDICATION

To my fabulous teenage grandchildren Delanie, Melina, and Alexander.

My thanks to the Design Team at CreateSpace, an Amazon.
com company for designing the interior and exterior of
The Almost Forgotten Wife.

THE AWARD WINNING MITCHELL PAPPAS MYSTERY/THRILLERS AND OTHER NOVELS BY GUS LEODAS

*The Forgotten Mission

(A WWII cold case mystery) "…Leodas promises action, drama and mystery. It is there." New York Daily News "Riveting. Written from the heart. An extremely tender perspective from the author's point of view." – Delray Beach Book Club

Eighteen-year old Melissa confronts four German spies in 1942 on Long Island.

What was the deadly secret of Shuller's Land? The last crop on the Long Island farm was planted in 1942, the year the land died from the horror of that one long night.

Decades later, the abandoned weathered barn that leaned precariously from old age still waited for a strong wind to complete the collapse before someone discovered its horrible secret.

Investigator **Mitchell Pappas** finds artifacts on the farm belonging to WWII German spies. So begins his mission to unravel the mystery of the forgotten farm and the disappearance of the spies and the farmer's teenage daughter, Melissa.

*Unsafe Harbor

"A great book." – *Writers Digest*

Selected as **Book of the Year Awards / Finalist**.

First Sentence: **He stood over her grave as a wilted flower.**

"*Unsafe Harbor* revolves around a series of unexplained murders at an exclusive yacht club. As **Mitchell Pappas** proceeds through the maze of possibilities, he isn't sure which way to turn. The outcome of *Unsafe Harbor* is a shocker, and it's a testimony to Leodas' writing skills that the reader is held in suspense until the very end." – *The National Herald – Books Supplement*

*Huntress (a revenge mystery/thriller)

Ah, yes! As Lord Byron Wrote – Revenge is sweet especially to women.

**KIRKUS Review – "Leodas sets up his novel with an intriguing premise; the reader is unsure of why exactly Victoria and Warren were forced to flee their home, and the quest for that answer is what drives the narrative forward. Once Victoria makes her fateful decision at Warren's funeral, the novel morphs into one full of action and excitement."

First Sentence: **The dreaded day may have arrived ending their secret life.**

Police and investigative author **Mitchell Pappas** team up again to solve a baffling and elusive revenge thriller.

"…and if you wrong us, shall we not revenge?" Shakespeare, *Merchant of Venice*

One of many 5-Star Reviews: By Dr. Franklin Montalban – "Been an avid Gus Leodas reader for quite some time now and he's STILL yet to disappoint. *Huntress* **keeps you guessing from beginning to end** and I promise that once you pick it up, you will NOT be able to put it down. Do yourself a favor and read it…you deserve it. An excellent book, possibly g.b.o.a.t."

A Sorority of Angels
Selected as Book of the Year Awards / Finalist

Several determined and concerned women in influential positions at the United Nations unite to help solve hunger and poverty in their countries. What they encounter, what happens to each in the service of their country was unplanned. **Theme: Women overcoming adversity**.

**KIRKUS Review – *"A Sorority of Angels* brings together the unique stories of five women working as aides to influential diplomats. In a successful literary device, each woman is embroiled in a dangerous, violent scheme of personal revenge. These women are more than entitled to their retribution, and their actions add a layer of legitimacy and intrigue to their mission. The effect is immediate and dramatic. The interesting premise makes for an entertaining read with more than one unexpected turn".

The Letter from Magda (a mystery/thriller)
'My dearest Johanna,
I pray you never have to read this letter while your father and I are alive.'

So begins Magda's letter to her daughter urging her to change identity, and to run and hide.

KIRKUS Review – "Johanna Wagner and Michael Warner become the unwitting catalysts in a tense conspiracy launched long before they were born. Both are children of wealthy parents and oblivious to the dangerous secrets of their parents' pasts. These secrets are soon violently revealed, as is their link to each other. The tension builds steadily as Leodas gradually pulls the storylines together **in a chilling climax full of twists and turns."

One of many 5-Star Reviews: **"This is one of the best mysteries I have ever read.** It is hard to believe what all goes on but that is what kept me interested. I just can't imagine having the talent to write a story with so many twists and turns. I would definitely read more by Gus Leodas and might reread this someday."

*The Devil Walks Besides Her

First Sentence: **Deanna Layne, a Suffolk County legislator pregnant with twins, fled to Fire Island terrified of being murdered before becoming a mother.**

Deanna Layne needs to survive a killer in an environment sated with unusual alliances, lethal relationships, and solutions. Police and **Mitchell Pappas** come together again to try to save Deanna in a devious and perplexing mystery thriller filled with love and hate that also turns Mitchell into a primary target, forcing him to research for clues to save Deanna…and himself.

Some 5-star reviews: "Love his style of writing and his storytelling ability." Demchuck/Scene East

"A well written **intense mystery**. Gus Leodas has added another hit to his list of books, and like the others, he has a surprise for the ending. If you like mystery, you will enjoy it." FBI Joe

"Excellent book by Gus Leodas. Suspense, twists, and strong women. Had to force myself to put it down so I didn't finish it on the same day. The kind of book you don't want to end. Another great one by the master." Texas Reviewer

*The Almost Forgotten Wife

*The Award Winning Mitchell Pappas mystery/thrillers and Other Novels by Gus Leodas.

** KIRKUS REVIEW is a leading book industry company.

SEE SAMPLE CHAPTERS OF *UNSAFE HARBOR* **a Book of the Year Awards – Finalist** at the end of *The Almost Forgotten Wife.*

Take this deal or they'll kill you.
Attorney Todd Hancock fled his home and practice on Long Island to save his life, and knew New York State would disbar him for disappearing during a rape/murder trial.

His case turned distasteful and terrifying with new and private knowledge that his client, Nancy Kiley never acted in self-defense as claimed.

Todd flew alone on a Sunday to Antigua to receive three million tax-free dollars in a secret bank account from conspirators who needed him to disappear. Todd termed their deal 'hush money'. With that amount, he'd start a new life in a different profession in San Francisco where no one knew him. Todd never regretted leaving his law practice of eleven years on Long Island, New York since his annual income remained insufficient to maintain a successful lawyer's profile without a burdensome debt.

Olivia Greene, Todd Hancock's friend and lover, presented the ultimatum and millions. He trusted and believed her when she pleaded for him to leave. Recent events replayed as his American Airlines jet headed for St. Martins, a stop before Antigua. When he landed in Antigua and arrived at the St. James's Club Resort, his restlessness ended. Todd no longer feared for his life. He made the right decision to accept their money to enter his own witness protection program.

Olivia Greene planned to arrive on Wednesday when they would taxi through the rain forest to the main town of St. Johns to Antigua Overseas Bank for deposits and transfers. Until then, Todd planned to pass time at the resort's beach under a palm tree on the Caribbean side of the island and enjoy evening steel drum music by the main outdoor pool.

Todd, a firm five-foot-ten and a handsome thirty-six with brown trimmed hair and wide face with narrow lips looked forward to four honeymoon style days and nights with Olivia. Then they would part to assure mutual security.

On Wednesday, Todd hurried to the resort's entrance at one o'clock. By two o'clock Todd waited with pacing and impatience for Olivia, who was late. Todd also wanted to visit the bank before it closed at three o'clock. Then he'd have a full day with her tomorrow at the resort. Olivia arrived by taxi a few minutes before three-thirty. Todd changed to happy and smiled. He motioned for her to remain in the taxi, entered the taxi, and joined her as he placed a finger over his lips to signal silence. He directed the driver to their two bedroom private villa that overlooked Marmara Bay and the yacht marina. Olivia, owner of a successful travel agency, placed their reservation for two in his name – no need for her to register.

Olivia Greene wore a broad rim white hat to cover dark curled hair. Sunglasses hid blue eyes and highlighted full lips. At the airport, she told the cheerful driver her destination then never spoke to him. She ignored him when he talked.

The lovers embraced in the villa.

"I suffered until you arrived." Todd whispered. "I missed you more than I imagined."

"And I thought of you all the way here. Still unsettled about the arrangement?"

"No. I trust you."

Olivia kissed him and pointed to the private pool in their terrace, "How do you like this place? Isn't it fabulous?"

"Perfect now that you're here."

She kissed his lips and separated. "You always say the right thing. Since I'm late the bank can wait until tomorrow." Olivia talked over her shoulder as she crossed for the bedroom. "I'm travel weary and need a shower. The delay on St. Martins took forever, why I hate indirect flights."

Todd shrugged an approval. "Won't make a difference about the bank. No problem."

Todd waited with his document at a glass top rattan table. Walls held tropical and nautical paintings fronted by rattan furniture on terracotta tile.

Olivia returned wrapped in a white bathrobe knotted in front. "I feel like a new person. First, our important business." Holding her briefcase, she sat opposite him, opened the case, removed bearer bonds, and counted them. She spoke in a business tone.

"For you, bearer bond certificates for three million payable on demand. I opened an account for you on my recent trip here. Present the shares for deposit, sign a form, and you own the cash to wire anywhere. I also opened a corporation for you at Bank in Liechtenstein AG. Wire funds there or to a corporation under your authority in the Bahamas. You can buy and sell stock through these tax haven corporations without accounting to the IRS when you trade as a foreign corporation and other transactions. Too basic, Counselor?"

"No. The tax haven procedures confirm my belief that a high percentage of America's private wealth hides in overseas banks away from the IRS and federal and state inheritance taxes."

"Potential exposures depend on the tax haven: foreign government criminal litigation for insider stock trading and drug and terrorist money laundering. Those don't apply to you, and you're no dictator or government official who escaped with national funds. But Switzerland now cooperates with our IRS prompted by the Madoff pyramid scheme and why I never opened an account for you there." Olivia pushed the certificates across to him. "Congratulations, Mr. Todd Hancock exceptional attorney and lover. You made the right decision."

Todd gathered his bonds. "And congratulations to you, Ms. Olivia Greene the new owner of my condominium in Garden City." Todd pushed his document to her side. "Signed, sealed, and delivered and backdated as agreed. I left a blank for your name or corporation as purchaser. You never said what name you wanted." She read the document as he said, "And also includes the furniture and electronics."

"All your other personal and Kiley case details completed?"

"My financial matters are all settled and the computers erased. I have vanished from Long Island and was thorough as you instructed."

"Since you paid three hundred thousand dollars for the condo and I got you five, you did okay. Here's your check for the condo."

"Thank you, darling." He accepted and set it aside. "I like the way you do business."

"Your ex-condo is my commission for acting as a messenger and convincing you to lead a better life."

"And because your mysterious client threatened to kill me and I needed to protect you, another reason I accepted. Who is your client that you call Uncle Max, and why his interest in the Kiley case? Can you tell me now?"

Olivia waved her head. "My arrangement compares to your attorney client principle and there's no advantage for you to know. Call me after the new Kiley case ends. I'll tell you then."

"Let me cheat," he grinned. "Do I know Uncle Max, your mystery man?"

Olivia moved her right forefinger as a metronome and smiled. "You know I won't answer."

"I appreciate the principle but concerned about you. You *are* in dangerous waters. If not for you, I would've notified the police and requested protection."

"I'm in no danger and you are totally safe." She looked confident. "He keeps his word and the fee is terrific. Enjoy the money and move on. Shut the past and forget everybody in it except me. Never look back. A perfect opportunity to change your life."

Olivia stood, walked around to his side, untied her bathrobe, and straddled his lap.

"Todd, sweetheart, our separation is beyond painful for me. I want and need you until Sunday, every minute, every hour."

He pushed the bathrobe wider and embraced her bare back. "Visit for a week in San Francisco without anyone knowing. Please arrange that."

Olivia kissed him and pecked his face. "I plan to my love. I love you too much to lose you so suddenly."

"When will you come?"

"In about two weeks."

"That will ease my pain and hunger for you."

"Call me as soon as you settle in. By shifting my schedule, I may come sooner. I promise."

Later, they ordered room service supper with a bottle of red wine and champagne to celebrate their love and financial rewards. They decided to remain in the villa that night and spend part of tomorrow at the white sand beach after their important trip to the bank located on the Atlantic side of the island.

Todd Hancock had a three million tax-free day and $500,000 for his condominium; a day filled with romance on a tropical island with the beautiful Olivia Greene; a day where he slept after a glass of champagne.

He had a wonderful day, and the last day of his life.

MEADOWLARK COUNTRY CLUB. HUNTINGTON, LONG ISLAND.

"Todd Hancock, a member of this club, disappeared while defending the daughter of United States Senator Austin Kiley. The Senator is a longtime member here. Days later, Hancock died possibly murdered at the St. James's Club Resort in Antigua," Attorney Stanford Crane said to his guest bestseller investigative author Mitchell Pappas after sinking a 16-foot putt for a birdie on the seventh green.

"Nice putt," Mitchell said. "Odd he'd vacation at that time." Mitchell shook his head at his own poor performance after four putts at the same hole.

"It's irresponsible and strange indeed, Mitch. No one knows why."

"How possibly murdered?"

Mitchell, a six-footer with broad shoulders, a long nose, brown eyes, narrow chin, and full brown hair that turned to middle age gray near the ears, picked up the flag and placed the pole in its hole.

"Unknown at the time. Hancock lived alone in Nassau County. A Nassau County medical examiner reexamined the body when returned to the States. He determined the *possibility* of foul play that Hancock was murdered but lacks proof, a perplexing problem and uncommon."

"Unusual in today's pathology."

They headed for their blue and white golf cart.

"Forensic medicine is inexact science, unlike the television shows where all is solved. Hancock wasn't the only attorney on this case to disappear. A replacement attorney disappeared two weeks into the new trial. He also lived alone and no one knows where he traveled. Questions to answer: Why did both abandon her? Where is the second attorney Laurence Bates and is he alive?"

Mitchell inserted his putter in the golf bag before sitting in the cart.

"And, who and what drove her lawyers away, one to his death? What's the Senator's daughter's crime?"

Stanford placed his putter into a Ping golf bag, sat behind the wheel, and drove on the paved path to the next hole. "She was raped in her dormitory at State University at Stony Brook and killed her assailant in self-defense, stabbed him in the neck with scissors. The district attorney pressed charges due to no signs of violence, penetration, saliva, or semen. She claims breaking free before he could ejaculate."

"Sounds like a difficult defense. Was he a student?"

"No, he was her boyfriend, Eddie Hawkins four years older and the son of a major Long Island contractor. The added tragedy is that the Senator and contractor are old friends."

"What now, a new trial?"

"She's out on bail. Because of her father and multiple trials, the new judge felt confident she won't jump bail and disappear. They are starting over with a new attorney."

"Does that mean a long delay?"

"A few weeks and depends on the court calendar with priority to begin due to the postponements. This new attorney prepares his case."

"Good luck to that fool. If this was a Perry Mason mystery I'd call it 'The Case of the Disappearing Lawyers'."

They approached the eighth hole, a par four dogleg left and waited to tee off once a foursome ahead cleared the fairway.

"The third attorney is the Senator's friend. The Senator asked him first to take the case and begged him to defend his daughter in both instances, but presiding judges refused to release him from his obligations to other ongoing cases."

When the foursome approached the green, Stanford set his Ping ball on a white tee and swung a practice swing at an imaginary ball.

Mitchell shouldered his driver, something serious golfers never do. The case continued to intrigue Mitchell, who said, "You'd think no one would want the case. Who's this sacrificial legal lamb who thinks he won't disappear and windup dead somewhere?"

Stanford swung a second practice swing.

"The best and smartest attorney I know." His smile expressed confidence. "He is the only person skilled to win against all odds...me."

"You're insane."

The murder case conversation delayed for tee shots. With the foursome safe, Stanford set his stance and drove his ball 275 yards to the middle of the fairway, a clear seven iron shot to the green, a par four.

Stanford, forty-six, an athletic and attractive five-foot-nine with a picture perfect golf swing and with blond hair and blue eyes looked satisfied with his placement. Divorced for two years, his wife left complaining about his constant work schedule. Incompatibility served as the official term. She relocated to Washington, D.C. when hired by a public relations firm as a lobbyist. They remained friends with no alimony.

"Perfect shot, Stanford. You should turn pro."

"I'll starve."

"Far better than being one more disappearing lawyer."

"I don't desert clients for any reason. My job as a defense attorney includes defending the guilty. You don't run from responsibility. My new client says self-defense and innocent. I believe her."

Mitchell set his tan tee and placed the ball. "What if you discover she lied?"

"Won't matter. I'll fight to get her off, my sworn duty to defend a client unless they release me. Take your shot."

Mitchell swung a practice swing and focused on the narrow fairway. "I wish my faith about staying on the fairway was as firm as your sworn duty," Mitchell complained approaching his tee shot.

He addressed the ball and studied the fairway for a target point on the fairway then drove the ball right about 230 yards into deep grass and scattered trees. "There's my game," he moaned as his ball disappeared. "Hit and search."

In the cart towards Mitchell's ball, Stanford said, "I want you as an investigator...may be a book for you here and I need your help as much as you can give."

"Aha! I wondered why a four-handicap golfer chose to play with a hacker again. You write the book if the lawyers' disappearance and Todd Hancock's murder connect. Other lawyers have written successful books on their court cases."

Stanford discarded the idea with headshakes. "I consider the book a conflict of client interest and self-interest to exploit a case. Without assurance of absolute confidentiality clients might withhold vital information to the detriment of the client's legal interest."

"Tell you what, I'll keep notes on the case then turn the notes over to you should you change your antiseptic mind."

"Don't bother. I won't exploit my client's confidence."

THE ALMOST FORGOTTEN WIFE

"I also have conditions. No pay or expenses. Compensation makes the arrangement official, biased, and obligatory. I need to function without limits and be unencumbered to talk with police. Why do you need me?"

Mitchell decided to help Stanford, no matter the need, or future book.

Stanford said, "This case has more than what's visible. What motivated them to abandon their professional ethics and legal standing? Who murdered Todd Hancock, if murdered?"

"If the police don't know, how do we find out?"

"Nassau County police have no reason to investigate Hancock's death; no evidence of a crime only a medical examiner's speculation. As a popular and objective investigative author, you have a wider leeway to probe than my private investigators. You know Detective Lieutenant Kenneth Mullins of the Suffolk Homicide Squad. He's a good source if Laurence Bates, the second attorney, turns up dead. Bates lived in Suffolk County."

They reached the approximate area of Mitchell's ball then separated and searched. Stanford located the ball near an oak tree in a grassless patch about thirty yards from where Mitchell searched.

"Do you know Lieutenant Manny Fernandez in Nassau County?" Stanford said as Mitchell approached. "I met him and I'm sure he'll cooperate."

"No. The few Long Island cases I worked on happened in Suffolk County. Perfect for me since I have a summer home in Amagansett."

"Meet with me on Monday to talk to my client who I've yet to meet."

"Can we see the coroner's report on Todd Hancock?"

"Monday morning. You're on the case, I see."

"Since you're insane someone has to protect you. Helene will thank you for this project to keep me out of her hair."

"As Helene's attorney, I would do anything to make her happy." He grinned.

Mitchell swung a four iron and lined the ball four yards short of the green.

"Terrific shot," Stanford said.

"An accident."

Stanford and Mitchell completed the 18 holes near 5:30. Stanford finished with a score of 75, Mitchell, 105 with three 'mulligans' and two 'gimmes' on the back nine – five free strokes. Stanford wanted him to score under 110, a respectable score.

An obvious random golfer, Mitchell appreciated and accepted the freebees. "Hacks have no pride."

They showered, changed in the locker room, and strolled to the clubhouse terrace lounge to await their dinner companions Mitchell's wife and Stanford's date.

Helene Pappas arrived at 7:00.

Olivia Greene arrived a few minutes later.

O livia Greene turned into the plush Meadowlark Country Club for her critical first date with Stanford Crane, an alternate to a lunch meeting on his home territory although she preferred dinner in a neutral setting away from people he knew. That evening with his friends served as a beginning to a friendship to prepare him for her killer champagne cocktail if he failed her client.

Olivia wore a black formal dress to reveal modest cleavage, a double string of cultured pearls to adorn the naked neck area, three-carat diamond studs in pierced lobes, and a Rolex watch. She needed to look attractive, successful, elegant, and less than sexy with understated makeup.

She sensed sex as a weak lure to busy and serious Stanford Crane – unlike the type to succeed with at first encounter. Her method needed 'aging' to succeed with intelligence, patience, and a professional demeanor.

Olivia stopped at a busy portico valet area, glimpsed in the vanity mirror for a last minute review, stepped out, and accepted an orange stub from a white jacketed college age attendant. Twin curved marble staircases dominated a cavernous lobby adorned with plants and flowers. Several members and companions gathered there. A CD of Mozart's Violin Concerto No. 5 added ambiance.

Her analysis of Stanford proved compatible with information in a dossier provided by her client, her 'Uncle Max'. Stanford greeted Olivia with a tender handclasp. She blended well with Helene and Mitchell, although younger. Evening flowed social, pleasant, uneventful, and strategic.

The ruse to call him – to introduce a special rate travel program customized for law firms. Stanford expressed interest in this incentive bonus plan but had no time during the week. Having met her before at various Long Island Business Association committee meetings, he extended the invitation to dinner at the country club with Helene and Mitchell. He wanted a dinner companion. His unexpected need arrived as good fortune for Olivia.

The travel concept arose. When Stanford inquired about the plan, she deferred the subject, an excuse to call him again next week and meet alone.

Olivia was impressed that Mitchell wrote bestsellers. The Pappas' made her feel comfortable, but had no interest to see them again.

They served as theatrical props to her evening and now expendable tools to achieve her objective.

Stanford offered to follow her home to assure a safe arrival. Olivia declined stating the trip as long for him in an opposite direction, continuing her strategy. She lived in a gated community on Shelter Rock Road in Manhasset, Nassau County. Stanford lived farther north in Huntington Bay, Suffolk County on a two-acre plot on the bay.

Separation that night prevented his finding reason to suspect motives other than business. She considered the decision appropriate and reconfirmed that.

Driving westbound on Route 25, she concluded that Stanford would want to see her again. Business and strategy aside, Stanford attracted her, handsome, successful, and masculine and looked forward to manipulate him as a short-term lover.

The Cold Spring Harbor road lacked other moving vehicles and she passed a red light no longer stopping at red lights late at night in quiet areas as self-defense against a carjacker. Her phone rang. She knew the caller.

"Hello, Uncle Max. I'm alone and thinking of you and impatient for your call."

"And a good evening to you, Ms. Greene. How did the evening go?"

"He had guests, as you know so I deferred our primary mission as planned."

"What's your timing?" he asked as she passed the waterfront Billy Joel Park in Cold Spring Harbor, a former whaling port.

"I'll call him soon for dinner alone. He definitely is interested in the travel plan."

"If he remains distant, don't make the initial offer. Unlike the others he may report your offer to the court and authorities will want to know how he knew."

"I'll also get guarantees up front like client privileges."

"Our objective must end with him. We may have to finish him here and forget the Cayman Islands. We must succeed with him."

She slowed for a red light at the Route 108 intersection then drove faster to avoid a potential theft or worse on a dark road.

"Killing Crane here risks a county police investigation. Avoid that direction," she advised. "That's dangerous exposure on home territory."

"We may have no choice…too much money is at stake without a good alternative. The others feel crippled to continue and are impatient to move on."

"I *will* succeed. The judge hasn't set a trial date and the longer the delay, the better for me should Crane delay."

"Not better for me. I found out that the Nassau County examiner suspects the use of succinylcholine on Todd Hancock."

She sensed concern in his voice as she passed the Cold Spring Harbor Laboratory.

"He's guessing and can't prove anything."

"I hope the examiner's diagnosis differs for Bates."

"Bates lived in Suffolk County. A different examiner has jurisdiction. Why should they communicate? Where's the motive? Who'll start an inquiry to claim collusion in two counties? Remember, no evidence."

"I agree, but time is an enemy."

"If I see Crane three times in two weeks he's mine."

"I don't doubt your confidence and determination."

He knew his lover. Responsible for expanding her travel business, he recommended Olivia to business contacts on Long Island and involved Olivia in the Long Island Business Association, an organization devoted to increase business on Long Island.

She abhorred 'mistress' preferring lover, his secret lover a month after they met three years ago.

"Do you have enough Rohypnol?" Uncle Max said. "I have more at home in my desk in the back of a desk drawer."

"It sounds risky and careless, my love."

"No one will look there. It's reserve if needed."

"I have enough for Crane."

"Want my company?"

"Do I want to breathe? I yearn for you always. I'll reach home within twenty minutes. Shall I have the hot tub ready for my Uncle Max?"

"Sounds perfect."

"In the meantime, think about what I'm going to do to you."

"I was about to say the same thing to you. Amazing how we think alike."

She blew a kiss. "Please hurry. I'll be in distress until I see you."

"Me, too."

* * *

The morning after she arrived in Antigua with a briefcase and clothe designer suitcase, Olivia taxied from the St. James's Club Resort to the airport. After the taxi left, she hailed another taxi to Antigua Overseas Bank Ltd in St. Johns. The change in taxis served as diversion to an investigation on Todd Hancock's mysterious death.

She had left the Do Not Disturb sign on the villa door. If the room cleaner heeded the sign, she wouldn't find Todd's body the next day. Unable to ignore the odor, the cleaner discovered Todd in bed two days later.

At the bank, Olivia deposited $500,000 worth of bearer shares into her account and wired $300,000 to her foreign corporation account in Liechtenstein. She never opened an account for Todd Hancock on her previous trip to Antigua to establish her account. She returned the balance of the bonds to her client/lover in New York.

She and her client conceived their perfect plan, including arriving late in Antigua to avoid the bank with Todd. The bearer shares and phony condominium check proved essential to get his condominium.

Olivia enjoyed a good financial windfall that day.

In Liechtenstein with Laurence Bates, she followed the same procedure with the bearer shares at Bank in Liechtenstein AG, deposited $500,000 into her account, and returned the balance of bearer shares to her client. Bates also turned ownership of his residence over to her as part of his financial arrangement.

When Bates's estate checked with the bank that held his mortgage, they would discover a foreign corporation owned the real estate in the Bahamas and the mortgage paid. The Bates estate should conclude that he traveled to tax havens to sell his property to avoid taxes and to deposit cash in a sheltered account. Finding no paper work to identify a secret account, the estate should conclude the money vanished.

Todd Hancock and Laurence Bates predated their real estate documents before they left the country. The Bahamian corporation transferred the funds to two corporations in Panama controlled by Olivia.

She learned the tax haven game from Uncle Max's international attorney.

SUNDAY MORNING. NEW YORK CITY.

The decision to meet Stanford tomorrow and participate in the Nancy Kiley murder case sent Mitchell to the computer to begin his note taking habit when on a case. He typed statements by Stanford regarding the two lawyers, Nancy Kiley, and the Nassau County medical examiner for future research for a book.

Mitchell's notes included secondary details: his and Stanford's golf scores, learning Stanford's acceptance of the case and at what hole, and dinner with Olivia Greene, travel agent and owner of Village Greene Travel Service. He noted the name as creative and marketing appropriate.

Mitchell grew eager to hear Nancy Kiley's version. A different mystery lurked in the background with her two former lawyers' disappearance – What motivated them to leave? Mitchell feared to think again – *Does that presage danger for Stanford? A murdered Todd Hancock would connect to the trial. If a medical examiner failed to prove murder how could I, an author? Was Stanford right about layers adding to this case?*

He'd keep notes of future discussions and events relative to the Kiley matter and maintain newspaper files. A case involving a United States senator's family piqued media, and for the third trial. Helene and her assistant, Alicia Velez could obtain past articles. He often recruited Alicia and Helene to research.

As Mitchell's literary agent, Helene was delighted that he explored a new book. A third trial for a United States senator's daughter intrigued and the two lawyers' disappearance was an added lure. If the dead lawyers weren't murdered or reason for his disappearance disconnected to the Kiley case, Mitchell could create excitement by adding fiction to make them murdered and write events as a novel. Fiction plots ran endless and he liked the concept and challenge.

The case would keep her husband occupied. Helene loved Mitchell beyond extremes yet on occasional days she swore to someday find time to write a book titled – *Why Idle Men are Preposterous to Live With.*

Mitchell was happiest when immersed in book projects. When idle, he grew restless to the edge of annoyance…sometimes. Helene gained numerous advantages: dinners out, theater, Lincoln Center, and enjoying the diversity of New York City. She enjoyed Mitchell's above average cooking when she worked late and overtired to eat out. She also needed space and time at home to evaluate numerous manuscripts when business surged.

* * *

In the morning, Helene read the delivered *The New York Times* at the kitchen table when Mitchell approached.

"Ready to go?" she said.

"All set."

Helene walked with him to the door where they hugged and kissed; a departing and greeting custom their partnership required when one left and when one returned from work or a trip. They believed tradition as a strong part of stability in a marriage. Mitchell turned and opened the door with his mind saturated with the challenges of the coming day.

"Mitchell?" She never called him Mitch. She reserved that for his friends. "Did you forget something?"

He turned back to ask, "Yes?" He realized why she called him. "Oops, sorry." He embraced her, kissed her mouth, and cheeks. The triple kiss evolved into another way for him to say...I – love – you.

Helene added extra that day. She kissed his lips and whispered, "Remember as you go through your day that you are my life and that I love you very much."

"On my working days?"

"Usually."

Mitchell left the building garage in his white Grand Cherokee to meet with Stanford and then his client. Passing LaGuardia Airport, he traveled the Long Island Expressway to Exit 49 South to the Huntington Quadrangle, four office buildings with parking areas and private roads. Stanford's firm was on the top floor of the first building on Route 110.

At the modern reception room of Crane, Schmidt & Birnbaum, the receptionist directed Mitchell to Stanford's corner office that overlooked Route 110. On the phone, Stanford motioned Mitchell to the visitor's chair. He sat. Plaques and professional awards dominated the wall behind a blue sofa. Stanford ended the call, checked his watch, and passed a folder to him.

"You're early," Stanford kidded. "Can't wait to get started on this intriguing case?"

"Ready to go. What's this?" He accepted and opened the folder.

"A copy of the Nassau County medical examiner's report on Todd Hancock, the first attorney and faxed this morning." Mitchell reviewed the document as Stanford continued. "He found traces of Rohypnol, a drug illegal in the United States. Familiar with this drug?"

"No. What does it do and is it deadly?"

"Termed the 'date rape' drug in this country, Rohypnol is odorless and colorless. The male puts it into her drink and she then feels queasy and passes out for hours, sometimes for days depending on dosage. When she awakens she cannot remember much and who raped her although awakening on and off during the attack. The Nassau examiner contends the drug mixed with champagne. He detected a needle mark and believes that Hancock was injected with succinylcholine, an undetectable drug that dissipates fast in the body.

"On occasion, remnants might settle at the base of the skull. He found none. Whoever murdered Hancock, if murdered, avoided waking him when injecting the needle. Looks like the perfect crime." Stanford reached to his left and picked up another folder for Mitchell. "The bad news. I know by a source in the Suffolk County Medical Examiner's office that Laurence Bates died late last week in his hotel room in Vaduz, Liechtenstein. The cause remains undetermined."

Mitchell opened the second folder and read about the second dead lawyer.

Stanford continued, "The autopsy in Vaduz revealed Rohypnol and champagne. In both, the amount of Rohypnol was insufficient to cause death. You could also call it the modern day 'Mickey Finn'."

"You found a connection to the deaths," Mitchell said impressed. "I still think you're insane to take this case."

"You know my reasons."

"Doesn't matter. You risk your life. Nothing is worth that."

"I asked the Suffolk examiner to provide me with a report after he examined the body to look for a puncture wound for the succinylcholine and to confer with the Nassau examiner. If he finds the needle mark, we made the link. We can advance a theory that the same person or persons killed Hancock and Bates. If positive I expect police will call soon to query how I knew."

"Good detective work...no, superb detective work."

"Necessary due diligence to preserve my life."

Mitchell's concern for Stanford deepened. "After we finish with your client I'll call Lieutenant Mullins to meet with him and say that I'm interested in the case. Maybe he can add more, or help with the investigations in Antigua and Liechtenstein. The more we all know may save your life."

"They chose to leave. I won't leave."

Mitchell returned the folders. "That doesn't lessen the danger."

"Do you want copies?"

"I'll note the meat of each report. I'll copy all your files if a book develops."

Stanford inserted the folders in a right hand drawer and stood saying, "Let's go save my life."

"Did Nancy Kiley's boyfriend give her Rohypnol?" Mitchell said rising.

"No, she was attacked, alert, and resisting all the time, overpowered until she used the scissors. She stabbed his left foot then in the neck after getting up." Stanford snapped shut his black briefcase.

"Has she testified in court?"

"No."

"Any eyewitnesses? Anybody hear anything?"

"No, to both."

"Will you have her testify?"

"A rape victim may prove advantageous to testify. I discourage clients from testifying. If the prosecution continues as before, I'll withhold her testifying, and depends on any surprises."

They left the office for Stanford's black Lincoln parked in a re-served space.

"She lives near here. Maybe you can visit Mullins today. Call him and save yourself a trip out here."

"Good idea. By the way, we enjoyed Olivia's company the other night. How long have you dated her?"

"Our first date if you call it a date, known her for years through the Long Island Business Association where she serves on several committees. She developed Village Greene Travel from a local travel service inherited from parents to an Island wide pleasure and busi-ness travel with numerous corporate accounts. I always considered her attractive and admired her from a distance. Our dinner was a good excuse to call her."

"I thought it mature and professional of her rejecting to sell you during our dinner. Do you always rob the cradle for your dates?" Mitchell kidded.

"No." Stanford laughed. "Will I see her again? Yes, to discuss her program."

Stanford placed his briefcase on the rear seat and sat behind the wheel.

"Since your client claims rape did she take a lie detector test?"

"No, and justifiable. New York State prohibits law enforcement of-ficials from subjecting persons who file rape complaints to polygraph tests. The word is *persons* because rape includes men. Victims' rights groups finally got the legislation passed – that polygraph or lie detec-tor tests subject victims to unwarranted shock and humiliation. Those tests discourage victims from reporting their rape. Rape victims might have emotional responses reliving attacks during a test and can result in false test readings. In our case the victim retaliated."

"Yes, but no evidence of rape. What happens to your defense?"

"I can make a strong case. Both previous attorneys prepared effective opening statements and cross-examination of others. We'll know more after we talk to our victim." Stanford reached the main road and turned north. "Her father, Senator Austin Kiley is a two term incumbent and a powerful figure in the Senate and state and Long Island politics. Her mother Madge is wonderful, charming, and pleasant. Her legal name is Margaret. I know she suffers over her daughter's anguish and sympathize for her. Nancy is twenty-two and a senior at Stony Brook University. She chose a dormitory to avoid commuting, and an independent sort according to the Senator. Nancy felt she'd appreciate college life more by living on campus. She came home for weekends and on breaks. The drive is fewer than forty minutes.

"The Senator left for Washington last night. Nancy stays at home with her mother afraid to leave the house and protected by round-the-clock security guards. I have to fly to Washington on Wednesday to meet with him again. If free come along."

"I'm free. Give me specifics later."

"I mentioned you agreed to help and he knows your literature, and appreciates your offer."

Stanford reached Old Country Road and turned left into the Tuxedo Park development, an upper middle class community near the Nassau County line.

"The Senator is a wealthy man who earned his money on Wall Street as a bond trader. He chose this upper middle class area for political modesty. He owns a 54-foot yawl that he berths at Cold Spring Hollow Yacht Club in Oyster Bay or in Three Mile Harbor in East Hampton. He owns a condominium in Georgetown."

After a few turns, Stanford slowed to approach a two story home with landscaped grounds. Security appeared tight at the one-acre Kiley residence; three eight-hour shifts with two uniformed guards each shift. SECURITY on their white Ford's blue stripe proclaimed that territory as protected.

Maurice Calvin and Tito Chavez, uniformed employees of Leviathan Security for the past five years and retired Nassau County and New York City police officers, watched the Lincoln approach. Tito exited the passenger side alert to any attack. Maurice remained behind the wheel weapon at ready.

One needed reason to drive on this street unless one lived here. The alien Lincoln approached.

"Good morning. I'm Stanford Crane, Ms. Kiley's lawyer. She expects me."

"I need to see identification and your passenger's."

Stanford showed a business card, Mitchell his driver license.

Tito accepted the IDs, checked his list, wrote in his note pad, and returned them.

"Okay, sir, pull into the driveway." He called the Kiley residence from his cellular and notified Mrs. Kiley.

Security alertness impressed Mitchell. "If guards on the other shifts are as cautious, your client should feel safe. Maybe she'll say why so frightened."

"If she does, this meeting will have succeeded by opening a wide door. We'll ask along with tough questions beyond an introductory meeting. Oh, and don't expect the expected."

Stanford turned into the driveway with Mitchell looking forward to the meeting...and the unexpected.

6

Madge Kiley waited with impatience behind a white storm door when Stanford and Mitchell approached. She tried to disguise a face etched by concern over the family trauma and to buoy her posture and aura. Upset stomachs turned into steady companions after her daughter's arrest. She met Stanford at the country club over a dozen years ago. She opened the door and smiled.

"Good morning, Stanford. I'm so relieved and ecstatic to see you again. I know you can end this ordeal. You must or I'll have a nervous breakdown. I can't think of anything else but what my Nancy is going through, like a one track mind."

"Hello, Madge." They hugged and touched cheeks.

Madge Kiley was striking, elegant, of average height, trim, with dyed blond hair pulled back in a bun, hazel eyes, and high cheekbones. She wore khakis with a button down green blouse that complemented the speckled green in her eyes.

"This wouldn't have happened if we had you from the start. I believe that. Austin should've postponed the trial until you were available."

"That would have been difficult, Madge. This is Mitchell Pappas, who will help in the investigation."

She extended her hand to shake. Mitchell accepted.

"How do you do, Mrs. Kiley?"

"Call me Madge, please. Austin mentioned you. God knows we need all the help we can get. Please come in."

Mitchell sensed the upbeat greeting as acting to straighten shoulders weighted by her daughter's ordeal. Her face displayed distress lines when the smile faded. Sorrow made her appear older than forty-nine years.

Madge met the Senator twenty-six years ago working at the same Wall Street firm in the bond department. They lived on the Upper East Side of Manhattan until pregnant with Nancy then moved to a condominium complex in Great Neck near the Long Island Railroad station, an easy commute to Penn Station in Manhattan. Madge resigned her job to raise Nancy. Her next two pregnancies miscarried and a third resulted in stillborn. These tragedies ended dreams of expanding her family and thoughts of adoption vanished. She chose to devote her life to her husband and child and was happy until Eddie Hawkins's death and Nancy's 'never ending' nightmare.

A maroon carpeted staircase led to the second floor. The dining room appeared to the right opposite the living room. Madge led to a high ceiling solarium whose glass wall faced the backyard pool, tennis court, and thick woods that extended into public land. Ample houseplants converted the room into a miniature greenhouse. Nature provided room warmth that offset the coolness of glass.

Stanford and Mitchell sat in pivoting black leather Eames chairs. Madge sat on the edge of the Italian black leather couch.

Madge looked troubled, the upbeat and actor vanished when she closed the front door. She appeared hesitant then spoke. "Stanford, forgive me but I need to hear that you'll see this trial through to the end to feel secure until this horrible experience ends. Nancy's agony affects our relationship and she hardly talks to me. She's antagonistic and secretive unlike the child I raised, as if I don't exist around here. Austin in Washington during the week adds to the problem. He tries to come home often whenever he can."

"I'm here to stay, Madge. I promise and to the end. Adding Mitchell as an investigator underscores my commitment. I will never abandon Nancy for any reason."

His statement inflated her withering optimism. Madge looked relieved and less burdened.

"Thank you. New trials distress Nancy and us like a bad dream refusing to end, a mental torture. It's bad enough she was raped and the legal process victimizes her. This horror devastates Austin and disables his responsibilities in Washington. I don't know when he's had a good night's sleep. He paces or goes out for long drives when here. How could Todd Hancock and Laurence Bates walk away? How could they? Did you know them?"

"I knew Todd from the club, never met the other." Stanford decided to withhold Bates's death in Liechtenstein. The Senator mentioned his family knew about Todd Hancock's death. "This trial will come to a happy conclusion. The jury will believe Nancy was the victim. She must think positive about the trial's conclusion. My team shall do all it can to make your environment happier."

Madge sighed looking uplifted with a better sense of security. "I'll get Nancy. She's terrified due to the mistrials..." She stalled. Anger for her child swelled as she said on the verge of tears – "She's afraid to leave the house, for god's sake. A woman can't defend herself without being punished." Her stomach acids churned. "I'm sorry." She breathed deep to calm.

Stanford let her settle then asked, "Any other reasons for her fright besides the mistrials?"

She stalled, evaluating. "I don't know why she stays in the house as a prisoner other than she feels secure. We're no longer close or have a relationship. All I can do is cook for her then we eat separately. I do what I can to make her comfortable including minimum questions."

"Does she have visitors?"

"Only Pilar Marisol, her college roommate. Pilar comes by often, almost daily, and stays the weekend sometimes. Pilar is good company for Nancy and me, a blessing to have around as a second daughter adding sanity to my world, and they also video chat when apart."

Mitchell wrote the name in his notebook and noted Madge's chameleon-like demeanor.

Stanford said, "I read Pilar's testimony. Today will be a review."

"Nancy is upstairs in her room," Madge said rising. "She spends time there with her computer and television. She used to read novels, but doesn't now." Madge shook her head to reiterate, "She hasn't left the house at all and turned it into her prison. Would you like coffee, tea, soda, anything? I'm sorry for forgetting. I'm so distracted."

"Nothing for me," Stanford replied. "Thanks."

"I'm fine thank you," Mitchell added.

"You're welcome to stay Madge."

Madge shook her head. "No, you should see her alone. She'll be comfortable without me here. The other lawyers agreed. They felt she would talk freer on a difficult subject. I'll remind her to speak open and truthful." She stood with both hands pressing her stomach and left.

Mitchell felt sadness for Madge as he watched her walk away with her child under siege threatened by the severe penalty for murder.

"Mitch," confided Stanford in a lower voice. "Again, don't show surprise if my questioning and statements aren't all diplomatic with Nancy."

"Consider me a fly on the wall."

* * *

The young woman entering the solarium with Madge appeared alert and ready to distrust two strange men.

Nancy dressed casual: white sneakers, washed blue jeans, and a gray loose fitting T-shirt with her university's name in a circular emblem; shoulder length dark hair framed a wide face, hazel eyes, a straight nose, and full lips accented with a light pink lipstick shade. Attractive and stunning, she looked her mother's daughter except for hair color.

About to stand and greet her, Mitchell realized Stanford stayed seated. Mitchell followed his lead of no diplomacy or courtesy. Madge guided Nancy to the couch with an arm motion.

"Gentlemen, my daughter, Nancy. Nancy, Mr. Crane and Mr. Pappas."

"Pleased to meet you both," Nancy said without a smile and sat with arms outstretched on top of the couch and crossed legs left on top.

Madge headed for the door as her stomach acted up. "I'm in the kitchen should you need anything." She left for her acid indigestion medicine in a kitchen cabinet.

Nancy felt calm and confident for the third trial to begin with a new lawyer. Her left foot started to tap air to stimulate thoughts.

Mitchell thought the tapping a nervous reaction.

Nancy readied for a familiar routine convinced that Crane would ask the same inane questions as the other stupid lawyers.

Stanford spoke. "I asked Mr. Pappas to assist me. Feel free to speak in front of him. Do you know of me, Nancy?"

Her monotone voice sounded bored. "Yes. My father wanted you as his first choice. He also mentioned Mr. Pappas."

"Why did you kill Eddie Hawkins?"

Nancy's mouth dropped and eyes widened at this enemy lawyer. She straightened and responded with an abrasive offensive.

"What do you mean *why?* Don't you know *anything* about my case? I cannot believe this. And how long will you stay before you leave like the others? Why should I trust you? And why do you interrogate me like a detective? Is that why you're here?" Nancy lowered her arms and turned away angry. "Incredible!" Both palms slapped the couch. "What the hell is going on here?"

Stanford deflected her arrogance. "Why did the other lawyers abandon you? Did you give them reason to leave?"

Ineffective in her irritable approach to the insensitive lawyer, she retreated to a less hostile position.

"No, they betrayed me for whatever their dumb reasons."

"Why? I heard they were responsible."

"I don't know!" she shouted. "They were irresponsible jackasses."

"Do you know that Todd Hancock died in Antigua?"

"Yes. Serves him right for abandoning me," she added, arrogant.

"Where's Laurence Bates?"

Stanford volleyed questions and replies with minimum delay – a staccato rhythm.

Nancy shrugged. "I don't know. At this point, I don't care. I hope he's in severe pain somewhere dying from an incurable disease."

"He was found dead in Liechtenstein."

Her composure changed, stunned, and she muttered, "I...I didn't know. From what?"

"Undetermined causes like Todd Hancock. Police suspect that both might've been murdered."

"My God!" Her eyes widened to a catatonic look.

Mitchell studied Nancy's reactions to Stanford's blunt approach. He sensed fear.

Nancy twirled her hair by the left ear; head tilted and left foot tapped air faster.

"Your attorneys fled from you and then possibly murdered," said Stanford.

"That's not my fault."

"If I have you testify I need to know you're consistent and telling me the truth. Arrogance won't get you through your crisis."

"My truth is consistent. I acted in self-defense. I'm innocent." She released her hair, foot taps ended, and legs uncrossed. "I want to testify. I was raped! The other lawyers said I could testify to appeal to the jury's sympathy as a victim."

"Forget the other lawyers' comments. I'm unconcerned with your innocence or guilt, only that the jury finds you innocent. I read the court transcripts, what *others* said. I want *you* to tell me what happened."

Nancy eased and lessened the arrogant attitude. Her voice changed to normal when she started her story.

"I was in my dormitory on a Saturday. I usually came home for weekends, but that weekend I prepared for an exam and needed privacy and time at the library. Eddie came in around noon. He was all over me wanting sex. I asked him to leave. He wouldn't. He was spaced on drugs and no way to reason with him.

"I said I wasn't in the mood. He insisted, grabbed my hair, and forced me to my knees. He put scissors to my throat and said he'd kill me unless I obeyed. I loved Eddie, but that day he was drug controlled.

He put the scissors down and restrained me from pulling away. During the...the act, I grabbed the nearby scissors and stabbed him in the foot to make him stop. He let go and backed away in pain. I got to my feet. Outraged, I was ready to prevent another attack. He swung at me and missed and I accidentally plunged the scissors into his neck when he lost his balance. When I regained my senses and realized what I had done, I panicked and cried, terrified." She hesitated as hands covered half her face and eyes grew wider.

Mitchell thought she relived her trauma, or a good actor. Tears never showed. Time passing and accepting the trauma might have held them back.

"Then what?" Stanford asked feeling she took long to continue. "Nancy?" Her name wiped the stare away.

"I called the police." Her hands lowered.

"How long before you called the police?"

"About two hours."

"That's a long time. Why? What did you do in the interval?"

"As I said, I was terrified. I didn't want to go to jail. I was also in shock. I killed a person I loved. It was self-defense wasn't it?"

She studied both men and sought absolution. They offered none.

"The prosecution disagrees," Stanford replied.

"Maybe he plans to run for public office and needs the publicity." The sarcasm changed to a plea. "You'll get me off? Promise you will."

"That's the goal. How long have you dated Eddie?"

"About three years."

"Were you intimate?"

"There'd be something wrong with us if we weren't after three years. We shared a good relationship and comfortable. We talked marriage. He held a good job at his father's company, a major construction firm."

"How was the sex preferred?"

Nancy turned to shocked. "You mean how did we do it?"

"Exactly."

"I'll never tell you that." Indignant she added, "That's personal."

"Not in court. You're on trial for murder and charging rape. The prosecution will probe every aspect of your relationship with Eddie."

Nancy hesitated, shrugged, and relented. "Er...oral."

"Who serviced who?"

"What! What kind of questioning is this?"

"Answer me, Nancy."

"I can't believe this!" She looked nonplused. "All right, all right. Yes, both."

"His favorite method or yours?"

"You're kidding!"

"Answer." He remained firm. Reluctant, she looked at Mitchell, embarrassed. "Mr. Pappas is on your side," Stanford added. "Everything you say stays confidential."

Nancy relaxed and said, "Mine. Afraid of getting pregnant, our sex leaned to oral."

"Him putting his penis into your mouth wasn't unusual?"

Nancy's jaw dropped again. "*You* are despicable! How do you live with yourself?"

Stanford stayed firm and ignored her emotion.

"No, the prosecution will be despicable. I don't want them to ask questions I haven't asked you. And they *will* ask these questions. We will have more meetings before going to court and unpleasant conversation. They'll claim Eddie expected oral sex...if he had sex at all that day. Your saliva wasn't on his penis. You had no visible bruises, no semen, and anything else to indicate a rape or an oral act. Why wasn't your saliva on him?"

Nancy sank into deep thought as her eyes roamed. "His finger-prints were on the scissors."

"An advantage for us, but insufficient."

"In panic and confusion, I washed it off. Stupid but distressed. I was going to say he tried to rape me. Then I realized I destroyed evidence of his attack. As I said, I was shocked, stunned, and confused. Please, I prefer not to testify to tell the world and my parents how we had sex. I would be mortified."

"You may wear an orange jumpsuit if you refuse. The New York State Legislature may reconsider the death penalty. You will testify only if necessary. What the world thinks of your sex practices is irrelevant compared to the penalty."

"I *am* innocent. It *was* self-defense. Why doesn't anyone believe me?" She looked helpless submitting to the relentless interrogator.

"I will make the jury believe you. Did anyone see Eddie enter the dorm or your room?"

"Few students hang around their rooms on Saturday on a nice day." Her voice lost its edge to more conversational.

"No one saw him stagger in, or in a drug stupor?"

The staccato rhythm played on.

"No one came forward."

"Did you scream or call out when you fought?"

"I yelled at him to stop. I guess no one heard me."

"My investigators will question everyone in the building. Did the police check the building?"

"Probably."

"After, what did you do? Did you call anyone?"

"I called my father in Washington and explained what happened – Eddie raped me and I killed him in self-defense. He said to call the police. He was coming home and to say minimum to police until he gets a lawyer."

"Did you listen to him?"

"When police came they asked what happened. I said Eddie raped me and I retaliated in self-defense. I refused to say anymore without an attorney present. The attorney was temporary until my father hired Todd Hancock."

"You told the other attorneys what you told me?"

"As I said, the truth doesn't change. Yes, except they didn't ask about my sexual preference."

"What haven't you told me?"

"What do you mean? I told you all I know."

"No, you haven't."

"I have. Why do you attack me? Do you have a plan, a legal strategy? What? Let's talk about you for a change."

Mitchell continued to take notes trying to keep up.

"Do you have a roommate?" Stanford asked ignoring her question.

"Yes."

"Then you haven't told me all have you?"

"She wasn't there."

"She lives in the scene of the killing. Where was she?"

"At the gym. She's a workout obsessive."

"When did she return to the room?"

"After the police came. She hugged and comforted me and kept me sane through the trials. She's there for me, a true friend."

"She has alibis at the gym?"

"Yes. The police checked."

"Her name is Pilar Marisol?"

"Right."

"A senior?"

"She's graduating soon. I'm not. The damn price of self-defense. I'm a continuing victim." She yelled, "Our legal system sucks!" Nancy vented anger by punching her left palm.

"Look at me." She did. "When did she leave for the gym?"

"A few minutes before Eddie arrived. He knew she goes to the gym around noon and that I'd be alone."

"Where does she live outside of school?"

"Her parents live in Argentina. Buenos Aires. She travels back and forth."

"An expensive trip."

"Her parents can afford it. She remained here since my arrest."

"Do you use drugs?"

"No."

"Ever?"

"I smoked marijuana in high school for a time. All my friends tried it. The peer pressure thing."

"How about Pilar?"

"No, she's a health freak."

"Talk to me about Eddie."

"I loved Eddie and I miss him, a wonderful person. If it wasn't for the damn drugs and..."

"How often did he do drugs?"

"More than casual. He promised to stop and I believed him. Drugs made him violent when he didn't get his way and impossible to communicate with. I now realize he was addicted."

"As we progress we'll concentrate on Eddie and his drug habit. Do you know his drug friends?"

"A few."

"We'll talk about them next time. Was this the first time he forced himself on you?"

"Yes. Why do you keep asking sex questions? What's your problem? Are you a deviate? Why?"

"Sex crime. Sex questions. Pretend I'm the prosecutor determined to win, to put you away for life, or worse. You never fought him off before?"

"No."

"Then he had reason to believe you would consent. Give in to him."

"Obviously, the way you put it."

"He never raped you before?"

"Never."

"Was he drug influenced at other times? On occasion?"

"Yes."

"You consented at all other times?"

"Yes."

Stanford paused to allow Nancy to digest his reasoning, the prosecutor's case to discredit her.

She looked analytical, nodding.

Stanford continued. "Do you begin to see where the prosecution will concentrate?"

"I know what you mean. He would've surprised me on the stand catching me off guard and undermining my credibility."

"Why different this time?"

Her acceptance of Stanford as her lawyer increased.

"I was under stress with studies and I had my period. I don't react well with that combination. I resented his ignoring my feelings; no passion or romance at all, a wham bam thank you ma'am like a stray dog."

"Is that the truth?"

"Yes, I swear. So help me God."

Stanford looked pleased.

"A good answer. Repeat it word for word in court if necessary. According to the transcripts, you were seen in the dormitory parking lot with Pilar Marisol at about the time Eddie was killed."

"I went to my car for a book and to place luggage with seasonal clothing in the trunk planning to drive home later that night. Pilar walked me to my car on the way to the gym before Eddie showed up in my room. You know everything now. Are we finished?" She slid forward on the couch expecting her release.

"Going somewhere?"

"No. Staying home. I watch television to pass the time. One of my favorite shows starts soon."

"We're almost done. What else is there? Avoid piece meal offerings."

"Nothing."

"Why do you insist on all the security? Why would anyone want to hurt you, frighten you? Your parents have no answers. You tell me."

"I guess it's my paranoia. My guilt for killing Eddie feeling someone will punish me."

"I see. Anyone specific?"

"No."

"Spare me the stupidity and do *not* insult me. Your family spends a small fortune for guilt feelings. Really? Your parents will do anything to please and calm you." He leaned forward and stared to penetrate. "I think you're throwing bullshit at me and your parents."

"Wha..." Nancy's mouth stuck in open as she glared at him. "How *dare* you insult me?"

Stanford was firmer. "How dare you insult *me?*"

Mitchell followed the encounter as a spectator at a tennis match at center court surprised at Stanford's coarseness, the initial strategy with this client.

"My fear is caused by paranoia," Nancy countered.

"Three people in contact with you are dead; Eddie Hawkins, Todd Hancock, and Laurence Bates."

"I didn't kill the damn lawyers."

"Do you know why they were killed?"

"No! I already told you. What's wrong with you?"

"Three parts surround you. The first is Eddie, the second covers Hancock and Bates, and the third is unknown to me. What is the unknown to your puzzle? For your sake, I need to know what frightens you. Why do you need armed guards? What's the threat? Who wants to kill you? I need answers." Stanford sat back in his chair and waited.

Nancy withdrew. The snappy attitude receded. She turned away from Stanford, mulling thoughts.

She thrust up, hurried to the door with her past, and left the room. In an instant, Nancy returned to the doorway and hollered, "You're not my lawyer. You're despicable and a pervert!" and disappeared.

Mitchell never expected her severe reaction. The case ended before it started. He looked at Stanford, raised his brow, and queried, "What now?"

"I expected that ending. The Senator warned me of her reaction regardless of what questions I asked. What now? We go on with the case at a full gallop. Let's say goodbye to Madge and leave. I'll call the Senator and confirm our trip to Washington."

As Mitchell stood he asked, "Did you believe her?"

"No."

Village Greene Travel Service's two story red brick building located adjacent to the Woodbury Commons shopping area on busy Jericho Turnpike in Woodbury. The first floor served pleasure travel customers, the second, corporate and professional. The staff included nine travel agents and three assistants.

Village Greene evolved into an important client to local media: radio, cable, presses, including *Long Island Business News* – a weekly where Olivia maintained a full-page advertisement each issue. Her marketing and advertising led to print and broadcast interviews, free publicity, and volume rates that promoted her to the Long Island community whose increasing population approached three million.

Born and raised in Syosset, Olivia attended Syosset High School. After graduating from C. W. Post College, she earned her Master's Degree in Education at Adelphi University. A position with the Levittown School System as a fifth grade teacher followed.

The next year, she married Dr. Bernard Morton, a dentist and divorced within a year. The reason explained to her parents – He was a dentist 'morning, noon, and night' in and out of the office and had no other interest or subject to discuss. At first, she found him fascinating then incompatible and boring.

"Every time he talked about dentistry my teeth ached," she mocked.

Olivia considered poisoning her husband during the closing months of marriage when he refused a divorce. She researched and abandoned the thought failing to find the perfect poison, the perfect murder. Then he agreed to the divorce that saved his life. She dropped his last name.

She had planted the seeds to sprout to a killer without a conscience as long as it served her wants and needs.

The following year, her father died of pneumonia. Olivia resigned her teacher position to help her mother run the profitable business. She returned to C. W. Post and studied travel management in evenings to add to her mother's guidance, and a karate class for self-defense. She reached an advanced status as a student in Asian martial arts and loved the workouts using them as a form of exercise.

Her personality and energy increased business motivated by her need to succeed. Her mother died two years later of a heart attack in the office. On her own with cash inheritance of $450,000 and property worth over one million dollars, she invested fifteen percent of the cash to increase advertising and promotion. The business grew.

Then Olivia met her client, the love of her life who helped her expand with new corporate accounts. She loved him and obsessed over him. Uncomfortable with the part-time and secretive arrangement, she wanted all of him hoping he'd divorce soon as he promised. They would meet during the week for a few hours in her office or her home with periodic overnights when both met out of town.

Marriage to her was unnecessary. If he asked her to marry him, she would rejoice. She achieved success, had financial comfort, and wanted children – no need for a husband to support or care for her.

Her beloved client, her love was the sole exception.
He embodied and possessed her future and her life.
She loved her business and success, but he was her career.

* * *

Olivia's prime objective that day was to communicate with Stanford Crane to further the process to his death.

She tempered impatience and would call him in early afternoon as opposed to morning. She again wanted to tone down an appearance of impatience to sell her travel program.

Her full-time secretary/assistant, Gwen Rhodes worked in an open reception area outside her office. Olivia had walls removed on the first floor to provide a spacious area for six desks and two conference tables, one at each end. Travel posters saturated walls and featured international vacation specials. Olivia dealt with management at her corporate clients. Her staff dealt with their employees.

She planned to attend a fundraiser that night at the Garden City Hotel to benefit The Heart Council of Long Island, an organization dedicated to the prevention and cure of heart disease and patient education, honoring Marshall Bradley of Bradley-Kahn Technologies. Olivia purchased two tables of ten for her company and client guests – a tax deductible working social.

Charitable fundraisers led as a choice method to network Village Greene's services. She always subscribed to a full-page advertisement in the event's journal, a standard procedure. Her company attended fundraisers for Meals-On-Wheels, The Kidney Foundation, The American Cancer Society, The United Way, and numerous others. Several corporate clients attended, an opportunity to socialize and to develop new business contacts.

Olivia reviewed her business plan for Stanford's firm for adjustments to suit a now familiar personality. She added lunch with Stanford and promote dinner for next week. She lacked the same confidence as with Todd Hancock and Laurence Bates. Stanford, principled and successful, achieved financial security with no weakness to exploit.

Would sex weaken his armor? Was that his weakness? Could I make him fall in love with me to become my next victim? What do you think? What...do...you...think?

She was unsure…*Would his involvement be simple or complicated if he took the lure?*

Either way, the result must end the same. She'd have to kill him to protect her lover and her lucrative fee, a third perfect murder but dangerous to inject her medicine here instead of the Cayman Islands.

Her assignments for her lover would end and her role as assassin over unless a fourth trial and a fourth attorney developed. She remembered that a fourth attorney should survive. Her lover's associates planned to resort to local violence if her mission with Stanford failed and to deal direct with Nancy Kiley then kill her and her roommate, Pilar Mirasol.

* * *

Olivia called Stanford's office. He was out and expected later.

"Please tell him Olivia Greene called to schedule a lunch for this week. Any day is good." Disappointed, she said her office phone number and ended the call.

Tempted to call Stanford again at 5:00, she decided to wait deeming calling twice in one day a strategy mistake. By 6:00, her call remained ignored. Annoyed, she drove home to dress for the fundraiser in Garden City.

She planned to call Stanford again in the morning.

* * *

Nancy Kiley was unsure whether the downpour and thunder, or the nightmare that left her in sweat shook her awake at dawn. Eyes wide with fright, she lay still and listened for movement in the dim room. Her heart raced as she scanned the room for an intruder and uttered a frightful question.

"Who's there?"

A tense silence.

"Who's there?"

She waited.

No one answered.

Convinced she was alone Nancy switched on a bedside lamp for assurance and prepared to scream for help. Seeing no one, she clicked off the lamp, and eased and tried to remember what frightened her in a dream that vanished. She attributed the invisible nightmare to fear living with her since killing Eddie Hawkins.

Nancy yanked the bed sheet aside, approached the window, and nudged the wooden blinds to peek.

Did *someone watch for me to appear, to shoot me?*

Rain clattered harder on the windowpane then retreated. Her fingers edged between two slats to look into the lit backyard and darkened and ominous woods beyond. A faint hint of daylight filtered through treetops. Security guards hid somewhere avoiding rain, probably in their car.

Her immediate surroundings grew fearful.

As she remained by the window, tears trickled as her heart started an increased rhythm. Hands shook as she pressed her back and slid against the wall, folded her arms around her knees, and wrapped herself in fear. Tears changed to crying and hands covered her face.

Nancy wished she could tell her mother the problem, needing her comforting at moments like this.

She didn't dare.

Nancy needed to keep Madge in the dark to keep her safe.

She felt that Madge would never accept or understand the truth.

The truth would destroy her.

She needed to treat her mother as an outcast.

Nancy cried for several minutes, wiped her eyes, and peeked the night again. The woods continued to frighten.

She saw no assassins or a guard.

Don't weaken, she urged herself.

Don't capitulate.

Don't create your own terror.

Nancy knew *they* would come after her in the night, maybe from the woods and backyard.

Their attack was inevitable.

She stole their millions…and crippled their operation.

8

The house in East Islip reeked with tragedy when Lieutenant Ken Mullins parked behind a flashing squad car. A perimeter crowd gathered, rubbernecking, and controlled by a police officer. The sense was the familiar violence and death when Mullins crossed the doorway. This dominant sense smelled of drugs.

"How many, Marv?" he inquired of Detective Sergeant Marvin Rose, commanding officer of the Suffolk Police Department Narcotics Squad who talked to a uniformed officer in the Ochoa family hallway.

Marv turned towards Mullins. "Four. Two adults. Two kids, a family."

Detective Lieutenant Kenneth 'Moon' Mullins, nicknamed after the cartoon character Moon Mullins, absorbed the body count with a painful wince. Of average stature in his early fifties with salt and pepper hair, he wore a blue suit, white shirt, and yellow tie with dark spots. A Long Island native, he attended the Half Hollow Hills School System in the southern part of Huntington, attended Hofstra University, married his college sweetheart, and moved to Commack where they raised three children now in their twenties.

The new surge in drug deaths and executions in Suffolk County connected to the vicious Rodrigo, a single name butcher.

"How killed?" he asked, although he knew the reply.

"Same for all four, left ear and circle."

"Anything stolen?" He looked around with a glare of disgust for Rodrigo and pity for the executed Ochoa family.

"All electronics are in place. So is the silver and ten thousand in cash in a slit in a mattress, plain and simple a Rodrigo execution, nothing stolen."

"South Americans?" Mullins asked.

"Ecuadorians according to neighbors."

Detective Marvin Rose was broad and compact with a frozen face with eyes roving with alertness contrasting his nonchalant attitude and speech. His lieutenant would soon see a signature assassination, Rodrigo's trademark.

Mullins nodded a hello to an officer by the stair to the second floor and headed upstairs. Photoflashes guided to the master bedroom. Three crime scene investigators collected evidence. He greeted the familiar team. The nauseating scene dried his mouth.

Mullins confirmed the patented Rodrigo execution; the four victims shot at point blank range in the left ear while kneeling. All lay on their right side in separate small blood puddles. The heart stopped bleeding when they died. The small blood trail meant the father's body moved from the killing spot. Four body bags waited nearby.

He needed to generate saliva.

Fear and death disguised the children's ages although both were younger than ten-years old. Mullins felt sadness and anger for the children, victims of the parents' sins or a parent's sin against a cruel and coldblooded killer who murdered children – a depraved piece of human garbage.

Blood printing on the wall advertised and confirmed a 'spare no one' killer, Rodrigo. Mullins knew this as a warning to Rodrigo's drug soldiers and customers that death, including families, followed disloyalty and stealing from him or failure to pay when due. The printing was inside a circle called a riata by gauchos in the Argentine pampas, their lasso.

Rodrigo defied authorities, contemptuous and blatant to accept credit for the extermination. A maniac, Mullins thought, thirsty for publicity as a terrorist group in the Middle East.

This made no sense to Mullins.

Why does Rodrigo call attention to himself?

Mullins assumed – to retain power by fear, to establish his base of operations, and damn the authorities. Mullins needed to know his identity.

He descended the stair.

Halfway down, Mullins asked, "Do we have anything, Marv?"

"Zero, including shell casings."

"Anybody hear the shots?"

"No, probably used silencers again."

Both assumed that Rodrigo fronted for the Colombian and Jamaican cartels. Rodrigo could never operate in Suffolk County without their knowledge and consent. Drugs channeled from other countries plus the Caribbean and South America. Although Suffolk County crippled the Colombian and Jamaican supply lines on Long Island, they resurfaced with Rodrigo who also channeled Ecstasy from Israel and The Netherlands.

"Just a matter of time before they spread to Nassau County. Alert Nassau, Marv. Call Manny and tell him I asked you to call. We have to involve them and to join forces."

"As soon as we're through here unless you want me to now."

"Clean up here first. I have a meeting at the First Precinct. Get the unit together in the morning. I want them all involved on Rodrigo." An acrid taste developed in his mouth and he wet his lips. "Rodrigo will make me sick. Find me answers."

Mullins returned to fresh air and his gray Ford sedan.

Mullins headed west towards Deer Park via Montauk Highway/ Route 27 reviewing previous Rodrigo cases and the increase in county drug activity the past year. On Deer Park Avenue, he called his office and learned that Mitchell Pappas called. He hadn't heard from Pappas in months. District Attorney Frank J. Laine also called.

"I know what Laine wants. What did Pappas say?"

"It has to do with the Kiley case. He wasn't specific. He's in Huntington today."

"Did he leave a number?"

"Yes."

"Tell him to meet me at my office around three o'clock." He ended the call.

Mitchell helped him to solve a few murder cases and gained experience working with law enforcement officials and procedures.

What is Mitch doing with the Kiley case?

9

Mitchell drove the expressway east towards Yaphank and Exit 66 to help uncover why Nancy's lawyers abandoned her. Mullins could access police files in Antigua and Liechtenstein.

He reached his exit, turned north under the expressway underpass, and followed signs to the John L. Barry Police Headquarters building, a modern two story structure amidst a sprawling field of manicured grass and parking areas. He parked facing east opposite the front entrance.

In the lobby, he told the unfamiliar detective behind the counter that he had an appointment with Lieutenant Mullins. He said his name and showed identification.

The detective checked and returned the driver license. "Lieutenant Mullins is out, but expected soon. Have a seat or visit our museum."

Mitchell decided to visit the Police Museum with an entrance from the lobby.

Finished with the museum, he strolled outside the building and read the plaques of Suffolk officers killed on duty. A young tree grew behind each plaque. Mitchell returned to the lobby and waited, saddened by the loss of those brave officers. Behind him at the other end of the lobby, four applicants waited to enter the Gun Permit room.

Mullins arrived ten minutes later and entered as a man in a hurry who never did anything at a slow pace. Mitchell sat and wrote notes.

"Hello, Mitch. Sorry, I'm late," he said with a wide and warm smile.

Mitchell stood and they shook hands."Good to see you again, Moon."

"And good to see you. Come on in."

They climbed the stairway to the second floor, crossed the squad room, and entered Mullins's corner office. Mitchell hastened to keep up with him. Mullins sat behind his desk where he could see activity in the squad room. Mitchell settled in a visitor's chair. Mullins's phone rang.

"Excuse me. Mullins...okay, Marv. Nine o'clock. No exceptions unless of an emergency. Where are you?...Get back here when you can. Declare it a Red Alert meeting. Bye." He looked exasperated.

"Did I catch you at a bad time?" Mitchell said.

Mullins adjusted reports on his desk."Man's inhumanity to Man never ends. Last year, Diane and I took our grandchildren to the Central Park Zoo. As we reached each exhibit, we came to an entrance whose sign read The World's Most Vicious Species. That intrigued us, and which species? When we stepped in front of the entrance, we stood before a mirror looking at ourselves.

"I visited a drug execution earlier. A family of four bound and shot at close range in the left ear. Two children included. We fight a new surge in drug traffic this year controlled by a new dealer called Rodrigo, an Argentinean. Drug usage among teenagers has increased especially Ecstasy, another addiction and craze, and other creations will probably follow. But," he slapped his desk, "those are my problems. What's with you and the Kiley case, how did you get involved and why?" Mullins pushed a bakery box of Danish mini-pastries towards his visitor. "Have a few."

"No thanks. Last time I ate your beloved favorites I got acid indigestion."

"I forgot. They're my fuel, why I gave up cigars."

Mitchell leaned back and crossed legs. "Go back to cigars. The two previous lawyers who defended Nancy Kiley abandoned her during trial, an uncommon professional practice. I thought to explore why."

"I don't have answers. No crime was committed, therefore no murder investigation."

"I believe I have information you don't on that subject." Mitchell grinned expecting Mullins's doubting expression, facial crunching.

He crunched."You have something I don't know?" His eyebrows arched. "That's impossible. This I must hear." He bit into a prune pastry.

"I assume so but confident it's new to you."

Mullins stalled, analyzing. He leaned forward placing elbows on the desk. "You're hedging. Plan to write a book on the trial?"

"I explore that possibility, but that's not why I'm here."

Mullins shrugged. "So, what is it you *might* know before me?"

"The first lawyer, Todd Hancock died in Antigua."

"I know Hancock died, Mitch." Disappointed air left him like a runaway balloon. His palms turned upwards to indicate a – So what? "He wasn't murdered."

"A Nassau County medical examiner's autopsy revealed Hancock drank champagne laced with Rohypnol and the examiner found a needle mark in the thigh area. Although the cause of death is undetermined, the examiner speculates Hancock might've been injected with succinylcholine, a deadly drug that dissipates in the body."

Mullins sat back in his chair disappointed at the examiner's conjecture.

"I'm aware of the drugs and their effects, but Hancock is out of my jurisdiction. He lived in Nassau County. If you wish, I'll call homicide in Nassau for you to talk to Lieutenant Manny Fernandez."

Mitchell raised his palms to indicate – hold on. "Checking further, Laurence Bates the second lawyer was found dead in Liechtenstein and the Suffolk medical examiner will do the autopsy."

"I also know about Bates. Liechtenstein authorities notified us." He sat up again intrigued. "How did you know about Bates? His announcement won't make the media until tomorrow, maybe the evening news."

"Aha! Did I get your attention?"

"Like a poke in the eye."

"My source contacted the Suffolk examiner to determine Bates's cause of death. The Liechtenstein autopsy revealed the use of champagne and Rohypnol. His cause of death was undetermined. If the Suffolk examiner finds a needle mark then identical modus operandi suggests the same person or persons could have killed them. Since Bates lived in Suffolk, you may have a murder case in your territory."

Mullins nodded at the revelation. "Good detective work, Mitch. You made a possible connection." He turned quizzical. "What caused you to check on their deaths as murder?"

"I need your help to save a friend's life. Don't if it's a conflict."

"How could saving a life be a conflict?"

"I refer to the new attorney for Nancy Kiley, Stanford Crane. His firm handles Helene's business."

"Saw Crane in court several times. He's damn good. Nancy Kiley is safe with him. He's not a conflict. Tell me more."

"With the lawyers gone, Stanford wants to know why they left. He checked the county examiners. If the Suffolk examiner verifies a needle mark, we must assume they were murdered. Will the killer go after Stanford? I'm here to help protect his life. Stanford is a Suffolk resident."

"If he feels the need, I'll provide him with around the clock protection. I cannot discuss the evidence against Nancy Kiley. The dead lawyers are a separate issue."

"They may connect to her and the trial."

"The case is a prosecution subject out of our hands."

"Maybe evidence we uncover will help justice – prosecution or defense."

"I don't see a conflict in a separate investigation."

"Good. Can you obtain the files from the Liechtenstein and Antigua police? I want to review them to see what else they found."

"I can get Antigua by tomorrow. Liechtenstein may take an extra day with the time differences. I'll call Nassau Homicide and see what they have on Hancock as well as the Suffolk examiner." He dialed the Suffolk examiner's office and turned on the speaker for Mitchell. "Dr. Marc Blumenthal, please. This is Lieutenant Mullins, Homicide."

A woman answered the connection. "Hi, Moon. This is Michelle, renowned medical examiner. Marc is out for an hour. Can I help you?"

"Hi, Michelle, I'm calling regarding Laurence Bates. The one shipped in from Liechtenstein. Have you finished with him? I know about the champagne and Rohypnol."

Michelle pulled Bates's chart. "We received a request from Attorney Stanford Crane to look for a needle mark for a possible succinylcholine injection. You know about that?"

"I know everything going on in this county." He winked at Mitchell. "The reason I'm calling. Whatever your results, I'm the first to know. The first."

"Guaranteed. As always."

"Thanks, Michelle. We'll talk later." He hung up and said to Mitchell, "You're a mile ahead on this one."

"More than two miles. What I can do with your approval and at my expense is visit Antigua and Liechtenstein to investigate. I might turn up something."

"If the medical examiners agree, we'll alert Antigua and Liechtenstein that we're investigating the deaths as a murder case. Let's see what their police reports indicate, who they questioned. Might save a trip. If their MO's are the same, a killer is loose on Long Island. I'm certain the killer thought no one would connect that Bates and Hancock died by similar methods, if they were. If right about the Rohypnol and succinylcholine combination, I'll leak it to the media to pressure the killer if on Long Island." He lifted the phone to call Nassau Homicide. "I'll call you. I have all your numbers. Thanks for adding to my workload, pal. I'll get back to you." Mullins smiled. "In the meantime, give my best regards to Helene."

"Last time I did that she stayed up all night thinking of you."

"Go home."

Mitchell left confident he'd find the lawyer killer with law enforcement behind him and the efficient Suffolk Homicide Squad.

* * *

Same day.

Mitchell worked at his computer accompanied by Mozart's Piano Concerto #19 in F Major. Mozart led the favored composers for background music to stimulate his creative process and to make words flow easier. When Mozart failed, he switched to Greek instrumental music; that always awakened his optimistic senses. When that failed, he listened to Bruce Springsteen.

Mitchell called Stanford's office earlier and left a message for him to call back. Stanford called back a few minutes after 7:00.

"How did you make out with Lieutenant Mullins? Will he cooperate?"

"The trial isn't a conflict. He'll investigate if the Suffolk examiner verifies a needle mark in Bates to confirm identical MO's."

"Contact him again. The Suffolk examiner's office called. They found a puncture wound in the thigh. They almost missed it because the body decayed. They confirm – champagne, Rohypnol, needle mark in the same area. No trace of succinylcholine. They'll consult with the Nassau examiner."

"I'm positive Mullins received the data before you did. Based on similarities, Mullins will investigate with Nassau Homicide. I told him your concerns."

"Also, the trial date is set and jury selection starts a week from this coming Monday. The process should take about a week then the trial. I'm pleased with the schedule. Still want to go to Washington?"

"Yes."

"I knew I was right," Stanford added.

"About what?"

"About getting you involved though you're a lousy golfer."

* * *

Mullins called as Helene and Mitchell prepared for dinner at a local restaurant.

"I thought you forgot me," Mitchell said.

"The medical examiner called and the MO's match across the board. I have the files from Antigua and Lichtenstein. Hancock and Bates were with a woman. That's significant, but no one could provide a good description. Both women wore hats and sunglasses...more sameness."

"What do you think as the plot thickens?"

"Could be the same woman. I think we have a femme fatale on Long Island. I'll conduct an investigation on Bates and ask Nassau to follow up on Hancock. We might get lucky and uncover the same woman. I should receive the detailed reports by week's end."

"The Kiley trial starts again in about two weeks. If Stanford's in danger, we have a week or so into the trial to find the reason Hancock and Bates left and why murdered."

"I might come up with substance on Laurence Bates by then. I assigned two men to investigate his background and that may lead us to the woman. We *will* find her."

TUESDAY.

The blinking answering machine light beckoned Olivia after her fundraiser where she met two potential clients – one a lawyer, the other a president of a Nassau County bank. She scheduled to call them tomorrow to set appointments. The sole message said "Max. Morning."

She erased the unsettling message.

Olivia's client/lover used the name Uncle Max whenever he called her office having agreed to avoid those calls unless necessary. She expected his call to forebode bad news otherwise why the cryptic message last night.

He called at 9:30 a.m. Gwen buzzed her boss. "Your Uncle Max is on line four."

Olivia set aside the file on Pakistan and the mountain climbing adventure to challenge K2 in the Himalayas. Last week, she received an interest in K2 from a member of a Long Island mountain climbing club for a potential trip next month by several of the membership depending on the internal politics there at that time. She was about to call her client to tell him to cancel the plan because the Taliban just killed nine climbers and a guide at a Himalayan base camp at a nearby mountain.

She prepared for bad news from Uncle Max with a long exhale, lifted the receiver, and pressed the security button.

"Good morning. Problem?" She crossed her fingers to forbid a problem.

"That depends on you. The trial date is set and jury selection starts in two weeks."

The news jarred. "It's too soon!"

"Our deadline and no more than a few days into the trial and absolute limit, and could change to earlier."

"Damn!" Her fingers drummed the desk. "I called Crane yesterday for lunch this week. He was out. I'll try again later."

"You must succeed. They prefer to bypass him and go to the alternative plan before the trial. They'll target Nancy's roommate Pilar Mirasol first to terrify Nancy to surrender."

* * *

Finished with Uncle Max, she dialed Stanford's office.

"Mr. Crane's office. Good morning. Rhonda speaking."

"This is Ms. Greene for Mr. Crane."

"Hold please." Olivia drew champagne glasses on a pad and printed C-R-A-N-E over one.

Rhonda returned. "Ms. Greene, he will return your call. He's in an important conference at the moment."

Olivia said her phone number and hung up disappointed. She refused to believe he wouldn't call back.

By 3:00, Stanford hadn't called. She grew restless.

Olivia devoted the next ninety minutes to think about Uncle Max, the court case, the Hancock and Bates involvement, and Stanford. Nerves devised and revised strategies on her approach to Stanford to coax him to lunch although she preferred dinner.

The judge slashed her time creating a need to move faster. Stanford lived alone, divorced, and based on his background dated no one steady. Absence of a woman companion may mean a potential Achilles heel. She thought about scenarios to lure him to sleep with her sooner.

At 4:30, Gwen, a mother of three grown children and in her fifties with honey colored hair, knocked on the closed door and entered holding flowers in a vase.

A surprised Olivia said, "Who from?"

"A card is inside." Gwen left.

Olivia pushed aside the crackling cellophane wrapping that surrounded white and pink carnations and red roses and opened a miniature yellow envelope expecting encouraging and loving words from Uncle Max. She read with delight -

Olivia,

Thank you for being my guest Friday night. I look forward to see you again, and soon, and to review your travel program.

Stanford.

Her smile tinged with victory that created confidence to succeed with the third lawyer, a potential lawyer 'hat trick'. She smiled at the hockey comparison of a player scoring three goals in one game.

* * *

The phone rang at 5:25. Gwen left at 5:00.

"Ms. Greene," she said. Brochures on Kenya's wildlife and safaris spread before her.

"Hello, Ms. Greene. Mr. Crane."

Elated, she made a fist and jabbed air. "Hello, Stanford. Thank you for the beautiful flowers."

"I appreciate your accepting my invitation on short notice."

"The pleasure was mine and I loved meeting Helene and Mitchell, a wonderful and accomplished couple. I love that category of persons."

"You excel in that category. I apologize for the delay to return your call – conferences and more conferences for a trial in and out of the office. I'm glad you work late."

"I called to thank you for a wonderful evening with the Pappas' and about the travel program for your firm."

"I haven't forgotten. I'm out all day tomorrow. Lunch on Thursday works for me. How about for you?"

Olivia checked her calendar. She had scheduled a luncheon conference in Babylon.

"Thursday is perfect. Do you have a favorite restaurant?"

"I'll leave that choice to you."

"I suggest Poseidon's Sea on Jericho. Best seafood on the Island."

"Been there. Is twelve-fifteen good?"

"Twelve-fifteen is ideal."

"I'll see you there."

"Thanks again for the flowers, Stanford. They're appreciated."

Short, sweet, and productive.

She wondered – Could I succeed to convince him to come to my house after lunch for a visit to the hot tub? That would be a home run.

WEDNESDAY. WASHINGTON, D.C.

Mitchell and Stanford reached Washington before 11:30 a.m. A taxi brought them to Palmer's on K Street, a favorite haunt for lobbyists, elected officials and staffs, and media. They sat at Senator Austin Kiley's favored table.

Twenty minutes later, Stanford spotted Senator Kiley greeted by the maitre d'. Stanford pointed the Senator out to Mitchell. They watched as the popular senator waved and greeted acquaintances as he approached. Room din swirled in a constant and even tone with dark wood walls unable to muffle the level.

An influential and powerful Washington official, attractive, broad shouldered, and six-feet tall, he wore a dark blue striped suit, white shirt, and yellow patterned tie. His brown curly hair showed gray traces. His Committee assignments were – Ways and Means, Commerce, and Finance. Those Committees placed him on a future road for Senate leadership that should add seniority and power.

Austin Kiley's smile widened as he charmed past diners to reach Stanford and Mitchell, who stood to greet him.

"Stanford. Thanks for coming down, a great convenience for me."

"Hello, Austin. Meet Mitchell Pappas."

"Mitchell, I can't thank you enough. I'm familiar with your work with Lieutenant Mullins and delighted to have you on Stanford's team."

They exchanged handshakes and sat. When Austin sat and was offstage as a senator, he looked hassled.

He waved to Sam the waiter, ordered prime rib end cut, and iced tea. His guests ordered chicken potpies, a specialty and mineral water. Sam bowed and left.

Austin said, "Did you meet my Nancy, Mitchell?"

"Yes, with Stanford. I also met Madge."

"God love that woman. God love her forever," Austin said sighing, shaking his head. "She's punished by this tragedy, this endless saga. She's a martyr, a saint. Madge doesn't deserve tragedy in her life. I hurt for her. I wish she wasn't so sensitive, but that's one of her many wonderful qualities."

"The hardship showed," Mitchell said.

"Stanford, was Nancy difficult?" Austin unfolded and placed a white linen napkin on his lap. "Predictable?" He grinned.

"As you described. Her departing words still echo: You're despicable and a pervert, at the top of her voice."

Austin laughed at his rejection prediction. "That's my new Nancy under duress. We spoke and she accepts you. She thought you were efficient and strong and exactly who she needs. What did you learn besides what I told you and from the transcripts?" He appeared impatient for Stanford's response and shifted his body closer to him.

"I had difficulty believing why she needs armed guards."

"She should confide in you before the trial."

"The sooner the better. Have you read about Laurence Bates?"

"What was he thinking to abandon the case like Hancock? How could two reputable attorneys act irresponsible? Bastards!"

"I did investigative work on my predecessors that included the medical examiners in both counties," Stanford said.

"That's impressive. Any evidence?"

"What isn't public is that both had traces of Rohypnol, a sleep aid and needle punctures. The Rohypnol didn't kill them. The Nassau and Suffolk examiners agreed an injected substance could have murdered them. Succinylcholine is their candidate, which dissipates in the body."

Austin's eyebrows arched widening eyes. "I'll be damned!" He sat back in his chair, palms on the table – distressed, absorbed, and massaged his thoughts. "No evidence to convict anyone? Only guess work?"

"Yes, and that worries me in various ways, Austin – if murdered, why? Does the reason relate to Nancy's trial? Is Nancy in danger? Does surrounded by security guards mean she knows why and protects herself? Questions she must answer truthfully."

Austin shook his head in rejection, unconcerned with Stanford's questions.

"Maybe I should have a martini. I'll be useless this afternoon from worry anyway." He searched for Sam, waved him over and ordered his usual martini with three olives and a dash of dry vermouth. "There's no mystery here, Stanford. Nancy has always been truthful. If she says Eddie raped her, he did. If she acted in self-defense, she did. I don't see a hidden agenda, or to use the term dominant in Washington, a conspiracy theory. If so, I can't imagine what. She is paranoid about unseen and unknown forces attacking her. First Eddie turned into a drug maniac and attacked then the DA. Are you confident you can help her?"

"I can build reasonable doubt by researching Eddie and his drug habit. His fingerprints on the scissors are an asset. Bates and Hancock headed in that direction then diverted to other witnesses. I need to find what motivated both to change their strategies, and possibly a third party."

"What the hell else is there?" Austin opened palms as his face contorted doubt. "She killed her boyfriend in self-defense. I approved guards to ease her fear, which I thought was psychological. I don't believe she's in danger, if so, I'll stay at home all week."

"Police in Antigua and Liechtenstein report Hancock and Bates were with a woman. Was she the same woman? They couldn't identify either woman. I'll look into their affairs on Long Island along with Mullins. Their families, friends, and staffs may tell us her name."

"You two make me nervous with this conspiracy theory. When do we go to trial, Stanford?"

"Jury selection starts soon. That should take about a week. I'd guess the trial begins the following week."

Austin appeared positive as his tension eased for him to say, "Something positive for a change. Who's the judge?"

"Robert Merckling III."

"Do you know him?"

"I appeared before him a few times, one of the best. Familiar with how Judge Merckling works, the case should end within the two-week period. After two mistrials, he'll hasten proceedings. Jury selection may take longer due to visibility. It would be difficult to find jurors who haven't heard of the case."

Austin offered a solution. "Will a change of venue help?"

"My associates and I decided it's to Nancy's advantage sympathy wise to remain in Suffolk, and the case is high-profile and known beyond Long Island. I need Nancy ready and cooperative and with the right attitude in court, no arrogance. She must appear as a victim. I need you and Madge to help in that regard."

"I'll see that Nancy does as you tell her."

"Did you know Eddie?" Stanford asked.

Sam returned with the martini and left. Austin drank a small amount.

"Ah, perfect. Met him several times. His father and I have been friends for over a dozen years. I talked to Beth and Randy Hawkins and they are devastated."

"Did you know Eddie did drugs?"

"No idea about the drugs until after the attack."

"The autopsy revealed a high drug level in his system substantiating Nancy's statement and helping our case."

"Beth and Randy had no idea their son used drugs. This mess created a double tragedy to destroy two families." He leaned on the table with elbows and pled, "Stanford, please don't let me down."

"Nancy is my sole focus and priority. I already switched a potential civil case to an associate."

"And thank you, Mitchell. I know you refused a fee. Allow me to pay expenses."

"I appreciate the offer, but no. My rules."

Austin raised his arms in mock surrender. "You win. I put myself and family in your and Stanford's hands. My high visibility nurtures media to hound Madge. She almost had a nervous breakdown during the first trial. What's happening to her kills me. Media will publicize the case again once the trial begins. I can handle the negative publicity, but will have continuing uneasiness for Nancy and Madge. I wish I wasn't a public official at times like these."

"Only if the prosecution exploits opportunities to mold public opinion will I talk to the press," Stanford replied. "I'll counter with the judge and media. The judge decides on television coverage. I'll request privacy based on the mistrials and potential for a circus atmosphere. We should get the decision. Do you know Eddie's friends?"

Austin shook his head and pursed lips. "Never met any or did we talk about them."

"Tell me about Eddie's father."

"Randy Hawkins is a successful business man on Long Island, influential, a community leader, and philanthropist. Eddie's death left him bitter, his only child, and the heir to his business and fortune. Randy won't seek revenge, or threaten Nancy. We talked in depth about the incident. He offered to reserve judgment on Nancy until after the trial. If self-defense, he will accept the verdict and move on. We remain friends and continue communications. Have you a strategy yet?"

Stanford nodded conveying confidence. "The strategy revolves around Eddie. If the prosecution presents any surprise information that strengthens their position, I may have Nancy testify. That might prove difficult for her because the prosecution will try to impugn her, question her morals, and activities. She may have to discuss sexual habits. Can you handle the difficult subject and exposure?"

"I can handle anything except a guilty verdict. Do what's necessary and hire whom you need. Nancy is strong and will bounce back. I cannot say the same for Madge. Madge is a strong reason for me to leave Washington to spend more time with her. Madge needs my support. And Madge will never be the same. I may lose the two people I love most." He blinked his eyes several times to control his composure that exposed love for his family.

Austin looked helpless when it came to his family. Nancy's crisis exceeded his power and influence...to help her, to exonerate her.

Stanford was in control now.

12

Pilar Marisol's life changed along with Nancy's, her university roommate for four years with a friendship as close as sisters. Her senior year grades crashed from straight A to C and D since Nancy killed Eddie Hawkins. To her parents, she used Nancy's arrest why she hadn't returned to Argentina. They understood Pilar's loyalty to Nancy. Pilar assured them that Nancy defended against his attack.

Nancy spent last year's summer at the Marisol mansion in Buenos Aires. Her mother wanted to visit during this trying period. Pilar convinced her that the trial would end soon – that Nancy would overcome the ridiculous charges brought by an ambitious and publicity seeking district attorney to prosecute a senator's daughter and that the Senator belonged to the opposing political party, a lie.

Pilar attended the trials and visited Nancy in prison as often as allowed. Judges denied bail to Nancy at the first two trials on the prosecutor's insistence. Austin's influence and a new trial's hardship prevailed.

Pilar's long dark hair, eyes, and Mediterranean skin shading connected to her mother's Turin, Italy heritage and father's from Madrid,

Spain. While her walk and model's height could have graced fashion ramps in Milan, New York, or Paris, she lacked interest in that career.

She parked in the Riley driveway, waved and smiled to the guards then rang the bell. A smiling Madge opened the door for Pilar, who she treated as her own. They touched cheeks and exchanged greetings before Pilar hurried upstairs.

"Tell Nancy dinner's at seven," Madge called after her.

"Thanks, Mrs. Kiley," Pilar replied, turning. "As always, I look forward to your cooking no matter what you prepare. I love everything and why I gained weight."

Pilar's visits delighted Madge. Pilar turned into the best medicine for Nancy – a constant and loyal companion who brought sunshine to a gloomy prison environment. Madge also remained a prisoner. Madge appreciated cooking for Pilar, who ate and praised her culinary talent and often came down and visited with Madge in the kitchen, and helped when needed. Madge always enjoyed Pilar's visits, a bright spot in the gloom and an infectious happy person that forced Madge to defer her problems unaware that Pilar deferred her own problems.

Nancy's bedroom situated in the rear left corner. Pilar entered after knocking, an automatic gesture. Nancy reviewed books on the Internet and noticed Pilar in peripheral vision.

"Close the door."

Pilar sat in the adjoining chair and edged closer to Nancy. Surfing the Internet, television, and tennis in the backyard occupied them every day.

"What do we search for today?" Pilar said.

"Time we acted smarter. What if your car is stolen? The mistrials work against us. I ordered a book on international banking. What we're doing now sucks."

"Moving into the rented condominium on Saturday will end the car theft problem. I prepaid the first three months in cash."

"Good. We're entitled to expenses. I called my father in Washington." Nancy changed pages on the screen, scanned titles, covers, and descriptions. "He approved that obstinate lawyer, Stanford Crane. I like him. Crane could end the court nightmare in a positive way. I hope he doesn't abandon me although he sounded committed."

"And having security guards works so far."

"That could change at any time."

"We did the right thing. You believe that should you weaken, Nancy."

"I'll never weaken. I haven't come this far to crumble. You still scared?"

"Scared, no, terrified, yes. Always until the nightmare ends."

"Me, too." Nancy reached out and hugged Pilar. "I love you. Let's both keep saying – Never weaken – to stay strong." She released her.

Pilar still felt unsafe. "I spoke to my mother last night and she wants to come up and stay with me. She needs to support you and your parents and regrets missing the other trials. I don't know if I can keep her away. What should I do?"

"It's okay. The trial should start on a Monday and my mother can use her support. I'm sure my mother will insist that she stay at our house."

Pilar and Nancy had dinner in Nancy's room.

Madge ate alone again.

Near 10:00 p.m., Pilar exited into the quiet neighborhood. The security car offered protection. She drove to Stony Brook University believing the third trial should end happily for Nancy...and her.

Pilar often checked her rearview mirror for suspicious cars, a habit since Eddie's death. She exited at two unfamiliar exits to assure no one followed and reentered the expressway. She reached the university grounds satisfied no one followed.

Nancy remained free if self-imposed house arrest under armed guards qualified as freedom. Pilar had it better than Nancy did – no prison, no trials, and no voluntary house arrest.

Only Nancy knew she was an accomplice.

Nancy being the rape victim was by mutual agreement. Nancy chose to act the victim. Nancy stabbed Eddie.

Pilar had no regrets with her involvement although as guilty as Nancy was under the law.

Pilar needed to help or Eddie would have killed Nancy the way he beat her.

Then Eddie would have killed Pilar.

THURSDAY.

Olivia awakened at 7:00, showered, left for work, and parked behind her office building leaving the front spaces for customers. Lunch with Stanford topped today's important items. Gwen brought *Newsday* and *Long Island Business* News and placed them on her desk with the business paper on top. Business news dominated daily priority.

She read the business paper and searched for client news and potential clients. An article announced a client's promotion to co-chairperson. She called her to offer congratulations. Olivia noted the conversation for her records and client history then communicated with other corporate clients to survive in a competitive business that included internet travel agencies and self-booking and seat selection airlines.

Olivia's alphabetical list reached her largest corporate client, the giant Computer Patterns Microsystems in Brookhaven. Village Greene handled business travel arrangements for twelve hundred employees. All employees and families received discounts for pleasure travel, a means for Village Green to combat Internet bookings by employees.

Her second largest client was Bradley-Kahn Technology, a Fortune 500 company headquartered in Memphis, Tennessee with a branch facility in Hauppauge, Long Island, the same Bradley honored at Monday's fundraiser for the Heart Council of Long Island.

Randolph (Randy) Hawkins, Eddie's father, obtained both accounts for her among others.

* * *

As Olivia prepared to leave her parking space to meet Stanford, Gwen called her cell to say that Stanford's office called to cancel. He had to go to court. She slapped the wheel and shrieked, *"Damn!"* Distraught and angry that she lost the week, she'd call him tomorrow to set a date for next week. If lunch failed, drinks after work or dinner. Maybe Stanford will agree to dinner at her house.

Then I've got him by the balls.

The delivered flowers meant interest and proved her wrong to prevent Stanford from following her home from the country club. She should have gambled. She scolded herself for failing to follow her instincts about men.

Olivia returned to her office. Gwen called the local Chinese restaurant and ordered brown rice and wonton soup for her boss. *Newsday* faced down on Olivia's desk. Having no interest in sports, she turned the paper to the headlines then to follow her procedures with clients.

Olivia gasped.

Laurence Bates and Todd Hancock's photos dominated the front page with the heading – Were Missing Lawyers Murdered? Autopsies Indicate Similarities.

She turned to the third page and read the full-page story written by reporter Adam Farmer and continued on Page 17 – 'Statements by the medical examiners confirmed the possibility of succinylcho-line, champagne, and Rohypnol. Police reports from Antigua and Liechtenstein indicate both lawyers were with a woman. The women remain unidentified.'

Her overseas activity came home with alarm.

How could it?

The impact was bomb bursting. Olivia stared out the window into the Commons as she wondered why the examiners communicated.

Who alerted them?

A knot formed in her stomach.

The informer could never be Uncle Max.

His associates? Am I in danger, a potential victim because I know too much and they fear my arrest?

The digital desk clock changed minutes. Olivia related that to the countdown to her life's final days. The thought of dying made her shudder then shook away the sensations. Fear attached as a companion. If a local investigation led to her, she'd be killed to prevent her from talking. *Threats must be eliminated* – why she killed Hancock and Bates. She was special, an insider, and rejected betrayal. No evidence existed that she'd been with Bates and Hancock including wiping her fingerprints where she touched.

Uncle Max would protect her.

Although concerned, she avoided panic but needed to protect herself.

At home in the garage, she opened the car's glove compartment, lifted the small pile of papers and car bills, and exposed the stainless steel Lady Smith & Wesson revolver. She had a permit to carry. She pulled the Lady out, closed the compartment, and returned to the kitchen with her security.

She'd get assurances from Uncle Max. To reassure herself and set aside the paranoia, she retraced her steps with pharmacist Troy Betson.

* * *

She had called Betson, chairperson of the Pharmacist's Association of Long Island to discuss a discount travel program for association members. He agreed to lunch. After the presentation, his dialogue slanted towards drugs as murder weapons in books and movies. She learned Rohypnol and succinylcholine's efficacy from Betson.

"Succinylcholine in small doses controls convulsions in cases of Strychnine poisoning. It is found in North and South America and Central America."

Betson, an avid Agatha Christie reader, said, "Agatha Christie used poisons in her mysteries. She had a background as a pharmacist. For example, Christie used cyanide in *Ten Little Indians* and *A Pocket Full of Rye.* She used other drugs also. In *Appointment With Death,* she used digitoxia. The classic film noir *D.O.A* starring Edmund O'Brien used a fictional poison called radium chloride. *Arsenic and Old Lace* was another illustration."

Betson discussed poisons administered by the Romans, Greeks, Chinese, and Egyptians and how Cleopatra used her slaves for experiments to find the perfect poison; then the notorious Borgias – Lucretia and Cesare – and their flagrant use, and to today's various and numerous poisonous products and drugs. Offering expertise on his favorite pastime excited him.

Olivia had this talk with him two months before she and Uncle Max decided on the procedures to eliminate Todd Hancock and Laurence Bates on the premise – *'Threats must be eliminated.'*

When she asked his opinion on how he'd poison someone, the probe linked to the conversation.

"All right," she remembered saying. "How would you poison a hated spouse? Had I known, I would've used it on my ex-husband." She laughed. "I'm kidding, of course, a severe wish at the time."

Betson was tall, in his early forties, bald with a dark beard, and wore wide rimless glasses. In lay terms, he explained how the drugs worked. "You use a small dose of Rohypnol, which is odorless and colorless in a drink to put the victim to sleep then inject succinylcholine. Too much Rohypnol can cause an overdose and death. Rohypnol is traceable and no longer a perfect murder drug. A little dose acts as a sleep aid. Succinylcholine dissipates in the body in a short time leaving no traces but speculation if the needle mark is discovered. An examiner might overlook the mark if injected in a non-obvious area. Skin texture changes after death and should hide any needle punctures unless you search for them."

"Where do you inject?"

"Succinylcholine chloride, also known as Anectine, affects the muscles. It is a white, odorless, slightly bitter powder soluble in water given intramuscularly or intravenous injection. It causes respiratory paralysis from seventy-five seconds to three minutes and has no antidotes or symptoms. I would inject it into the thigh muscles towards the back near the scrotum. That *might* avoid detection if one doesn't suspect murder."

"Your deadly knowledge scares me. Remind me to always remain your friend."

"And remind me never to marry you now that you know how to murder me," he joked.

She regretted never having this perfect murder information while married to the dentist.

Betson bought the travel discount plan.

He called her a month after their lunch. The Association's board of directors approved her program. As chairperson, he signed the proposal.

Several weeks later, Olivia called him again for lunch to discuss the program. He agreed. They met at a restaurant in Hicksville near his pharmacy.

"The conversation we had last time," she said after the travel plan discussion ended, "was about pharmacology in books, movies, and history. You spurred my interest in mysteries and pharmacology. You talked about a perfect murder using two drugs I cannot pronounce and had no reason to remember. Succi something or other."

"Succinylcholine and Rohypnol."

"Right, Rohypnol, the illegal date drug. What about the other? All drug stores carry succinylcholine?"

"Several do. I keep mine refrigerated in the prescription section." He smiled. "Do you have an enemy in mind?"

"No," she chuckled. "I have an idea for a mystery novel and thought to write on weekends. A perfect murder is a challenge."

They separated with Olivia having her drug information and a new account.

Uncle Max provided the Rohypnol. He obtained a supply through European connections.

Two days later, a break-in at Betson's pharmacy activated the alarm. The police and Betson couldn't determine what was stolen. They assumed the alarm scared the burglar.

Uncle Max also provided the efficient burglar who obtained the succinylcholine for her.

* * *

She contemplated the *Newsday* problem and rehashed her thoughts about Stanford, the lawyers, and Betson. He called. The coincidence amazed her.

"Your call is timely, Troy, coincidence. I just reviewed our arrangement."

"I must have picked up your vibrations. Why I called. Did you see *Newsday* today?"

She tensed. "No, I haven't had a chance. What's going on?"

"A front page story about two attorneys in the Kiley trial. Both disappeared during the trial and found dead. Police believe them murdered because of Rohypnol and possibly succinylcholine in both bodies. I mentioned those drugs to you. I thought to bring it to your attention. Have you started your mystery yet?"

"Yes, but I haven't gotten to the poisoning part yet. What a coincidence. I'll have someone run out to get *Newsday.*"

"Read the article if you continue with your mystery." He laughed. "I know it's not funny, but you came to mind once a woman was involved who could live on Long Island."

"Maybe if they were my husbands," she said faking a throaty giggle.

"I'm sorry, bad joke. Read the article. The reporter did his research on how the drugs work and there's an interview with a medical examiner about his methods. Good material for your book. Is everything else going well? Have my people responded?"

"Excellent, Troy. A few dozen have been active. Thanks again for your help."

"Any time. Let's get together again."

"We shall. Soon," she encouraged.

"I'll call you next week. And I should review your manuscript for accuracy when you're ready."

"Good idea. You're a sweetheart."

"Hold it, I forgot. I read a recent article in NewScientist.com about a plant referred to as 'suicide tree' as a perfect murder weapon in some communities in India. Authorities believe the plant kills many more people in those communities than previously thought. I'll read excerpts of the article to you. Could be a replacement in your book."

"Great, go ahead."

"Also known as *Cerbera odollam,* which grows across India and Southeast Asia, it is used by more people to commit suicide than any other plant. But toxicologists also warn that doctors, pathologists, and coroners fail to detect how often it is used to murder people. Three quarters of Cerbera victims are women. This might mean that the plant murders young wives who do not meet the exacting standards of some Indian families. It is also likely that many cases of homicide using the plant go unnoticed in countries where it doesn't grow naturally. End of article. It also goes on to say how to mix it for use. How does that sound?"

"Wow! Hold on to that for me. Sounds like a perfect weapon for the clandestine operations for the CIA or international counterparts. Troy, I promise we'll get together soon. All my extension lights are flashing."

"Go. I'll look forward to seeing you again."

Dazed by the first part of their conversation, she replaced the receiver, and focused on Betson.

Alarmed, Olivia switched to the sofa to massage her thoughts. *Newsday* and Troy made her vulnerable; a remote witness who connected her to the drugs. A decision arrived.

Returning to her desk, she dialed a private number. She stayed firm, determined in her decision – no turning back and no regrets. The response came.

Olivia pressed the secure button and said, "We have a problem...a serious problem."

* * *

A man turned into a mini-mall a few streets before the railroad overpass and parked near Troy Betson's pharmacy. He entered and headed for the prescription counter at the rear of the rectangular store where an elder woman waited for her prescription. Other customers browsed towards the front. The man stopped and reviewed the prophylactic display. Betson completed the prescription. The woman signed, paid a co-pay fee, and left. Betson approached the man studying the variations.

"Sir, can I help you with anything?"

"Oh, no thanks, doc. I need something new, you know?"

Betson grinned and returned to his work. He turned his back to fill a prescription for Coumadin.

The pharmacist fit the description: tall, bald, beard, glasses. The man opened his jacket, pulled out a silencer, and shot Betson twice in the back. Betson bashed forward against the counter and slipped to the floor, his white jacket turning red.

The killer walked casually out of the store.

Uncle Max provided the killer.

* * *

Olivia received assurances from Uncle Max when she called and awakened him at 3:00 a.m. She had awakened to answer nature's call and betrayal thoughts preyed, and deterred a return to sleep. The subject of her assassination refused to leave her thoughts clinging as barnacles to a hull in seawater.

"You're hallucinating, sweetheart…no reality to your fears. Everybody appreciates what you did. From what I learned, the mess started with Stanford Crane to find out why his predecessors bolted the trial. He persuaded the medical examiners to compare notes. I will kill anyone who even dares threaten you."

"I never thought anyone would make the connection, or have reason. I'm carrying a revolver with me at all times to defend myself."

"Needless, but if it makes you feel better do it. Crane protects himself."

"There's no evidence, only coincidences," she reassured.

She refused to tell him police questioned her travel agent regarding the Todd Hancock and Laurence Bates bookings. The police left satisfied about the coincidence.

"I'll be more creative with Crane," she said.

"I believe you will, my eternal love. Remember, time is running out."

"I hear the clock ticking."

FRIDAY.

Pilar and Nancy missed the *Newsday* article yesterday. When Madge read the dead lawyers article she hid the paper to avoid distressing Nancy, a protective act, but bad timing and inappropriate to deal with conjecture. When Nancy asked for *Newsday*, Madge said, "It wasn't delivered today. I forgot to call and complain." For Madge, the article was another invisible nail hammered into her world of misery.

Pilar never read *Newsday* when she returned to her room to pack. She discovered the stunning article in the morning while wrapping newspaper sheets around glasses. She called Nancy and read the article.

"Their lawyer tactics failed," Nancy said. "I think they won't bother with Crane as they did with Hancock and Bates, but come after us instead."

Pilar gasped from fright. "Oh, no!"

"I'm guessing. For them to continue the same procedure on Crane is illogical. But desperate people do desperate things. We must act cautious. After you move to the apartment tomorrow move in with me. We're safe here until my trial starts."

"You think that's necessary."

"Pilar, they are vicious. You don't want to live alone and unprotected. Get real."

"I agree. Oh, be friendlier with your mother. She needs you to need her now. I know you protect her. Your rejection is another problem for her."

"When the time comes, I'll explain and she'll forgive me. She doesn't store anger or hold grudges and is forgiving. I love and respect her."

* * *

Having difficulty with sleep after the conversation with Uncle Max, Olivia ignored the 7:00 a.m. alarm, moaned with fatigue, rolled over, and slept for another hour.

Feeling lethargic, Stanford spurred her thoughts as she drove towards her office. At 9:00, she called Gwen to check if Stanford called. No one called.She settled in traffic flow and called Stanford's office as she passed the Willis Avenue exit and an orange Astro Moving and Storage van. Rhonda put her through.

"Olivia, good morning." said an upbeat Stanford. "I was about to call your office."

"I'm headed to a meeting. You *know* I'm calling for the rain check." She sounded cheery.

"Again, my apologies. The judge needed to conference with both sides as an out of court sidebar."

"Shall we try again?" she asked as traffic slowed between Exit 39 and Exit 40.

"We'll have to wait. Send your proposal to me. I promise to read it first chance I get. I have no time at all next week. I start a case the week after and must prepare. We can meet after the trial."

She urged, "Then let's do dinner away from the disruptive business day and away from your club like a quiet bistro, and this time you're my guest and that's fair." She tensed for his reply that came without hesitation.

"A positive solution and do-able."

"How about this evening?"

Stanford laughed at her prompt initiative appreciating her sales effort.

"I can't at all this weekend. I'm going to Vermont for the weekend. Friends have a home in Mount Snow. How about Monday night?"

Success! "Ideal. There's a second element to my hospitality. Have dinner at my house. I'll provide the food and you provide the wine. What do you say?" *...said the spider to the fly.*

Stanford hesitated.

"I say I look forward to seeing you."

She guessed right and beamed. The flowers expressed his interest.

"Great. Here's my address." She said the address.

"What time is good for you?"

"Seven. Seven-thirty," she said.

"I'll be there with bells. I'm in Long Beach that day, but I should finish by six-thirty.""I also offer choices. You prefer Italian, Chinese, Japanese, Greek, American, what? I operate an international kitchen."

"You're that versatile? I'm impressed."

"I don't cook, darling. I cater from terrific restaurants. I learned from my mother. Take your choice."

He laughed again. "Make it Italian. You select the menu. I eat everything."

"I promise you'll love the selection."

"And you'll love the wine."

"And the Italian dessert will be spectacular," she said.

"What is that?"

"I'll surprise you."

Enthused at the outcome, she beeped Uncle Max and conveyed her progress with Stanford. *That should ease his pressure.*

* * *

In late afternoon, Mullins called Mitchell.

"Forget visiting Antigua or Liechtenstein. I have detailed reports from both authorities. Two taxi drivers in Antigua remember a woman passenger with the hat. One drove her from the airport, another to the airport. No facial descriptions other than that she wore sunglasses and a hat. St. James's Club employees didn't see Hancock's companion, or could offer descriptions. A bellhop in Liechtenstein escorted a woman to Bates's room. He couldn't describe her. I have lists of the various people interviewed." Mitchell wrote notes.

"Regarding airlines," Mullins said. "Hancock booked a one-way trip to Antigua on American Airlines. Bates booked a one-way trip to Vaduz, Liechtenstein. Neither one planned to return to the States, or make their own arrangements for elsewhere. We'll run a credit card check for reservations. Why would two attorneys plan to go to a tax haven? Hancock sold his condominium before he left meaning he never planned to return. An anonymous foreign corporation using a law firm in Nassau in the Bahamas purchased the condominium. It's already rented for two years. All papers are legal. The estate executor failed to locate the money."

"You work fast. How about Bates? Did he have an asset to sell?"

"The bank received the papers on his house last week. Consensus is they received payment in cash overseas to avoid taxes. The relevant point is that the same attorney in the Bahamas filed the sale with the Bates bank."

"The MOs continue the same as if given similar instructions."

"The same travel agent booked airline and hotel reservations for both – Marilyn Schroeder, who is their exclusive agent under a travel discount program with their firms. My people accept that coincidence. If you want to talk to her, you can reach her at Village Greene Travel Service in Woodbury."

Olivia Greene!

The unexpected lifted Mitchell's eyebrows.

* * *

After Madge said goodbye to Pilar, she returned to the kitchen to finish preparations for dinner. She expected Austin soon to offer comfort and assurance in the turbulence. Tuna steaks waited trimmed and basted with a lemon and white wine sauce with a touch of ginger, an Austin favorite. She always prepared a favorite dish to welcome him home after an absence to remind him there's no place like home, crisis and all.

The country style kitchen had a fireplace and early American furniture and decor. Madge loved the culinary arts and her kitchen. To escape these stressful days, she prepared her personal cookbook to pass on to Nancy. Her kitchen evolved into a haven to help overcome loneliness when Austin stayed in Washington. Nancy turned into more of a concern than a companion did and remained withdrawn in her room.

Madge perked when the garage door opened, a signal her husband arrived early. He parked a car at LaGuardia. Austin looked troubled to Madge when he came into the kitchen through the garage and laundry room. She knew his moods and nuances. He always entered upbeat and bright leaving Senate problems in Washington happy being with Nancy and her. Austin wore a glum face.

"Is she upstairs?" he said and headed for the foyer.

The slight jolted Madge. "No hello, after a week? Austin!" she called out.

Austin stopped. He lacked reason for anger with Madge.

"I'm sorry, Madge. I have too much on my mind. My apologies." He embraced her and kissed her cheek. "Always know I love you no matter how I act. The constant pressure here and in Washington over-whelms me. Please understand."

She conveyed understanding with a hug. "Nancy's in her room, as usual. She comes out when Pilar arrives. I'm glad you're here."

"Is Nancy alone?" He hoped for a positive answer.

"Yes. Pilar left a while ago. They played tennis and swam today." She studied her husband's face. Something wasn't right. "What's wrong, Austin? What happened?" He turned to leave. She held him firm. "Tell me. Please." Her eyes widened.

He ignored her. "Later." He pulled away.

"Don't do this to me, Austin!" she stated in a louder tone. "I have enough to put up with already. You're away and I have a daughter at home who's always in her room, and I'm living in an armed encamp-ment. I don't have a family. Don't you brush me off. I'm not a house-plant. If there's something wrong, I need to know." Her eyes flared. "I can't stand being ignored. I'm drowning in rejection. I can't breathe! I need a life when you're here. *Please* give me a life!"

Witnessing rare anger from Madge, he returned and hugged her. "Madge, you're right. Please calm down. I'm sorry." He held her to console. "I need to see Nancy. She's been lying why she needs the security guards."

"Lying?" Her face contorted. "Why?"

"Stanford is concerned. He believes there's more than she's admitting. I need a serious talk with her that can't wait. Satisfied?"

Madge nodded and headed for the stove confused...once again a spectator to the crisis.

"What's for dinner?" stalled her.

He treated the question as a throwaway stage line.

"Tuna steak and salad," she mumbled.

Austin nodded approval. "Great. Back soon with Nancy."

Austin left and hurried up the stair to Nancy's room. Without knocking on the closed door, he entered, and slammed the door.

Nancy, at the computer, jumped up and yelled, "What do you want? Get out. Get out!" She rushed towards him to open the door to throw him out.

Austin swung a slap that sent her reeling sideways into the bureau and to the floor. He stood over her.

"Tell me the truth!"

"I won't."

Their yelling reached the kitchen. Madge stopped her activity when she heard the muffled yelling and undistinguished words. She heard them argue in the past, but less strident. Alarmed, she hurried to the staircase.

The door to Nancy's room opened and slammed. Austin raced down the stair his right hand behind his back to hide bloodstains and said, "Go back, Madge. The matter is settled." He passed her. "I'm going to my boat. Forget dinner. I'll discuss Nancy later."

Exempted from another family crisis, confused and concerned, Madge rushed upstairs to Nancy's room. She knocked. No answer. She opened the door.

Her hand covered her mouth to stem the shock.

Nancy rested on one knee about to rise in pain holding her bruised arms close to her body. Blood flowed from her nose.

Madge ran to her child.

"O God! What happened? What's going on?"

"Mom, forget it. We argued and I slipped against the bureau. I'm fine. I need ice."

"But why did he leave you bleeding?"

"He didn't see the blood."

"Did he ask about the security?"

"Mom, I told you why I need them. Forget it. Please." She entered the bathroom for the medicine cabinet and closed the door.

Cast aside, Madge returned to the kitchen and set a table for two. When dinner was cooked, she notified Nancy. Nancy entered the kitchen, filled her plate, and left to eat in her room.

Madge lost her appetite, deserted again by her family, and still lost in a strange land.

She cried.

When done and eyes dabbed dry, she ate alone again.

She cried again before dinner ended.

SATURDAY.

Olivia received an invitation to a Saturday afternoon cruise on Randy Hawkins's yacht in Sag Harbor with cocktails at 1:00 p.m. plus a roundtrip cruise on Sunday to Newport, Rhode Island. She looked forward to this social with delight and great expectations for the weekend.

Randy, a business force on Long Island, volunteered to help Village Greene Travel Service and introduced her to a few major clients. His company signed as a travel package client. Randy never hesitated to do all he could to please her. Olivia knew his wife Beth.

Nancy Kiley killed their son Eddie.

Weekend weather forecasted as ideal and seasonal with lower temperatures at night. Olivia packed her needs. She wore a blue denim shirt, matching blue jeans, and white docksiders.

She reached the commercial center, Main Street and the thick flowing mosaic of tourists drawn to the waterfront. President George Washington designated the famous town an official port of entry in 1797, growing into a major whaling port comparable to New Bedford and Nantucket on the Atlantic seacoast.

Olivia crept with slow traffic on Main Street, turned right on Bay Street, and parked in the marina parking lot on the left. Randy's yacht was visible from there. She followed the dock that skirted the dockside restaurant then passed through the gate alongside Long Wharf and headed for the yacht.

The impressive 72-foot *Golden Hawk* tied to cleats on her starboard side.

Captain Walker Conniver, dressed in whites, and acting as a maitre d' greeted as she reached the boarding steps.

"Permission to come aboard, Captain." She made a comedic salute as she smiled.

"And permission granted. Always a pleasure to see you, Ms. Greene."

"Hello, Walker, same here."

Captain Conniver accepted her designer duffel bag. A steward, dressed in whites, carried the bag below to her assigned stateroom. Captain Conniver was thin, thirty-seven years old with blond hair. A professional private yacht captain, he captained the *Golden Hawk* over a year.

Randy, in his mid-fifties, exuded authority with a general's demeanor and social grace of a practiced host, medium built and stocky with broad shoulders, blue eyes, a sharp nose and an outdoors sculptured face, now an executive no longer dirtying his hands from construction work.

Randy's construction business varied – from private homes, commercial buildings, to road and bridgework. His state and county contracts totaled in the hundreds of millions. Austin Kiley's political power proved helpful and influential to Randy in those areas.

Aboard, Olivia turned aft towards the salon where four men and two women sat in a semicircle nursing cocktails. Randy excused from his guests and approached her.

With arms outstretched he said, "Welcome, my dear Olivia. Glad you could make it."

"I would never say no to your invitation or for anything, darling."

"That's my girl. You look lovely as usual." He kissed her cheek and added a firm hug. "How was your trip?"

"The traditional summer weekend traffic, ugly."

"Come, let's get you a drink."

"The usual Black Label and mineral water. I don't see Beth. Is she below?"

"She refuses to socialize until after one year from Eddie's death, her religious nature. My business life must go on and on."

Randy prepared Olivia's drink and escorted her to the semicircle. The men stood almost in unison to greet her.

"This is Olivia Greene travel agent extraordinaire. Never leave home without her. Olivia, you know Janet and Bob Graham. This is Susan and Congressman Anthony Bianchi. Greg Morris you know."

Bianchi, thirty-six and a lawyer, served as a congressional representative from Randy's district. His wife, eight years younger, smiled looking uncomfortable in a new environment of wealth and power.

Janet and Bob Graham owned a home mortgage organization and summered at their home in Sag Harbor. They also owned a home in Kings Point in Nassau County. Olivia was familiar with their television commercials and their slogan – 'When the banks say "Uh, uh," we say, no problem.'

The Grahams, Nigerian Americans in their mid-forties, met in law school in Lagos, Nigeria. They fled Nigeria twenty years ago during a military coup and came to America where they changed their first names for business purposes. The Graham ancestors had adopted the name after a beloved Englishman. Their wealthy parents – her father prospered as a corrupt public official – remained in Nigeria, but managed to smuggle four million dollars to Switzerland for their use. Once settled in New York City, Janet and Bob Graham wired for money when needed.

Greg Morris, forty-two, handsome, and tall was an executive vice-president at a leading Wall Street bank and Randy's personal financial advisor and wealth manager.

After he greeted and embraced Olivia, Greg remained next to her 'claiming' Olivia as his escort for the day. She often met Greg at fund-raiser benefits where he accompanied Beth and Randy Hawkins.

Randy herded his guests to the top open-air deck where a steward worked a mini-bar. Another steward served hors d'oeuvres. A disc by Frank Sinatra provided background music; "...*exchanging glances. Strangers at first sight, what were the chances...*"

Randy entertained his guests with his storytelling and jokes setting an atmosphere for joviality and informality, the center of attraction. Appetizers and cocktails continued.

At three o'clock, Randy announced they would weigh anchor for their cruise into The Long Island Sound and up Connecticut's Thames River when the guest of honor, Senator Austin Kiley arrived. Senator Kiley called ahead to apologize for a delay.

Randy spotted Austin alone and in casual wear, and with a blue overnight bag.

"There's Senator Kiley now," he said for all to hear. Austin looked up and waved. Randy turned to the bar steward. "Tell the captain the Senator is here." The steward left.

Olivia nudged Greg as Senator Kiley approached and whispered, "Senator Kiley is quite a hunk, isn't he?"

"Hey, you're with me, remember?" He smiled.

"I won't forget, darling."

Austin boarded, greeted by the captain. Randy waited by the steps. Austin reached the top deck, shook hands with Randy, and they hugged as friends experiencing a similar tragedy.

"Austin, you know the Grahams, the Bianchis." Austin touched cheeks with the women then approached Olivia and Greg.

"Hello, Greg. How did I know you'd be here?"

"You know me, Austin, at the right place at the right time. Free rides, food, and drinks are a specialty." They laughed. "This is Olivia Greene."

"How nice to meet you," Austin studied her, stirring his memory. "But you do look familiar. Have we met?"

"I've seen you at a fund raiser where you spoke, Senator. I also do commercials for my travel agency. You might have seen those. Village Greene Travel Service."

He formed a contemplative face and grinned. "No, that's not it. I know I've seen you before. I'll think on it."

"Come over here, Austin," Randy interrupted. "Let me fix you a drink."

"Excuse me," Austin said to her. "Our host beckons."

Greg wrapped his arm around Olivia and led her towards the stern.

Golden Hawk flowed forward until her stern cleared the pilings. Captain Conniver pivoted her to face the channel. He followed the channel, passed the breakwater to starboard at 6-knots, shifted to neutral on and off to approximate 5-knots channel speed until he reached Gardiner's Bay. He increased to a moderate cruising speed at 12-knots.

The large yacht burst a wide wake as it glided with muffled diesel engines. They exited the bay at Plum Gut and cruised across The Long Island Sound and up the Thames River past New London, Connecticut and the United States Coast Guard Academy with its many buildings sweeping up the hillside along the western waterfront.

Austin sat next to Randy and Susan Bianchi across from Janet and Bob Graham, who sat next to Olivia. Both Grahams had a British leaning speech pattern, were social, outgoing, and smiled and laughed with ease.

After two hours, *Golden Hawk* turned for the return cruise. A comfortable camaraderie enveloped *Golden Hawk's* guests.

During the cruise, Bianchi asked Austin about Madge, who needed to remain home with Nancy. Mentioning Nancy was the sole reference to the joint family misfortune. The guests knew that Randy and the Senator's long friendship transcended the tragedy.

Stewards established a buffet: grilled bluefish fresh from the Montauk docks, pasta salad, sliced filet mignon, shrimp, green salad and *Golden Hawk's* private label wines Cabernet Sauvignon and Chardonnay.

They reached Sag Harbor after 8:00, berthed on the starboard side, and continued their social in the salon after a cooler evening breeze arrived.

At midnight, Janet and Bob Graham left *Golden Hawk* for their home in the Sag Harbor hills to return in the morning for breakfast and the trip to Newport. Olivia hugged and touched cheeks with both as old friends. Austin retired to his stateroom a few minutes later complaining of exhaustion and tried to stifle yawns. Susan and the Congressman excused themselves and left for their stateroom.

Randy, Olivia, and Greg remained.

"I'd better be going, also," Randy said. "I'll see you two at breakfast." He left for the master stateroom.

"Did you enjoy the day, darling?" Greg said reaching out to hold her hand.

"I always do being with you."

"Wait here," Gregg said. "I'll check below to make sure it's safe. If I'm not back in twenty seconds, come down. Stateroom Two."

Greg left the salon. Olivia studied the luxurious and spacious salon decorated in American Southwest tones – a clams and seashells motif, waiting for the seconds to pass. She loved the luxury of the yachting life. She'd extract more invitations from Randy.

After waiting for nearly a minute, Olivia left and reached Stateroom 2 and opened the door. She entered, closed, and locked the door.

With a white robe covering his naked body, he waited by the bed and watched her, impatient for her, and admired and devoured her movements with a hunger building all day. She leaned against the wall, kicked off her shoes, and undressed with slow motions, pants first then unbuttoned the shirt.

"Want some?" she whispered as fingers beckoned. Liquor and expectation of his embrace heightened passion.

United States Senator Austin Kiley obeyed the fingers and leaned his body against hers as he kissed her neck, face, and lips. His touch sent electricity to her nerve endings. She pressed closer, body yielding, and his lips tender and roved as he unbuttoned her shirt. He removed the shirt and flung it across the room.

Austin released the brassiere and dropped it. His thumbs pulled the panties downwards as he lowered to his knees to reach her ankles. She stepped from her clothes.

Austin caressed her legs.

Austin kissed her thighs as he ascended to stomach and navel then chest.

He stood and tongues met. Olivia moaned as he whispered passionate words to force their embrace to grow tighter and stronger. Austin lifted her and walked backwards to the bed. Her legs wrapped around his body and captured him. Olivia embraced his face and whispered as she kissed and pecked his mouth with fervor.

"My love, my love. We're together as we should be."

"You missed me?" Austin teased.

"I always miss my Uncle Max."

PART II

They slept the comfortable sleep of exhausted lovers in each other's arms until Olivia awakened before dawn. Her stirring to make love again awakened Austin to take advantage of their part-time togetherness. She then left to sneak to her stateroom opposite Austin's before the Bianchis awakened. The Bianchis knew Madge.

Randy, Greg, and the Grahams knew of Olivia and Austin's affair.

If there, Greg acted as Olivia's escort when she and Austin attended the same business or social function. She kept her distance from Austin in Greg's absence. They then met at her house if Austin arrived at the function without Madge. He concocted a phony excuse to Madge when he arrived home late.

Olivia resented Madge taking up his time and often wished her dead.

Janet and Bob Graham arrived at 8:10 and joined Greg and Randy for breakfast in the salon. At 8:15, Austin arrived. Susan and Congressman Bianchi entered at 8:22 and Olivia, wearing an orange T-shirt and white pants, happily greeted all two minutes later.

Captain Conniver started engines when stewards removed breakfast remains and guests settled on the top deck.

Day remained sunny and mild, perfect for cruising to an exciting international port.

Susan, mother of two young children, postponed her career in the research department of an advertising agency in Melville. She said to Olivia, "I'm not excited about going back. I love staying home with my kids. We live half the time in Washington. When the kids reach school age, I'll find something in D. C."

"Your husband is an effective congressman. I understand that Randy's a huge supporter. That means a lot up here." They sat on the bow bench cushion. "I'm sure Senator Kiley also supports him."

"Randy's great. We see the Senator at functions. I prefer raising the kids than working in an office. I don't want to be viewed as a ladder climbing elbow wife for my husband because that's how that scene plays out down there."

Olivia removed her business and ambition hats to communicate on Susan's interests. Olivia thrived as an executive – happy to sell, promote, advertise, wheel and deal, and make money. She grinned at her next thought – And kill lawyers and pharmacists – 'Threats must be eliminated'.

Janet joined them as they neared Block Island and conversation changed to fashion, imports, and retailing. Janet specialized in fashion imports from Nigeria. Olivia floated with the social flow.

Two hours after departing Sag Harbor, they docked in world famous Newport Harbor at Harbor Bay Hotel Marina, a facility that accommodated large yachts. This busy harbor throbbed with life. Sailing vessels, local and from foreign waters, saturated harbor moorings from Newport Yacht Club on one end to Ida Lewis Yacht Club and Brenton Cove on the other. Numerous foreign flags flew at sterns;

England, Australia, France, South Africa, Venezuela, Sweden, and others unrecognized by Olivia.

Newport's skyline featured church steeples, the tallest structures – no tall buildings or skyscrapers. She visited Newport before; four times last year. She visited on a Saturday and registered at a waterfront hotel to wait for Austin. Twice, he came alone for the weekend.Other times, he came with guests and Madge. Austin left his guests and Madge for an hour and a half saying he was going to jog, twice on Saturdays – then hastened to Olivia's hotel. On Sunday, he visited her in the morning. She left Newport to play blackjack at Foxwoods Casino in Connecticut for several hours before returning to Long Island.

Olivia wished Madge dead at least a dozen times since.

I should force Madge to take the perfected champagne cocktail. Maybe it's time to implement that terrific idea to end a major obstacle.

Susan, Congressman Bianchi, and Bob Graham left *Golden Hawk* to stroll the town. Randy, Greg, Janet, and Austin gathered in the galley for a 'closed door' meeting.

Olivia remained on the bow with a novel and propped against the bulkhead.She needed to stay on board during the important meeting. Austin asked her to stand by if he needed her to attend the meeting. She knew the cruise to Newport wasn't the main reason, but a subterfuge.

The trip served as an excuse to conduct business.

Two stewards lowered the top deck launch. Captain Conniver boarded with a case of Budweiser in cans, undid the line, and headed out towards the mooring field across the channel. He idled to allow a sightseeing boat to pass. Olivia watched him weave at harbor speed among moored boats.

Olivia knew his mission. She watched as he slowed and tied up with a 56-foot schooner moored near Goat Island. The American ensign flew from the schooner's stern.

Conniver passed the case of beer to an unshaved sailor and boarded. Olivia watched the schooner for ten minutes. Captain Conniver and two men appeared. Conniver lowered into the launch and the men passed down twelve cases of assorted foreign beer in aluminum cans.

She watched as Conniver weaved his way to *Golden Hawk*. Stewards waited on the dock. Conniver unloaded the beer on the yacht's stern platform and boarded as the stewards tended to bring the launch about.

Only Conniver handled the beer cases. Putting them in the salon, he closed the stern door. Carrying two cases at a time, he stored the beer in the engine room against the bulkhead where guests wouldn't pry.

Olivia knew the procedure.

The beer case Conniver brought to the schooner contained money. The beer cases he brought back contained drugs in cans. Clever, she concluded. Austin had said the schooner arrived from the Azores after stopping at Annapolis to supply Baltimore and at Cape May, New Jersey then up the Delaware River to supply Philadelphia and Trenton.

The schooner would then head south to Nevis to deposit the cash in a numbered account after several more stops with no rush or urgency in the entire operation. Numerous sailboats kept the operation moving coming and going with ocean transfers, and avoiding the Caribbean when carrying drugs. Cash differed.

If exposed, Conniver would accept all blame. He'd take the fall, the terms he accepted – that he ran his own private operation unbeknownst to *Golden Hawk's* owner. Conniver excelled as a successful drug runner in the Florida and Caribbean area and came recommended by the Colombia and Netherlands networks for the Long Island operation. Conniver's philosophy required small batches at a time and patience.

Whenever Conniver made a drug run, Randy made sure he had a public official on board should the United States Coast Guard want to conduct a random search, empowered to do and had often in this area famous as an international sailing destination. *Golden Hawk* identified as a familiar vessel from Long Island waters to Nantucket Island. The public official served as insurance that *Golden Hawk* might bypass a search. The familiar Congressman Bianchi from Long Island fronted as this trip's insurance. Austin served as an added bonus today motivated by his need to be with Olivia.

The galley meeting of Randy Hawkins, Senator Austin Kiley, Greg Morris, and Janet Graham merged as a foul gathering.

The cabal that financed the Long Island drug trade met in session on *Golden Hawk* in Newport, Rhode Island.

They formed the person who Mullins sought, the notorious Argentinean.

They were Rodrigo.

Olivia waited for the Rodrigo board of directors' meeting to end. Wealthy persons who should have found a better investment with their money, she bemoaned. The decision amassed their collective moments of madness to converge at the same time. They never should have allowed Janet and Bob Graham to persuade them to finance the drugs from Colombia via Asia, The Netherlands, Nigeria, and The Azores. First, the Grahams persuaded Greg, who managed their finances, who persuaded Randy, who persuaded Austin – all assured Austin of safety, secrecy, and foreign banks.

Olivia's outrage matched a mother's scolding of her child when Austin confessed his involvement after Nancy killed Eddie. When her fit passed, she devoted herself to help and keep him safe although her persistent efforts failed to persuade him to resign from Rodrigo.

"There's no getting out," he stressed.

Bob Graham, their field general, established the distribution channels in Suffolk County. Former channels reopened once he recruited Tomayo Suarez. Austin felt safe, hidden, and that nothing was traceable to him; a cash and numbered accounts world. Olivia believed the others felt the same.

How naïve.

How greedy.

After an hour, Olivia remained nervous and concerned. The novel failed to divert her thoughts although she continued to read. The starboard door opened and closed. She set her novel aside hoping Austin's meeting ended.

Austin appeared on deck, dejected. "It's over," he said in a low voice as he sat next to her and faced forward.

"What? The meeting?"

"Waiting for Nancy. They've lost patience. Time ran out for me to protect her."

Her face showed disappointment. "Did you mention I've dinner planned with Crane tomorrow night?"

Austin shifted position to face her. "I did but they prefer you leave Crane out. Cancel him. The *Newsday* article panicked them. They never expected those overseas events to return home. Telling Crane the procedure invites exposure. Janet is jittery. Have your dinner with Crane to sell only your travel package."

"Crane will never violate a secrecy oath."

"He may. You don't have the legal protection clients have." Austin squeezed her fingers. "I don't want you jeopardized any longer."

"You should've let me talk to them. Did they all agree?"

"There wasn't an opportune moment for you. Greg and Randy agreed to give me more time. Janet opposed. Anything to go forward must be unanimous, as you know. She wants it to end now. I can't fault her. They respected my wishes and waited a long time. Her husband pushes for closure. Nancy stalled his profitable programs.

"A shipment is due next week at Block Island from Bermuda on a sloop called *Mandalay. Mandalay's* homeport is Norfolk, Virginia. American based boats arouse less suspicion. Because of Nancy, they can't complete the transaction, a larger shipment. Randy believes he can get *Mandalay* to lay over an additional week the latest. I must succeed with Nancy by next weekend. I'll be more forceful with her tonight. In the meantime, Walker will sail my boat around to Three Mile Harbor then go to Block."

"Austin, listen to me." She extended her right arm to coax his face to turn towards her. "Stanford will never violate secrecy. He'll wonder who approached me to give him the message. I'll say my life was threatened if I didn't. He won't tell the judge, or the police. He's a legal purist."

"That's a helluva lousy gamble."

"Well, if he does or threatens to I'll kill him."

Austin shook his head in despair. "Is killing so easy for you?"

"Yes, for you. All I do for you will always come easy. I need you free from prosecution so I can love you forever, to be with you always. For that, I have no boundaries when it comes to doing for you."

"Then for me, no more killings."

"If that's what you want, yes. Maybe the lure of three million dollars plus may entice him. Few can resist that amount tax free."

Austin remained pessimistic. "I doubt money will alter his ethics. I might have thought so once. Different now. Best direction is to exert pressure on Nancy. She must see the danger that she's jeopardizing her mother, Pilar, and me. She's dealing with Graham's vicious people. The next step is up to me." He gazed at the clean fiberglass deck and glittering rub rail, his thoughts in turmoil. "Janet was crazed with impatience, the bitch. Did you hear us argue? Sometimes, she's more vicious than her husband."

"I couldn't hear from here."

"Her moods are impossible to deal with. Her husband is no better. She's the brain and he's the executioner. His hardball tactics with dealers keeps the operation running and secure. Graham has whole families wiped out if anyone crosses him. He's a butcher. He has their mouths, hands, and feet taped then shoots them in the left ear, children first. That's their trademark to establish Rodrigo as a person."

"You already told me his methods. And the bloody name Rodrigo inside the riata. You can add me to your family. They can't afford to have me live if they turn on you."

"That won't happen. Randy and Greg will never approve. Remember, all decisions must be unanimous. They consider you an important member of the team and trust you. They all ordered your pharmacist eliminated because you labeled him a possible threat. You proved yourself."

"I assume nothing. The Grahams will receive my special champagne cocktail if you think they might attack you. If anything happens to you, I'll kill them all. I have a gun and know how to use it."

"The gun won't help. If they kill me, you run."

She hesitated as anger and determination crept on her face. "I'll never do that. I won't run, no matter what. If they kill you, I don't want to live without you. I swear, I will avenge you."

"Enough. This is a crazy conversation. There's more to life than me."

"Not for me."

"All will turn fine once Nancy confesses. Let's get ready to leave. I hear them now."

Austin stood and scanned the immediate Newport surroundings. He approached the rub rail and leaned against it.

Olivia failed to speak, in a trance, and distant. Her silence made him turn. "Are we going to town?" He nudged her stupor.

"Wha...oh, yes". She stood and approached him. "I need to visit the marine supply store. An aside, the captain completed the transaction with a sailboat across the harbor. I watched the transaction."

"Simple, wasn't it? Easy."

"Yes, but dangerous."

Olivia searched for the schooner near Goat Island. The mooring bobbed unoccupied. She searched towards the channel in time to see the schooner turn to leave Newport Harbor and wondered where the next load of poison headed.

The door slid open again. Randy, Greg, and Janet in a jovial mood joined them on deck and they all left *Golden Hawk* as if the meeting never happened. Olivia and Janet walked arm-in-arm and conversed as old friends, actors to each other. The men followed.

At the marine supply store on America's Cup Avenue, Olivia and Austin peeled off to catch up to the others later. She purchased nautical binoculars and night vision binoculars.

"Why buy binoculars?" Austin asked.

"Gifts for employees, two boaters who reached certain sales levels."

Olivia lied. She needed binoculars for a counteroffensive to monitor their activity day and night if Austin felt threatened.

She wouldn't run.

She would counterattack.

* * *

Austin's distressed state angered and depressed Olivia as she watched him grapple with futility regarding his daughter. Often, he ignored her words with his mind occupied.

Olivia wanted to hold and comfort him, to assure all would turn out all right, that all was surmountable, and everything negotiable.

Her man reached the point where he couldn't protect his daughter and himself.

And me. To hell with his wife and daughter.

Austin's condition worsened when he called Olivia at one in the morning after they returned from Sag Harbor. When she answered the awakening phone, a long pause followed after he said her name.

"What is it, Austin," she mumbled into the phone. "What happened?" She pushed the white satin sheet aside and sat up.

"I pleaded and begged Nancy tonight to end this madness." He hesitated again. "She refused unless I withdrew."

"There's always Stanford Crane and my program."

"He won't do any good." His voice lacked conviction. "He could tell Nancy he knows, that he'll tell the court and police what she did, or as reason to withdraw."

"Come to me. Let me comfort you. We can discuss Crane further."

"No. I'll call you during the week. I need time to think. Goodnight."

"Wait," she urged. "Do you want me in Washington? I'll take the week off."

"No, my considerate love. You have a business to run. Sorry to have awakened you. I needed to talk to you."

"And I need you to always need me and to never need anything or anyone else."

"I'll always need you as I have every day since I met you." Olivia savored his statement. "Bye, for now," Austin added and hung up.

* * *

Olivia's thoughts faded to the coming evening with Stanford Crane.

What should I do?

Mention only the travel plan?

And trivia?

Or confront him with the truth about Nancy and why she killed Eddie Hawkins – requiring me to poison Stanford...a threat that must be eliminated.

Olivia remained confused after wrestling with the complexities.

MONDAY.

Mitchell left the city in midmorning to talk with Marilyn Schroeder and Olivia regarding the dead lawyers. When Mullins mentioned Village Greene, he stunned Mitchell with Olivia's connection to the three Kiley defense attorneys. He thought – *If Marilyn Schroeder wasn't helpful to Mullins's people, how could she be helpful to me? How could Olivia?*

Olivia answered Gwen's buzz.

"Mr. Pappas is here to see you."

What could he want? Why visit?

She opened her door and emoted, "Mitchell! What a wonderful surprise."

"Good morning. I was in the neighborhood and wanted to say hello and discuss a travel package."

She rejected the 'in the neighborhood' line. As for the travel package, he could have called from Manhattan. "Please come in." Before closing the door she said, "Gwen, hold my calls," to underscore his visit as important.

Mitchell occupied a visitor's chair, Olivia the desk chair.

"How's Helene?"

"Fine, thank you. She sends regards."

"So, where do you plan to go and when?"

"Next year. June. We want to divide a month among Australia, New Zealand, and China. Keep the trip first class. If I left that to Helene, I'll be backpacking."Mitchell passed a business card to her. "You can forward the itinerary anytime within the next month. I'll have the actual dates for you after Helene checks her calendar."

"The earlier the better to assure better seats and rooms. My people travel often. I have a few who visited your locales. They'll personalize your itinerary including the best restaurants. In today's world of personal computers where one reserves plane tickets and hotels from home, we offer extended services. You name the country; chances are we've been there."

"How did you do with Stanford and your discount travel program?"

"He's busy with a new case and hasn't had a chance to meet. We had a few phone conversations. I nearly got him to lunch but he had to be in court the last minute." She had no intention to reveal she'd see Stanford tonight. And why would Stanford tell him?

"Keep after him. He's taken on the Nancy Kiley murder case and the trial starts soon. Are you familiar with the case?"

"That case has gone on forever. Nancy Kiley did the right thing. Every raped woman should kill her attacker and given a medal for preventing him from raping anyone ever again. Men made the rape laws they deem fair to men, and when the woman defends herself the laws defend the rapist, questioning her integrity and character and lawyers call them whores or nymphomaniacs. I abhor men who abuse women. I remind you that American women never had the right to vote until about ninety years ago and almost pay equality recently. I'm rooting for Stanford to free Nancy Kiley and women to govern the world. And any educated woman who thinks differently is brain dead."

"I believe Stanford will succeed."

"I understand you might be involved with him. I'm sure he can use your help."

"Intriguing is the *Newsday* story about the two previous lawyers who allegedly were murdered. If so, the killer might be a Long Island resident. Stanford needs to know if there's any connection to the trial. What happened to the lawyers could happen to him. It's safer to check."

"I read the article. Police visited since the attorneys were clients. I signed them to the same travel package I plan to present to Stanford. We revealed all travel arrangements with them, but nothing relevant to help the case. It's scary that both were clients."

"Can I talk to Ms. Schroeder about them?"

The suspicious Olivia asked herself – *How did he know Marilyn was their agent? You revealed your visit's true purpose, Pappas. You're connected to the police.*

"I'll have her come in and talk." *Only with me here.* Olivia dialed Marilyn's extension.

"Bring all the records you showed to the police on Todd Hancock and Laurence Bates. Someone in my office needs to talk to you." She ended the call. "Marilyn works on the second floor with the corporate and professional division."

"I can't imagine what I'll learn that the police don't have, but my involvement makes Stanford feel safer."

Marilyn knocked and entered with two file folders, in her mid-forties, average stature, rimless glasses, and short blond hair. Olivia introduced Mitchell and said to Marilyn, "Start with Todd."

Marilyn sat in the visitor's chair next to him, folders on lap. "Todd Hancock was our client for about three years," she said, all business. She showed him the various places they booked for Hancock with appropriate data; all trips to the Caribbean. "He asked about Antigua and I recommended the St. James's Club Resort because my husband and I vacationed there last year and loved it."

Mitchell said, "I understand he booked one way," added conviction to Olivia that he communicated with police.

"He wasn't sure how long he'd stay," Marilyn said, "and that he'd make further arrangements through the hotel. He came by and picked up his ticket. Laurence Bates..." She opened the file. "...Let's see. I booked to Liechtenstein via Zurich and a connecting flight."

"Did Bates ask to go to Liechtenstein?"

"Yes. He also requested a one-way ticket. In both instances, I recommended an open end round trip and both said no."

"Did either offer a reason for their destinations?"

"No. I have never been to Liechtenstein. No one here has as far as I know."

More sameness, Mitchell thought.

Marilyn showed him Bates's various itineraries. "I booked all of his trips. I provided this information to the police."

"Is there more you need, Mitchell?" Olivia said.

"No. Thank you for your time, Ms. Schroeder. I appreciate your professionalism."

"Marilyn's been to the Great Wall and Beijing. She'll plan your China itinerary. Okay, Marilyn, thank you."

Marilyn left and closed the door.

Olivia wanted to know what he knew or surmised. "Mitchell, any remote idea what caused Todd and Laurence to leave the trial? Have you and Stanford any speculations? I'm astounded that they'd violate their obligations."

Mitchell shrugged. "No idea."

"For Stanford's sake, I hope you find the answers."

Mitchell stood saying, "Good to see you again. Add me as a new client."

She escorted to the door happy to see him go. "Thanks for visiting, Mitchell. I look forward to seeing you again."

Olivia returned to her desk no longer considering Mitchell a threat, but a possible informant. Her clandestine world increased momentum as a volcano readying for eruption.

* * *

At home, Mitchell noted his meeting with Marilyn and Olivia and added to the Kiley files. He reviewed similarities and listed them: the champagne, Rohypnol, needle mark in thigh area, possible succinylcholine; both seen overseas with a woman; both sold their real estate through overseas channels through the same Bahamian law firm; both on the same murder trial; both had one way ticket routing to tax havens and both used the same travel agency.

Mitchell concluded the same person murdered them.

A preponderance of coincidences existed.

The questions continued – Who? Why? Olivia knew Hancock and Bates as clients. She sold them the discount travel package. Olivia knew Stanford and attempted to sell him the same package.

Another similarity to add to the list. Coincidence?

He underlined the word and added two asterisks. But Marilyn did say no one at Village Greene traveled to Liechtenstein.

Something Olivia said stirred his curiosity. Stanford can verify her words. If he could, was her statement less than meaningful? If he couldn't, should Stanford beware Olivia?

Was she the femme fatale?

Am I creating fantasy, dreaming to solve the case before the trial?

He started to sense an enemy behind every rock. Paranoia spurred him to call Stanford's office. His anxiety increased waiting for the phone to answer. Stanford had left for the day. Mitchell called his home. No answer. He left a message for Stanford to call him tonight, important. He'd call Stanford again before going to bed and in the morning if necessary.

Did I find the killer?

Regarding Olivia, he'd remain cautious and alert for Stanford. He'd protect Stanford's back while he concentrated on Nancy's trial – an official bodyguard to find the lawyer killer.

O livia reached a crossroads; one direction was passive – to obey
Austin to ignore Stanford and let Austin and his associates solve
their problem; the other assertive – to go ahead with Crane after he
promised secrecy. Austin's burdens with his associates and bitchy
daughter obliterated optimism to solve his problem. She knew what
was best for him and their future. Certainty was going ahead with
dinner with Stanford to pave the next step to her champagne cocktail.

* * *

Olivia received the food delivery before 7:00 and placed aluminum
trays in the double oven ready to reheat. She dressed, set the dining
room table, and checked first floor rooms for neatness. Satisfied, she
climbed the marble and stainless stairway to her bedroom to turn on
the hot tub ready for her next victim scheduled to arrive at 7:30.

Her phone rang a few minutes after seven. With trepidation, she answered hoping it wasn't Stanford with another last minute cancellation.

He wouldn't dare, or I'll find and shoot him for wasting my time and efforts.

"Hello," she said with restrained anger, and ready to provide several reasons to continue with dinner.

"Your dinner still on with Stanford?" Austin said. "I have a few minutes before I go out."

Strange for Austin to call to ask that, she thought, but relieved he wasn't Stanford canceling.

"Still on unless he calls and cancels. How do you feel? You sounded defeated last time. I don't want you that way."

"No more. I'm confident that I'll persuade Nancy this weekend. I'll be forceful and adamant and convince her to relent. She's so damn stubborn or determined."

She never believed he was confident. "And I'm confident I can sell my travel package. Crane should arrive in fifteen to twenty minutes." She knew he called for more than to ask about dinner. "My love, is this call to make sure I stick to the script? Do you doubt me?"

He waited several seconds before saying, "Too obvious?"

"Remember, my darling, whatever I do, I do for you. How can you not trust me when all I want is to make you happy?"

She walked farther away from the hot tub area to avoid him hearing the running water.

Austin hesitated at her astuteness. "The thought crossed my mind. Sometimes your love for me amazes me."

"I don't withhold my love for you. I tell you what I feel. Do you prefer less?"

"Don't consider the thought."

"Then don't ever doubt my love or me. I have to prepare for my guest." She decided the call screamed for help, sought blanket security, and groped at straws in a tempest...but inappropriate for a long conversation to vent and make him feel better. "I'll call you later, Austin, okay? We can talk all night."

"I'm leaving for a dinner meeting with the President. I'll call you after that."

Perfect, she thought, he won't be alone tonight. "Call me when you get home no matter what time and tell me who attended – all the inside gossip."

"I will. Give Stanford your best sales pitch. I know you're super at selling, the best salesperson, and why you're a success."

"He won't refuse. And I'm super at loving you. No one has ever loved or will ever love you the way I do. And put your mind to rest. I won't make offers on your behalf unless you approve. I know what I have to do."

"Good luck tonight. I love you."

"And I love you more...and I want to hear that more from you. Goodnight." She needed to lighten his tension. "When will you say you love me again?"

"The minute I see you."

"Now you got it right. Enjoy your evening." She ended the connection.

The call depressed. A sinking feeling enveloped her stomach, angry at Austin's mental anguish. She wanted her man to stand tall. Uncertainty chiseled his call and weakened by failure to succeed with his daughter. He feared retaliation by associates and was on the edge of crisis bordering his family's life and death.

Olivia wondered – How could Austin withdraw as Nancy demanded? He couldn't or they'd kill him, a threat to eliminate – unless all agreed to end the Rodrigo operation. And that was doubtful.

Unless the miserable Grahams agreed.

Austin needed her more than ever...*a certainty!*

She must provide comfort, instill confidence, and do all she could. A visit to Washington would help and to exercise discretion to avoid seen in public with him. She'd stay outside The Beltway or probably in Arlington since it was risky to stay overnight at his condominium. If he needed a crutch, she'd turn into a crutch for him to walk tall, limp or no limp.

Olivia cradled the receiver unhappy with Austin's mental posture.

She straightened the bedroom and bathroom again and turned off the hot tub faucet. She set the controls to keep the water warm as her thoughts focused on Stanford on how he could help Austin.

Olivia made a final visual inspection before going downstairs. She turned on the audio system to soft instrumental music and balanced the music level in each room. An instrumental CD of Italian love songs would play when he arrived and restarted during the Italian dinner.

She wanted perfection to win on all fronts.

At the bar, Olivia placed a bottle of Moet-Chandon in the ice bucket and added ice. Another bottle chilled inside.

She placed the Rohypnol on a shelf behind the bar and hid it behind a bottle of Johnny Walker Black Label scotch.

She checked her watch.

Stanford, where are you?

Don't you dare cancel!

Stanford finished his civil matter meeting at 6:30 with an associate in Long Beach. He looked forward to a quiet dinner with Olivia, who he thought of often since their 'date' at the country club.

Late, he sought a local liquor store on Park Avenue near the Long Island Railroad station for the promised wine. He purchased two bottles of Brunello di Montalcino from Tuscany as a complement to dinner and added Dom Perignon champagne as a house gift, a habit he followed when a guest for the first time.

The gate guard buzzed Olivia after checking his visitors list. Mr. Crane arrived. After a victorious smile, she turned the ovens on to warm, lit two candles on the dining room table, and placed the travel package presentation on the living room cocktail table.

Olivia smoothed her black silk pants in the foyer mirror, checked the matching black silk blouse, and loosened a button to expose a deeper neckline. She wore pearls – earrings, necklace, and bracelet. Makeup remained understated. The Opium scent should stir when he came close. She needed to display a warm, friendly, and humorous personality to lure him to the next step.

From a living room window, she could see her target turn into the driveway. Olivia formed her best smile when the bell chimed.She opened the door and exclaimed with animated arms.

"At long last! We're together again. Some events are fated. Welcome."

"Buono sera, Signorina Olivia. How do you say your name in Italian?"

"I have no idea. I didn't know you knew the language."

"Only a few popular words."

They touched cheeks, unlike the tender handclasp at his country club. He entered. She closed the door satisfied and accepted the champagne. He held the wine.

"Come, enter my villa on Lake Como and follow me." Stanford followed through the living room to the bar in the spacious family room.

"How was your day, Stanford?"

"Better than hoped. I love your home." He surveyed the modern professional designed decor: white walls with ample color, marble, stainless steel, and softened with abundant greenery.

"I wanted a free flowing, high ceiling home without corners, and plenty of windows. To my taste, rooms without corners work better with contemporary style furnishings."

"My compliments, your home is almost as beautiful as its owner."

"Thank you, Counselor. You're off on the right foot. Compliments will get you everywhere."

She sometimes addressed Todd Hancock and Laurence Bates as Counselor.

They reached the bar where a bottle of champagne chilled. She placed the new bottle on the bar. Stanford added the wine.

"This beautiful evening must begin with champagne to celebrate our fated reunion," she said.

"Sounds like the right beginning."

Olivia placed two champagne glasses on the black granite counter and lifted the bottle out of the bucket. He undid the foil and wire cage, uncorked the bottle without spillage, poured then forced the bottle into the ice bucket. He raised his glass. "Here's to you, bella Olivia."

"To your health and success on your next project. Cheers." They touched glasses and sipped. "Let me have your jacket. This isn't Enrico's fancy restaurant." He removed and draped the jacket over the stool next to him. "Much better," she added. "Loosen the tie or take it off."

Stanford loosened the tie and white shirt's top button. "Am I ready to relax yet?" he kidded.

"You look better, more at home. Come, you must see the menu. If you prefer something else they deliver pronto."

Stanford laughed. "I'm sure whatever you ordered will be outstanding." Stanford held on to his glass.

She reached for his hand, held tight, and led him to the spacious, modern kitchen designed for efficiency with black and white speckled granite counters, stainless Viking appliances with a stainless Bosch dishwasher, and wide windows overlooking woods, pool, and backyard. She lowered the double oven's top door and inhaled the flavorful aroma.

"Taa-rah!" she mocked, slid into a beige oven glove, and pulled out the middle grate. "For your special Italian menu, we have calamari with linguine and marinara sauce. And here we have chicken scarpariella, all white meat off the bone with yummy scrumptious sauce." She stirred the food with a long wooden spoon. "And..." She inserted the grate and pulled out the lower one. "...behold...baked stuffed artichokes, clams casino, and we'll add escarole. What do you think? Are you jumping for joy?"

Stanford shook his head, unbelieving. "You have enough here to feed a small army, and they're all my favorites. Perfect. How did you know?"

"You lie." She playfully punched his arm, inserted the grate, and closed the door. "If you're hungry after your long day, we can eat now."

"I'm in no hurry. The night is yours."

"You are *too* easy. Here's tonight's special program, and changeable at your request," she said with a smile. "We'll finish our champagne in the family room and have appetizers and dinner in the dining room then coffee and dessert in the living room plus Italian music everywhere. Do you approve, Counselor?"

An orchestral version of *Romanza* ended and *Con te Partiro* started.

"An exceptional travel agent always at work. Whatever you say. I feel like I'm in beautiful Florence again. Ever been there?"

"Yep. I did a month in Italy during a summer recess from Venice to Sicily and loved it."

They returned to the bar. Olivia lifted the champagne bottle, wiped it with a towel, and said, "Let's go."

Stanford carried the ice bucket and towel and they settled in the black leather cushions after Stanford topped off the glasses.

Olivia's offensive started. "Mitchell Pappas came to see me at the agency – a wonderful surprise. He and Helene plan a vacation next June in the Far East and asked for an itinerary."

"Probably pursued leads."

"He said he's helping you as an investigator on the Kiley case. Good luck and success with the outcome. He also talked to my vice-president, Marilyn Schroeder, Laurence Bates and Todd Hancock's agent. We told Mitchell and police what we knew. Not much substance, I'm afraid."

"I wasn't aware they were your clients. That's quite a coincidence."

"It is. Mitchell knew. They subscribed to the travel discount program for their firms. Todd was a client for three years before that and Laurence much longer." She switched subjects to indicate a lack of interest. "After I fatten you up and fill you with wine and soft music, I'll present the package during dessert. I intend to take complete advantage. You're hard to get, and I gotcha!"

Stanford laughed, finding comfort with her. Being with a woman with humor felt good, a trait his former wife lacked, and thought Olivia appeared beyond stunning when she opened the door.

She reverted to Mitchell. "Oh, something else. Mitchell said that you're concerned why they disappeared and turned up dead."

"As the new attorney, it's important I know why. It's the self-preservation part of my due diligence."

"Any ideas?"

"None. We may never know."

"Frightening. You think you're in danger? Does your client know why?"

Unlikely that Nancy Kiley would reveal what Bates and Hancock told her.

"She says no. I'm meeting with her again Wednesday. I'll raise the subject. Someone or something motivated Hancock and Bates to leave. They may try to motivate me. I'll hear what they have to say then arrest and investigate them. I don't abandon clients for any reason."

Olivia wasn't happy with his response although knowing Stanford as difficult to persuade. Her approach to him proved correct. She'd act diplomatic but aggressive and emphasize a client type of relationship.

"That's courageous and dangerous." She switched to analytical to show concern. She stayed on the subject. "Stanford, what if they had valid reasons to leave?"

"What could be valid? They violated their client and profession. If they didn't leave the country they would've been disbarred."

"Suppose they discovered facts to leave the case. Todd and Laurence were decent guys. Something motivated their action. My perception of them was that they weren't irrational though I didn't know them that well."

Stanford massaged a long contemplative sip."You make a good point. That doesn't change they were murdered in the same manner. A question arises. If they had reason to withdraw and didn't go overseas, would they be alive?"

She said to the core question, "You have to assume the cause for withdrawal rests with your client. Maybe she's lying."

"Possibly. Another good point by Signorina Olivia. She might relent if she has something to hide. Let's change this depressing subject. Tonight there's only you and me...and your travel package."

Olivia created doubt and planted the seed without self-exposure. Goal number one, accomplished.

She changed the subject to exotic vacation locations, a travel and vacation trend, and a new world to Stanford. Fifteen minutes later she suggested, "How about appetizers?"

"I'm ready."

"We'll keep the rest of the champagne on ice for later."

Stanford returned the ice bucket and bottle to the bar. Olivia returned to the kitchen, switched the heated food to serving bowls, and carried appetizers to the dining room. Stanford entered with an uncorked bottle of wine.

"Have a seat," she ordered. "I run a self-serve restaurant. Dig in and eat hearty. I suggest you loosen your belt."

Stanford poured the wine. He lifted his glass and said, "To the best chef in the best Italian ristorante in town."

They exchanged histories, more travel locations, Long Island's problems and politics, former spouses, the Kileys, Helene and Mitchell, and an abundance of humor. He lacked interest in public office. They enjoyed each other.

Stanford knew he wanted to see her again, having much in common.

"You served enough to feed the Seventh Army, forget the small army. I'm stuffed," he said holding his stomach. "Tell you what. I'll clear the table."

She raised her hand. "Don't you dare."

"I have a suggestion. Let's delay dessert for later and discuss your travel program right here."

She acted excited. "I'll plug in the coffee, get the proposal, and be right back. For that, I'll change the schedule."

She left and returned with a folder.

Stanford almost cleared the table. "We need a clean table." Finished, he poured a glass of wine. Olivia refused more wine.

He sat back with folded arms, pretending as a difficult barrier. "Okay, give it your best shot. I'm a tough sell."

"If you don't approve, don't worry. I'll come after you tomorrow. I know what's good for you."

Stanford smiled. She forged a friendship with her light banter.

All business, Olivia unfolded her presentation, reviewing advantages and benefits to his staff, and spectrum of international travel. She included the new division and Village Greene's personal services and mentioned several of her largest satisfied clients on Long Island, an impressive list. Background music enhanced her sales pitch.

Her presentation ended. "Do you have any questions?"

He nodded. "The obvious."

"What's obvious?"

"Where do I sign?"

She laughed. "You are *so* easy."

"An intelligent program and a value."

"Not that I'm impatient...here's a pen and the contract."

He scanned, signed, and returned the uncomplicated contract.

"Ready for espresso and zabaglione?" she asked.

"Ready."

Olivia set aside the paperwork and left for the kitchen. She returned with the coffee and dessert. He tasted the soft dessert.

"How is it," she inquired.

"Excellent. Fantastico."

"In Italy, that's called the dessert for lovers."

"Why?"

"It's soft and spreads easily. Use your imagination."

Stanford grinned, using his imagination.

Dessert and coffee ended. "Now that you've been wined and dined and signed up, you need the ultimate relaxation; to digest your food properly. Follow me." She left.

Stanford followed, obedient. "Where to?" he asked.

"I'll show you what I do after a long meal and when tired. You need to see something upstairs – and more than the bedroom. You already signed the contract so there's no need to be nice to you any longer." She laughed.

"Another Village Greene Agency tour. Lead on."

Romantic music continued through the upstairs speakers. Holding his hand, she led him to her bedroom and raised hot tub area. She added hot water. Water flowed and gurgled.

"What do you say? Are you game?" she asked looking devilish.

Stanford stalled, inquisitive. "Are you serious?"

"Of course. This is the perfect conclusion to a perfect evening. Do it. No other Italian restaurant in town has this amenity. Even the owner is friendly." She approached him and kissed his cheek.

"A great idea but I didn't come prepared for this. I would've brought a suit."

"Oh, don't be silly. You can do that next time. Time to assert...and to improvise."

Olivia returned to the tub and undressed with slow motions; shoes, blouse, and pants then continued until naked without hesitation or tempting gestures. Before his exploring eyes, she removed the jewelry. Her fingers waved encouragement.

"Improvisation, Counselor. I'm sure you do that in court now and then. Exciting moments develop when unplanned and unexpected. Or do you just want to watch?"

Her brazen action surprised him.

To encourage, she pivoted into the tub and sat. "Come on in, Stanford," she beckoned. "The water's fine."

Reluctant, although pleased at her initiative, Stanford undressed removing everything except for briefs and headed for the tub.

"Okay, you win." He smiled, happy to lose.

"Take the plunge. Take it all off." With spread fingers, she covered her face. "I promise I won't look."

Stanford laughed at her act and removed the briefs.

She smiled a victory smile.

He approached and pivoted into the tub near her. "Ah, this is great, perfect" he said immersing with a contented sigh. "Your establishment is unbelievable. You know how to treat a customer."

"I know what's good for you." She slid next to him. "I said I'd have a special dessert for you. This is it. The famous Roman Baths. So Italian, ala Signorina Olivia." She emoted, "When in Rome, do as the Romans do. It wasn't the zabaglione. Isn't this better than eating zabaglione off somebody's body? How boring is that?"

He laughed. "No, I don't think so. That's tough to beat."

"It will be. All you need is patience and imagination, or do this."

She leaned over and kissed him on the mouth, a soft pat to test his reaction although confident she primed him.

He did not move. Stanford hadn't been intimate with a woman since his divorce.

She whispered, "You know what?"

"What? More surprises?"

"Something you should know or felt by now." She kissed his lips. "I think I love you, Stanford. No, make that I do love you." She kissed him again on the lips. "I really do."

Olivia said the same words to the other lawyers before the first sexual encounter.

He embraced her and reciprocated with a kiss.

Without leaving his lips, she maneuvered to face him and sat on his lap. She hugged his head and tongue kissed him, and swayed her body as she moaned.

He responded.

Stanford was hers.

Amidst gurgling, swishing, and steam they tangled as longtime lovers. Wine lowered Stanford's barrier making him comfortable.

She achieved her second goal, one more to go.

She kissed him again. "How's that for dessert?"

"Much better than zabaglione, and as I said, great restaurant, exceptional dessert. Put that on your next menu." They laughed.

"Always for you. Be right back. I'll get the rest of the champagne."

She left the tub and dried with a yellow towel as he watched.

Naked and smiling at her conquest, Olivia returned to the bar, and poured champagne.

Then she reached behind the scotch for the Rohypnol.

O livia loaded the Bosch dishwasher when Austin called a few minutes past midnight. She stayed up to await his call. If he failed to call before 1:00 a.m., she planned to call until he arrived home to assure him of her success with Stanford and to analyze Austin's mindset, wanting a positive attitude. When the phone rang at 12:30, she answered the first ring.

"The President turned the evening into a social with twenty guests. I couldn't call you sooner. Did I wake you?"

His voice sounded positive to her. "No, darling. How are you feeling? You had me worried earlier. You sounded down. I need you strong again, to be your old self."

"How did your evening go?"

"Couldn't be better. Stanford bought the package and signed the contract. He left about three hours ago." She added a dishwasher soap tablet, selected the cycle, pushed the start button, and closed the door. "Did you know he scheduled a meeting with your daughter on Wednesday?"

"No. That's normal pretrial diligence. I'm impressed he talked about the subject." Austin's voice now lacked enthusiasm.

"The subject focused when I mentioned Mitchell Pappas stopped by my office to schedule a vacation."

"Maybe Stanford will weaken her stubbornness."

Satisfied with the kitchen's neatness, she primed the house alarm as she talked, turned off the downstairs lights, and headed upstairs with the phone.

"Until then, think of me instead. My love will keep you strong. I'm not a port only in a storm, or a lighthouse on a dark night sailor."

"No need to remind me. Talking to you is a cure. I have to rise early tomorrow for a Committee briefing."

"Austin, your crisis convinced me that we must be together. Can't you talk to your wife? You did promise me you'd divorce her. Walk away now and we'll go elsewhere." She expected a no, but wanted to reinforce his promise.

"I did promise and I will. I can't as long as Nancy's trial continues."

"I'll remind you when the trial ends."

"You won't have to. I'll tell Madge then. My lying and deceiving her must end."

Olivia reached the second floor. She considered asking about the President's social, but lacked interest in Washington party gossip. The White House gathering served her purpose, kept Austin busy, and distracted negative thoughts and depression.

"I love you, Austin. Nothing must ever happen to you. I always want you happy and positive. We will win. Believe the same with Nancy. Call me tomorrow." She entered her bedroom.

"I shall, without fail."

"I'll be home before seven. Goodnight, my love. Dream of me."

She disconnected, placed the phone on her bureau, and headed to the hot tub area.

The tub emptied, wet towels thrown in the hamper, and moisture evidenced a bath. She brushed her teeth and flushed with mint-flavored mouthwash.

Olivia loved Austin, her ultimate man, yet couldn't find fault having sex with another man since she did it for Austin, a sacrifice. Although unacceptable to others, it was right for her. Sex with Todd, Laurence, and Stanford never diminished her love for Austin; it deepened. She accepted the premise from the start to do anything for Austin including kill for him. During sex with the lawyers, she pretended they were Austin to make acceptance easier.

She'd never at random violate her love for her Uncle Max. The lawyers were tools, implements to benefit the man she loved, to keep him from harm's way, and to have him for life.

When the Nancy nightmare ended, Austin would be hers as long as he lived. Losing him hung as an eternal nightmare, a suffering for life...or she'd rather die. The thought of losing Austin lingered as horrible and she shivered it away.

Olivia turned off the ceiling lights. At the night table, she set the alarm for 6:30 a.m., turned off the lamp, shed all clothing, pulled the sheet aside, slid into bed, and lay in the darkness and thought about Austin, her great and obsessive love.

Olivia shifted, rolled over on her right side, and put her arm over Stanford Crane's body.

Olivia stirred as the 6:30 a.m. alarm sounded. She stifled her reveille and left for the bathroom. Returning to bed, she pulled the sheet, pressed against Stanford's body, and kissed his face.

Stanford stirred. His eyes opened to her face and daylight.

"Good morning, Counselor."

Groggy, he realized he slept over. "What time is it?" Stanford embraced her nude body as she pecked at his neck and face.

"Six thirty-seven."

"My head weighs like an anchor. What happened? When did I come to bed?" He rubbed his eyes to clear cobwebs.

She thought of sex again to solidify the relationship, but last night proved sufficient for her purpose. Breakfast qualified as an extension.

"I'll tell you later." She hugged him again. "When you're ready, come down for breakfast. There's a man's electric shaver in the medicine cabinet. Former husband."

Stanford watched the trim and beautiful body flow to the bathroom. When she reappeared, he sat up, and watched her dress.

"Don't tell me you have breakfast catered."

"No. That's homemade. Like the entertainment."

Closeness with Stanford satisfied Olivia. Her aggression burst his barriers. Intimacy produced a common bond. To ensure the bond, she decided to extend dinner to breakfast to achieve her third goal. She felt him primed to do her bidding, and to control his future.

She needed Rodrigo's approval.

Olivia assumed it difficult to convince him to stay over after the presentation. Undressing before him opened the door to physical contact.

To ensure that he stayed over, she laced his champagne with a small amount of Rohypnol as a mild sleep aid. After the hot tub, he felt woozy and tired. She led him to bed and suggested he lay down to rest. Stanford lay and passed out.

At breakfast, he apologized for drinking much wine.

* * *

The Olivia Greene theory created turmoil for Mitchell, who sat at his desk after preparing breakfast for Helene and kissing her goodbye at the door. He decided that a visual aid might help for clearer analysis.

Mitchell drew a wide circle and three smaller circles – a planet and three moons. He wrote Olivia Greene in the planet, the three Kiley lawyers in each moon, and a line from each moon to the planet.

Is it a coincidence Olivia Greene is the hub?

She might have slipped when they met – a mistake on her part or was it his runaway fiction oriented imagination.

Mitchell drew another moon to connect to Planet Olivia Greene. He left the moon blank for a name to offer a solution to his mystery.

Mitchell called Stanford at home. The machine answered. He called Stanford's cell phone. No response. He called Stanford's office.

The automated system answered and he left a message. He'd call again later.

Mitchell remained troubled.

As Mitchell thought to call Stanford's office again, Stanford called."I got your message this morning. What's up?"

"Mullins told me that Todd Hancock and Laurence Bates had the same travel agent, a Marilyn Schroeder of Village Greene Travel. Hoping to discover why those two traveled overseas, his people learned nothing relevant from the agent. Helene and I talked about a vacation next year and thought I'd kill two birds with one stone and interview Marilyn.

"I discussed my travel plans with Olivia and Marilyn and talked about Hancock and Bates. Here's the problem. Before I mentioned to Olivia that I helped you, she said – 'I understand you might be involved with him. That is excellent. I'm sure he can use your help.' The reference was to you. My point is – how did she know of my involvement? Who told her? Did you? If you did, end of discussion."

"No, I didn't tell her."

"Who else knew? Mullins, the Kileys, Pilar? I'll include the security guards at the Kiley residence that asked for identification. Would your staff tell her?"

"I don't know who on my staff would talk to her, other than Rhonda and she's a clam. You have a puzzle. Are you certain you didn't confuse your notes?"

"Positive. What are the chances that Olivia knows the Kileys? The Senator? Maybe she knows him."

"I'll ask Austin. Maybe in his involvement on Long Island, he met her and the subject arose. I'll call him and solve your puzzle. If he didn't, what are your suspicions?"

"Village Greene and Olivia connect to the three Kiley attorneys. She might be more involved than appears."

"Why don't you ask Olivia who told her?"

"I caught her off guard. I'm sure she'll deny saying it, and alert her contacts."

"If any," Stanford corrected. "We had dinner last night to discuss her travel program. Nothing she said indicates involvement in the trial. She lost two clients and signed me up last night. She has dozens of clients and other law firms, so dozens of other lawyers connect to her. How could she connect in a devious way? And she didn't want to talk about the Nancy Kiley trial and changed the subject to travel."

"My notes are correct. Beware Olivia, Stanford. I'm suspicious of her connection to both dead lawyers. Please talk to Austin."

"I'm seeing Nancy tomorrow and want you with me. Are you free?"

"Yes. What time?"

"Around noon. Come to my office and we'll go together."

After hanging up, Mitchell placed a question mark in the empty moon.

"You're the link to the solution, nameless moon." He darkened the question mark. "I *will* find you."

* * *

Wednesday.

Stanford said to Mitchell, "I called the Senator to request permission to be forceful with Nancy today. He said to do whatever will free her. He hasn't talked to anyone about your association with me. So, I didn't pursue further. I can't imagine Olivia as other than talented and pleasant. I plan to call her for dinner next week." He hesitated and added, "Maybe sooner, and I'll stay alert. Regarding Nancy, I told Madge that I wanted her in the room this time. Pilar Mirasol has moved in with Nancy. I also told Madge to have Pilar there and warned her of a difficult meeting ahead for her. And no matter what, she must support us. She agreed to the leeway."

"What do you want me to do?"

"Observe and analyze Pilar and Nancy's reactions. Pilar might be up to her neck on Nancy's secrets. Nearly all will be ad lib. Watch their eyes, demeanor, and reactions. Focus on Pilar. I'll focus more on Nancy. Look for the hidden truth."

"Climbing Mount Everest will be easier based on the first meeting."

"We have to know why she demands protection. Let's throw everything at her, including all kitchen appliances not just the sink."

Stanford decided they would stand for psychological impact – Nancy and Pilar to sit while they looked down on them as interrogators, the strong dominating the weak. He needed answers and cooperation from both girls and the truth.

The process reminded Mitchell of the executive with his desk on a raised platform as his visitors sat lower than he sat, which conveyed authority and dominance. When Mitchell related the story, Stanford said, "Mind games, Mitch, all part of negotiations."

The door opened. Madge came in alone as a messenger.

"They'll be down in a moment. Anything I should do or say? I want to help." Madge looked uncomfortable in what she again deemed a legal setting, unsure on how to contribute yet eager to help. "How can I participate without screwing up? Thinking about what to say is making me nervous."

Stanford touched a chair opposite the couch. "Sit here to face the girls and feel free to ask them questions or say what you wish no matter what the reaction. You are an integral part of this meeting. No need to feel insecure."

Stanford wanted Madge facing her daughter to make the moment difficult for Nancy.

"Thank you for assuring me. I'll do what I can to help." Madge sat.

Stanford walked around to face her. "Also, I need you to listen and to look at Nancy and Pilar. Look at Nancy's eyes when she talks to you. Your presence may encourage the truth."

"Which you believe they're hiding?" Madge queried with a frown that rejected deviousness from the girls.

"Yes."

"But why lie? Nancy was always forthright, and knows you're here to help her."

"To help her will be difficult without truth. We must learn their secret or secrets."

"I will support anything you say and do. I can't believe she'd lie. That's not the daughter I raised. Ever since the incident, this house has become alien. She's been a stranger and keeps me away from her new world. I know I repeat myself and I'm sorry to complain. I just don't know what to do." Madge clasped hands in her lap still feeling confused as a stray lamb, a spectator to a difficult family problem.

"If I lose my temper with Nancy, understand it's necessary. And support Mitchell. We must function as a team, as one voice."

"I understand," she nodded and sat up ready to participate.

Nancy and Pilar arrived. Nancy smiled. Pilar appeared somber and tenuous to meet with suspicious strangers although they looked friendly. Pilar planned to support Nancy when needed. She tried losing nervousness. Both wore rainy-day-gray Stony Brook University sweatshirts, white sneakers, and tennis shorts.

"Hello, Mr. Crane, Mr. Pappas. This is my ex-roommate and friend, Pilar Mirasol. Pilar this is Mr. Crane and Mr. Pappas."

Pilar nodded greetings to both.

"Nancy, sit on the couch like last time," Stanford ordered pointing. "Pilar, sit next to her." The girls sat as directed.

Stanford repositioned to stand behind Madge to force their focus in a line with Madge. Mitchell stood behind the adjacent empty chair. "Nancy, a subject we spoke about at our first meeting won't be discussed. No need for that today."

Nancy looked puzzled. Stanford pointed to her mother. Her face widened with revelation that he referred to the oral sex questions.

"Right." She smiled making a thumb up signal, having accepted Stanford as her attorney. Her face showed minimum evidence of the fight with her father. Ice reduced the swelling and makeup disguised a small bruised area.

Nancy appeared relaxed, casual unlike the first meeting. Pilar appeared nervous, fidgety with subtle body shifts, and eyes down away from the interrogators.

Stanford said, "Certain events happened regarding your former attorneys. Mr. Pappas, investigating with Suffolk police, found troublesome similarities to their deaths and he'll update you. Has anything changed since we spoke no matter how trivial?"

Nancy pursed lips and swung her head from side to side. "I haven't left the house since we spoke. Pilar moved in over the weekend. We're roommates again. That's all that's different."

"Did anyone, from anywhere, friend, stranger, or foe make any attempt to contact you besides Pilar and your parents?"

"No one."

"Madge, do you take all calls?" Stanford's staccato rhythm started.

"Yes, I do. I screen them all," she said without turning. "Or the answering machine when I go out, a security procedure."

"Any calls you haven't told Nancy about? Strange calls?"

"No."

"Has any media called?"

"Not for a while. They'll call again when the trial starts or just before."

Stanford patted Madge's shoulder as a thank you.

"Nancy, do you answer calls?"

"I do when Mom leaves and Daddy calls."

"Pilar?"

She tensed. "Yes sir?" She swallowed. Her nerves refused to settle.

"Why did you move in?"

Pilar cleared her throat and sat up. "School ended, Mr. Crane. I want to be with Nancy until the trial ends and return to Buenos Aires where I live with my parents. Or stay for postgraduate work."

"Is there anything you should tell me to help Nancy?"

"I don't know anything other than what I told the police and my testimony, sir." Talking calmed her like passing stage fright to an actor.

"Nothing different, no strange thing happened to you since the last trial?"

"Nothing."

Stanford accepted their replies. He returned to Mitchell. "Mr. Pappas, tell them about your meeting with Lieutenant Mullins regarding Todd Hancock and Laurence Bates. Madge, if news to you, accept what is said then we can talk after we finish."

Madge nodded, obedient. "I understand."

Mitchell said, "By taking your case, Nancy,Mr. Crane risks his life considering your other attorneys are dead. If you know anything to protect him say so."

Stanford liked the opening that confirmed his belief on the occasional unrehearsed method.

"There's no danger," Nancy said.

"If he *is* in danger you'll inform him?"

"Yes."

"I'm an investigative author trained to find clues and killers and an authority on evidence evaluation. I'm also a trained detective although a civilian. Mr. Crane asked me to participate to save you – and him. I blow my own horn to assure you everything connected to you will become known for your sake. If you have any doubts read my books." He spoke slower to underscore importance. "I will find the connection to free you. You can help by being open, honest, and cooperative. You weren't last time."

"What do you mean by...everything?"

"Any subject that connects to your case's heart and solution."

"Oh," she replied. "I see." She and Pilar exchanged guilty glances.

"The Suffolk and Nassau police departments are involved in the Hancock and Bates murders because I provided evidence to start the investigation. The police didn't find the evidence. *I did.* I investigated the Nassau and Suffolk agencies to make the connection." He stared at Nancy and Pilar. "Have I convinced you both?"

Stanford silently approved of Mitchell usurping credit to make his dramatic point.

Nancy nodded. "Yes, Mr. Pappas."

Mitchell turned to Pilar. "How about you, Pilar?" She assented with two nods fearing exposure.

Mitchell came out from behind the chair and paced as a lecturer. "My meeting with Lieutenant Mullins..." He continued for several minutes to describe all similarities in Antigua, Liechtenstein, and here.

"Since you know the overall sameness regarding your former lawyers' murders, let's go to the next level."

The 'next level' stirred Nancy and Pilar's curiosity.

"I want you to picture a large circle." He drew a large circle in the air. "A planet we'll call Nancy. Around Planet Nancy, we'll orbit three smaller circles. Moons. In each moon, we'll place your lawyers: Bates, Hancock, and Crane. Envision a line, a tether from each moon to the planet. Add another moon that we'll leave unnamed and add a line to make two halves. Let's add question marks to each half. Soon, we'll name this fourth moon. I assure you, we *will* name the two parts. And when I do we'll know why you need security guards and who killed the lawyers." Mitchell finished and returned to stand behind the Eames chair.

Silence.

Nancy and Pilar froze – their secrets and lies threatened.

Madge grew perplexed, an alien wandering in unfamiliar territory. She turned her head to plead with Stanford to let her ask questions. Stanford touched her shoulder.

"Go ahead, Madge. Ask all you want."

Madge turned to her daughter who twirled her hair with her right hand with eyes away from her mother. Madge recalled what Stanford said about eye contact.

"Nancy, what about the security guards?" Madge asked. Nancy turned away, twirled hair, and her crossed foot tapped air – refusing to look at her mother. Pilar crossed her arms to withdraw and sank into the couch. "Look at me, Nancy. What's going on?" No response. "Look at me!" Madge shouted and moved to the edge of her chair.

Nancy stopped her nervous actions and sat up irritated.

"Mother, this is fantasy. Fiction. I'm frightened that's all. There's no conspiracy stupidity like he claims."

"Are you lying to me? Look at me!"

Anger from her mother was rare.

She looked at Madge. "I'm not lying!"

Uncomfortable, Pilar peeked at Nancy. Madge appeared lost as to what to ask next or whether Nancy told the truth.

Stanford distracted Nancy, calling her bluff. "Tell you what we'll do, Madge. Release the security guards. Tell them they're no longer needed."

"If that's what you want, Stanford, all right," Madge replied. "I'll do that right after this meeting."

"You can't cancel!" snapped Nancy at her mother. "Only Daddy can do that. He knows I need them."

"No, he doesn't," countered Madge, her voice louder than Nancy's voice. "Your father believes Stanford. That's what you argued over last week."

"Mother, you know nothing. They make me feel safe. I need to feel safe. I suffered enough with all these damn trials and accusations."

"That's part of the problem. I don't know *anything*. I want to know what's going on. Why must I yell to get answers?" Her face flushed. "Talk to me!"

Nancy ignored her.

Stanford spoke. "Remember, Nancy, what Mr. Pappas and I said earlier – you and I are in danger. You know why. I don't." His piercing eyes stalled Nancy. Stanford let the silence linger then continued. "Two persons have already died defending you. Doesn't that bother you?" He turned to Pilar and hollered, "Pilar!" His loud voice jolted her. She sat up. "Why does Nancy need guards?"

The opportune opening arrived to help Nancy and participate in a positive manner. With a voice soft, calm, and confident she said, "She's frightened. They offer security and she feels safe in here."

"Of what? Who?"

"Shadows," she replied and shrugged without hesitation.

"Shadows?"

"Yes, shadows. She's scared of going to jail. Her security need is psychological emanating from her experience and constant prosecution, trials, and questioning – nothing physical or anyone, just shadows, all mental."

"You believe that?"

"Yes. I minored in psychology. I know her problem." She looked at Mitchell. "There's no conspiracy, an X name in an orbiting moon."

Stanford walked around Madge's chair and stood between Nancy and Pilar. Part of the mind games syndrome to ridicule. "You two remind me of the monkeys See No Evil and Hear No Evil if you deny the danger. Pilar, if you care for Nancy, if you love your friend don't lie for her. Truth will help me to protect Nancy."

Pilar straightened...adamant. "I'm telling the truth, sir."

"Time will tell. Mr. Pappas and I will talk to you again before the trial." He turned to Nancy. "You can't tell the truth to your mother. Why? I don't expect you to volunteer the truth to me...yet. But if I were your father, I'd kick your ass for lying to your mother."

Nancy raged, "I said I'm not lying!" She thrust up.

Stanford shoved her back on the couch and leaned his face close to hers. "I," he pointed to himself, "am the person between you and life in prison. Do you understand?" No response. "Hello! Are you home?" His face withdrew.

"Don't insult me," she countered less arrogant. "You're a lawyer. Act dignified." She crossed her legs again and tapped air.

"You...are going...to prison. I must have the truth. If found guilty, your life is over."

Nancy appeared to withdraw into her own world. She stopped twirling hair and ended tapping air. Stanford watched her conflict as she evaluated his words. All eyes focused on Nancy waiting for her internal meeting to end.

He must know, Nancy concluded.

Who told him? They both know waiting for a confirmation from me. They know, why they're arrogant and demeaning.

She said, "When are you going to ask me?"

She baffled Stanford. "Ask you what?"

"What the others did..." She paused. "You know...where it is."

Nancy studied his confusion. *Why didn't he understand?*

She realized she spoke out of turn, made a mistake. He *didn't* understand her cryptic reply. The solution energized her and no longer felt as an interrogated prisoner.

"You don't know, do you? They haven't reached you yet have they?"

"What don't I know, Nancy? Who hasn't reached me? Who are *they?*"

"Nothing and no one," snapped Nancy confident, in charge. "You know *nothing*." Nancy stood with arrogance. "Get up, Pilar. We're leaving." She turned to Stanford and pointed her right forefinger. "And don't you *dare* touch me again."

"Sit!" Madge hollered. "Sit down!"

Nancy turned to her mother and raged, "And you shut up!"

"How dare you!" retorted Madge. "How dare you!"

Nancy ignored her.

Air fled the meeting.

Stanford realized the situation crumbled. The tide receded. He tried his weapon again to shore up his defenses. "You're saying I should quit?"

"You won't quit. You can't quit. My father will never approve. He wouldn't dare." She turned. "Move Pilar. We're outta here." The girls left and slammed the door behind them.

Madge felt disoriented and humiliated.

Stanford looked at Mitchell and shrugged.

They gambled.

They lost.

"Stanford, you can't resign. She doesn't mean it. Nancy's confused," Madge said on the edge of desperation.

Stanford sat on the couch and faced Madge to assure her. Mitchell sat next to him.

"I won't quit, Madge. I hoped she'd confess to who or what the question marks represented in Mitchell's example."

"Shall I release the guards?"

"No. I wanted to scare her to confess the truth. Keep them in place to maintain her security needs just in case."

Madge's confusion continued. "You believe there's more and that she's lying?"

"I believe so. So does Mitchell. She's frightened and feels threatened." Stanford's calm tone relaxed her.

"Nancy almost confessed," Mitchell said. "Others approaching her means a third party persuaded Hancock and Bates to question Nancy."

"Any ideas on this third party?" Madge said.

"Not yet," Stanford replied. "I'm certain Nancy knows, and Pilar. The lawyers' similar deaths accuse a common third party. No one has approached me to confront Nancy to ask – Where it is. If they do, I'll have the answer. Talk to Austin about today. You two may persuade Nancy to tell the truth. Does she protect the people who frighten her? Makes no sense. Jury selection begins on Monday. I'll call Austin when I get back to my office."

"Pilar knows and protects Nancy?"

"She knows. They're in this together."

Madge wilted in the chair. "Oh, my. I have been naïve, deceived, and useless. I'm last, out of step with what's going on as if I don't exist around here, a part of the furniture."

Nothing Stanford could say would allay Madge's disappointment and damaged pride. He felt bad for Madge, well intentioned and pure thinking who bore no evil for anyone and expected none.

Fraud, deceit, and disrespect in her home remained inconceivable to Madge.

Stanford said, "Mitch, we should go."

Mitchell stood with an idea and said, "Madge, stay alert and listen to Nancy and Pilar's conversation. Maybe you'll hear what they're hiding. That is our best source of information."

She sat up feeling needed. "To spy on them?"

"Yes. It's necessary."

"If I don't, I'll never know what's going on around here. I have a problem coping with rejection. An initiative helps." Madge felt aggressive. "I'll call Austin and ask him to come home from Washington. And it's time I changed to cope with reality and to smell the foul stench in this house. I cannot remain ignored and invisible. I'm ready to burst from this rejection outrage."

* * *

Wednesday evolved to a busy day for Olivia: attending a breakfast meeting of Women with Hearts, a program by the Heart Council of Long Island, and lunch with two female executives of Ralston Employment Services, a multi-million dollar organization. After lunch, she returned to Ralston with the executives and ran an hour seminar on 'The Executive Woman' for forty-one Ralston clients. Olivia had written several articles on the subject and published in local newspapers along with her photograph.

She returned to the office at close to 5:00, checked her mail and messages then left for home. Exhausted, she needed to stretch out, to nap or use the hot tub. She stopped at Waldbaums for groceries.

Once home, Olivia stored the groceries and changed business attire for casual. She boiled water for tea. She lacked appetite. To tide her over, she opened a blueberry Greek yogurt to have with green tea and honey. She turned on the television for local news, sprawled on the sofa, and released a much-needed sigh. Her body eased to decompress from the business world. She needed a do nothing evening.

After a while, television failed to penetrate her hearing. Her thoughts refused to stop about Austin. Occupied all day, she had no time to focus on his problems. Austin should call soon.

Stanford Crane was hers to mold. She reflected on him with a smile. Stanford responded to her advances and promised to call next week, the perfect time to begin the process towards her champagne cocktail.

Olivia might persuade Janet Graham and her husband to allow her to go ahead with Stanford and lie if necessary. She would embrace and challenge any risk to save Austin, her future. She believed Randy Hawkins and Greg Morris would agree if Janet approved. Although Bob Graham had no vote he influenced his wife's thinking and decisions, the power behind the power.

When Olivia presented the lethal cocktail strategy to Rodrigo, Bob Graham persuaded Janet to implement the plan and agree to her high fees. They needed a trusted female assassin. Cost never mattered. They accepted the death method as untraceable and unique. Olivia's willingness to help Rodrigo and Austin and kill for them impressed Bob. When she completed her journeys, Bob lauded her commitment.

The Grahams respected her.

Olivia knew it.

The Grahams were untrustworthy and kept at a social distance.

What if Austin failed with Nancy this weekend? Would Bob Graham's drug guerrillas attack? Would they go after him and his family? And me?

She envisioned their method; taped mouth, on knees, hands and feet taped behind the back, tormented before shot in the left ear, and a blood ring on a wall.

Would they force Austin to watch my execution?

Their execution style meant a drug hit, Rodrigo's trademark. Headlines and the world would consider her a drug pusher and user. Olivia rattled her head to clear the ugly thoughts. She swore that must never happen.

Never!How could Austin be dumb enough to get involved with Rodrigo? Why did he? Did he feel safe because he also lived in Washington?

She scolded him when he told her – now late for regrets.

She concentrated on solutions.

Olivia sought answers for the next half-hour analyzing variations including extreme solutions and rejecting none. Her review ended when the phone rang. She muted the television and reached for the extension.

Austin said, "Stanford Crane called me earlier after meeting with Nancy. Stanford and Mitchell made their best effort and failed. Madge pleaded. Stanford and Mitchell were forceful. Nancy didn't care."

"Did you speak to Nancy?"

"Yes."

"Did you emphasis that Rodrigo will kill her and Madge?"

"Nancy doesn't believe me. She thinks it's a trick to get her to capitulate. Her misplaced love for me will cause destruction. I'm leaving in a few minutes to go home tonight. Madge is too weak to stand up to Nancy. Madge is nonaggressive and passive. Three people couldn't break Nancy. How will I? Any ideas?"

Austin's futility knotted her stomach.

"This phase in your life *must* end. The threat to our lives is reality. If Rodrigo attacks Pilar as predicted, Nancy may go to the police with the story or yield. I know she'll try to protect you. What if she slips? What if she makes a mistake? You'll go to jail and I'll never see you again. I can't have that. I can't live without you. I told you that dozens of times. Austin, you must win. You must succeed or I'll die."

"Don't go dramatic, please. Damn. I was sure Stanford and Mitchell's pressure could force her to reconsider." His frustration vibrated through the phone line. "I'll make a plea to Pilar if Nancy remains intransigent."

"Pilar must know all."

"I'll call you first chance I get. We'll work this out."

"Have a safe trip. Don't let anything happen to you. Goodnight, my love. Be strong."

"Your voice is my energy."

She smiled and blew a kiss into the microphone loving his words.

He added, "In my darkest moments, when I can't sleep from restlessness, I think of you."

"Don't ever stop."

Austin's quiet panic blared. Olivia knew every change in tone, his inflections in speech, his breathing, and sighs. She could visualize his expressions as he spoke and when he listened. A three-year study of the man she loved, the man she obsessed. Olivia refused to envision life without him, a month without him. She expunged the horrible thought.

Olivia couldn't sit by and wait for him to solve the problem on his own. Others failed with his daughter.

She needed to help.

Somehow.

For the next hour that is all Olivia thought of. Five minutes later, she changed clothing.

She was going out.

The time and solution had come to solve Austin's problems.

Olivia left her home on Shelter Rock Road as the overcast dispersed. The GPS directed her to Janet and Bob Graham's house on Kings Point Road near Long Shore Drive in an area of spacious home sites near The Long Island Sound. She turned into the Belgian block driveway. The quiet neighborhood had no one outdoors. Exterior landscape lighting silhouetted an oversized Tudor. First floor lights were on inside. Olivia assumed that the Grahams disapproved of unannounced visitors. She wasn't a stranger and had a problem and they should at least tolerate her...and felt confident of persuading them to approve her mission.

As Olivia reached the bend in the circular driveway, motion detector lights around the property turned on. A buzzer activated inside the house alerted the owners of visitors or intruders.

A curious Bob Graham hurried from his television program to a window. He recognized her exiting her car. Bob called out to his wife in the family room that Olivia Greene was here.

"Did you know she was coming?"

"No!"

A surprised Janet wondered why she visited. Olivia hadn't been here before. Why didn't she call first? Had she, Janet would have said bad timing and lied that she had company. Janet had no interest to socialize with her without Austin. Olivia classified as Rodrigo business, an employee. Janet slammed shut the novel by Toni Morrison and hurried towards the front entrance, guarded and angry. Olivia wanted something from her and felt certain it had to do with the third lawyer to change her decision.

Crazed with the interruption, she now wanted to be free of Olivia, who was no longer useful to her and knew too much. *'A future threat that must be eliminated.'* She'd talk to Bob later to have her killed Rodrigo style. Then she included Austin and his daughter after they get their money back...and his wife.

Bob opened the door before Olivia pressed the bell. He smiled as Olivia approached scanning her as if to detect her purpose. "Well, well. What a nice surprise. What brings you here?" Barefoot, he wore white jeans with a multicolored Nigerian shirt.

"Hello, Bob." They hugged. "I need to talk to you and Janet. It's important to bother you at home. I've so much on my mind that calling escaped me. Sorry. It's been a troubling day."

Bob accepted her gratuitous comment.

"Olivia!" An enthusiastic Janet called out reaching the door with a happy face. "Come on in." They touched cheeks. "I'm delighted to see you," she emoted.

Janet wore an ankle length, loose fit orange Nigerian boubou, an import from Nigeria that highlighted her smooth facial features. She looked elegant and attractive in Nigerian fashion – a deceptive international drug runner, a soft and beautiful image in a violent trade of death and money.

Bob turned off all motion detector lights.

The Graham home mixed contemporary and African furnishings and Nigerian art, paintings, statues, and numerous sculptures by the renowned Ben Enwonwu. The Grahams displayed expensive taste that complemented their high priced home.

Olivia, a self-styled interior decorator was impressed and said so. Janet, suppressing anger, quickly toured the first floor with her. To Olivia the tour served as a social gesture to soften Janet before her needed request. She complimented each room, being diplomatic. Bob waited in the family room suspicious. Janet and the intruder entered.

Janet sat with her husband on the zebra striped sofa with quiet suspicion and arrogance. Olivia settled in the leopard skin covered chair. African artifacts on walls included ancient ceremonial masks, shields, and spears.

"I love your home," Olivia said. "I wasn't aware Nigerian art was so vibrant. And my image of the country isn't anything like those cities."

Low aerial views of Lagos and the new and modern capital Abucha hung on the walls.

Janet formed a gratuitous smile and said, "The Western world now turns its head toward Africa the awakening giant. The largest black nation, Nigeria has over one hundred and forty million people. Brazil is second then the United States. The slave trade bled Africa."

"That's a revelation, Janet. I never considered Brazil."

"The majority of Nigerians are educated. Nigeria has a trained and modern army. Did you know Nigeria provided the majority of peacekeeping troops around the world prior to the Bosnia crisis in the nineteen nineties? And is a leader in the economic development of Africa?"

"I'm surprised. And a well kept secret."

"Nigerian custom excludes bragging about achievements. But in the fast moving world of international investments the image has to change. Nigeria is a surprising country and will soon take its place as a great nation, a few internal political matters to fix first. Bob and I are Nigerian Americans as opposed to African Americans. We know where we came from, similar to saying Irish American or German American as opposed to European American."

"The country is important and not the revolving governments. Maybe I'll come with you next time you go, for professional reasons."

Janet wasn't enthused. "Nigeria hasn't developed their tourist industry as they should. Best you wait."

Bob waited for the chitchat to end. What did she want, a higher fee, the third lawyer? She didn't come here to talk about Nigeria. When the women finished he sat up. "What did you want to talk about? What's important to visit opposed to a phone call?"

"An important subject. I need to speak to both."

Bob shrugged turning his palms. "Go ahead. What's the subject?"

Janet crossed over from a social attitude to a leader of the Rodrigo world where Olivia served as a freelance soldier. Olivia wanted something, she reiterated, an effective Rodrigo operative, a perfect killer, and an established and successful businessperson no one would suspect as an executioner. She paid her dues. Now she'd pay with her life. But Olivia earned an audience with her.

"Regarding Stanford Crane, Austin conveyed your decision to me. What you and Austin don't know is how I managed to get Hancock and Bates to do my bidding without risk to Rodrigo. The risk was mine. Here, in Antigua, and Liechtenstein – risks achieving a goal. Austin mustn't know my methods. I want to help all I can without losing him while promoting Rodrigo."

Janet guessed sex as her weapon. "What you say stays private."

"I was intimate with them and fulfilled my assignment without hesitation or regrets. I've killed for Rodrigo and have a right to make a request, and granted my request. I consider myself a loyal member of your team and know that you agree with me."

Bob readied to interject when Janet stopped him by touching his leg, a signal to let her finish.

"I'm at a point with Stanford Crane to act by next week. This past Monday night, he came for dinner at my home to discuss my company's travel discount package for his firm. He stayed for breakfast. Jury selection begins this Monday, the trial the following Monday. In between, I can get him to listen to me without reporting to the court or police. I want you to approve my initiative with Crane."

The Grahams exchanged looks. Bob knew the reply belonged to Janet. She cast the dissenting vote in Newport. Janet studied Olivia, who expected an answer.

"A difficult request," Janet said. "If Crane doesn't act as you prescribe then what?"

Olivia replied without hesitating, "He goes the way of Bates and Hancock in the Cayman Islands or on Long Island."

Janet's expression grew pensive and approving, emoting by compressing her lips, and raised eyebrows although the answer wasn't a revelation.

Bob rejected his wife's facial reaction. "The *Newsday* story no longer makes your procedure viable and secure. They linked a potential plot. To reveal the procedure to Crane will tell him why Hancock and Bates died. In light of the publicity, it's giving Crane and the police the key to our secret world."

"I'll say a third party contacted me, that we were seen together at his country club and to pass the information to Crane. He threatened me if I didn't do as required. First, I'll get secrecy from Crane. If he rejects the offer, it's over. He won't suspect me or tell the court. Let me try. I will succeed."

"No good, Olivia," Janet said and waved a finger like a metronome. "I agree with Bob. The concept is no longer a brilliant idea. Exposure is now suicidal. We cannot risk Crane's devotion to you no matter how often he stays for breakfast. We protected you against the pharmacist, a potential threat. Crane is different."

Olivia received the decision without showing disappointment. "I should back away and let your people resolve the matter?"

"It's the best solution," Bob said. "We've been more than patient to accommodate Austin's wishes. His miserable daughter affects our business. We need an immediate solution before our distribution chain falls apart."

"Won't violence create attention? Violence is a worse option."

"It should jolt Nancy Kiley to end her stupidity. She won't give up her father to authorities. She'll back away and all forgiven and we can continue our business."

Olivia digested Bob's logic. She knew better. He lied about forgiveness. Forgiving wasn't part of his brutal world. She retorted, "If the decisions were mine, if I walked in your shoes, I'd eliminate Nancy. And Austin. And those connected to them including his wife, Nancy's roommate...and me."

Janet acted appalled. "That's absurd. *An outrage!* Is that what you think of us? That we'd kill all the Kileys and you? That's lunacy. How dare you insult us?"

As Bob prepared to support his wife's protestation, Olivia stood and acted disappointed. She reached into her shoulder bag and pulled out the Lady Smith & Wesson.

"Don't get up or move," she ordered.

The stunned Grahams obeyed the weapon.

"I won't allow you to kill Austin and me."

She extended her arm towards the Grahams and they leaned back, arms raised to protect against the bullet.

"You...you're overreacting," stammered Janet.

"We won't harm Austin," Bob pleaded. "Put the gun away and let's find an alternate way to work with Crane."

"I don't think so."

Olivia reached into her bag again, pulled out the silver duct tape, and tossed it to Janet, who used both hands to catch the unexpected throw.

"Bob, down on your knees, hands at your side then move away from the sofa or I'll shoot Janet." She motioned with the revolver. "This discussion is between me and Janet only."

Bob dropped to his knees and scrapped four knee strides away from the sofa saying, "Olivia, this is crazy. You can go ahead with Crane. We approve! Go and meet with Crane and set your own time-table. Do what you want to do to him."

"Quiet. You have no options thanks to your know it all mentality. Call my visit a preemptive incursion, a warning that you should listen to those who render a service to you. Janet, tape his mouth then his hands behind his back then his legs. Isn't that how your people do it, Bob?"

Janet, no longer looking confident and elegant, was scared to disobey, no longer the general, the decision maker, and now the frightened prisoner. With nervous fingers, she unrolled an eight-inch piece and covered his mouth.

Olivia waved the revolver. "Don't do anything stupid. I know how to use this. And won't hesitate. Accept the possibility I may change my mind from punishing and humiliating you to killing you."

Bob put his hands behind him. Janet unrolled several strips and taped the hands together at the wrists. Olivia kept a safe distance from both to inspect the awkward taping.

"Put another two wraps on the wrists, tight." Janet taped. "The legs next. Also tight." Janet obeyed. "Connect the hands with the legs. We don't want him standing." The grating unrolling tape vibrated within Janet. The long strips secured her husband. "Sit, Janet." She hastened to the sofa, an obedient prisoner. "We can talk now woman to woman without his interfering opinions. You *are* the brains in this family. He's the stupid brawn."

"Why are you doing this?" Janet said. "We've made you rich and supported what you and Austin wanted to do with Nancy and the other lawyers. We have *always* supported you and Austin, especially with his daughter. He asked for the time to solve the problem and we approved."

"All I've done and do is for Austin, and only Austin. If it meant you making me poor to help him, I would have accepted."

"I love Austin." Janet's eyes glared, emphatic. "We'll never hurt him. Please! He's valuable to the organization, an important partner. And we need you. I won't tell him you came here. I agree with Bob. Do whatever you want with Crane."

"Austin is more valuable to me. Your violent ways against his family will put me at greater risk than my way. Violence against the Kileys will launch a countywide investigation. He's a public official, a United States senator. You'll invite a federal investigation. Your genius husband didn't think. Then we're all in danger. My way would have been quieter and might've proved effective. You must erase your plans."

Her offer thrilled Janet that may eliminate the threat. "Will canceling all violence satisfy you? That's it?"

"Yes. Doing nothing is better. That'll satisfy you and Bob and satisfy me...and definitely Austin."

Easy and naive, thought Janet. "I agree. We'll change strategy. You have my word."

"Excellent. We're on even ground. We needed to talk without interference. The next important question – Do you have cash in the house?"

The question confounded Janet, softening her fear. "This is a robbery? This is about money?"

"It's evolved to money. Answer me." She pointed the revolver at Janet's face.

"We have cash."

"How much?"

"About thirty thousand. In hundreds."

"Where is it?"

"In the study, in my desk under papers. Lower right drawer."

"That's an unsafe place. Is there a key?"

"No. We figured no one would look in an unlocked and unsafe place." The possibility Olivia wouldn't kill them nurtured in Janet, considering her visit as a robbery. Olivia knew she wouldn't report the robbery.

"How about negotiable instruments – bearer bonds and shares?"

"We don't keep those here."

"Where are they?"

"On *Golden Hawk* in a waterproof container hidden in the bilge. The rest are in the office safe."

"How much on *Golden Hawk*?"

"About six million."

"Four of you, one point five million apiece."

"Yes, all equal."

"Jewelry?"

"Upstairs in a safe and in my linen closet. The combination is..."

"I don't need it or your cash. Do as your husband did. Get on your knees and face him. First, tape your mouth."

Olivia looked at Bob, who tried to free an arm to fight his assumed death sentence. She pointed her weapon at him.

"Settle down, Bob. Settle down."

Bob settled uneasy, eyes showed fear, and helplessness.

His alarm jolted Janet as she taped her own mouth.

"Kneel about five feet away from your husband and face him." Janet cowered and knelt, terrified to refuse. "Put your feet together and bend them upwards." Repositioning the revolver in her hand, she unrolled a long strip holding the edges only and wrapped it around Janet's legs careful not to leave fingerprints. She taped a second strip and watched the Grahams for sudden movement. "Put your hands behind you, stretched out."

With one hand, Olivia wound the tape around Janet's wrists, ignoring her muffled pleas.

Comfortable that the tape secured Janet, she put the revolver on the floor behind Janet and added more tape to her legs and wrists. She connected the arms and legs. The Grahams were immobile prisoners of war.

Olivia picked up the Lady Smith & Wesson, put the tape back in the bag, and stood next to Bob's left side.

Bob's eyes reflected he knew the procedure and panicked, fighting the tape.

She lied!

"Janet, do you know how your husband executed his enemies?" Janet nodded several times, wide eyed. "A horrible way to watch someone you love be executed. How dare you even *think* of killing Austin? What would you have done, executed me before his eyes, or him first to torture me? What would've been your sadistic pleasure? But now that the incursion is completed, it's time for the preemptive strike."

Olivia put the revolver to Bob's left ear and fired.

Thunder and terror rumbled through Janet.

Olivia made a fist and pushed Janet's husband over on his right side. His ear hemorrhaged blood and body quivered.

Gunpowder scented the room.

Janet's terror increased as Olivia approached. She inched backwards on her knees. Olivia ignored her muffled wailing.

"Calm yourself, Janet. He'll never interfere with our conversation again. Now you know how I would've felt if you killed Austin. After his men killed the families, they left a second trademark. If you haven't seen it, I'll show you."

Dipping a finger in Bob's blood several times, she printed R-O-D-R-I-G-O on the near wall and drew a riata around the name. She wiped her finger with a handkerchief retrieved from her bag then returned the bloodstained handkerchief.

Janet cried, hysterical and tried to talk for Olivia to hear her muffled and terrified pleas. Her upper body collapsed held by tape.

The writing on the wall blared her life was about to end.

Her husband's dead eyes stared at her as if to apologize he couldn't save her.

"Why I asked if you had money and jewelry in the house was so this appears as a drug execution committed by Rodrigo, the vicious Argentinean. With valuables untouched, police shall exclude robbery as motive. Be brave, Janet. Act like a leader and stop crying. Generals don't cry. I'm promoting Rodrigo's notoriety. Isn't that the goal so police could chase a phantom? With you two out of the way, Austin is safe. Randy and Greg wouldn't hurt him. I'll convince Austin to persuade them to end the madness, to let Rodrigo die."

Olivia avoided touching anything in the house. With her sleeve, she wiped where she sat, and wiped the tape on Bob's mouth. She kept her fingers away from his shirt when he greeted her. She felt positive of erasing all prints including all tape surfaces.

Janet released a muffled shrill when Olivia came towards her.

Her body vibrated.

Olivia stood by Janet's left side and put the revolver to her ear ignoring Janet's sounds, her terrified and wide wet eyes, and vibrating body.

Throughout, beginning with the taping of Bob's mouth, Olivia remained detached and cold.

She felt no sympathy for her and Austin's future killers.

That is how Olivia continued to feel when she pulled the trigger, pushed Janet over, and walked away.

Olivia peeked outside for life and threats before opening the front door.

Did anyone hear the gunshots?

She did not think so being in the middle of the house and distance from neighbors who might be away.

In Janet's study and holding a tissue, she opened the lower right hand desk drawer and removed papers covering the $30,000. Olivia snatched three $5,000 wrapped piles, cautious about prints saying, "I may need the cash Janet for the Third Act and saves me a trip to the bank. Call it a convenience donation."

She placed the papers in the middle drawer leaving the cash balance exposed for police to find. With cash in her bag, she closed the drawer, and returned to the front door ignoring the executed Grahams.

Olivia surveyed the secure night before opening the door.Fresh cool air diminished the gunpowder scent that invaded her pores. She hurried to her car, left at normal speed, reached the deserted road, and drove away.

The ride home was peaceful and with a smile...the Grahams no longer significant to her future. Their cash contribution was paltry and spiteful but felt good to steal from them. The $15,000 balance she left behind should convince police that Rodrigo killed the Grahams instead of a robber.

After closing her home's automated garage door, she returned the duct tape on the garage shelf, pulled down the ladder to the unfinished attic, climbed up, and hid the Smith & Wesson under fiberglass insulation near an exhaust fan.

Olivia soaked her handkerchief in hot water, changed into the same casual clothing as before, sprawled on the sofa to watch television, and waited for Austin to call. His call came during the 11:00 p.m. news. She muted the television and answered the third ring.

"Hello, my love."

Austin said in a lowered and unenthused voice, "When I told Madge I needed a drive, she wanted to join me. We had a difficult time with Nancy tonight. She's locked in her room with Pilar. I'll try again with Nancy tomorrow. Madge insisted on joining me to talk about Nancy, a tough night for both."

She ignored his despair. "Tomorrow's a new day Austin. Don't think about it. Things might change." She nearly burst to tell him.

"Nothing seems to work with Nancy."

"Think about me instead."

"I'm driving to Oyster Bay. Captain Conniver came in with crew on my boat then sails tomorrow morning to Three Mile Harbor for the Block Island pickup this weekend. I'll go over a few things with him since I'm committed to a drive with Madge. I also need supplies they can pick up in East Hampton."

She wanted to say the trip to Block Island was unnecessary, Rodrigo was dying, and he was free. He'd realize that after the media announced the Grahams' execution. She thought – *He'd better realize it!*

"I'll call you tomorrow," he added.

"Afternoon is better. I have a few errands in the morning and should return around one o'clock."

Olivia envisioned the Grahams day maid finding the bodies, a police presence, and news of the drug execution in exclusive Kings Point on the midday news.

He'd miss the news if he called in the morning leading to an inane conversation.

* * *

Olivia's first act awakening with the 7:00 a.m. alarm was the local television news station. She never expected to hear about the Grahams, but someone might have come by late in the evening. In Newport, Janet said that her day maid came in at eight, cleaned, washed, shopped, prepared dinner, and left.

She decided to stay home and check in with her office. No meetings were scheduled. Today she'd rejoice at home without arousing Gwen Rhodes's curiosity at the office. Austin must continue his turmoil until the announcement.

The minutes slid as molasses on bark for Olivia adding to impatience, minutes no longer counted down to her Rodrigo style execution. As noon neared, impatience raised as a crescendo to a symphony's ending as she savored Rodrigo's demise and continuing life with Austin her eternal soul mate, her breath.

Noon came and passed without news regarding the Grahams. Within the disappointing hour, she also listened to radio stations and searched cable channels.

* * *

On a clear day with a favoring moderate breeze, Captain Conniver, in civilian clothing, left Oyster Bay with Austin's yawl, *Caucus*, for the nine to ten hour sail to Three Mile Harbor in East Hampton. He'd arrive at Austin's slip by 5:00 p.m. after riding the favorable current at Plum Gut, refuel, and add the supplies listed by the Senator. Minor repairs deferred to the following day. *Caucus* would remain in East Hampton for the season. Conniver expected to return to *Golden Hawk* and Sag Harbor after 10:00 p.m. that day. The second steward would meet them at the *Caucus* dock with a car for shopping and the return trip to Sag Harbor.

Conniver scheduled a meet with *Mandalay* on the eastern side of Block Island's Great Salt Pond at noon on Saturday to exchange four dozen beer cases provided Randy Hawkins approved the rendezvous that now hinged on Nancy Kiley.

* * *

Detective Marvin Rose rushed into Mullins's office.

"Rodrigo hit Nassau up in Kings Point. I got a call from Manny Fernandez. He asked if we could come and verify the crime scene. It's the same execution style, same writing on the wall, and both victims lying on their right side."

Mullins wasn't surprised that Rodrigo expanded. "I'll go with you." He stood and speculated, "More Ecuadorians?"

"No, Africans this time, Janet and Bob Graham, Nigerian Americans prominent and successful. You might have seen their commercials on TV. They owned a home mortgage company."

"Drugs have no economic barriers Marv. Let's take your car, sirens and all. The time has come to create a bi-county narcotics unit. I'll recommend to Manny that you head it up. That shouldn't pose a problem since you know more about Rodrigo than his men."

Marv formed a huge smile. "Good decision, Moon. Does that mean extra pay?"

"Just my usual extra pat on your back."

Lieutenant Detective Manual Fernandez of Nassau County Homicide stood outside the Graham residence talking to one of his men when Mullins and Marv arrived. The usual crime scene activity was present along with media vans with roof antennas and broadcast hardware. Fernandez saw the Suffolk detectives enter the driveway after waved in by a Kings Park officer. Fernandez approached as they exited the car.

Lieutenant Fernandez, Mullins's counterpart in Nassau and in his late forties, looked determined and burdened as he stroked his mustache. One inch scars in the forehead and left cheek near the ear marred his handsome face – remainders from his youth as a Puerto Rican gang member in the South Bronx to survive his gang violent neighborhood. Police work lured, led in that direction by a neighborhood patrol officer who changed his life's course with persistent lectures.

"Thanks for coming." They shook hands. "Let's go in. It looks like your man has crossed our border. We found the Grahams bound and gagged with duct tape and shot in the left ear. The circle and printing in blood are there."

"Anything stolen?" Mullins asked.

"Everything's in place according to the maid. The safe is intact, all silver and electronics in place. We found fifteen grand in cash in a desk drawer. This looks like the genuine thing, Moon, drugs all the way."

"Any witnesses?" Marv asked.

"Neighbors heard nothing."

After they reviewed the gory crime scene and verified Rodrigo's methods, the three detectives returned to the front yard and stopped inside the yellow tape away from reporters who called for Manny's attention.

Mullins urged, "Manny, that Rodrigo garbage will make it to Queens, Brooklyn then all of New York City as their numbers increase. We couldn't stop him in Suffolk; you might lose in Nassau. Let's have the DEA research Rodrigo – who he is, where the drugs come from, and who provided the finances. I recommend they send a task force to assist us. I need to know how the drugs come into Suffolk to stop the flow. Rodrigo's demise extends beyond our resources."

* * *

Tomayo Suarez waited for two hours to meet with Bob Graham at the Parthenon Diner in Massapequa. Suarez grew annoyed waiting for his $100,000 monthly allocation for the pyramid organization he put together for Rodrigo. Suarez kept half each month as his management fee before disbursing the balance to lower management. He lied to Graham that he kept twenty-five percent.

Suarez ran the operation with six trusted lieutenants who filtered others to the street. Today was payday. Two hours late meant two hours late and disrespect. The meeting was scheduled for 10:00 a.m. Four cups of coffee and two apple pies cost him his appetite at noon. Besides being paid, they would discuss the organization, talk strategy, and insist on a greater supply to meet demand. The meeting was important to both for Rodrigo's expansion.

Impatient, he called Graham's house. He hung up when the machine answered.

Where's the damn maid?

He called the Grahams' mortgage office. The person who answered said they closed for the day.

Suarez considered calling Randy Hawkins, but was forbidden to contact him by phone and to meet only in special situations like the payoff for killing the pharmacist. He never dealt with the Senator or Greg Morris for business but knew them. Suarez was trusted, an insider, a field commander. Rodrigo's distribution depended on him.

Livid, Suarez couldn't condemn his golden goose. He left the diner and returned to his bodega in Brentwood. Keep your temper under control, he urged himself. This was the first time Graham failed to show.

He must have a good excuse.

The Grahams attained fame at 1:00 p.m.

Olivia rushed to increase the television sound level when the news opened with, "An execution in Kings Point..." The Grahams consumed eight minutes including a media 'autopsy' of their lives, with pictures, their business, background, and home. "...A terrible ending to two business success stories." The comprehensive report included an interview with their maid providing added material.

Satisfied with the publicity, she waited for Austin to call. *Police should give me a medal for eliminating a major drug ring.*

The curtain closed on Act I of her scenario to separate Austin from Rodrigo. The curtain for Act II readied to rise and revisions that sometimes write them may improve her drama.

* * *

Austin worked at his study/library desk reviewing his investment portfolio with his investment advisor Reuben Birnbaum, and was pleased with the 12% increase in investments for the year. Austin paid the month's expenses on their residences and boat. By delving into his finances, he hoped to escape for now the conflict with Nancy. Nancy refused to see him earlier that morning. Intent with finances, he failed to see Nancy in the doorway. She knocked on the open door.

"Daddy, I have to see you. It's important."

Containing his elation, he replied, "Of course. Come in and sit."

He pointed to the visitor's chair and studied his daughter's troubled face. She shuffled unsure steps to approach her father who remained wary of her purpose.

"I came to tell you something serious that concerns you."

At last, he reasoned, did she relent to his wishes, their war ended? "What is it, Nancy? What's more serious than our dispute?"

She stopped halfway between the chair and door stuffing her hands in her jeans' side pockets. "Have you watched TV today?"

"No, I haven't. Why?"

"Your associates Janet and Bob Graham were executed in their house. It just came over the news."

A whack across his head with a blunt instrument would've had less impact than her news... his ignorance and shock were obvious.

"You didn't know?" Nancy said.

Austin shook his head and slumped in his chair tongue-tied. He clicked on the wall television to his left.

"Daddy the news ended and should repeat at two o'clock. Channel Twelve News usually does that."

Austin ignored her and flipped to the Long Island news channel. An interview with a college professor neared conclusion. He clicked to the major channels from New York City – no news. He clicked off the television and adjusted his posture to appear strong to his daughter.

"Shocking. What did it say, Nancy?"

"They were killed after bound with heavy duty tape. Shot in the left ear. The police call it a drug execution by Rodrigo." Eddie told her about Rodrigo before she killed him.

Austin turned silent, immobile, analyzing his quiet alarm. He thought Tomayo Suarez, Rodrigo's executioner as responsible.*Why kill the Grahams?*

"Daddy?"

"Eh...yes?" He focused on Nancy.

"Why were they killed and who did it?"

"I don't know." His voice faded. "This is a disaster and a surprise. I have no idea."

"Did you have anything to do with it?"

"No, no. I swear."

"They're dead, is it over? Will you withdraw? Please tell me you will."

"I don't know what to think right now. I'll know later."

"I'll give in if you do. Let's put an end to it."

"I need to find out who killed them."

He strode forward to hug her.

Nancy backed away towards the door, leery from his attack – the first time he ever hit her. His violence shocked her.

Austin's hands thrust up offering safety. "Don't be frightened, Nancy. I will never strike you again. I'm sorry I did. Please forgive me, a moment of temporary insanity from frustration with your firm position."

She stopped. He stopped.

"With the Grahams dead are you in danger?"

"No, I'm sure. Does Pilar know about me?"

He surmised she'd known based on their closeness, but wanted to make sure.

"Yes. She sustained me."

"Does anyone else?"

"No."

"Good. Make sure your mother never knows. Our problem will destroy her. She's too weak to handle adversity, not as strong as us. You need to protect her."

"She'll never know."

"Can you trust Pilar?"

"With my life. She's kept me sane. I just thought you should know about the Grahams. Bye." Nancy turned then turned back. "I love you. I don't want to lose you, why I'm doing this."

She rushed up the staircase to her room.

Austin couldn't answer Nancy. He must know – Who killed the Grahams? He'd give her an answer after talking with Randy Hawkins and Greg Morris.

A bigger mystery for Austin: Who issued the orders?

The 2:00 p.m. news repeated the deaths as he absorbed every word and visual. During the newscast and after the Grahams segment Randy called...as confused as Austin.

* * *

Madge listened to the perplexing and cryptic conversation that shed only a speck of light for her on the dark family secret.

Madge followed Mitchell's suggestion that she try to eavesdrop on Nancy and Pilar when possible. On several occasions, she meandered near Nancy's room, but their conversation seemed irrelevant. She lost confidence in eavesdropping convinced that wouldn't yield any substance. Then Austin came home.

Madge hastened on tiptoe to return to the kitchen when Nancy readied to leave. Madge knew Austin worked in the library. She turned curious when Nancy came downstairs alone and entered the library.

Madge played spy again confident of overhearing the family secrets. She removed her shoes and tiptoed to near the library's doorframe. She pressed against the wall and listened...lost as ever.

From what was Austin supposed to withdraw? I am drowning in ignorance!

* * *

At 2:34, Austin called Olivia. When the phone rang, she positioned an acting attitude expecting Austin the lead actor in her script.

"Are you all right? I called your office and Gwen said you're ill then I remembered you said you'd be home."

Didn't he hear the news? Why ask about me?

"I had a headache. That time of the month."

"I'm home also. Have you heard the news?"

"No. What's the subject? I napped. Had a sleepless night. Your problems are contagious."

"Janet and Bob Graham were murdered last night in their home in Kings Point."

"O my God!" she emoted alarm. "I can't believe it. By whom?"

"They were executed Rodrigo style. I spoke to Randy who's as shocked, and Greg. Randy called an emergency meeting at six o'clock this evening on his yacht. I trust Greg and Randy and positive they weren't involved. Our first thoughts were that Tomayo Suarez killed them."

"Who's Suarez?"

"He's Graham's executioner, a field captain responsible for the distribution channels. He worked with Bob Graham. Maybe Graham tried to screw him."

"Austin, listen to me. I don't care who killed them. This is an opportunity, a perfect opening. Get out now. Dissolve Rodrigo. Don't waste the opportunity. The Grahams' killer may kill you three. Maybe a crisis or a conflict happened with the Grahams' overseas connections. They screwed up somewhere."

"I'll see how the meeting goes."

"Austin, what's to think?"

"There's no getting out you know that."

"If you all agree it's over."

"I doubt it."

"I'm coming with you."

"Out of the question. This is a matter for Randy, Greg, and me." He hesitated. "But you're right. The opportunity is perfect to end Rodrigo. You want me out. My daughter wants me out. And I want out. With the Grahams gone that's possible."

"Come by and let's talk about what you should emphasize."

"I won't have time...and stop mothering me. I know how to handle those two."

"Quit. Please pull out." She needed to pound out her message. "Nancy won't implicate you. Then you're free again. We're free. We can go on without fear that someone is out to kill us. Please my love, for me. We can go away for a few days." The cash from the Grahams covered the costs, a long trip sponsored by the ungrateful Grahams.

"I'll do anything you want after I meet with Randy and Greg."

Olivia thought it an opportunity to plant another seed.

"Including divorcing your wife?"

"After the trial. Don't start with that dammit."

"Persuade Randy and Greg that Rodrigo *must* die. When are you leaving for Sag Harbor?"

"About four thirty. Greg's flying in from Teterboro Airport."

She hounded him into perfect position – lost, worried, and stressed – perfect to manipulate him.

"I'm scared, Austin, and I don't scare easily. I'm terrified for us." If with him, she'd cry for impact. "I did your bidding with Hancock and Bates. It's your turn to do mine. I'll never want anything else from you besides your love. Please. You must tell me you will."

"I must know who killed them and why. I'll call you later, okay?" Austin grew impatient with the lecture and persistence.

"Don't hang up. I want your promise. I insist."

"Stop with the hounding."

"If you have money with Randy get it back and get out."

"Bearer bonds and cash."

"The bonds will prove to me that you withdrew. I want to see them after."

"You're relentless."

"That's all I ask. I love you. Please win for me."

"For you, for me, and Nancy," he said – a reminder that his daughter was important to him, more important.

"Call as soon as possible."

"Yes, yes," he reaffirmed.

She hung up and grinned; satisfied he had direction.

She expected an emergency meeting in Sag Harbor before she killed the Grahams to start Rodrigo's demise to free Austin. Persuading Randy and Greg to release Austin remained and that shouldn't be an obstacle. Randy already sacrificed his son on Rodrigo business. He'd be crazy to continue with Rodrigo. Greg had more money than he could spend in a lifetime so why risk exposure with the possible police investigation that could destroy them all.

The Grahams were dead. Their mysterious execution should alarm them and hasten Rodrigo's dissolution.

Olivia's script unfolded and progressed beautifully and about to end with a firm capstone.

She changed clothing to go out…to reach Sag Harbor before Austin.

Olivia parked on Bay Street in the town marina parking lot abutting *Golden Hawk's* marina. A narrow building separated marinas. She decided that Randy, Greg, and Austin would park in the closer other marina where they couldn't see her or her car.

Golden Hawk's starboard entrance was open. Knowing Conniver and a steward sailed *Caucus* today, she concluded that the second steward remained on board and was to meet Conniver later at Three Mile Harbor, or Randy arrived earlier.

Olivia could view the security gate and dock to *Golden Hawk*. She settled in to wait with day and night binoculars at her side. She regretted not stopping at Dunkin Donuts for a latte. Night binoculars served as contingency if their meeting extended into evening.

Why should it? The decision should be easy – It's over!

The marinas remained passive during the week without weekend boaters and visitors. She waited for minutes to pass and watched a picture-postcard harbor stir with three local boaters motoring from the small boat marina on the bridge's other side. They whirred into the harbor's channel continuing northeast to Peconic Bay.

At 5:15, the second steward in civilian clothes came out and locked the door. He descended the boarding ladder for the security gate and marina parking lot. That confirmed to Olivia that Randy had yet to arrive.

At 5:30, Randy passed the security gate. He boarded his yacht, unlocked the door, and left it open. He also opened the portside door for cross-ventilation and headed to the galley. Olivia focused the binoculars to his movements. He hurried past the door headed for either the salon or the stateroom stairway. She scanned salon windows. He must have gone below.

Randy searched below to assure the crew left.

Austin arrived five minutes later and hustled to board. Olivia rooted for him to be determined to withdraw and persuade them to end the venture. She felt confident her man and two persons she admired would make the intelligent decision.

Within seconds, Randy entered the salon and they talked by the bar.

Greg arrived ten minutes later.

The view from Olivia's location proved unfavorable for spying. She decided to move next door to *Golden Hawk's* parking lot. Olivia envisioned Rodrigo's demise. She started her car and relocated. The three decision makers sat – three friends conducting an important life and death decision. With binoculars, she could see three heads through the half-drawn drapes. Olivia imagined their conversation, baffled by the Grahams' death scaring them back to sanity. She wished Austin had worn a wire for her to listen in, or purchased a portable listening device to aim at a window.

Austin thrust up waving his arms looking mad. Greg jumped up and shoved Austin.

Olivia panicked. She lowered the binoculars, placed them on the passenger seat, grabbed her bag, and fled the car with her panic.

She sped to the boarding ladder. She climbed and stood by the entrance, leaned in toward the bulkhead to hear Randy, "...and if it wasn't for your damn daughter this wouldn't have happened. We're screwed because you couldn't control her. We granted you time and you failed."

"Bullshit! She didn't kill the Grahams, did she?" retorted Austin. "Maybe one of you assholes did."

"And maybe you did," countered Greg.

"Greg, enough," Randy said. "Graham might've screwed one of his dealers and he turned on him. We'll go on without him and Janet."

"Randy, I told you I'm out!" objected Austin.

"Wake up, Austin," Greg said. "Persuade your daughter we want it to end by Sunday. Or so help me God I'll have her killed."

"Don't you threaten her you son-of-a-bitch," Austin said before he punched Greg's face sending him backwards to the sofa.

"Randy, don't be stupid. Put the gun away. Are you out of your mind?"

Olivia's panic forced her to call out, "Randy! Hello! Are you there? Hello!"

Her voice paralyzed them.

She retreated to the dock.

Randy appeared at the door without the gun looking cordial. "What are you doing here?"

With an innocent look she said, "Austin mentioned your meeting and thought I'd drive out for him to take me to dinner at my favorite East End restaurant."

Randy hesitated, suspicious of the interruption. "He arrived a few minutes ago. Your timing is perfect."

My timing is better than you think.

"Permission to come aboard, sir," she said saluting and smiling.

"You never need permission."

His composure changed to social for her, a friend. He tolerated her intrusion. He'd tell Austin later and in private to come alone tomorrow to finish the meeting.

Olivia boarded and entered the salon smiling. Scanning the room, she missed the gun and assumed it behind the bar or a cushion. Greg and Austin sat faking a conversation. They stood in unison smiling at her. Austin hugged her and kissed her cheek.

"I'm glad to see you. Nice surprise."

"Shall I wait outside till you're done?" she said innocent and nonchalant knowing she exploded the meeting.

"The meeting ended," Randy said going to the bar. "Have a drink. The usual?"

"Yes."

"Black Label and mineral water coming up."

She left with Randy saying, "Greg, I'll be right back. Don't go away."

Olivia waited for her drink then approached Greg.

Greg greeted her with a forced and tight smile. "Hello my darling, always wonderful to see you no matter what the circumstances."

She hugged him. "How's my favorite escort? What happened to your face? It's all red." She reached up to soothe his punched face.

He pulled away. "A minor accident," Greg lied rubbing his face.

Austin's tension lessened pleased that her love for him turned her into an aggressive person to assure his safety. "Good timing. I was about to leave. You have an uncanny instinct for showing up at the right time."

"I'd have reached you on your cell phone. You weren't getting away from me tonight. As soon as I finish my drink, we can go. I had a tough day at the agency today. Nothing seemed to go right."

Randy left the bar holding his drink and sat. Greg and Austin also sat. She drank and placed her glass on the cocktail table.

Olivia delayed to sit. Approaching her chair, she reached into her bag and pulled out the Lady Smith & Wesson that astounded her three most admired men.

"What the hell!" said Randy stunned.

"Randy put your hands on your head and don't talk," she ordered. "You too, Greg. And remain seated. You two don't know when to have an intelligent and objective discussion, or when to seize the opportunity to avoid prison due to your greedy madness."

Greg's mouth closed ending his potential protest. They obeyed unbelieving as she put her finger to her lips.

"Please no talking. I don't want to hear your outrageous exclamations about what I'm doing, that it's an irrational and emotional female thing. Austin, lock the doors. Hurry!"

He reacted and locked both doors.

Randy continued his protest. "What the hell are you doing? Put the gun down for chrissake." Randy thought her act as a female emotional moment.

"The worst kind. Be quiet. You'll make me nervous and shoot because this is a hair trigger."

She reached into her bag, pulled out the silver duct tape, and tossed it to Austin. "I'm sure you all know the procedure. Where's the gun, Austin? I don't see it anywhere."

"Behind the bar," he replied pointing.

"Throw it in the harbor. Make sure no one sees you."

Austin did, on the port side close to the hull after he assured no one could see him. He returned.

"Tape their mouths," she ordered. Austin unrolled a strip and taped Greg then Randy. "No more questions. You didn't listen to Austin,

Randy. You don't want to hear good advice. I believed you would read-ily agree to dissolve Rodrigo. Why go on with the insanity? You don't need the money. Austin wanted to resign and you threatened to kill him. How stupid of you. I want Austin out. No strings attached. Either that or I'll kill you." He failed to acknowledge her glare. "Randy? We're all friends and should forgive each other." She pointed the re-volver at Randy's face.

He nodded approval. He'd go along with her. They'd been friends for too long to fear her pulling the trigger, and a major force in help-ing to build her business. She owed him. He never feared her. Then he thought – *But she's a woman and she could get irrational.*

Olivia turned to Greg, who nodded before the revolver pointed at him. "Excellent, Greg. You and Randy can go on with Rodrigo if you must. Austin and I are out. And forget eliminate the threat slogan with us. Do we have a deal? We won't talk and your secret world will remain private. I don't want you doing to us what you did to Janet and Bob Graham."

Both issued prolonged muffled denials. She ignored them chuck-ling to herself.

"All right, Austin. Let's get your portion and go. Where do you keep the money, Randy?" He hesitated. "Greg? You guys have to com-municate better." She removed the tape from Randy's mouth.

Austin, taking a back seat to her initiative replied, "Don't bother, I know."

"Where?" She continued to act ignorant. Austin would want to know how she knew about the bilge.

"In the bilge."

"How about cash?" She checked her prisoners for a possible attack. They looked resigned to their position unafraid but tentative, both cer-tain she wouldn't kill them.

"Under his bed."

"We're going below. Randy, stand up." He stood with rising panic. "Austin, tape his hands behind his back."

"Come on," protested Randy. "You made your point, no need to continue this nonsense. It's over and we didn't kill the Grahams."

"Yes you did," she said. "You just threatened Austin. You would've killed him if I wasn't here. I'll tell you when it's over." She taped Randy's mouth again before he could start his protest.

Austin unrolled tape. "He's secure."

"It's your turn, Greg." Greg stood and Austin taped him. "Austin, lead the way down single file and don't let them pass you. Randy might have another weapon below." She looked at her prisoners. "He'll count his portion so you two can't claim he cheated you though I know that as old friends you won't."

They filed downstairs: Austin, Randy, Greg then Olivia. Austin opened the master stateroom door. The others followed. The spacious bed held numerous colored throw pillows – all pastel shades of the Southwest: orange, pink, blue, and violet. Pillows leaned upright on the white bedspread and pressed against a maple headboard. All bureaus and closets were maple.

"Randy, get on your knees. And you too, Greg and face each other." Greg lowered and Randy knelt objecting with muffled protests. "Tape their ankles and connect their arms and legs Rodrigo style."

Austin completed the assignment. Randy continued to complain with his muffled sounds. Olivia wasn't interested in what he had to say enjoying their panic and suffering.

"Austin, get your money and let's leave. Captain Conniver should be back by ten o'clock to set you two free. Relax and get comfortable. We'll part as friends and forget Rodrigo ever happened. All I ask is that you exclude Austin and me from your thoughts and future. Is that too much to ask?"

They waved their heads. Austin searched under the bed and pulled out a dark blue overnight bag.

She pulled the tape from Greg's mouth and asked, "How much is there, Greg?"

"Six hundred thousand dollars."

Olivia pressed the tape back in place. "Austin's portion is one fourth, right Randy?" He nodded.

Austin left the stateroom. She studied the two who threatened Austin; men she adored and determined they would've killed Austin. That wasn't in her tame script. They altered the plot and rewrote a violent Act II.

Killing the Grahams failed because of greed by two stupid and wealthy persons who knelt before her. The opportunity to dissolve Rodrigo died. She never wanted her killing the Grahams wasted.

Damn!

Austin returned from the bilge with a thick manila envelope. He unclasped the metal prongs and emptied the contents on the bed. Learning the amount from the Grahams, Olivia continued her acting, the leading lady in her drama.

"How much is there, Austin?"

"Six million."

"Nice round sum. One point five is yours?"

"Correct."

"Leave everything on the bed. Randy, do you have another overnight bag?" His head motioned to the closet. "Austin, do the honors." He opened the door. The overnight bag lay on the shelf.

"Take half the cash and put it in the bag," she ordered. "Call it interest and a donation from the Grahams." Austin followed directions and shifted approximate half from the Grahams' portion without counting. "Austin, count out your and the Grahams' shares." Austin counted the total, intent on his assignment. "We concluded our financial transaction. I thank you Randy and Greg," she added. "Civility is a wonderful word. You needed to act civil, to accept Austin's resignation with civility and friendship, and saved yourselves the embarrassment of being on your knees before a woman. I know that doesn't sit well with your macho ass, Randy – a woman having advantage over you."

Olivia picked up the soft, pastel orange throw pillow with her left hand, and stood by Greg."I want you to know, Greg that I love you as a dear friend. And Randy, I owe you for helping me with my business. You both are instrumental to my success. I'll always thank you for that. It's time for us to leave. I hope you benefit from this lesson. Finished, Austin?"

"In a minute," Austin answered without looking up.

Greg's breathing grew heavier, eyes frightened, inching on his knees away from her.

"It's unfortunate," she continued. "You were going to kill Austin and underscoring the old saying – With friends like you, who needs enemies?"

With sudden movements, she put the pillow against Greg's head, pressed the revolver into it, and fired into his left ear. The muffled shot echoed in the enclosed room and reverberated through Randy and Austin. Austin couldn't believe she killed him. The amount he counted left his head pushed out by shock.

Randy swirled in chaos struggling to break free to move backwards away from her.

She looked at the startled Austin. "They were going to kill you, Austin. Don't forget that. They're your enemies."

Austin tried to speak. His mouth moved but couldn't form words.

She turned to Randy, who cowered. "You had the chance to let him go. You chose to pull a gun on him. You wanted to kill my Austin knowing how much he meant to me. And after you killed him then what? Was I next? Or try to take me as your lover? To go on killing for Rodrigo?" Randy shook his panicked head. "You don't measure up to him. No one does. And you never once considered how I'd feel did you?" His terrified eyes widened. "I loved cruising with you but our voyages ended torpedoed by your greed."

Olivia pressed the pillow to Randy's head and fired in his left ear.

Austin's body locked, numbed by her violence.

She pushed her new victims over on their right side.

"Let's go, Austin. Take all the shares and cash and a bag. I'll take the other." Austin shook his stupor and reacted to her commands. "Wait," she said and turned back. "Mustn't forget." Olivia dipped her finger in Randy's blood and made the Rodrigo trademark. "Rodrigo is a bad dude, isn't he? No one to mess around with."

She stuffed the pillow into a bag for disposal later.

"Austin, wipe our prints off the tapes."

He did. Austin looked out a starboard window and signaled all clear to leave. They left *Golden Hawk* closing the door. Activity increased on the waterfront and none near them. They left the yacht and walked with innocence to their cars.

"Meet me in the Bridgehampton Common parking lot west of Bridgehampton on Route 27," Austin said.

"I know it. Don't think about what happened. You're alive. Rodrigo's dead. Is that a happy conclusion or what? I did it for you my love, for us." Olivia glowed.

They entered their cars for Bridgehampton via the Sag Harbor-Bridgehampton Turnpike.

The man in the car several spaces away raised his lowered body, hidden to avoid discovery until both cars pulled away. Recognizing the Senator, Tomayo Suarez watched them leave *Golden Hawk*. He did not recognize the woman.

He arrived minutes ago from his bodega to confront Randy Hawkins for his money after the news announced that the Grahams were murdered.

Austin continued unsettled over Olivia's coldblooded killing. Muffled shots echoed within. Driving south, he started to accept her actions when the focus and location shifted. She saved his life and he shouldn't feel sympathy for his ex-associates. His drug world equated to death and violence. Hiding in Washington never hid his crime.

Austin labeled himself a criminal, a drug dealer, and a murderer, an accessory to pharmacist Troy Betson's murder, and connected to Randy Hawkins and Greg Morris's executions – and conspired with Olivia to kill Todd Hancock and Laurence Bates – and as violent as Bob Graham and his associates. His delusional safe distance from exposure faded and he accepted reality.

Olivia and Austin conceived the ploy for Hancock and Bates. The lawyers would receive three million dollars if they confronted Nancy and extracted the truth. Had they succeeded, she would've lured them to the tax haven after the trial to establish an account and exchange the bearer bonds as their reward. The lawyers then must die with the champagne cocktail overseas to eliminate the threat for knowing much. Failing, she persuaded them to leave the country and sell their properties, that they failed, and their life was in danger. They accepted the irresistible financial offer and new lifestyle and left Long Island to their death overseas.

Placing facts before him, Austin concluded his acts as evil and ruthless. He couldn't hold to a higher standard than Olivia. He failed society and his family. Olivia acted out of love for him. He did it for money and might have lost his daughter. That pain would last a lifetime.

He thought of Madge – innocent, 'see-good-in-everybody' Madge, who he betrayed and kept distant in his life and needs. He didn't care about losing Madge. After all these years, Madge was just there, a part of the house, a convenience for him, and his politics. He should've been less cruel and divorced her long ago to let her live a better life, possibly with a man who'd appreciate her wonderful qualities. Madge was a terrific mother and a devoted wife. He never deserved her, he concluded. Austin needed to make amends with Madge and Nancy.

Austin reached a major fork to his upcoming decision. He massaged his future options – Does he surrender to the police? Does he run and hide? He had money to live in a foreign country in luxury and change identity. Would Olivia leave her successful business to come with him to hide? Yes, no doubt. Would his confession help Nancy in her trial? He'd do anything to help her. Should the prosecution condemn Nancy because her father destroyed lives with his poisonous drugs? Guilty by association, the prosecutor would claim. Like father, like daughter. They're both killers. For Nancy's sake, he couldn't surrender and confess to police.

A third option spawned.

Rodrigo belonged to him if he wanted it. He could continue to run the operation with Captain Conniver and Tomayo Suarez.

And Olivia.

* * *

Day approached its final hour as Austin led to the Common. He parked at a vacant area facing Montauk Highway/Route 27. Olivia stopped next to him and left her car for his green Cadillac.

Following Austin to Bridgehampton, Olivia knew Rodrigo would receive the blame for the Rodrigo style executions on *Golden Hawk*, and Randy and Greg labeled as drug users. The media should connect Randy with his son who used drugs before Nancy killed him. The bridge would be – Like father, like son – an advantage to help Austin's uncompromising shit of a daughter.

Olivia was pleased as she thought – *Who could prove that Janet, Randy, and Greg were three-fourths Rodrigo? Who could connect Austin as the last puzzle piece? Austin was free and Rodrigo neutralized, the body still in place, and the heads chopped off.*

But her script had yet to complete.

The Third Act curtain would soon rise.

* * *

Expecting to explain the drastic actions, Olivia was surprised when she closed the car door and Austin said, "Thank you for saving my life. And thank you for loving me."

Austin leaned over and kissed her mouth with a long kiss that had more gratitude than passion.

"How daring kissing me in public." She approved. "You don't look rattled anymore."

"More surprised than anything."

"They would've killed you then gone for a ride and dumped your body in Gardiner's Bay with weights."

"What made you follow me?"

"Intuition, that you might need me."

"Tell me something more believable."

"I wanted to make sure you resigned – a part of my future plan as an eternally romantic pair. I wouldn't know how to live if something happened to you. I have no future without you. I told you that many times, and will continue to tell you that."

He kissed her again. "We have decisions to make. One includes my having a discussion with Nancy tonight. The others concern our future, options to discuss, and decisions we can't delay."

Olivia and Austin left Bridgehampton for their homes. Night arrived when Austin reached his armed encampment. Decisions about the future with Olivia concluded after a lengthy discussion.

A conversation with Nancy remained for Austin.

Madge wasn't in the kitchen. The solarium television attracted Austin. Nancy and Pilar watched a rented movie. Tortilla chips and Paul Newman's Own salsa were on the coffee table. When he entered, Pilar tensed and nudged Nancy, who said "Hi, Daddy."

"Where's your mother?"

"Shopping. The stores are open late tonight."

"I had my meeting and need to talk. Come into the library." He avoided eye contact with Pilar.

Nancy accepted the good news with quiet enthusiasm. "Sure. Pilar, excuse us," she said and stood.

Pilar clicked the Pause button.

Nancy followed her father and expected good news.

He turned to her. "Shall we close the door? Are you uncomfortable?"

"No longer." Nancy closed the door.

Austin sat behind the desk, she, in the visitor's chair. His daughter appeared more relaxed than last time. He leaned towards her with elbows on the desk. "I have a dilemma. First, the good news. I withdrew from Rodrigo." Nancy's face gleamed, having won. Her insistence paid off. "If I tell the police that I participated, the prosecutor will exploit that you're the daughter of a drug financier – a murderer, like her father."

"I never wanted you to tell anyone, Daddy. I don't want you going to jail. I just wanted you out. I'm glad I insisted but there's a problem now."

"What problem?"

"What do I do with the luggage?"

"You're right. It's complicated." Austin searched for a solution. "Three pieces?"

"Yes."

"Keep one for your mother. We'll return the rest."

"To who? Where?"

The questions stymied him having a mental lapse. No one remained to receive the luggage. The answer came. "Stanford Crane. Tell him the truth. He must also know about you and Eddie. Don't keep anything from him."

"You mean tell him about you?"

"Especially about me."

"And the truth about Eddie? Why I killed him?"

"Yes. Stanford won't violate your trust. He'll know what to do with the luggage without revealing my role. Your best defense is the rape charge. He may proceed with that. He may not. Do whatever he tells you. For your sake, he must know the truth to avoid being blindsided by the unexpected in court. You're courageous beyond brave for me. You don't have to worry anymore. Rodrigo's over, dead."

"The others have withdrawn?"

An inappropriate time for her to learn they were dead, he said, "Eddie's father and Greg Morris are out. With the Grahams dead there's no need for the security guards anymore."

"Who killed the Grahams?"

"We suspect their people in the distribution system."

"What happens now? Mr. Crane will know about you."

"My future will take care of itself. I don't want you hurt anymore. I leave for Washington tonight for a morning meeting with the President. I'll be in Washington for a few days, and then a week, possibly two, for conferences in other states. For your protection, it's best I'm off Long Island if I'm implicated to Rodrigo."

"What do I tell Mom?"

"Tell her I had to return to Washington tonight for important meetings. Give her one luggage *after* your trial is over to protect yourself during the trial. Your mother is honest, pure, and innocent in these matters. She'll want an explanation."

"I'll never tell her or the truth about me and Eddie."

"Do that after or during the trial and after consultation with Stanford Crane. Make every effort to know her better. Your mother is a wonderful person and needs you to love her and to get closer as you grow. You will soon discover that she's a special person."

"I have to keep her at arms distance. When should I tell Mr. Crane? The jury selection process starts on Monday."

"Call him Sunday, not before. I have my reasons. Are you comfortable with all this? Will you be okay?"

"Yes."

"All right if I hug you?"

"Yes."

Austin came around and she stood to meet him. They embraced. He kissed her forehead.

"I love you, Nancy. I'm sorry I put you through this and disappointed you." They stayed embraced. "Thank you for loving me."

"I did it to myself." Nancy hugged her father tighter. She always believed her tenacity would win.

"Yes, and you won. You beat me and I'm happy to lose." The embrace opened.

"I'm thankful I did." Tears came. "You had to stop before getting deeper. I'll never understand why you joined Rodrigo."

"I made a horrible mistake, honey, a very weak and naive moment when I should've known better. I'll call you often. You'll win again and in court this time. Mr. Crane is a good man, a brilliant attorney, why I wanted him in the first place. I have to go."

They left the library. In his bedroom, he collected personal items and packed an overnight bag. The conversation pleased Austin. They were back on talking terms, and positive she'd endure the trial and listen to Stanford Crane...and pleased that Madge wasn't home.

He didn't want to face her to say goodbye.

Austin had parked in the driveway and left the garage door open. He ignored the guards and clicked the garage door closed.

He reached Old Country Road without noticing the white car following him. He turned left and entered the Long Island Expressway at Exit 48, Round Swamp Road.The pursuer followed. Westbound traffic flowed above the speed limit with sporadic decreases in the construction zones until he reached Exit 36. The white car followed, its driver concentrating on the Cadillac's taillight design to prevent losing it to the night.

Austin traveled the north service road to Shelter Rock Road and made a right turn. The white car kept a distance about a football field length. Austin never suspected someone followed. Behind him, the headlights looked alike and unimportant.

The white car slowed when the Cadillac's turn signals and brake lights lit. The Cadillac turned right into Olivia's gated community and guardhouse. The Cadillac passed the security gate, turned a bend, and faded.

Madge passed the entrance to the guardhouse and made a U-turn to return home.

Returning from her shopping, Madge recognized Austin's car in the driveway. The open garage door meant he planned to leave soon. Madge turned in the opposite direction and waited for his departure to follow him to LaGuardia Airport, his normal destination for Washington.

Or was he going on one of his restless night drives?

She turned defensive, suspicious of her husband, and Nancy's collusion that made her an outsider.

Was he going to Washington? Elsewhere? Austin never mentioned he'd leave.

Madge wondered whom he visited on Shelter Rock Road.

When Nancy said he'd been here and had to return to Washington tonight for a morning meeting with the President, Madge had no comment, only a quiet rage.

Madge could no longer believe anything her husband said, and angrier for the lies and what he hadn't told her.

She needed to settle her stomach before sleep.

Upsets and nausea were frequent visitors during the past several weeks.

31

Madge had grown accustomed to sleeping alone. That night's restlessness emulated sleeping with a crowd, nudged, and kicked in a packed New York City subway that thrust her awake just before sunrise to a stomach that screamed for relief. She rushed to the bathroom cabinet for an antacid tablet. Rejection continued to attack as her head throbbed.

Why did they consider her an outsider to the family problem, she asked her tormented soul. She knew that stomach problems and headaches would greet her from now on every morning.

Why did her husband and daughter consider her *that* weak? What had she done wrong? Was she to blame? Madge felt rejected and scorned, deemed unimportant, her advice and counsel irrelevant, all grating weights sinking her deeper into depression to make her feel demeaned and useless.

She needed to solve her mental distress on her own and without a psychiatrist.

Differences between awakening yesterday morning and that day were the blatant lies and betrayal from her family. The insults added to the lingering stings that aroused ire and hurt to stab her soul. The overheard conversation between Austin and Nancy replayed.

Your associates Janet and Bob Graham were executed – The police call it a drug execution by Rodrigo – Did you have anything to do with it? – Are you withdrawing? – I'll give in if you do – Does Pilar know about me? – Make sure your mother never knows – She'll never know – I don't want to lose you.

They understood the disguised conversation; she hadn't, separated from the current family mystery. Nancy wasn't honest with her. Austin wasn't honest with her and disloyal if he cheated on her.

Did he visit a woman last night? Why didn't he fly or drive to Washington?

Madge remembered more – *Don't be frightened, Nancy. I will never strike you again.*

More lies, Madge added.

Austin beat Nancy during last week's argument. *Why did Nancy protect him? What secret did they share?*

She couldn't ask Nancy. Nancy would lie again. Pilar was also involved in the charade.

Distraught at her family's lack of confidence in her and their rejection, she felt alone, cast off, and insignificant to the crisis. Hopeless and feeling irrelevant, Madge cried, sinking deeper in her pit of despair from her family's disrespect. Her distress lasted longer that day.

Recovering, she decided to accept the cards dealt and to allow the hand to play out and to stop the crying and stop feeling sorry for herself. No matter how hard she'd try to uncover their secret they weren't ready to include her. Madge decided to accept the obvious.

Don't waste your time in that direction.

Madge must devote time and energy to find who Austin visited on Shelter Rock Road. The mission motivated her out of bed to the kitchen for a cup of coffee and toast then to the library and house files enthused to start her mission, her offensive for knowledge to brighten the darkness.

Madge opened the files in the study/library, pulled telephone bills for the house and cells for the current and past year, and sat at Austin's rosewood desk to search. Austin paid all bills and kept records and files. She needed to review calls made to the Manhasset and North Hills areas, uncertain which area. She started to review and scrutinize all bills carefully, confident she found the right track, and determined to uncover his secret life if he had one. As she searched, the more she believed his unfaithfulness.

Madge discovered a number called often each month in Manhasset and circled each with a red pen. She checked her kitchen calendar where she marked the weeks and weekends Austin lived home for that year. Austin had called the suspicious number on all weekends with ample calls during the week, when Congress recessed, and on holidays.

She wondered whom Austin called often. Madge called the Manhasset number. She checked the clock – 10:25 a.m.

What would I say when the party answered? Why I called? My name? Was there caller ID?

No matter, Madge must know hoping she made a mistake, and that Austin never violated their marriage. She could live with his collusion with Nancy, but never with his betrayal – the ultimate insult and degradation.

She dialed the suspicious number. The phone rang and connected to the answering machine – "This is Olivia. We're unavailable. Message for now." Madge ended the connection.

Olivia.

Madge knew half a name. Encouraged, she pulled Austin's thick Rolodex closer to her. The search would've ended sooner if Austin maintained a computer address file.

He should've hired a secretary for a day.

She flipped the cards and studied the last name or any name that matched the phone number.

The cards had a similar pattern: name, business, and phones. She had no success from A to F. In the Gs, she found an Olivia Greene in Manhasset and Village Greene Travel Service, and pulled the card. She checked the phone number with the telephone bills. They matched – Olivia Greene on Orchid Drive in Manhasset – no need to search the internet.

Madge looked in the Nassau County Street Map binder and found Orchid Drive in Manhasset off Shelter Rock Road. She knew that was where Austin turned into the gated community. Although not surprised, her heart sank. Olivia Greene. The name sounded familiar.

Where have I heard the name? Did I meet her in the past?

Satisfied and depressed that she found her husband's destination curiosity reviewed the telephone records. She envisioned Austin calling her the past two years. Earlier years waited in the basement files; no need to search those. Madge had her *absolute* evidence beyond a reasonable doubt in legal terms.

A scorned wife's curiosity refused to let go. *How long had he called her?*

She rushed from the library muttering mild obscenities. In the basement, she uncovered another year and a half of calls. Her breath fled weakening knees that forced her to lean against the black metal file.

"You bastard!" she whispered. "You miserable bastard! You despicable son-of-a-bitch!"

Madge felt nauseous with revulsion, returned to the kitchen for coffee and an antacid tablet then sat at the table with *Newsday* to help erase the betrayal and her destructive thoughts. She never turned the newspaper pages. Grinding thoughts led her in a different direction.

Madge decided to make an emboldened visit to Village Greene Travel Service to see what Olivia Greene looked like...this...*this loathing parasite of other women's husbands...this marriage destroyer!*

For the first time, Madge nurtured hate...for Olivia Greene and Austin who violated her marriage and dignity. She shuddered to believe that on Austin's long drives at night when unable to sleep that he left to see her. She concluded, yes.

Oh, yes, you deceiving snake!

Deception altered her psyche from naive and innocent to alert, suspicious, and angry. Hate carved a niche creating a new personality. The alien posture felt uncomfortable, but essential to force her to solve her problems.

Wake up!

Madge drove north on Round Swamp Road turning left at Jericho Turnpike for the short trip to Woodbury. She slowed with traffic backed up at the busy intersection at Woodbury Road. The white Village Greene building was on the right. Noon approached.

Madge turned into the parking area and had second thoughts. She should have waited until after 2:00. Olivia Greene may be out to lunch. She read the sign in bold lettering – Open 7 Days for Personal Service.

Nervous, Madge summoned the strength to go in to see Austin's lover, where this lowlife worked.

What should I say? Do I accuse her and threaten her to stop?

No, no, let's see what she looks like. Then I'll develop the strategy.

Several agents at their desks serviced clients.

Which one is she?

The two conference areas held meetings with many brochures on the tables. The young woman behind the counter asked to help.

"I'd like to see Olivia Greene." Madge's voice lacked strength and confidence.

"I don't think she's in." She turned towards the rear. "The lady in the corner is her assistant."

"Thank you."

Madge approached Gwen Rhodes. Gwen had turned to file a folder and finished as Madge neared. "Hi, can I help you?"

"Is Olivia Greene in? My name is Madge Kiley, Senator Austin Kiley's wife."

"It's a real pleasure to meet you. I'm sorry, Mrs. Kiley, but Olivia is on vacation for three weeks."

"Oh," Madge said looking unaffected.

"Is there anything I can help you with?"

"No. No, thank you. The Senator suggested I talk to her to plan a vacation for next year and he insisted only with Olivia. I'll wait till she returns." Madge forced a light laugh. "Maybe we should go where she goes. She must know the best places. Where did she go?"

"I don't know. She left a message on my email that she'd call later. I'll tell her you stopped by. She communicates with the office."

"Don't bother her vacation. I'll see her when she returns."

Madge returned to her car unhappy and disappointed to wait three weeks to meet Olivia Greene while waiting for the next family deception to unfold...three more weeks of treated as useless and scorned.

* * *

In Sag Harbor, Tomayo Suarez waited for a few minutes before he left his car to see Randy for his monthly fee. He called out when he boarded *Golden Hawk*. His calls unanswered, he began looking for Randy. Going below, he found the bodies. His first thought urged him to flee…the next was to wait for Captain Conniver. He lived on board but he should return unless he quit the operation. Suarez decided to wait until midnight.

Conniver and stewards arrived at 9:30. Suarez showed the bodies to Conniver and said he'd seen Senator Kiley and a woman leave. Conniver searched under the bed for the cash and in the bilge for shares and bonds.

"Looks like the Senator cleaned us out. We can handle the problem tomorrow. The Senator killed them and the Grahams. He wants to take over. He can't without us. We'll switch boats and use his. Let's be smart and join him. He's the man. I'll call the police for them to see another execution by Rodrigo. Tomayo, go home and keep your mouth shut about this. We'll talk later. Do you understand?"

"Si."

* * *

Detective Marvin Rose and Mullins were summoned from their homes by police to witness the latest Rodrigo slaughter in Sag Harbor.

* * *

At mid-afternoon, Captain Conniver turned off Old County Road into the Kiley community with an urgent need to talk to Senator Kiley for him to explain the whereabouts of the $6 million in cash, bearer shares, and bonds missing from *Golden Hawk*. This wasn't a subject for a phone conversation.

Conniver wore his white uniform. The Kiley security hailed him. Conniver asked for the Senator. Guard Tito Chavez called Madge. Madge came to the screen door with a cordless and studied the man who asked for her husband.

Conniver exited watched by Tito Chavez and his partner, Maurice Calvin. Tito passed the phone to Conniver.

"Mrs. Kiley, Captain Walker Conniver. I work for Mr. Randy Hawkins. It's important I see the Senator."

"Ah, yes, I remember you. He left for Washington. Anything I can do?"

"No. I have news to tell him personally. Thank you. I'll call his office. Do you have the number?"

Madge said the number.

Conniver memorized the number. He left the area to plan new strategy. The trip proved a waste, but he verified security guards protected the house.

* * *

That evening, Madge saw the beautiful and younger Olivia Greene and thrust forward in her chair, alert.

"Hi, I am Olivia Greene," began the television commercial for Village Greene Travel Service.

This attractive bitch has been stealing Austin for over three years. Wake up, Madge, you dumb shit. She violated you. She stole him, obsessed over him. You...lost...him...forever. Forever!

Madge, who never permitted foul language in her home or conversation until recently, felt that thinking the F word very loud was appropriate for her thoughts and anger. She felt better.

* * *

Nancy and Pilar spent the day playing tennis then settled in the solarium. Since her father withdrew from Rodrigo and back on talking terms, the threat from Rodrigo vanished – no need to confine herself to her house any longer.

At the front door, Nancy hailed Tito Chavez. A surprised Tito met her on the lawn.

"Mr. Chavez, I want to thank you and your crew for being here. Things have changed. After tomorrow night, I have to cancel the arrangement. Can you stay only through Sunday morning?"

"As you wish. The shift will end at ten o'clock on Sunday morning."

"Perfect. Again, I thank you."

"I'll notify my office. I need the request in writing."

"I'll bring the authorization in one minute."

* * *

The 5:00 p.m. news crushed Nancy.

The drug execution of Randy Hawkins and Greg Morris captured the lead story. Nancy listened along with Pilar aghast that her father might have murdered his former associates.

A reporter covering Randy Hawkins's history, a prominent Long Island resident, included Eddie and Nancy – reminding that both father and son were involved in drugs. The reporter also mentioned the Nancy Kiley jury selection scheduled for Monday and her two former lawyers allegedly murdered overseas.

Nancy cringed when hearing her name, a reminder of her pending ordeal. She agreed the father and son connection added to her claim of self-defense.

Randy Hawkins and Greg Morris died.

The Grahams died.

Rodrigo died.

Her father lived.

Was he next? Was he the survivor...or the murderer?

Nancy rushed to the phone to call his office.

"The Senator hasn't come in today," said his secretary Rosella. "He said he wasn't feeling well."

Nancy called his apartment. The answering machine wasn't connected. The phone rang ten times. No answer. She tried again three times before going to bed.

Daddy, please. Where are you?

* * *

When Nancy and Pilar listened to the news about the executions, Madge worked in the kitchen preparing dinner and listening to the same channel. Madge stopped peeling carrots, listened, and absorbed after hearing Rodrigo. Austin and Nancy used the name when she eavesdropped. Madge knew Randy and Greg. Nancy referred to Janet and Bob Graham as Austin's associates.

The Grahams were executed in the same manner as Randy and Greg. His associates? All murdered. Nancy asked – "A drug execution by Rodrigo?" If Austin's associates were involved in drugs, wasn't he?

Madge lacked evidence, but convinced herself with – Yes!

Austin never talked to her about his involvements or finances. She wasn't sure of their worth. He said several million and never to worry about finances. He handled the finances. Nancy's words in the library repeated – "They killed the Grahams. Are you in danger?" Austin said no.

At that moment, Madge no longer felt anything for Austin, whether he lived or died.

He ripped the love out of her, gouged it out of her.

His betrayal overwhelmed her soul.

Disgust also drove him out of her.

Madge's life with him shattered. A future confrontation waited when he returned.

At the appropriate time, she'd take the initiative to divorce him, no sense in questioning Nancy about her secrets. Nancy wouldn't confide in her. Confronting Nancy with Stanford, Mitchell, and then Austin failed.

What good could I do alone?

She'd stay alert, suspicious, and analyze the phone bills.

Madge wouldn't be distant, angry, and argumentative with Nancy. She would continue pleasant and treat her and Pilar the same as before; oblivious to the problem; the naive mother; cook and chief bottle washer; part of the furniture, and an irrelevant houseplant thirsty for water.

She had exceptions: analyzing their conversations, eavesdropping more, and reading between the lines. Assertiveness won as her motto.

But to descend to a level where divorce was mandatory to go on with her life churned her stomach and forced her to vomit.

Later, Nancy told Madge that she released the guards effective Sunday at 10:00 a.m.

"Thank goodness," Madge replied. "I'm glad you got over your psychological feelings. That's a relief."

Madge decided to lie.

Why should I be the exception in my house?

Mitchell and Lou Stafutti, Stanford's associate, completed interviewing dormitory residents. Four residents departed for home. Mitchell interviewed two at their homes, a male and female who lived in Upper Brookville and Woodmere, and two females covered by Lou in Riverhead and Flanders.

This information wasn't new except for one resident who focused on how distressed Nancy looked. The resident, nearly raped years ago, knew the emotions.

The attacked girl heartened Stanford. The prosecution would challenge her statement, but the jury would've heard. Ready for jury selection on Monday, he asked Mitchell to be there and to attend the trial. Mitchell agreed looking forward to the procedure. He never experienced the jury selection process.

* * *

Nancy and Pilar left the Kiley residence in the morning convinced the threat ended. When Nancy notified her mother that she and Pilar were going shopping at the Walt Whitman Mall, Madge had no opinion. Madge never knew what spurred Nancy's turnabout and no sense in asking. If the threat vanished, Nancy should go out. How nice if the girls had asked her to shop with them. Madge had no choice but to accept the exclusion. She wasn't 'one of the girls'.owH

In Pilar's car, they headed east on Jericho Turnpike to Commack to the furnished rental condominium apartment on Commack Road. Although Nancy felt safe, she checked for following cars. They scanned Commack Road for the enemy after parking.

The second floor apartment served their purpose: two bedrooms, a long living room, and a kitchen/dining area. Full moving cartons lay scattered in all rooms. The look advertised – Just moved in and haven't had time to unpack.

Pilar unlocked the closet door. A male friend who helped with the move installed a lock. The opening door revealed three identical pieces of dark tan luggage, the only items in the closet.

Nancy stared at what caused her problems. She said nothing new to Pilar as if talking to herself. "They served their purpose."

"Your father said to give one to your mother and the rest to Stanford Crane. What's Crane going to do? Give them to the police?"

"Maybe or another authority."

Pilar pulled out and opened the three pieces exposing the contents. Each piece contained approximately $4 million in cash, some bearer shares, and bonds. Nancy turned bitter at the byproduct of her father's madness.

"Let's take the one with more cash," Nancy said and zipped the luggage and placed two in the closet.

Pilar closed the door and turned the lock. "What should we do with your mother's suitcase?"

"Store it in an unused bedroom at home under the bed. When it's time, I'll say Daddy told me where to look and that the money is for her."

"How do you explain four million dollars?"

"I don't know. I'll think of something."

They loaded the money in two cartons and placed them and the empty suitcase in Pilar's trunk.

Nancy called Stanford Crane."This is Nancy Kiley, Mr. Crane. It's important we meet. There's something you must know. I want to meet tomorrow at four o'clock in Commack."

"Commack? You're leaving the house?"

"Yes. I don't need protection anymore. I'll explain when I see you."

Nancy provided the address and apartment number.

"I want to bring Mr. Pappas since he attended our other meetings."

"Okay. You can have Mr. Pappas with you. Pilar will also be there and I trust her."

Nancy and Pilar returned to the Kiley residence, parked in the garage, and closed the garage door. Nancy needed to locate her mother to avoid her seeing the boxes. Madge sat in the backyard at a table by the pool reading a biography on President Harry S. Truman. Reading served as a refuge away from her immediate world.

They shoved the boxes under the bed in an unused bedroom. When Madge asked what they bought, Nancy said, "Nothing reached out to talk to me. I'm no longer the impulse buyer. I'm learning to control myself."

* * *

Pilar slept while Nancy stared at the dark ceiling in conflict over tomorrow's meeting with Stanford Crane. She ignored the heavy rain that scratched at windows and hummed on the roof.

She massaged the question – *Could I give the $8 million to Crane without implicating Daddy?*

If she told Crane and he told authorities after the trial, her father would be a murderer and a disgraced senator. She refused to destroy her father on a gamble to save herself. She'd say the money belonged to Eddie, that he wanted her to hide it for him. Her mind stalled – *How would I answer if Crane asked – 'Why late in returning the money? Were you planning to steal it? The prosecutor will claim you killed him for the money'. And why did Daddy want me to wait until Sunday afternoon before telling Stanford Crane?*

She'd ask her father when he calls.

More questions preyed – *What if I continued to hide the money? Then Daddy would be safe. Or, what if I give Crane the money after the trial without mentioning Daddy? How do I explain 'Where it is?' from my conversation with Crane? How do I explain what the other lawyers asked me?*

The debate continued inside.

Rain continued outside.

Sleep ended them at 2:10 a.m.

Nancy and Pilar arrived at the apartment in the morning to finish unpacking and straighten. Nancy prepared for her lawyer after reviewing her thoughts and decision with Pilar about her father. Pilar agreed with the conclusion.

* * *

Pilar answered the knock on the door.

"Come in, Mr. Crane, Mr. Pappas."

Pilar closed the door. Nancy entered from the bedroom.

"Thank you for coming. Please have a seat." Nancy pointed to a blue and white patterned couch. The red oak floor lacked a rug.

Nancy and Pilar sat in chairs facing the men.

Nancy said, "Certain events transpired since we met that you should know. I'm able to answer questions you asked the other day, and know why I couldn't respond. Regarding the 'where it is' discussion, do you recall?"

"I do," answered Stanford.

"Todd Hancock and Laurence Bates asked me – Where's the eight million dollars Eddie had on the day I killed him?" Nancy made an extra effort to get the number right and not say twelve.

"Eight million?" Stanford said astounded by the amount.

"Both lawyers insisted knowing I killed Eddie for the money. And if I didn't tell them where I hid the money they'd resign the case and I'll be found guilty. This explains why Bates and Hancock were killed because they knew about the money and the person or persons for who they acted as agents." Nancy captured their attention. "Before I say more, I need to initiate a client-lawyer secrecy agreement. Everything I say from here on is confidential, germane to my case, or is that automatic? Yes?"

"You had that from the start," Stanford said.

"Mr. Pappas, also?"

"He's included. Your secrecy is assured, Nancy."

"I have one more item to add as a preface, an umbrella type background subject exempt from secrecy. A drug organization exists on Long Island headed by Rodrigo."

Mitchell reacted to Lieutenant Mullins's nemesis.

"Recently," Nancy continued, "several drug related deaths were attributed to drug dealers. Janet and Bob Graham were killed in Kings Point. Randy Hawkins, Eddie's father, and Greg Morris were killed on a yacht in Sag Harbor."

"I read and heard about them," Stanford said. "I noted to talk to you about Eddie's father. Randy Hawkins underlines Eddie's drug use, a weapon in court to strengthen our case against Eddie; a father and son connection."

"What isn't public, Mr. Crane is that the Grahams, Hawkins, and Morris are, or I should say were, Rodrigo. They provided the funding.

Rodrigo is not a person...but a front. With their deaths, the Rodrigo organization is over."

Stanford turned skeptical.

Mitchell leaned forward, curious. "Who could've killed them?"

Nancy hesitated to answer having speculated the killer might be her father. "I don't know. I know they were Rodrigo. I stated a major disclosure, and fact."

"Do you know why they were killed?" Mitchell said.

"No."

"Who told you they were Rodrigo?"

"Everything so far has been exempted from secrecy," Nancy replied to avoid the question. "I don't care who knows about the Rodrigo management. Mr. Pappas, since you communicated with the police tell them if you want. I don't care."

Mitchell liked the permission, an opportunity to inform Mullins again with new and stunning information.

Nancy added, "My answer to your question and subsequent statements must include secrecy. Privilege."

"Again, you have that," Stanford said.

"Eddie told me."

"He knew about the Rodrigo hierarchy?"

"My father left for Washington and then he's going on tour for a week. He won't be around. I asked him what I should do about the truth. He urged me to tell you, that you would know what to do. I have to get something. Excuse me."

Nancy disappeared into the bedroom. Pilar looked away from the men, uncomfortable, alone.

"Pilar, do you know about this?" Stanford asked. She hesitated. "You can answer. The secrecy will include you."

Pilar nodded, hesitant. "Yes, I do."

"You protected her?"

"She's my best friend. I'll do anything for her. She comes first above all else."

Nancy reappeared. She dragged the luggage and placed both near the oak coffee table. She unclasped and opened the luggage whose contents surprised the men.

"Eight million in cash and bearer bonds and stock," she added. She left the luggage open and returned to her seat. "My father said to give the money to you to give to the authorities after the trial ends. He felt the prosecution will accuse me of killing Eddie for the money."

"Your father's right. The prosecutor would use the money against you."

"My father wanted me to tell you the truth."

Stanford's suspect attitude lingered. "Good advice. Why did you take it in the first place?"

The question stalled her. "Allow me to defer the answer. You have sufficient background to see how the rest fits in." Their silence meant approval to continue. "I worked in my dormitory studying for an exam the coming week. Eddie came in stoned and happy. He coaxed me from my desk. I stood and he started to dance with me. He bragged about how much money he had in his car and we should go out and use some. He told me about his father, that he helped him by transporting the money, about the phantom Rodrigo, the Grahams, and Greg Morris. That these people...and my father...were Rodrigo."

Nancy paused to watch the men's astonished reaction.

Stanford reacted. "Your father?"

"Yes, Mr. Crane. Eddie said my father turned into a drug dealer."

"Did you tell your father?"

"Yes."

"What did he say?"

"He denied it and that he and Eddie's father were friends and Eddie was confused. The drugs affected him."

"Did you believe your father?"

"I know him. If he were a murderer, he wouldn't have said for me to tell you this. Eddie insisted he and I had more in common and that our fathers were in business together. Outraged, I told him to stop abusing my father. He laughed with his drug mentality. I got angry. I slapped him. He kept laughing. Then he turned into a vicious animal and started to hit me."

Stanford turned suspicious again.

"You had no bruises, Nancy. Remember?"

"He used his knuckles, beating my head. Pilar came in and leaped on his back. He pushed her to the floor. He again came at me. My head hurt like hell. Crazed with pain, I grabbed the scissors and swung wildly to keep him away. Eddie came towards me, laughing again. He lost his balance and I hit his throat by accident. That's how I killed him. He never raped me. You rattled me with your oral sex questions."

Stanford looked to Pilar for confirmation. "Do you agree?"

A reluctant Pilar said, "Yes, the oral sex story is fantasy, contrived. What she just said is the truth."

Nancy continued. "We sat shell-shocked until I came up with the rape theory. Once we agreed, I stabbed him in the foot to substantiate I was on my knees. Whether he raped me or not my actions were self-defense. I was attacked, assaulted, and I struck back. Self-defense."

Nancy paused and Stanford probed for inconsistencies.

"Why did you remove the luggage from his car? Why take the money?"

"I wasn't sure if Eddie lied about my father. If he were involved then I'd return the money to him to encourage him to resign, to take his portion, and return the rest to Eddie's father. The police came and I told the rape story.

"I told my father the truth, why I stabbed Eddie. He reiterated denying having business dealings with Randy Hawkins. Eddie talked through his irrational drug influence and behavior. I told the police the rape story. I had the money and was stuck with it. My father feared for himself and me if he returned the money to Hawkins. Hawkins would know my father knew about his drug dealings. That's a death warrant.

"Hawkins will have blamed me for killing his son for the money – and that my father returned it to make amends. My father knew why I needed protection at home. He insisted I do it before the trial, to give the money to you for reasons already explained. This is the truth."

"Let me ask. Do we continue with the rape defense?"

"The rape is my preference."

"To protect your father or yourself?" Stanford asked.

"He was never involved."

"He's why you attacked Eddie."

"True. What should I do, Mr. Crane?"

"We'll defend your rape self-defense. It's your best chance though Pilar is a witness. Technically, you're turning the money over to Mr. Pappas for safekeeping. Mitch, is that acceptable?"

"Yes," he said, ignorant of any legal consequences, if any.

"When appropriate, we'll present the money to the authorities as evidence uncovered during my investigation of Eddie and his connection to Rodrigo. The money is the problem. Where did Mr. Pappas get it and what evidence is there that it belongs to Rodrigo. Nancy, from here on you never connected to this money. There is no one to connect you except Rodrigo people. The leaders are dead. Any survivors won't tell authorities. We'll make the transfer when appropriate. Your father was correct. After the trial is best. Anything else I need to know?"

"I covered everything. I swear."

"Your father is privy to our secrecy. I'll call and discuss the subject with him. Do you object?"

"No." She'd try to reach him first.

"Pilar, anything you want to add?"

Pilar switched to confident with Nancy's good presentation.

"Mr. Crane, Eddie would've killed her if I didn't come in when I did. He was vicious. If she didn't stab him accidentally he'd have killed her, and me. We agreed to the rape story and added Eddie's fingerprints to the scissors."

"You realize you were an accomplice?"

"More important, we survived Eddie."

"Anything else on this subject?" Stanford looked at both.

Pilar responded. "Nancy and I were at Eddie's car where witnesses saw us together before I left for the gym after removing the luggage from his car."

They stayed another half-hour.

Mitchell closed the luggage and placed the two pieces in the Lincoln's trunk after they left the apartment.

Driving back to Stanford's parking area, they reviewed the surprising turn of events and the difficult position and onus Nancy placed on Stanford.

Stanford agreed to store the luggage in his lockable office closet.

Reaching his office building and parking next to Mitchell's Jeep, Stanford asked, "Where's the hidden motive? Is there one? You're the analyst."

"I believe Nancy protected her father, who lied to us from the start when we met in Washington."

Nancy protecting her father seemed logical to Mitchell and suited his moon theory. He unpinned the planet diagram from the corkboard hung behind the computer. Nancy's fourth moon split between Senator Kiley and Rodrigo. He wondered if the same names could apply to Olivia's moon.

With a pencil to erase if necessary, he renamed Olivia's moon Kiley-Rodrigo. The cast of characters for her universe included – Austin. Rodrigo. Bates. Hancock. Crane.

He thought and probed – How did Olivia know he helped Stanford? Did Austin tell her? Was Austin a part of Rodrigo? Why would a United States senator get involved? Did Nancy disassociate him?

If so, he named Olivia's moon correct assuming the Senator told her.

The huge question glowed in neon – Was Olivia the femme fatale?

Did she persuade the lawyers to ask Nancy – Where was the money? Having failed, did she travel with them to Antigua and Liechtenstein? Why go overseas besides to sell their real estate? Were they to receive a fee from tax-free money?

If correct, he may be able to trace her credit card purchases via Mullins. Maybe she never told Marilyn Schroeder about her trip to Liechtenstein. If on a covert mission, why tell her employees?

No evidence, speculation, and more speculation.

But Austin was the key, the connection with his daughter and Rodrigo, and with Olivia and Rodrigo. More thoughts about Austin added to belief that Austin connected. The premise felt logical. Mitchell erased the pencil writing from Olivia's fourth moon and left it nameless again until he obtained a closer connection through Mullins.

A moon for Olivia covered with mist.

* * *

Monday.

Block Island, Rhode Island.

At dawn, *Mandalay* raised anchor and motored out of Great Salt Pond to head for its next destination. Captain Conniver planned to contact them again to arrange a meeting in Annapolis, Maryland on *Mandalay's* southern route to the Caribbean and Nevis. Drugs at Annapolis were destined for Baltimore. Once past the entrance buoy, *Mandalay* turned to starboard in full sail and sailed towards Buzzard's Bay and Cape Cod Canal to the Atlantic Ocean then up the Massachusetts coast to Boston Harbor.

* * *

Three Mile Harbor, East Hampton...On Board *Caucus*.

Tomayo Suarez arrived at the peaceful marina before 8:00 a.m. and boarded *Caucus*. He couldn't care less about the nautical beauty of the tree lined cove and harbor. He was expected. Captain Conniver, in civilian clothes and having breakfast, greeted him with raised eyebrows and a limp wave. He knew Suarez came to whine, why his reception lacked enthusiasm when he came below.

Tomayo poured a cup of black coffee in a blue mug and sat on the opposite bunk looking nervous.

"What the hell do we do?" he asked.

"Without the eighteen million we're stalled." Conniver remained passive accepting the disaster.

"Sheet, man. You're putting me outta business."

"Tomayo, without that money the Long Island operation stopped breathing. My sailboats won't come here anymore. I'll try to deliver goods to you from Annapolis by car with double deliveries to cover you if you have cash. I'm leaving for Annapolis tonight. I'll communicate with you from there when I'm ready to deal."

"We gotta get the money back, man."

"I couldn't reach the Senator all weekend. I'll keep trying. And his daughter's under guard. He has to come here if he wants his damn boat. You can use it or guard it."

"Man, he zapped Hawkins and Morris and stole the six million and his daughter has the rest. Maybe the Senator and his daughter planned the whole thing. What do you suggest?"

"I don't have answers, Tomayo. I'm as lost as you."

"What do my people do?"

"Do?" Conniver shrugged and mulled the question. He had to offer a direction to this nitwit or he might never leave. "Woods are behind the Kiley house. Have your men watch the house for the Senator to pay him a visit. If we can't locate him, attack the house, take out the guards, and go after his wife and daughter. If they don't tell you where the money is, shoot them. If they tell you, shoot them anyway Rodrigo style. Killing them should get the Senator's attention. Call me if you find the money."

Tomayo Suarez slapped the table. "You're talkin' my lingo, amigo." He left, happy to have direction.

* * *

Madge grew nervous for Nancy, mad at her but nervous for her. Jury selection started that day. Madge would have Nancy answer incoming calls and listen on the extension, her best method of learning, and probably her only method. She called her husband in Washington several times, including when she awakened that morning. No answer. She'd call his office at 9:00.

At 9:10, Madge called. "He hasn't arrived yet, Mrs. Kiley," Rosella said. "Shall I have him call you?"

"Yes, please. I'm home all day."

At noon, Madge called again impatient. Rosella said he hadn't come in today. At 5:00, Madge called again. Rosella confirmed the Senator never came in and she hadn't heard from him.

The phone rang at 8:00 when Madge prepared a shopping list in the kitchen. Madge called out to Nancy in the solarium. "Nancy, get that. My hands are wet!"

They weren't wet. This was her opportunity to eavesdrop hoping to learn answers to the crisis.

Nancy stopped the fourth ring. Madge listened on the kitchen phone as her hand covered the microphone.

"...good, honey. How are you doing? Did you see Mr. Crane?"

"Yes. Everything's fine, Daddy. He's holding the luggage until after the trial."

"How about Eddie?"

"I told the truth. He's staying with the rape defense."

"I knew he would."

"Why did you want me to wait until Sunday to talk to him?"

Austin couldn't admit he wanted time to make his plans. Sunday suited him. "Did you tell him what we discussed?"

Should Nancy say she disobeyed by failing to reveal his connection to Rodrigo? Nancy changed her mind. *Not now.*

"Yes. How are you doing?" A quick subject change might detour him.

"Busy, busy. Lots of work over the weekend and the office today was a nightmare, people coming in and out all day. I just got home. The jury selection started?"

"Mr. Crane is satisfied with the progress."

"Do whatever he says. I'll call you again soon, Nancy. Be strong."

"I am. Bye."

Madge replaced the receiver with continuing disgust and frustration.

Her husband continued his lies. She dialed their condominium phone in Washington. Seven rings registered before she hung up confirming the lies with each ring a death knell to her marriage. "You lying bastard," Madge muttered. "You're not in Washington. Where the hell are you?"

Massaging an upset stomach, Madge sat at the table to calm, to find the elusive solution to her exile from the family crisis, and to preserve what self-dignity remained.

Madge concluded again that her marriage died.

Get strong, accept it!

Acceptance was difficult for a stomach that forced her to rush to the sink and vomit...again.

PART III

35

Mitchell phoned Mullins, who answered. "What's your problem today that you couldn't sleep?"

"I'm heading for Riverhead. Kiley jury selection starts today."

"Sounds like a boring day ahead."

Mullins sipped coffee while selecting pastries from a bakery box before him.

"Moon, I know you hate hunches, but I have a hunch regarding the former Kiley lawyers. The answer to who killed them."

"A hunch. No evidence?"

"Not yet."

"And you want me to help you with your hunch, a potential wild goose chase at the expense of overtaxed Suffolk tax payers?"

"I think my hunch will prove correct."

"If your psychology makes you feel better, I'll find some patience to listen, shoot."

"The lawyers' common link including Stanford Crane is Olivia Greene, owner of Village Greene Travel Service in Woodbury. Your men questioned her regarding Bates and Hancock's plane tickets."

"I remember, Mitch. What's your hunch?"

"I believe she was overseas with them. Would you trace her credit cards for trips to Antigua and Liechtenstein at the approximate dates the lawyers were there? Also, check the Village Greene corporate card. She might've charged the trips to that account. Can you make your inquiry legal by connecting her to the Kiley case?"

"As continuing investigation in a murder case or possible case it's a fine line but achievable. Do you have any idea which credit card?"

"No idea."

"Why make it easy for me?"

"How soon will you have the information?"

"If we get lucky, it could be before end of day."

"I'm also pursuing leads that may lead to the identity of Rodrigo."

"What?" He thrust to his feet. His mouth nearly expelled the pastry. "Get outta here. What leads and who are you pursuing?"

"I'll hide behind the First Amendment as a writer. If the information proves correct, I'll tell you after I get the Olivia Greene data."

Mullins sat with obvious disappointment then encouraged, "You can hide behind the Constitution and anywhere else you want. Get me Rodrigo and I won't ask questions about anything. Act as your own judge and jury and lord of the manor."

"One more confirmation and I may tell you by tomorrow."

"After the credit card check?"

"Bad timing."

"You've been right since I've known you though some theories you throw at me don't stick to the wall. I know you'll be right again. I just hope it's soon."

"Have a great day, Moon and keep grinding."

"Mr. Writer protected by the Constitution please pursue your leads at top speed without hitting pedestrians."

* * *

Mitchell received permission to sit with Stanford as an advisor. The laborious day for lawyers, prospective jurors, jury selection advisors, and judge ended at 4:30 with agreement on three jurors. Stanford considered it progress; nine more and six alternates to go.

About to enter the westbound expressway at 4:50, Mitchell called Mullins.

"How did you make out?"

"You struck out, game over, the effort a waste. Olivia Greene did *not* use her personal credit cards for plane fares to Antigua and Liechtenstein. You owe Ms. Greene a mental apology."

"How about the corporate card?"

"She didn't use that card within a month of the dates Bates and Hancock were overseas."

"I can't believe it. Something's wrong."

Mullins laughed saying, "Look in the mirror. Maybe it's your thinking. You can have sunnier days if you change your thinking."

"Thanks for your effort and your humor, Moon."

"Wait, wait, not so fast. What about Rodrigo? That's more important – the lottery for me."

"Tomorrow. I'll make your day tomorrow."

"I'll be waiting. Eat, sleep, and think Rodrigo night and day along as you try to save Crane. Bye."

The call ended. *How could I be wrong?* Mitchell wondered.

A thought prompted a call to Mullins again.

"One more question."

"Go ahead." Mullins lacked enthusiasm. "Good thing I like you."

"Did anyone else on the corporate card go there?"

"Let me pull the file...got it. Yes. A Noreen Gilbert made a trip to Geneva, Switzerland two days before Bates died. Close, not close enough."

"How about Antigua?"

"Noreen Gilbert flew to Antigua about a week and a half before Hancock arrived and returned in two days, and a second trip to St. Martin two days before Hancock's murder. No evidence she traveled to Antigua from St. Martin on the second trip. Close on both but no rings. Are we done?"

"One last shot."

"Give it your best. No more hunches after this, please."

"Do you have a list of Village Greene Travel's employees? Do your men have the list in the file?"

"Hold on." About forty seconds later, he said, "I have the list and looking for Noreen Gilbert...and no Noreen Gilbert. Is that strike five or is it six?"

"She was omitted, or is no longer with the agency."

"Are you having another hunch I should waste my time following? That I trace her disappearance?"

"No."

"Your hunches are over?"

"For now."

"Hallelujah! Don't forget Rodrigo. And I won't count this last hunch as a mistake. Your record remains safe."

"Tomorrow definitely on Rodrigo."

"And no more hunches but facts. I don't have the time for wild goose chases. Do I have your word?"

"Only the facts."

The ride home rehashed notes and conversation yesterday with Nancy. Maybe he evaluated wrong about Olivia Greene. Mitchell stalled, tentative on the next step where to look, and felt depressed.

As he opened his front door, the phone rang. He hurried to answer, "Hello."

"Mitchell, this is Madge Kiley. I'm sorry to call you at home. I didn't want to bother Stanford...with the trial and all. I must speak with you about my husband. It's very, very important. Can we please meet?"

36

Madge and Mitchell agreed to breakfast at 8:00 a.m. at the Huntington Hilton on Route 110. Mitchell arrived a few minutes early. Madge waited inside by the entrance and revolving door, impatient. She preferred to reveal the important information in person. A reserved table waited in the restaurant that overlooked a glass-enclosed pool a floor below. Mitchell waved to her through the glass door before entering. He remained curious.

She approached him saying, "Thank you for coming, Mitchell."

"Morning, Madge."

"I reserved a table. Let's talk there. I do appreciate your coming all the way out here to meet me."

The host, in her forties, with short red hair, and a fixed smile picked up two menus and escorted through the crowded restaurant to a table near a plant cluster. She offered menus and poured two coffees.

"So Madge, what's very important that we couldn't discuss over the phone?"

She leaned closer to the table. "I...I believe Austin isn't where he said he'd be."

The cryptic opening baffled. "Where *was* he supposed to be?"

"I eavesdropped as you suggested. I listened in on their phone conversation last night. I also learned she talked to Stanford on Sunday. She told Austin."

"I attended that meeting with Stanford." Mitchell added milk to his coffee and stirred with a teaspoon.

"Can you tell me what happened at the meeting?"

"I must honor my secrecy agreement. Some parts are confidential. Nancy will tell you, eventually."

"I doubt it."

He wanted to steer her to the meeting's purpose. "What did you mean about Austin not being some place?"

"Last Thursday night, Austin left the house as I returned from shopping and decided to follow him. I followed to Manhasset where he turned into a guarded private community on Shelter Rock Road. When I returned home, Nancy said he left for Washington. I called his apartment and office on Friday, Friday night, several times on Saturday, and Sunday. Yesterday, his secretary told me he was out all day. Last night he called Nancy – that's when I eavesdropped – and he said that he had a busy day at the office and just got home. I called his apartment seconds later. No one answered."

"He's missing but not missing?"

"I suspect he left with another woman and not to Washington. Austin has been unfaithful to me for a long time." With the difficult admission, Madge sat erect ignoring her coffee, focused on her complaint.

"How do you know about another woman?"

"I did some research to locate whom he visited the night I followed him. I reviewed our phone bills and found an often-called number in Manhasset. I called the number. The answering machine said her first name. I checked his Rolodex for that name. I found her then drove to her business to see what she looked like. She started a vacation last Friday. It's logical to believe they're together." She deviated from the mistress. "I suspect collusion between Nancy and Austin and I'm afraid it may hurt Nancy."

He tried to be patient with her meandering and attributed it to her family crisis."Madge, take a deep breath and slow down. You're all over the place. Based on my meeting with Nancy, Austin isn't interfering with the trial."

Madge looked around to assure no one listened. Her voice lowered as precaution. She leaned closer to Mitchell.

"Nancy and Austin are keeping important information from me. Nancy said to Austin that *they* – whoever *they* are – killed the Grahams. And she asked Austin – Are you in danger?"

"Was she referring to Rodrigo?"

"I don't know. Who killed the Grahams?"

"Rodrigo, as alleged by the police."

"Then I heard the news that Randy Hawkins and Greg Morris died the same way. Nancy worried about her father, a main point of what they discussed. Something's wrong there. Can you find out if and how Austin is involved with Rodrigo?"

"Maybe after the trial. I'm busy helping Stanford and that must be the priority. Shall I try and locate Austin?" he said to avoid slighting her information.

She shrugged and shook her head. "If he's gone, he's gone; an inappropriate time to run off with another woman. He should be *here* to support and comfort his besieged daughter as she prepares for trial." Her anger expanded. "The phone records indicate he called his lover for over three years. No wife likes to admit her husband is unfaithful. They left together. Maybe he left to escape from being killed by

Rodrigo. She's with him and I won't have him back." Her eyes widened. "God! Three years! I can't believe I've been duped and naive." She stopped for a deep breath. "You and Stanford need to know about Austin's possible connections to Rodrigo, whatever they are. He may alter the trial's outcome by affecting Nancy negatively."

"Madge, there's no evidence Austin connects with Rodrigo and no evidence he ran off with that woman. Who is she? Can you say?"

"Her name sticks in my throat like barbed wire full of peanut butter. Her name is Olivia Greene and she owns Village Greene Travel Service."

Bam!

"Mitchell, what's wrong? Mitchell?"

Everything in Mitchell's body froze as an ice sculpture with Madge's revelation, lost in a universe of his planets and moons. *Incredible*, he thought.

Incredible! From the mouth of the innocent.

Madge was the last person he expected to solve his mysteries. "Sorry, Madge. I met Olivia Greene with Stanford and while investigating Laurence Bates and Todd Hancock's deaths. They bought their tickets at Village Greene. I had no idea Austin knew her, a stunning revelation."

"Include me until now." She forced a wry smile. "How oblivious can a wife get? What a pathetic jackass I've been. Unbelievable. Everyone in my family is devious with me like I'm a leper to avoid. Worse for me, one who doesn't see what's happening in her home. If I were blind, I'd see more."

"The problems aren't your fault, Madge. Don't go in that direction. You *have* been helpful. More than you know."

"How?"

Mitchell wanted Madge to feel better. Olivia hadn't won.

"The Suffolk police and I investigate the possibility Olivia Greene might've killed Hancock and Bates using Rohypnol and succinylcholine on both. The latter is almost undetectable, difficult to find."

Madge's eyelids lifted from joy. "My God, You exist! A touch of payback. Maybe she'll do me a favor and do the same to Austin. He deserves it."

"I know you don't mean that."

"I do. Or I should. After what he's done to Nancy...and to me, he deserves an unhappy ending. I hope he and his lover go to hell after Nancy goes free. His mistress is gloating at my failures while Austin considers and treats me as an idiot."

Mitchell refused to reason with a woman scorned.

"What I have to tell you is confidential. The police will never trust me again if this got out. So everything we discuss here has to remain here."

"I promise silence. We're still a team aren't we for Nancy's sake to free her?"

"Yes, we are."

"And thank you for making me feel better even if it isn't all true about that woman."

"I told you the truth. In time, the police will arrest her. I believe she was with the lawyers overseas when they died. That option is still open to investigation."

"There's no evidence you said," Madge countered thinking him condescending.

"We'll find it knowing her involvement with Austin, who might be involved with Rodrigo. If he is, that's another nightmare to live with during the trial. Madge, you did a good job. I'll mention your discoveries to Lieutenant Mullins and Stanford that you've been helpful in opening new investigations."

"Yes, a nightmare and I feel better that I'm helping. Can you keep me informed?"

"Stanford has to approve everything before I mention it to you – legal protocol in Nancy's defense. Call me if you learn anything new."

"It shall be my pleasure. I haven't had much of that for a long time. You made me feel useful again. Thank you."

"You did good Madge, for Lieutenant Mullins, yourself, and your daughter. My compliments."

She cleared the mist from Olivia's moon.

Madge also did 'good' for Mitchell.

Day bloomed sunny and clear as the 47-foot sloop pushed white water on the blue and protected waters of Sir Francis Drake Channel in the British Virgin Islands as the 12-knot trade winds powered the sailboat towards Virgin Gorda and the Bitter End Yacht Club Resort. The sloop had sailed from its home base Trunk Bay Plantation on St. John in the United States Virgin Islands and chartered in St. Thomas at Yacht Haven Marina. Road Harbor, the main port and center of commerce on the island of Tortola, lay to port as a hibernating bear. To starboard were the chain islands: Norman Island, Peter Island, Salt Island, and lesser islands.

Wind heeled the craft to starboard at a comfortable angle providing the invisible fuel flowing between the jib and main sail to provide lift and forward force, the Bernoulli principle at work.

Olivia, standing behind the wide stainless steel wheel protected from the sun's heat by rope braiding, could feel the boat's need to migrate windward as she applied opposite wheel pressure to the skeg rudder to keep the sloop on a straight line and on course. She wore a black two-piece bathing suit and Austin's white T-shirt to cut sun and wind. Austin sat next to her facing forward.

Looking satisfied with controlling the boat, she learned how to handle large sailboats from Austin sailing off Newport when he managed to get away from Madge. Austin felt safe with her behind the wheel in open water. He controlled the helm in crowded harbors and docking. Docking made her nervous.

"Pure heaven. A top ten loveliest area on earth," she said as the winds massaged her face and rustled her hair. "Almost as good as sailing the Greek Islands in the Aegean. People should live where they vacation. What do you think? Shall we do that?"

"I want to live where you are." He rubbed her right thigh.

Olivia beamed and blew a kiss.

They passed Virgin Gorda and Mosquito Island to starboard. Darker and aggressive Atlantic Ocean sprawled to distant port. The low island of Anegada lay as a flat line on the horizon. Without a chart, one couldn't tell its location from a distance.

Olivia soon steered southwest cautious of the Colquhoun Reef to starboard to the red and green buoys that marked the entrance between reefs to Gorda Sound, a protected body of water with a shallow opening between the yacht club and Prickley Pear Island. She turned the engine on. Nearing the yacht club, she turned the bow into the wind to neutralize the sails as Austin lowered and furled the sails.

"Slow down and drift by the club until assigned a slip. The dock master should have seen us coming in."

The dock master waited for them on the first finger and assigned them to a port berth in the middle of about two dozen power and sailboats. He left for that slip to help secure the lines to dock cleats. Austin steered.

Once docked and at their lunch destination at the seaside restaurant, they sat at a table by the beach with a panoramic view of the islands.

Thought Olivia – *This and Austin. Heaven.*

* * *

The curtain closed on Olivia Greene's revised Third Act.

She attained her perfect ending winning Austin in the last scene to sail into perfect days and blissful tomorrows...fade to black, the end.

Olivia achieved her goal with unwavering perseverance by committing seven murders to win her obsession.

She hadn't thought of the math while achieving her missions: Todd Hancock in Antigua, Laurence Bates in Liechtenstein, pharmacist Troy Betson indirectly in Hicksville, Janet and Bob Graham in Kings Point, Randy Hawkins and Greg Morris on *Golden Hawk* – all in the past and irrelevant today in her new world. In her delusional mindset without a conscience or compassion, they never happened.

The dead served as a stream's steppingstones to ford her ultimate goal.

That segment of history vanished and the law had no evidence she connected to their deaths.

She thought proudly – *How sweet is that?*

In Bridgehampton after leaving *Golden* Hawk and Sag Harbor, Olivia persuaded Austin to leave their world behind and begin anew away from possible criminal charges. They had the Rodrigo money plus what both owned in tax haven accounts. The decision was the best overall option. She protested when Austin suggested taking over Rodrigo to run the organization and won with persistence. She

wanted to assure their future now that Austin, her cherished possession, belonged to her. Olivia would kill anyone else who threatened
that future.

She recommended bare-boating the Virgin Islands – renting without a professional captain – then plentiful days sailing the Windward
Islands and lower Caribbean. Austin loved sailing. She used sailing as
a lure, her way to ease him towards another country and identity and
a life together.

They traveled incognito as Noreen and Austin Gilbert.

Plane and resort reservations were under Olivia's credit card issued
in the Bahamas and the sailboat paid cash in advance for two months.
When sated with sailing, they'd leave the boat at a major island, notify
the charter company, and pay extra for the convenience.

Austin told her last night that Nancy met with Stanford Crane on
Sunday. She told all to Stanford including his involvement. Stanford
knowing equated to a huge blunder. Austin was her exclusive passion
now and never wanted to lose him.

Ever.

Olivia slept each evening embracing Austin and clung to him
afraid someone would take him away wanting to remain tethered to
him never to part or be far from each other. She turned her monopoly
into an obsession to shape and mold to control his never having a need
to stay away from her.

When Nancy's trial concluded, they'd leave for a less curious
country or one that won't seek a missing senator. Australia and New
Zealand rated as prime candidates. She'd also research countries absent of extradition treaties should evidence surface against her or
Austin...or both.

Her movie ending led to reality as long as no one knew their location or recognized them especially Austin the public official.

No one knew she associated with Rodrigo and left with Austin, and no evidence she committed anything illegal. When leaving the Virgin Islands, she'd honey color and straighten her hair, and wear glasses in public. He'd dye his hair black with gray touches and grow a beard. When settled on land, she'd have their child, maybe two.

Thinking ahead, motherhood brought impatience to start her family. Children offered them more to share, the ideal eternal triangle. Olivia thought about Susan Bianchi's conversation on *Golden Hawk* on the cruise to Newport how she loved motherhood. She'd "...prefer to raise kids than working in an office."

Each day was romantic, passionate, and exciting. Olivia felt complete loved by the man she loved and having him all to herself.

Madge was history.

Another time.

Another place.

An ugly memory.

See ya, Madge. You're on your own. You and your daughter can go to hell.

* * *

The second day of jury selection unfolded without incident. Mitchell drove the expressway at Riverhead and called Mullins as promised to discuss Rodrigo. To tell Mullins that Olivia Greene and Austin Kiley were together would be valueless without evidence, an inappropriate time for Mullins to react to another hunch. Mullins should ask, "Did anyone see them together?" Mitchell couldn't discuss Austin.

The discussion might defer until Mitchell had evidence or a clue to their location. Madge, the determined and motivated sleuth, may help.

Rodrigo was the subject – more information without evidence, but sufficient to direct Mullins's investigation in the proper direction to end chasing a phantom.

"I've been sitting on broken glass all day waiting for your call regarding Rodrigo. My rear end is bleeding," Mullins kidded happy to hear from Mitchell. "I know you're busy, but don't put my priority on the backburner."

"What I'm about to tell you will soothe the pain and stop the bleeding," Mitchell said. "It's gospel. Believe everything I tell you."

Mullins's pause ran three seconds too long.

"Does that mean you have no evidence? Are we revisiting Hunch City? Did you buy a condo there?"

Mitchell took that to mean – Say it isn't so. "It's much, much more than a hunch." He tried to sound consoling.

"Can I have Detective Marvin Rose listen? He heads my narcotics unit and leads the Rodrigo investigation. He's also working with Nassau County and heading up our joint drug task force to find Rodrigo."

"Put him on. He'll be glad to hear what I have to say. You, I know will be thrilled."

"I hope so. I'll get him and put you on speaker. Stand by."

Mitchell smiled breaking Mullins's defense against theories. Detective Marvin Rose and Mullins were ready.

"Detective Rose is here. Thrill me, baby."

"Hello, Mr. Pappas," Marvin Rose said.

"Greetings, Detective. Rodrigo isn't a person. Rodrigo is a consortium that included Janet and Bob Graham, Randy Hawkins, and Greg Morris. They supplied the financing for the drugs in Suffolk County. A good guy will soon turn evidence over to you through an attorney – the funds Rodrigo used to purchase the drugs, about eight million dollars. You will know that person at that time. You're curious to ask – Who killed them? I don't know.

"You should experience a slowdown in drug traffic. From what I hear, Rodrigo is crippled. A few goons may continue to function without those funds. You may want to investigate the Grahams, Hawkins, and Morris. Please let me know the results when you search their homes, yachts, banks, and brokerage accounts for money movement. Any questions?"

"I believe you," Mullins said. "Do you have any other names?"

"Not now."

"Any idea how the drugs were brought to Suffolk," Rose asked.

"No. I'll continue to seek answers for you. By sea is a good guess. Hawkins owned a yacht."

"You won't tell me your source or sources?" Mullins asked.

"You know I will when I can."

"You won't hide behind the Constitution?"

"I won't hide. I'll call back regarding the other matter we talked about yesterday."

"You mean your hunch on Noreen Gilbert? I'm here till six today, and you have my home number."

"Then goodbye from me. Oh, did I deliver as promised? Are you thrilled?"

"You the man, baby, you the man!"

* * *

Mitchell called Village Greene Travel and asked for Gwen Rhodes.

"This is Gwen Rhodes."

"Mrs. Rhodes, this is Mitchell Pappas. Do you remember me?"

"I do, Mr. Pappas."

"Is Olivia there?" He wanted confirmation that she left.

"She is out of the office. Can I help you?"

"Yes. Does a Noreen Gilbert work there and does she travel or vacation often?"

Mitchell heard her light laughter before she said, "Olivia uses Noreen Gilbert as an alias when she scouts a resort or hotel. This way, she doesn't get preferred treatment and can evaluate the place better. How did you know about Noreen? That's like a state secret around here."

Good question, Gwen. How do I answer you?

"When there, I talked with Marilyn Schroeder. Olivia must've been pulling my leg for me to also talk to Noreen Gilbert, who travels extensively. When I called and asked for Noreen, the girl said no such person worked there." *A pretty good tale.*

"Olivia pulled your leg."

"Thanks, Gwen. Give her my regards when she comes in."

"In about three weeks. She's on vacation."

Madge was right. "Good for her. Where did she go? I'm sure she vacations at the best places."

Can I get lucky?

Gwen laughed. "She hasn't called in yet so I don't know where she is. She should be calling soon."

Mitchell thanked Gwen and hung up saying he'd call back again in a few days. Maybe Gwen may know by then. He called Mullins.

"You're quick," Mullins said impressed with the response time.

"I just received confirmation from Gwen Rhodes, Olivia Greene's secretary at Village Greene Travel Service. Noreen Gilbert is an alias Olivia Greene uses to travel incognito to evaluate resorts she recommends to her clients. How's that for a hunch?"

"You're a magician."

"Is my credibility intact?"

"Better regarding Noreen Gilbert."

"Olivia is on vacation. As Noreen Gilbert, she was close enough to the crime scenes and could have traveled to Vaduz and Antigua by other means. I'll call you as I acquire additional information."

"You provided enough to keep my people busy for a few days, but remember no more hunches. Keep up the good work."

"You know I will, as always."

They cast off from Bitter End Yacht Club Resort at 2:30 p.m. for their return trip. They turned into Pillsbury Sound and Trunk Bay Plantation to their assigned mooring.

Austin launched the gray inflatable dinghy, started the outboard motor, waited for Olivia to descend the stainless steel stern ladder to sit then he whirred towards shore. They passed the office and public telephone area and followed a tropical plant landscaped path to their private waterfront beach house. They avoided other guests and always hid behind sunglasses.

They napped in an embrace after sharing a bottle of wine and cheese on the veranda before leaving for the hillside restaurant for dinner at nine with a view across to St. Thomas and the ferry town of Red Hook.

On the way to dinner, Austin stopped at a public phone and called his daughter, ready to hang up if Madge answered. Nancy answered in the solarium while remaining intense over a television drama series forgetting to check the caller.

"Hello," came out mechanical.

"It's me. Is it safe to talk?"

"Mom!" she hollered. "I got it!"

She paused the television. "Yes, Daddy. Mom is inside or upstairs. Where are you? Please tell me."

"In Washington."

"No, you're not. Mom and I have been calling your apartment and office."

Silence. He stalled to buy time to recover from his lie.

"I had to leave for a few days."

"To where?"

"I can't tell you yet."

"Daddy, there's no need to hide," she pleaded. "If that's what you're doing. I didn't tell Mr. Crane about you. I gave him the luggage and told the truth about Eddie. I protected you."

"I must be away for your sake. Anything else new?"

"And I need to know where I can reach you. My trial starts next week and I'm scared. I need to know you're close. I'll call only in emergency. Pilar comforts me, but need you."

Austin hesitated before relenting. "All right." He said the phone number. "It's the Trunk Bay Plantation. Ask for Mr. Gilbert and wait several minutes. They have to send someone to get me. The rooms don't have phones."

"Where's Trunk Bay Plantation?"

"It's on St. John, in the U.S. Virgin Islands opposite St. Thomas."

Nancy wrote the information with a pen on the newspaper's edge to transfer later to a memo sheet in her room.

"Why there?"

"I'll explain another time."

"Why are you using an alias?"

After a brief delay, "A few senators and I chartered. We're traveling incognito and supposed to be on a cross-country trip."

"I wish you had given me specifics. What if I needed you in an emergency?"

"I'll always be in touch. If I'm out sailing, I'll call you when I return from day trips."

"I love you, Daddy. No one will know about you. Come home."

"I love you. And I know you'll be all right. I'm concerned that some unknown fact might arise with Rodrigo. If during the trial, I shouldn't be there if I'm subpoenaed. My negative publicity may overwhelm your self-defense. Stanford Crane can deny and reject rumors. I'm avoiding the like-father-like-daughter accusation."

"I understand. I feel better knowing I can reach out to you."

"I have to go. I'll call regularly no matter where I am, but if Mom answers I'll hang up."

"I'll be alert. Bye, Daddy. Enjoy your sailing. And never forget to call."

* * *

Madge remained at the library desk after putting the phone down and after listening to her husband and daughter, happy she lifted the receiver a second after Nancy to spy.

"And Madge now knows," she whispered. "Madge finally knows your secret. Good old naive and abused Madge is no longer in the dark. She has a lit candle and will no longer function as an ignorant houseplant."

Madge sank to a deeper layer of abuse, no less than if beaten. Her husband was a cheat, a liar, and a murderer, a Rodrigo – a drug dealer who ran from police and those who killed his associates.

He was getting away with murder, a drug dealer going unpunished protected by Nancy and Pilar.

Madge remained in the library for a long time evaluating herself and her family. Her daughter mentioned telling Stanford the truth about Eddie.

What did that mean? She wasn't raped? What was in the luggage? Austin lied about being in Washington. He probably lied about being with senators.

Austin traveled with his mistress, she concluded. Her husband hadn't communicated with her for days because Olivia Greene had him.

That bitch got him!

"May you two get the punishment you deserve, you despicable things," Madge said to herself aloud.

They weren't humans anymore, but repelling 'things'.

* * *

Helene answered the phone at home.

"Is Mitchell there? This is Madge Kiley. Nancy Kiley's mother."

"Hold on."

After a short pause Mitchell said, "Hello, Madge."

"Austin called Nancy again. I have specific information about Rodrigo and Austin's role. Nancy was supposed to tell you and Stanford, at Austin's request, that he was a member of Rodrigo. He's in the Virgin Islands at a Trunk Bay Plantation on St. John. He told Nancy his telephone number. I have it. Austin said he's with senators. I believe Olivia Greene is with him. We know why he ran and a better than good belief he's with her."

"That's solid information, Madge." She advanced the case another step forward.

"Can you get the police to arrest them?"

"There's still no evidence to implicate him...only hearsay and hunches that Olivia Greene killed Hancock and Bates. I already talked to Lieutenant Mullins of Suffolk Homicide and he's investigating Olivia Greene, who used an alias traveling to Switzerland and St. Martin; two areas near the murder scenes. A Noreen Gilbert."

"I'm right! I'm right!" she exclaimed. "That's it! That's another connection. Gilbert is the name Austin is using in St. John. She's with him. They're *together*."

"Then you were right about them, Madge. Mullins investigates the Grahams, Hawkins, and Morris. He may find evidence Austin did business with them or how they connected."

"You mean nothing can be done?" She sounded outraged. "How could that be possible?"

"What can be done is being done."

"That's ridiculous. They're guilty."

"I'll suggest to Mullins that he investigate Austin's finances. The movement of funds may help implicate him. Are you comfortable with that investigation?"

"I'll give authorization, if necessary, and do whatever is needed. Austin always kept good records at home."

"Madge, the police work with evidence, physical clues, and leads. After they finish investigating the others, I'll suggest they investigate Austin. I'll do that after the trial ends to protect Nancy."

Her disappointment magnified every word when she said, "The drug dealer and his mistress will go unpunished?"

"For now. We need to stay focused on Nancy. She must continue as the priority and that includes you. It's more important that she's exonerated. Austin can wait till then."

"There's something wrong with our system then. It's wrong, all wrong for them to get away."

"Our system is fine."

"I agree we must protect Nancy, but somebody has got to do something about that woman and Austin. I'll force Nancy to confess about her father after the trial. I don't know how yet, but I'll find a way."

"You know she'll never confess. Look how long she held out under armed guards."

"Well, I won't protect him." She sounded firm.

"Your statement will be hearsay."

"Justice will never be served, Mitchell. For all I know, Austin will never come back. He abandoned us. What's to keep them from running off to another country and disappear? The jail threat is gone and the proverbial 'other woman' has him."

"I'll talk to Stanford and Mullins; the best I can do. Forget your husband and Olivia Greene and concentrate on Nancy's trial and eventual release. She needs you. Be there for her. Don't add to her problem."

Madge's answer delayed. Her voice changed to failure and disappointment from her unconvincing conversation.

"No, she doesn't need me...she hasn't at all during her crisis. I'll focus on the trial and concentrate on positive matters. Please stay in touch, Mitchell. I'll continue to do the same with you."

Madge lied.

Madge couldn't let go of Austin and Olivia who ate her insides as piranhas.

* * *

Mitchell expended an uneventful day at jury selection. The process should end tomorrow. Stanford needed three more jurors. He updated

Stanford on his findings about Austin and Olivia Greene, knowledge that could undermine his case to defend Nancy.

When Mitchell related the connection between Olivia and Noreen Gilbert, Madge's investigation that Olivia might have gone on vacation with Austin, Stanford felt used. Olivia set him up with her fraudulent romance as she had Hancock and Bates with plans to kill him.

Stanford retained focus on his defense. Olivia can wait. He'd confront Nancy about her father and Rodrigo before the trial starts and his being in the Virgin Islands. Any lies prior to trial were intolerable. Truth never varied.

Mitchell arrived home before 8:00 p.m. Helene had prepared Hungarian goulash, his favorite. He devoured more than his usual share.

"You're tense and troubled," Helene said. "You're overeating and rushing. You poured your wine and never touched it. Where's your mind? Do you remember who I am? Say my name."

Her voice penetrated. "I'm sorry, honey. It's been a day. I had a light lunch."

He opened the refrigerator for a hunk of feta cheese and Italian bread to have with his wine and briefed Helene on the case. He talked for over thirty minutes.

After reviewing with Helene, he sat at the computer to update notes. He unpinned Olivia and Nancy's planet systems and filled in Olivia's fourth moon: Senator Kiley and Rodrigo.

Her moon filled.

And had a name.

Mitchell no longer doubted she killed Hancock and Bates, and that Austin joined the Rodrigo cabal.

Olivia's planet and moons resolved thanks to Madge.

Madge provided answers without proof. Could he find evidence? He couldn't. Lieutenant Mullins could with his authority to investigate deeper.

Mitchell reminded himself that he wasn't a cop.

Mariano and Luis, with Tomayo Suarez at the Ochoa family executions in East Islip, sneaked their way through dark public woods at 1:00 a.m. to the Kiley property. With the backyard lights on, the prowlers needed to stop farther away from the tree line to avoid light splash.

"No guards," Mariano said to Luis in Spanish looking through binoculars. "Go around to the front and make sure." Luis left following the neighboring backyard fence and headed for the dead end street. Guards in front were gone. Luis returned and informed Mariano. Mariano called Suarez on the stolen Verizon cellular number. They left the area the way they came – through thick and darkened woods.

From her bedroom, Madge thought she saw a man in the woods hurrying in the shadows from her house to the neighbor's house. She waited for more movement. A few minutes later, a crouched figure returned and stopped then the figure disappeared. Was it a deer? She wondered – *But deer don't live in this populated area.* She should have put on her glasses.

Madge leaned against a window with the slats part open in the darkened room. She stared into the night after Luis's moving figure sounded her inner alarm and grew scared and queasy. She checked the armed house alarm to assure it was on. She thought about calling 911 to report a prowler, but that would stampede unwanted media publicity that may affect Nancy's trial.

Madge hurried downstairs to the library closet for the shotgun and loaded the chambers. She checked the first floor windows. Front lights were on. Madge avoided the solarium's large windows. She would be an easy target there. On red alert, she guarded the darkened house waiting for a burglar, or the enemy Nancy expected, and primed to call 911 – to hell with the potential publicity if attacked.

An hour later, Madge slept in a chair in a darkened kitchen with the shotgun across her lap. In the morning, Madge attributed her alarm and defensive scare to an imaginary burglar. She blamed stress, and for feeling queasy. Good thing she never called the police.

Madge stood ready to kill to protect her child, a lioness defending her cub.

* * *

At 9:00 p.m. Wednesday, Suarez rang the phone in the darkened Kiley house. He expected someone home to torture to get results and to kill by shooting into the left ear.

The answering machine connected. He clicked his cellular phone and cursed, accepting the Senator, his wife, and daughter weren't home. He sent Luis to the car. Luis returned fifteen minutes later with the equipment.

They jumped the fence, crouched in the former guards' path, and ran to the solarium inside the U-shaped rear structure. Once inside the U, neighbors couldn't see them, a perfect hiding place.

Mariano placed two suction handles on the window, cut a 4-foot oval with a glasscutter, taped, and removed the glass with Luis. They climbed in with flashlights and silencers. Suarez searched the solarium and kitchen. Luis and Mariano searched other rooms. Suarez waited in the solarium for his abettors going upstairs to the bedrooms hoping the daughter slept to beat her and have sexual fun before they killed her.

In the spare bedroom, Mariano found the two cartons with the approximate $4 million under the bed. Each carrying a carton, they came downstairs to tell their boss the good news. Suarez checked the contents.

"There's much more. Search the basement. The rest of our money must be here. Find it. Hurry!"

Luis and Mariano left leaving the cartons near the coffee table.

The amount the Senator and his daughter stole branded in Suarez's mind. He assumed they found the daughter's portion, and that the Senator stashed the other $8 million here or elsewhere. He asked himself – *And where did he hide the $6 million plus cash from Golden Hawk? Was it in the basement? Did the woman with him on Golden Hawk have it?*

She must be his wife.

He'd kill her after torturing her to confess.

Suarez turned on a flashlight to count the money again in the dim light when the writing on the newspaper on the coffee table distracted him. He picked up the paper and read Nancy's writing: Daddy. Trunk Bay Plantation. St. John, V. I. - A.K.A. Mr. Gilbert, and the phone number.

"Buenas noches, Senor Senator Gilbert. We'll meet soon. I found you and the rest of the money if we don't find it here."

He folded the page containing Nancy's writing and put it in his pocket. He guarded the house wanting the rest of the Kileys to come home to confess and to die. Mariano and Luis returned from the basement without money.

"I know where the rest of the money is," Suarez said. "Mariano, ever been to the Virgin Islands?"

"Never."

"You'll be going soon alone. On small islands, it's best to work alone." Suarez had a better thought. "Maybe I'll go instead. The Senator deserves me to punish him."

They stole the two cartons and left temporarily satisfied with their limited success.

The thieving senator escaped to St. John. Thieves must be punished to maintain discipline in his organization, without deviation, punished like the Ochoa family and others, no matter where they hide. Tomayo Suarez would maintain that effective Rodrigo procedure.

The Senator must be executed!

The four million put Suarez back in business. Early tomorrow morning, he'd tell Captain Conniver the good news to contact *Mandalay* for the new delivery, that Rodrigo lives.

A half-hour later, Madge, Pilar, and Nancy returned from the theater complex in East Farmingdale. The girls asked Madge along. She agreed, happy to be included at last and to see her favorite actor, Tom Hanks. Mad and annoyed at Nancy were insufficient reasons to remain unsociable now that Austin abandoned them for his lover. Madge hadn't gone to a movie in months. She loved movies and happy endings.

They parked in the garage and entered through the laundry room. Madge entered the kitchen first and turned on the lights.

"O my god!" The sight thrust her backwards with hands covering mouth.

The kitchen imitated a war zone – cabinets opened and contents scattered on the floor. "Mother, what's wrong!" Nancy and Pilar rushed into the mess.

"Nancy, call 911!" ordered a horrified Madge. "We've been robbed!"

Nancy ignored her mother to run upstairs to the unused bedroom to check on the money under the bed. Pilar dialed 911.

* * *

On Wednesday morning, Olivia and Austin set sail for St. Croix, the largest United States Virgin Island forty miles from St. John. The sunny day calmed the sea to an ideal cruising day. They planned an overnight in Christiansted and return to St. John by late afternoon on Thursday.

* * *

Police searched the Kiley residence. They checked the grounds and the burglars' entrance and exit.

Madge, mystified, could not verify anything missing. Jewelry in the bedroom remained in place.

When asked by an officer if she noticed anything missing, Nancy said, "My room is a mess but nothing is missing."

Nancy knew Rodrigo's second layer had struck and now controlled the drug business. They attacked for the money and her. The total had to disappoint them. She couldn't tell her mother that Rodrigo broke in and that going to the movies saved them from torture to confess then death. Tomorrow, she'd recommend they move out for a while, or rehire the security guards – that criminals return to the crime scene.

After the police left, Nancy and Pilar helped Madge straighten the kitchen and library where books covered almost all the floor. Pilar and Nancy returned to Nancy's room to straighten and to discuss the stolen $4 million belonging to Nancy's mother.

"Just as well," Nancy said. "Probably blood money." She found justification to feel unconcerned over the loss.

Madge started to tidy her bedroom, but surrendered in disgust and left. She removed the shotgun from the library closet and returned to the kitchen.

She blamed Austin for her home's rape.

She felt violated. The burglars had to be Rodrigo men after something Austin had. They stole nothing else. Madge checked the basement's cement enclosed disguised safe. A dummy waste pipe connected to the removable top. She lifted the cover and dialed the combination confident the thieves never discovered their secret safe. She opened the lid. They kept fifty to sixty thousand in cash there, legal documents, expensive jewelry, gold coins, and certificates. Austin used the cash for casino play. All secure, she closed the safe, replaced the cover, and left.

In the library, Madge studied the files for assets, besides brokerage and bank accounts. At Austin's desk, she searched drawers looking for what the burglars might have sought. She could not interpret the various financial dealings, which Austin recorded. Nothing there or obvious that connected Austin financially to Rodrigo's associates. The police would have to research the records after Nancy's trial. Mitchell was right. Nancy had priority.

Her ire continued to manifest with her husband. Maybe he hid the financial evidence elsewhere in the house. Madge labeled Austin guilty. Mitchell believed her. What she, Mitchell, Nancy, and Pilar knew about his connection to Rodrigo seemed inconsequential without evidence or a confession from Austin or Nancy. Neither one seemed likely.

I'm a houseplant and hearsay.

If Austin wasn't coming home for Nancy's trial, he wasn't coming home at all, she confirmed – a fraud with her and Nancy. He vacationed, hiding in a love nest leaving his family unprotected, potentially assaulted, and killed. His cheating paled compared to his flight from his family responsibility and justice.

Austin abandoned his family in crisis.

What lowlife of a man does that?

Lacking evidence, authorities wouldn't force their return. A troublesome question repeated – How could those two, responsible for the direct and indirect deaths of many people go unpunished?

Madge paced into the night in her dark house with the shotgun, often checked the taped wood covering the hole, and again churned Austin's three-year romance with Olivia Greene, their crimes and conspiracies...and her own ignorance.

Madge prepared to protect Nancy and her home from another intrusion with her shotgun, as the turmoil within collided.

She felt nauseous as an eruption stirred.

Madge reacted and ran to the bathroom and vomited with a grotesque sound before she reached the sink.

PART IV

40

Continuing good weather, plentiful sunshine, and the trade winds enhanced sailing the Virgin Islands. Olivia and Austin cruised back to St. John, the rugged and hilly island with an unspoiled national park. Austin connected the automatic pilot, compensated for sea current drift, and locked the compass heading. With the nearest boat miles away, she lay topless in the center cockpit seeking an even tan. Less exposed body areas had turned sun pink.

In bathing suit, Austin sat with feet stretched out surveying his surroundings to search for unseen submerged hazards; dock pilings, tree stumps, and cargo containers that toppled off container ships during storms. These lurking container monsters were a major navigation hazard floating below the surface made visible by the Caribbean's azure and clear waters. Containers sank or damaged many boats, more at night.

Austin providing Nancy with the Trunk Bay location and phone number panicked Olivia, who deemed it a major mistake. She no longer felt safe in this area and needed to manipulate a change.

"Austin," she said without moving or opening her eyes. "When do we leave this area?"

"Anytime next week on the best weather day."

"Can we do it sooner?"

"Why?"

"Just a thought. Why don't we leave earlier and go through the Panama Canal to Cabo San Lucas, Baja California, and the Sea of Cortez. I read that the sailing there is spectacular." There, she'd persuade him to continue north to San Diego or Los Angeles and a plane to New Zealand or Australia.

Austin countered with, "We're better off in the Aruba, Curacao area. We're in the hurricane season. The Panama Canal is a long run. South is safer away from the hurricane path."

That also worked for her. They could board a plane from Caracas, Venezuela. "Let's leave tomorrow morning. Let's up and go."

"Wait until Sunday. I want to visit Peter Island and sail St. Thomas. What's your rush to leave a great sailing area?"

Two more days won't make a difference, Olivia reasoned. As consolation, she's getting him away from here earlier than planned. She changed the schedule. "If it's Sunday you want, Sunday it is."

"I look forward to the trip – new islands, new ports, and new challenges – an exciting phase of sailing."

"Make sure you don't make a stop in Antigua, that's all."

"It's a shame to bypass one of the great sailing islands in the Caribbean, the sailing center, where major sailing races are held."

"It's a reminder of Todd Hancock. An Antiguan proverb says – Absence of body better than presence of mind."

She shifted position. Her head lay on his lap, body stretched out, looking up at him.

"Are you happy, my love? You got the best of both worlds: me, and a sailboat. And if you need more, ask and ye shall receive."

Austin grinned. "More than I deserve." He lowered his face and kissed her vertical mouth, and lingered there.

For Olivia, she was on her honeymoon, a blissful romantic adventure with changing scenes, new places to visit and explore, and full-time alone with her Austin, more than a few stolen hours each week. She closed her eyes and felt the sea's rhythm. She planned to call Gwen Rhodes when in port to say she was in Barbados. Olivia decided to abandon her business. She'd advise that her employees continue without her, continuing their salaries. She'd designate Marilyn Schroeder as its leader with a sizeable salary increase and maintain a profit escrow account until her return. Olivia wasn't concerned as to what they'd do with the escrow when she never returned.

Her house and acquired lawyer properties were secondary. Let them sit. She may contact her Bahamian lawyer to sell her real estate. Those funds could move to one of her international bank accounts. Olivia and Austin hid more money around the world than they needed. Once settled and hidden, they wouldn't risk surfacing again for unneeded finances. She closed the past, erasing her murders again. They served their purpose; never happened – *today and tomorrow mattered.*

She sat up and embraced Austin resting her head on his shoulder as he monitored the course ahead. A contented smile flushed her face.

As the boat sailed on, Austin thought about the upcoming trial and concern for his daughter. Never to see Nancy again would turn into a tragedy. No matter where located with Olivia, he'd find a way to meet with Nancy. He loved his daughter to exclude her from his future, and was willing to sacrifice for her by having her confess to Crane about his role in Rodrigo.

Madge would be hurt and shocked he abandoned her. She never knew about Olivia, that they were together, and would move on with her life.Madge would forgive him in the end. What choice now that Rodrigo crumbled...and he might turn into a wanted criminal? Madge was kind, sensitive, and a forgiver who never held grudges but hurt easily.

If proved innocent in court and Nancy never exposed his role in Rodrigo, he'd go back, resign as senator, tell Madge he wanted a divorce and live elsewhere with Olivia – the perfect timing to end the marriage charade. He'd know in two weeks. Until then, he'd follow the Windward Islands south to the Leeward Islands' chain and call New York for news updates on the trial.

Olivia's philosophy differed, he thought – to keep going, to never look back, and settle down somewhere with new identities and have a family. Let her believe that until the trial ended. After the trial, he'd call Nancy and decide what to do.

As wind soothed his face, Madge and the happy life they shared in earlier years returned. Austin betrayed her, more than once and loved Olivia for over three years. Madge never knew about the four other women he had over the past twelve years. One lived in Locust Valley, and three from the Washington area, and why he often stayed weekends in Washington until he met Olivia. As a public official, he had selected discreet married women. Once Olivia stole his soul, he excluded all others. His marriage never mattered.

Madge seconded as a necessary companion; a part of his Long Island life, a part of the household. An elected official, family stability appeared important to his constituents. Whatever intimacy they shared happened always on Madge's initiative. Turning her down could have aroused suspicion. His marriage lacked romance and passion.

He no longer loved Madge, but never wanted to offend her when together.

He failed as a husband. He never openly hurt Madge. He would soon, believing she'd forget him in time and go on with life in financial security, as she should.

* * *

They reached St. John and their resort at 5:20. They tied up to their assigned mooring. She connected the loop over the bow cleat. When the dinghy reached shore, Olivia placed her phone call by the office building. She informed Gwen Rhodes that she vacationed in Barbados and promised to check in often, and to have Marilyn Schroeder make the decisions in her absence. She refused to provide her hotel saying she wanted to enjoy a vacation. She also spoke to Marilyn regarding her new salary and management.

Austin called Nancy. The phone rang four times and the machine answered. Unable to talk to Nancy, he rejected leaving a message and hung up disappointed. He'd call later before dinner or thereafter.

During their calls, a stalker spied on them from a distance.

Holding hands, Olivia and Austin strolled to their private beach house carrying a blue overnight bag.

The stalker strode to keep them in sight following from a distance until they turned at a bend in the path to their front door. Olivia and Austin entered the beach house.

The stalker lingered in the path until the door closed, kept close to the vegetation and tree line, and approached the front windows. The woman's voice penetrated through the window screens, fading to the veranda that overlooked the bay, the Sound, and St. Thomas.

Peeking in the window, the stalker could see the back of the woman's head as she sat in a rounded high back rattan chair on the veranda facing out. The Senator then left the bedroom for the kitchen, opened a bottle of red wine, and prepared a tray of assorted cheeses and crackers. He poured two glasses.

Austin carried the tray to the veranda, returned for the wineglasses, balancing to avoid spillage, and sat next to Olivia to enjoy the solitude and approaching sunset. Water lapped the shore. Wind nestled palm trees. The lovers clanged glasses.

"Here's to our future, Olivia, wherever we may go." They sipped.

"As long as it gets better with each day. I promise you it will be. No unhappiness about anything."

"We can't miss," Austin replied.

She sighed leaning into the chair. "My favorite time is watching the day wane with the sun, and so peaceful. Wine and cheese are perfect at this time of day." She sipped the wine.

"I'll get the wine bottle."

"It can wait. Relax. Put your feet up and absorb this paradise, how we should live every day."

"Let's make it a mandatory procedure."

The stalker crept to the front door, placed the gym bag in the corner, and turned the knob. The door opened. Moving as in a minefield and convinced the Senator wouldn't return soon to the kitchen, the stalker crouched, approached the wine bottle, and added Rohypnol guess measuring the amount to add for them to pass out for a long time. A reserve was essential if they failed to drink the wine, to wait for a new opportunity.

The prey's continuing conversation and occasional mild laughter were audible in the kitchen. Guarded, the stalker retreated and left the beach house by the front door carefully closing it, picked up the gym bag, and returned to the resort's main area – to wait, diligent if they came by for their 9:00 p.m. dinner reservation. The restaurant confirmed their dinner hour.

The stalker waited for night when safer. Making a mistake risked stranded in the resort if security forbade buses from leaving. Dinner at the restaurant should use up over an hour, closer to two hours.

Day waned, fading, dissolving into a magenta sky that proclaimed a good day for tomorrow – 'Red sky at night, sailor's delight'. Night approached and lights lit the resort's paths. Glow of the hillside restaurant's lights illuminated night in this sparsely populated part of the island. Steel drum music drifted over the resort to blend with droning night insects. Across the Sound, lights speckled St. Thomas, except for the light cluster in Red Hook and the ferry landing.

The stalker waited for the prey to make their dinner date if they did not drink more wine, a possibility and a disaster requiring new opportunities to use the Rohypnol again. A new opportunity may never arise.

They were late.

Another half-hour passed as guests strolled the paths and grounds.

The stalker meandered to the beach house, acting as a guest. Steel drum music faded near the beach house. A couple passed headed for the main area. The path emptied again.

The Senator's beach house was dark, the night eerie, and full of insect chatter.

The stalker turned into the property and tiptoed along the side of the house listening for voices from within; none. Trees and vegetation hid the house from passing guests and neighbors who couldn't see the beach house at the end of a curving path. The stalker approached the rear on tiptoe to peek the veranda. Dark outlines indicated the woman and Senator sat in awkward positions.

Did they drink the wine?

Returning to the front, the stalker entered on tiptoe, closed the door, waited for minor eye adjustment to the dark, and crept to the kitchen. Dim moonlight revealed the wine bottle was no longer on the counter.

Wearing rubber gloves, the stalker approached the veranda holding a weapon in the gym bag and cautious although the prey seemed immobile.

Sailboats tied to moorings and anchorages about a football field distance in deeper water, a few with lights below. The veranda was dark, softened by moon reflections on the water. Waves reaching shore rolled soft and hushed unaffected by a warm tropical breeze.

The stalker approached on toes, each step measured hoping the floor wouldn't creak to announce the intrusion. The stalker continued approaching until able to reach out and touch the Senator – gentle as if he was electrified then a nudge. Repeat nudging failed to stir the Senator and woman still in bathing suits. The wine bottle stood on the rattan table between two empty glasses. Cheese and crackers remained.

The bottle was empty.

The stalker, walking normal and feeling comfortable, returned to the kitchen and sat at the table listening to the night sounds, watching the sleepers through the door opening…and waited.

The stalker now stood by the front window – waiting, looking out from the darkened room and then a return to the kitchen table.

More waiting.

Night insects sounded louder.

Then the stalker bolted to the veranda and plunged scissors into the Senator's neck.

The shock shuddered Austin Kiley's drugged body – then stillness, darkness, and blood.

The killer looked at the Senator's moonlit and distorted face without remorse or conscience, a human that needed to stop breathing, a weed discarded in a necessary mission.

The killer nudged the woman. Harder. The woman slumped in a deep stupor. The killer guessed she'd sleep for many more hours – ideal, allowing sufficient and ample time to flee from the island.

The Senator was the mission's only target.

41

Madge awakened at 6:30 a.m. after another nauseous and restless night, and with a horrible taste in her mouth, and hadn't recovered from the grotesque vomiting that growled from the end of her toes to a violent and ugly eruption as if she needed an exorcism, a part of her recent morning routine from her family's rejections.

She sat at the edge of the bed, rubbed her eyes, and stood weary with a moan on rubbery legs whose ligaments made crackling sounds like wood in a fireplace. She complained to herself.

"You're getting old, Madge. You're getting old."

Her stomach turned acidic. Madge inhaled deep several times and hyperventilated to rush oxygen to her lungs. The thrust of oxygen to blood cells strengthened her and she stood holding her stomach then pressing her abdomen.

Madge smacked her lips several times to change the taste in her mouth, and rubbed her face hard to erase grogginess. She shivered involuntarily and stretched on toes several times, as her arms wrapped the body to stimulate heat. The room was warm, Madge felt cold – like a February day.

Her ears rang. That never happened before. She yawned. Her mouth waved the jaw sideways a few times to end the noise. Ringing dominated although she never suffered from the medical problem, tinnitus. She reached an age when her stressed body needed at least six hours of uninterrupted sleep to function as demanded without naps.

Madge needed to begin an exercise regimen to get back into shape. She'd never keep up with the younger crowd in a gym or dance class. She'd start with a private trainer at home. Her body needed help and exercise would serve as medicine for her stress and family's neglect.

This wasn't the time to think of these matters, she said to herself. *Not now. Not now – later, much later when you feel better. Think good things, something positive and happy to erase the upset stomach.*

Madge shuffled to the bathroom to revitalize her mouth, and face, and seek an antacid remedy. She searched – no antacid. She studied the stranger in the mirror leaning closer, unhappy with the stress signs. She stuck her tongue out. It looked normal. The eyes streaked with red lines from lack of sleep.

Who are you?

Who the hell are you?

What have you become?

When her crisis reached reality again, she left the bathroom, and returned to bed – and sat for a minute deep in thought. Madge stood with a moan to confront the day, and inhaled deeply three times to lessen the acidity.

Madge delayed going out to the veranda to see the body and the blood and Austin's dead wide eyes that had opened to darkness when the scissors struck.

Before entering the veranda, she had checked for potential witnesses. No one appeared on the moored sailboats nearest to the beach house and farther out.

She slid on the rubber gloves again and checked on Olivia, who breathed and remained sedated.

Madge avoided looking at Austin.

All would go as planned when Olivia awakened to find Austin murdered.

Madge smiled and calmed at the thought, the ideal and perfect thought that Olivia Greene would get the blame for killing Austin.

In the bedroom, Madge opened her ex-husband's wallet and counted $2,000 in hundreds. She hadn't looked inside his wallet before and never curious about the contents of his private property. Hate spurred curiosity.

Nancy's photo was in the first plastic slot. His driver license, credit cards, and miscellaneous professional cards followed, including his identification as a United States senator. Olivia Greene's smiling photo insulted from beneath a leather flap. She didn't expect to find her own photograph, and did not. Madge cursed at Austin's continued rejection that made her feel ugly and undesirable. She returned the cash.

Madge searched an unlocked Debussy designed luggage, new and unfamiliar. She discovered American Express checks plus two $5,000 packets in $100 bills. She assumed Austin unlocked the luggage to check for possible theft. She ignored the money to comply with her strategy.

The successful mission must never appear as a robbery to have any focus shift from Olivia killing him.

Finding receipts of wire transfers to foreign banks, she kept those for future use and investigation. If he had money offshore, she wanted it. She'd search those sources after the funeral and after comforting Nancy.

Madge uncovered the manila envelope that contained the $6 million in bearer shares and bonds underneath new T-shirts and familiar laundry. She gladly confiscated the envelope. She'd mail the envelope to herself from St. Thomas to avoid a Customs check. The envelope qualified as a 'gift' from her former husband. The ex-wife owned their assets. Madge grinned as the trip brought a financial windfall and a deserved reward.

She controlled the family's finances. The house burglars probably searched for this envelope, she thought. Whatever, the contents belonged to Madge. She closed the luggage.

Madge opened the closet door and saw his new pants, sports jacket, and shirts. The rest belonged to Olivia Greene. She wondered how much cash she had then avoided searching. Madge had no interest in her possessions. She wasn't a thief. There wasn't anything Olivia might have taken from the Kiley house.

Only Austin.

And she could have him now – with Madge's blessings.

Madge turned away then remembered an important final act. From the gym bag, she removed the unlabeled plastic prescription size container with the remaining Rohypnol and placed it in Olivia's handbag. To assure success to her mission, she tore paper and printed ROHYPNOL, and placed it in the container facing up for easy detection by police. She hid the handbag behind luggage in the closet to assure Olivia overlooked it. Madge hoped local police would conduct a thorough search for evidence.

To linger on the island lacked advantage.

Madge needed to make a successful escape to New York, a long and hazardous journey with no exits to seek refuge.

The return trip frightened her and gripped as a vise.

Madge opened the front door to expose herself to tropical growth, birds, and the clear and pleasant day. She turned for a last look at the veranda. With contempt, she dry spit towards its occupants and said in a lowered voice, "Have a nice day, you shit." She closed the door and left the beach house.

Acting as a casual beach house resident, she headed for the main area to begin the return trip home and wondered with her fogged mind if she forgot something, or left anything behind including fingerprints. Madge kept going, every face an enemy.

* * *

Following the house burglary, Madge discovered the plastic bag labeled Rohypnol in Austin's desk behind the last file drawer. She knew about Rohypnol from the *Newsday* articles. Her earlier visits to the Internet and local library provided added research regarding dosages, efficacy, and effects.

Todd Hancock and Laurence Bates swallowed Rohypnol. Austin's supply suggested his responsibility in providing the illegal drug to his mistress. Mitchell proved correct in saying Olivia killed the lawyers, she concluded. Her discovery verified hers and Mitchell's beliefs.

The Rohypnol strengthened her, the catalyst for her daring mission, and her perfect assistant acting as motivation to proceed.

Madge decided what she must do – to render justice without legal evidence and couldn't deny motivational revenge. Finding the Rohypnol did not mean he used it to commit a crime. She refused to accept her bitterness at his treason as a motive and realized that was delusional.

The day after the burglary, she awakened at dawn. Awakening Nancy and Pilar, she told them to leave the house until the guards returned. They agreed. Nancy reached the same conclusion right after the robbery. Nancy and Pilar drove to the Commack apartment after notifying Stanford Crane's office and calling security.

Madge left for the early American Airlines plane to the Virgin Islands. She told Nancy and Pilar she was going to New York City to shop, to get an early start on the day, and stay until the security company reinstituted the twenty-four hour service. Then home would be safe again. She'd call when settled at some hotel.

Madge's decision to board the Virgin Islands plane required a leap into courage, and was difficult to find. She needed to consider the following – How could she possibly succeed and escape? When would the situation occur to use the Rohypnol? Was she unrealistic? Would she have to stay on St. John several days to seize the moment? Where would she stay? How does she account for her absence for those days?

Austin said to Nancy that he made day trips. His absence from the resort would allow time to scout for opportunity. She entered the resort as Mr. Gilbert's sister and planned to visit for a few hours. She showed her and Austin's photo on their yawl to the casual guard who boarded the bus to check the dozen or so passengers. He checked his guest list for Mr. Gilbert then focused on the next passenger. Madge wasn't concerned about the guard remembering her. Buses traveled the short trip back and forth to Cruz Bay all day. The photo served as her pass. Besides, the resort welcomed guests in the relaxed environment.

A male office clerk directed her to Mr. Gilbert's beach house. At the dock, a busy dock assistant confirmed the Gilberts sailed to St. Croix for an overnight and should return before dark. Charter companies, he offered, banned sailing as part of the rental contract when the waning sun obscured the coral reefs. She had the run of the facility and blended with hundreds of guests.

Madge had strolled to the beach house to reconnoiter. She tried the front door to his love nest. The door opened. Suitcases stood by the closet in the neat house. The open rear door exposed the veranda. She assumed security as tight since the resort had one road to Cruz Bay – a burglar couldn't go far, or stealing wasn't a concern on St. John, a vacationland away from business and crime. Doors remained unlocked in the relaxed and calm environment. No one had reason to suspect her in a paradise far away from mainstream thieves, terrorists, and fanatics.

Madge explored the grounds when a sailboat approached the mooring and anchorage field. She put on her glasses and confirmed Austin behind the wheel. She watched and waited hidden from view behind a tropical garden.

Panic overwhelmed her as she entered the beach house for the second time after following her husband and the *thing* he called his lover. What could Madge say if caught…that she spied on them? The confrontation would be awkward. She'd leave as a puppy with tail between its legs. Without the Rohypnol, she was helpless. Worst case, she had an out if caught – a jealous wife who sought her husband.

Madge swirled in incomparable terror before she plunged the scissors and battled to find the grit to implement her conviction. Nancy used scissors to kill Eddie Hawkins. Aware of airport security, Madge purchased the pointed scissors in St. Thomas.

The difficult part passed – finding opportunity to use the Rohypnol. The execution should be easy, she thought, lacking confidence.

Madge spent three hours in the beach house fighting her ethics, her morals, her self-dignity, her religious teachings, her hate, and her weakness.

Everything good she stood for lost the battle to forgive Austin, although she tried to forgive the unforgivable.

That should account for something on judgment day.

Madge attacked quickly to succeed as a trained terrorist assaulting her objective without concern for consequences if caught.Her attack created terror for an hour before the fright subsided after realizing the consequences. Her heart raced hard as if she ran up a hill. Fear caused vibrations and her body revolted against her, condemning her, and finding her guilty. She threw up in the bathroom before falling asleep.

She murdered Austin.

I'm no better than Austin and his mistress who murdered.

Madge convinced herself and accepted that she acted as agent for justice and personal revenge. The justice part made her feel better and justified. Her inner yelling voice repeated, "What you did was right!" It echoed as a strength stimulant.

Accepting the justice premise, she left the beach house without regrets. Remaining was to leave, survive the bus ride to Cruz Bay without stopped and questioned, survive the ferry ride back to Red Hook, St. Thomas and the long plane confinement without reason to be arrested at the airport.

The plane ride created mental torture, every minute an hour.

Is a United States marshal on the plane?

Madge tensed whenever an attendant came near her expecting her to say, "The captain needs to see you in the cockpit." She worried. Would the busy bus guard remember her? She found comfort in think-ing – *Hundreds of guests and visitors came and went at the resort.*

Paranoia.

She remembered to place the Do Not Disturb sign on the door, needing time to get away. Having the maid miss today added an advantage – more time to be forgotten, or connected to the stabbing by the guard and others.

Madge reasoned no one on Long Island knew she flew there.

Who would check?

Why should they?

They would have to be some kind of psychic.

She tried hard to sleep, to escape her mind. The ongoing terror won. Thankfully, the seat next to hers stayed vacant.

When the plane landed at JFK International Airport, her heart jogged. Madge delayed departure when the plane stopped, putting off the confrontation. She reached the International Arrivals Building, and Customs and Security clearing area that churned active with arrivals.

Madge tried to look relaxed as she waited on line to submit her duty declaration form. She summoned all her strength to get past the stern and cynical looking agent. He scared her. *He* was the United States of America.

The agent personified the law, society, and government, her St. Peter on earth.

Would he let me through his gate? Did the St. John police issue an All Points Bulletin for my arrest? No, too soon.

Madge braced for her first test to appear casual, an innocent and ordinary American traveler. She waited third on her line.

He wasn't smiling when he finished with the first couple who passed inspection. The man next in line failed and moved to another area. Her turn came.

Her heart rhythm jogged faster.

Do I look guilty?

She hated her inability to control her fright from guilt. She envisioned herself caught and in prison clothes, to pay her debt to society for killing her husband. Her hands vibrated. They clasped together to stop.

The agent looked at her, looked at her passport, looked at her, looked at the form, and looked at her again. She stiffened with each of his looks waiting for him to yell, "Murderess!" Madge wondered if that was his way to find guilty faces in an environment of heightened security. She straightened her body and offered her best political smile to act as a United States senator's wife. She gained some control.

"No declaration? No purchases?" he questioned.

"No sir." Her throat dried as a desert. "I didn't have time to buy anything." Her knees shook. She cleared her throat. She regretted forgetting to buy gum to keep her throat moist.

"Was this an overnight business trip?"

"I visited a friend."

"A long way to go for a short visit. Did you visit any foreign territories?"

"No, my stay was in the U.S. Virgin Islands. St. Thomas."

"What's in the bag?"

"Personals." Madge unzipped the gym bag. She had thrown the yellow rubber gloves, from her kitchen, in a trashcan in the women's room at St. Thomas Airport.

He probed the bag containing clothes and personal items for several nights stay. Madge felt thankful she mailed the envelope.

"Any relation to the actor Richard Kiley?" he asked while probing for dangerous items.

"No, I wish I was."

She screamed to herself.

How much longer? Do I look like a terrorist?

He said, "I still remember him from the original *Man of La Mancha.* I saw the play three times. The music was perfect."

"Wonderful play and a beautiful musical score by Mitch Leigh," she replied. "I saw it twice."

He continued to probe, sullen and official. "How about the jewelry you're wearing? The watch?"

Madge wore her diamond Rolex watch. "I owned this for years, an anniversary gift from my husband." She readied to remove the watch to show a few scratches, that it wasn't new.

Before she could unclasp the watch he said, "Thank you. Welcome back, Margaret. We missed you."

She thought he smiled. He zipped the gym bag and smiled.

Madge escaped like her tension, cleared a major hurdle, and heart eased back to normal.

Reaching the taxi stand, she felt safe – distant from her husband's deserved execution. Perfection would be Olivia charged with killing Austin as she planned. In her euphoria, she included a $50 tip for the cab driver when they reached her hotel in New York City.

Madge checked into the Palace Hotel on Madison Avenue. She called the phone number Nancy had given to her and mentioned the hotel, phone, and room number. The conversation was brief, informational, and excluded her father. Madge dreaded the next call to Nancy after Austin's murder reached the media.

Madge Kiley rewrote the ending to Olivia Greene's script.

Madge's happy ending.

Brava! Brava! Brava!

Dawn crept over the horizon in the Virgin Islands nearly thirty hours after Austin's murder. Light leaked into Olivia's darkened world as she stirred and eyes blinked as her vision fogged from stupor. Her arms felt heavy and body weighted as she rubbed face and eyes until the fog receded, and the Sound and sailboats focused.

Her mouth dried. She needed to roll her tongue and smack lips to generate saliva to eliminate an alien taste.

Olivia sensed a foul odor and her kidneys complained. She realized being on the veranda next to Austin. They had cheese and wine and dozed. But why did they sleep all night? Confused, she couldn't fathom how dawn arrived so fast. It must have been bad wine. Her body ached all over, mind hazy, and dulled.

She pivoted her legs to reach the floor to rise, her back to Austin and the table where she had open space. Olivia needed to get to the bathroom to relieve her kidneys and bladder, to ease the body pains, and hangover, and to cold water her face for some relief. Preservative sulfites in wine always induced a deep sleep to her system, but never this bad.

Olivia unfurled, stood holding her head, and staggered inside to the bathroom where she realized her bathing suit was damp. She shrugged away the fleeting thought that she urinated while passed out. She hadn't done that in her sleep since the age of four and blamed spilling the wine when she dozed. She felt better after brushing her teeth, had a cold shower, and changed clothes for another sailing day – white short-sleeve top and shorts. Cold water rejuvenated her drugged body although movements remained lethargic. Head and muscles still ached.

Olivia headed for the veranda.

Although her vision remained hazy in the early light, she could see Austin asleep in the chair. Early to awaken Austin, Olivia decided to wait until 8:00 then go to the restaurant for breakfast. In the meantime, she'd clear the veranda table and refrigerate the cheese, and make needed strong coffee. Austin also enjoyed a cup of fresh coffee upon rising, a habitual way to start the day then sail to Peter Island and its beautiful beach after breakfast. The way she felt, a nap on the beach would be ideal.

Olivia approached the veranda.

A distorted vision opened her eyes wider when she reached the door. Rubbing her eyes did not help to change the vision.

What was that in his neck?

Crunching her face with curiosity, Olivia approached the chair, and leaned forward with eyes wider to see clearer.

Her body bent over with the horror she tried to hide by covering her mouth and face with both hands when she saw blood...then from the sailboat moorings and anchorages, from the resort office to the restaurant to unseen neighbors and guests...Olivia's screams ruptured the morning and echoed across the serene bay.

Again.

And again, louder, and longer.

* * *

The St. John police notified Lieutenant Ken Mullins at 6:00 p.m. at his home by a call patched in from his office. He'd receive reports tomorrow. They detained the Senator's protesting companion, Olivia Greene, as a possible suspect. The information staggered. Mullins called Mitchell, who worked at his computer station.

"You were right about Olivia Greene and Senator Austin Kiley. You're back on track with solid information."

"What brought you to that conclusion? Do you believe my theories?"

"I just received a call from the U.S. Virgin Islands police. Senator Kiley was murdered in a beach house on St. John and Olivia Greene is held as the primary suspect."

The news thrust Mitchell out of his chair. "How murdered...like Rodrigo?"

"With scissors in the throat as he sat in a veranda chair. The attack came from behind. Also, the motive wasn't robbery. Traveler's checks and over twelve thousand in cash weren't taken leading the authorities to exclude robbery. Looks like Olivia Greene killed him in a lover's quarrel."

"This is incredible. What about an autopsy? He could have been drugged or asleep like Hancock and Bates." He paced the room.

"That's pending. I alerted authorities to check for Rohypnol and to hold Olivia Greene until the autopsy completes. They offered full cooperation and compliance with our jurisdiction for the United States senator from New York. If there is traceable Rohypnol, we connect Rodrigo and Olivia to the Rohypnol murders. What an incredible turn of events." Mullins changed subjects. "Also, somebody broke into the Kiley residence. Mrs. Kiley and daughter reported no losses."

"I didn't know about the burglary. Tragedy has a firm grip on the Kiley family."

"I'm starting to get ahead of you," boasted Mullins. "As it should be."

"Maybe Rodrigo searched for missing money."

Mitchell thought of the $8 million Stanford Crane held in his office.

"Possibly. His murder doesn't mean the Senator connected to Rodrigo," Mullins said. "We can speculate he connected if Rohypnol shows up."

"Would you believe Senator Kiley was involved with Rodrigo if luggage full of money belonging to Rodrigo showed up?"

"You mean from the good guy? If you can prove the luggage was in the Senator's possession, I might. I would even hug you."

"Spare me, please. Maybe in two weeks. I'm busy with the trial until then. Have your people uncovered anything on the others?"

"We found about four hundred thousand dollars worth of drugs in the Graham Sag Harbor home in beer cans. The bastards are creative. I alerted the Coast Guard to check beer cases on boarding missions. If involved with Rodrigo, the Grahams might've stolen or stored the drugs. That's solid evidence. We need to confirm the connection. You've been helpful there. Thanks."

"I may confirm the tie-in." He sat the computer desk.

"And you can't tell me?"

"Need to verify something first. I don't want to present more theories to you. Please be patient. Rodrigo is dead."

"All right. And I agree. Please, no more theories. How you get your information is startling."

"No, Moon. I'm good at what I do. You need me by your side."

"I think you underrate yourself." Mullins laughed. "I'll wait for your call."

"Have you notified Mrs. Kiley?"

"Not at home. I'll call again later."

After Mullins, Mitchell called Stanford. The breathless news shocked Stanford.

"Does Nancy know?"

"I don't know. Mullins can't reach Madge."

"Nancy is at the Commack apartment. It's best her mother tell her. I'll call Madge also, maybe go and see her to console then call Nancy together."

"Is this reason to delay the trial?"

"No. The Senator's death might prove beneficial to Nancy with the jury."

Stanford called Madge at home several times within an hour. Failing to communicate with her, he called Nancy, who almost collapsed when told and couldn't talk. Pilar continued the call. Stanford explained what happened and how he died. Pilar said she was about to call Mrs. Kiley. He suggested she give Nancy a sleeping pill and that he'd call Mrs. Kiley. Pilar provided the hotel number.

Olivia and Austin deceived him. Austin hired him as the sacrificial lamb to find his money and free his daughter, and Olivia with phony emotions and her body.

Why did she kill Austin?

Stanford thought about them then focused on her. Stanford enjoyed the evening and morning with Olivia and often thought of her and wanted to see her again.

Stanford felt a loss.

He felt relief having survived their deceit.

Good riddance to both.

44

S tanford spoke to Madge right after he contacted Nancy and Pilar with the tragic news.

Madge acted with shock and 'crocodile' tears while bemoaning her family's continuing tragedies. Stanford apologized for telling Nancy first. When he couldn't reach Madge, he needed to tell Nancy before she learned of her father's murder from media. Madge thanked him for his consideration. Stanford repeated Nancy's phone number and address.

Finishing with Stanford, Madge faced another major hurdle – calling Nancy. She reached for the phone and hesitated needing to find courage after causing her anguish. Madge never considered Nancy's feelings when she killed her father. Then, she was a terrorist, a judge and jury, and a vengeful wife...and an agent for justice. Madge reached for the phone twice before she grabbed and held it.

Madge must revert to a mother again.

She wasn't ready.

Madge procrastinated and deferred the call for several more minutes hoping Nancy slept, hoping Pilar answered, hoping she had the strength to act as a fraud, and hoping she could handle Nancy's grief without facing her, a better option.

Madge dialed slowly to delay the inevitable. The phone answered on the third ring. Pilar said a low and mournful hello.

"Pilar, this is Mrs. Kiley. Mr. Crane called me."

The stalled silence burst by Pilar's crying. Madge's stoic facade cracked at Pilar's inability to talk. Her lips quivered.

She heard Pilar's sniffling.

"Mrs. Kiley. I'm sorry about Mr. Kiley. I'm so sorry." More sniffles. "Nancy's sleeping. Shall I wake her? Mr. Crane told me to give her a sleeping pill. She cried almost all night."

Madge had difficulty responding to her child's pain.

"No, Pilar. It's best she sleep. I'm returning immediately and will come by in the morning. Goodbye, Pilar. I'm glad you're with her."

Madge couldn't go on, emotion prevented talking.

"Goodnight, Mrs. Kiley."

Madge had tears when she hung up and cried for Nancy's grief... and for losing her father. When the crying stopped, she accepted being a different person; her psyche changed, no longer living in her husband's shadow and as observer to Nancy's gyrations with her father.

Madge needed to survive her self-justifiable act and must continue the lies.

And deny, deny, deny if anyone accused her.

* * *

Stanford called Mitchell to update and discuss Austin's death. Stanford mentioned that Madge returned to Long Island from New York City. He named her motel in Commack and why she's staying there.

* * *

The mysteries to Mitchell's planets and moons solved; everything interrelated in his equation. Who killed Austin remained, if not Olivia?

Mitchell assumed the burglars at the Kiley residence were Rodrigo men looking for the cash held by Stanford. Did the new Rodrigo management track Austin to the Virgin Islands? How did they know he stayed at a resort in St. John? Did they monitor phones, or was it by an Olivia contact?

He couldn't exclude Rodrigo. They had purpose and resources to kill him. Why didn't they kill Olivia? Did they arrange to have her take the blame? Who else knew the Senator's location besides Nancy and Madge?

Mitchell typed those questions and other thoughts into the computer.

Nancy Kiley – Her father was murdered in the same manner she killed Eddie Hawkins. Her whereabouts accounted for.

Pilar – With Nancy at all times. Not a suspect.

Madge – In New York City.

Mullins, Stanford, myself – exempt.

Rodrigo – Strong suspect. How did they learn the Senator's location?

Gwen Rhodes – Never knew Olivia's location.

Did Madge know people in Rodrigo? Did she relay the information? No, that unrealistic concept doesn't apply.

Reviewing Madge...she had motive.

By eavesdropping, Madge discovered the truth about her husband and Rodrigo. He cheated for three years and deserted her for another woman.

Madge had motive, he typed, but wasn't the type to kill for revenge, or any reason. She wasn't the strong, determined, and ruthless type.

Madge wasn't an Olivia Greene.

Where would Madge get the Rohypnol? That drug is banned in the States. If the autopsy on the Senator indicates Rohypnol was present, Madge wasn't involved.

I'll reserve final judgment on her until the autopsy results come in.

If the killing were a Rodrigo hit, wouldn't they have followed their execution pattern? I don't think so, he typed, talking to the computer. How do you get guns through airport security? Security would cause a change in execution style. That doesn't exclude Rodrigo, especially if Rohypnol was found. Rodrigo's international connections must have provided Olivia with her Rohypnol.

His notes continued.

- The Rodrigo financial consortium died, the leaders murdered.
- The Nancy trial remained from their activity.

Mitchell remembered Mullins saying, "Get me Rodrigo and I won't ask questions about anything." He already exposed Rodrigo to Mullins. The rest could come after the Nancy trial.

When the trial ended in Nancy's release due to reasonable doubt, Stanford would turn over the $8 million to Mullins. Stanford believed he would win the decision.

Stanford would have Nancy tell Mullins about her father and Rodrigo. With her father dead, would Nancy tell the truth about the people in Rodrigo? If so, that should satisfy Mullins in the Rodrigo case having received eyewitness testimony.

Mullins can then close the case against the Rodrigo financiers. The case against Olivia remained due to the Rohypnol connection, if found, and killing the two lawyers. Probing her finances and assets should be included for possible irregularities and profit from illegal drug activity. A criminal investigation, foreign governments should cooperate and provide her records and she might have profited for killing the lawyers in Liechtenstein and Antigua.

His commitment to Stanford ended with the conclusion of Nancy Kiley's trial. Then he'd settle in to write the book. Sufficient book substance existed negating the use of fiction. Further investigation and Olivia's trial would be included. By then her trial may reach the sentencing stage.

He molded a better thought. Olivia may plead guilty. If Rohypnol was in the Senator, she may accept the Rohypnol as damaging and plea-bargain for a lighter sentence, a better option than life imprisonment.

Mitchell preferred a guilty plea to avoid a prolonged trial and continued suffering for Madge and Nancy.

When the phone rang at 10:20 p.m., Madge thought about her terrifying future as a potential fugitive from justice and her relationship with Nancy. Austin's death should bring them closer; one more reason added to her justification. She assumed the caller as Pilar or Stanford and readied a funereal demeanor until she read the caller's name. She tensed because Mitchell was an investigator, a friend but a potential enemy and obstacle.

Hesitant to answer, she lifted the receiver with confidence and a widow's grieving voice.

"Yes?"

"Hello, Madge. Mitchell Pappas. Sorry to call this late. Stanford told me your number. I have a bad habit of calling right away when there's a death in the family of those I know. I needed to reach out to you. I want to express my sympathy for the good years."

Madge sat on the bed, guarded, and continued to perceive the call as a threat.

Could he suspect me?

How could he possibly know?

Keep talking.

"No, it's all right," Madge replied monotone. "I'm glad you called. Being right about Olivia Greene and Austin is no consolation. We had many good years. You know something Mitchell, it's justice." She eased on the grieving tone. "Austin's drugs murdered people and she murdered Todd and Laurence and Austin. Maybe she killed others. Someday, I'll sit and cry for him. My concern is to rebuild my life and Nancy's and pray she's declared innocent. Austin deserved to die like all drug dealers. I look at his death as fate and punishment for his crimes. I thank you for calling me."

Madge wanted Mitchell to take the hint and sign off although important to Nancy's trial. She'd remain courteous and act normal if he continued, and hoped he wouldn't accuse her. She knew Austin's location on St. John.Mitchell may believe she had motive as a jealous wife.

"I can't blame you, Madge. He's put the family through hell. When will you return home?"

He didn't attack or accuse. Her comfort level increased and tone eased to normal.

"Tomorrow. We've had a burglary and the guards return then. We need them again. We know why Nancy needed them."

"Stanford mentioned the burglary."

"Another hex on the Kileys. When it rains, it pours, right? Nothing was stolen. I assume Rodrigo's men searched for what Austin might have had that belonged to them. I'll fine comb the house tomorrow to check for drugs. If I find any, I'll call you and Stanford for advice. And we know he was a drug dealer, don't we, Mitchell?"

"Yes, he was, Madge thanks to your exposure of Olivia Greene and alertness at home."

Mitchell's friendship attitude continued to ease her tension against a potential accusation.

"Considering the many years I lived with him, I never really knew him. God, what a fool I've been and Nancy wouldn't speak against her father. Austin and the Greene woman would've disappeared and gotten away with murder. Is it better for them to go unpunished? I don't think so."

"Madge, it's difficult to disagree with you."

His response encouraged Madge. "It's time to erase the past. What's left is to bury him. I'll give him the best funeral for Nancy and the good times and the world will know he cheated on me. I can handle that. I grew immune to what anyone thinks about me, the rejected and jilted wife. My life will go on with new thoughts and with my daughter."

"I'm glad you're at peace with all this."

And I'm glad you never pointed a finger at me.

Maybe it's too soon?

"I am, in every way. It's the right ending. Perfection means Olivia Greene going to jail. Let's close the book on Austin's death and solve Nancy's problem. I may sell the house so Rodrigo's men don't know where we are. I'll see how Nancy feels about selling after the trial. The condominium in Washington can wait. I'll sell the sailboat."

In her firmness, Madge seemed a tower of strength.

"Will you attend Nancy's trial?"

"Everyday hoping my presence will help my daughter. I know Stanford will win. I believe he's the best."

"I agree. Maybe we can sit together to help support you."

"I'd love that. Thank you for being so considerate."

"Goodnight, Madge. I'll see you soon."

"Goodnight. Again, I'm glad you called."

Madge found solace in the conversation, but he was an investigator and a lurking threat. Madge passed the encounter as she had with

the Customs and Security encounter. Doing so provided a dim sense
of added security.

Madge overcame two hurdles, and confident of facing any others.
Don't self-destruct.

* * *

Mitchell felt like a rowboat attempting to head upstream without
oars, held in place by conflict, punished by white water, and an inde-
cisive conscience.

He returned to the computer and the keyboard, resolute -

- To let Mullins come to his own conclusions on Olivia and Austin
if Rohypnol is in Austin's body, or found in the beach house in the
Virgin Islands.

- To avoid speculation and mistakes by letting events unfold with
police investigation and the outcome of the Nancy trial and the Olivia
trial. They are the determining reasons.

- And if authorities accuse Olivia of killing Austin, to no longer
pursue hunches on the Kiley tragedies as the credit card checks that
failed to prove she visited Antigua and Liechtenstein. Mullins's words
still echo – "No more hunches after this."

Mitchell decided to make a stand, to take a position he could live
with, and move on to the trials without theory interruptions and devote
time to the manuscript. He began his confession to the computer:

'Senator Austin Kiley got what he deserved. Olivia might connect
to the Rohypnolmurders. If so, an aggressive prosecutor may blame
both for several Rodrigo murders.

In reference to my unofficial investigation and my curiosity about
Rodrigo, Olivia Greene, and Senator Austin Kiley and those lurking

and troublesome questions, I can with a comfortable conscience, say –
Case closed. Likely...but the unexpected always lurks.

Murders have no time limitations.'

* * *

United States Senator Austin Kiley's death captured headlines in
media and shocked Washington and the nation. Olivia Greene featured as the lead suspect in a high profile case.

* * *

Olivia vehemently proclaimed her innocence as she sweated and
paced in her 6'x9' detention cell that included a bunk bed, sink, and
toilet. She screamed at every police officer who came near her cell and
condemned the Virgin Island police system as incompetent and lazy
to search for the real killer.

Authorities turned deaf to her rage to await test results for
Rohypnol. She refused to eat, threw her food at guards, and banged
the food tray against the bars in protest. Olivia appeared innocent with
her screaming persistence and long crying jags that left her exhausted
after several hours. The guards thought she lost her mind.

Convinced she'd be cleared of the Rohypnol charge, her emotional
agony pained for losing Austin.

*Who killed him just when my world was perfect? The Grahams,
Randy, and Greg were dead. If it wasn't for Nancy Kiley withholding
the money to force my beloved Austin to resign, none of my killings
would have been necessary, and Austin would be alive. Austin spoke
to his shitty daughter. Was she to blame for Austin's murder? Yes!*

When cleared of the ridiculous and unthinkable accusation that I killed Austin, my love, I'll return to the States, confront the little bitch, and kill her. No one else knew we were in the Virgin Islands. She killed her father the way she killed her boyfriend. It had to be her. And include her weak and pathetic mother who used up Austin's time when it could have been mine.

How could anyone left in Rodrigo management know we were here? Who had motive? Captain Conniver? I'll take care of him, also. Those three have to die.

Olivia returned to anguish and more crying for her shattered future. She pounded the bed with her fists as she wailed.

* * *

After a bad night's sporadic sleep that clothed her with paranoia that she'd be caught and punished, Madge prepared for her role as a distressed widow. She'd play out an encounter with Nancy knowing they'd hug and cry to each other.

The role of family liar would reverse.

Madge would have her daughter back, and her child would again need her.

* * *

Leaving Nancy and Pilar a half-hour after Stanford arrived, Madge decided to drive to the expanded Roosevelt Field in Westbury to shop while Stanford conducted pretrial briefings with Nancy and Pilar.

Madge stopped for a last minute review in the mirror, approved her stressed physical presence then hesitated leaving to study the different person.

Stay strong, Madge. Everything is perfect. Believe that. Don't become a frightened lamb. Act strong and secure and control your life. You're on your own. Avoid panic. Austin's lover will be charged and convicted. Your plan was perfect.

Perfect, perfect, perfect.

Convinced, she prepared to leave satisfied, hesitated again and chastised her reflection.

That's it, Madge, take a good look at what you've become – what a family you raised. What a home you made. Your husband was a murderer and a drug dealer who cheated on you, your daughter killed her boyfriend, and you killed your husband. God! The only bright light in your new and fraudulent world is for that 'thing', that Olivia Greene to receive blame for what you did.

She added for reassurance – *And blamed she'll be. That will happen. Yes, that will happen. And someday you also will be judged on earth or in heaven, or will it be hell?*

Madge felt almost comfortable with her acting role with Nancy and herself as avenger and judge dispensing justice, and as an executioner of a drug dealer and kingpin.

She'd remain alert and guarded until several weeks passed and much longer until Olivia Greene's conviction for killing Austin. The Rodrigo case would then close and her survival chances increased.

Nobody suspected her.

Eventually, many criminals are caught – and I am a criminal – by a slip up or the unexpected. Let it be later or never. Many cases go unsolved, not everyone is caught. This case will solve and close when Austin's lover is proven guilty, a killer. Then the champagne comes out to celebrate, shutting the door to the past. Yes, indeed, the champagne will flow. I'll even bathe in it.

A sudden thought brought a smile. She'd attend Olivia Greene's trial to watch her squirm and to relish the revenge.

Hate...tasted...good.

Maybe the prosecution would allow her to testify against the husband stealer. But...her future wasn't secure. A record existed of her flight to St. Thomas and back. Who besides Mitchell Pappas could find reason to check?

Why should anyone consider me a suspect?

After all, I didn't kill Austin, did I? Olivia Greene did.

She added questions – What if someone discovered the trip? What could I say? She had answers – When the plane landed in St. Thomas, she decided to return from St. Thomas considering the trip unnecessary, a jilted wife's temporary madness, and who accepted her husband's cheating.

There's no record she visited St. John. The island shuttle ferry never kept passenger records. *Where did I stay overnight?* A problem. *Should I say the airport?*

She'd think of something. Or whatever innocent concocted tale while continuing to blame Olivia Greene.

And Madge believed for it provided strength – *If necessary, Stanford Crane will defend me and be found innocent.*

Stanford knew Austin and Olivia's history. He'd make the case against Olivia, the Rohypnol murderess.

Madge's mournful charade would continue prior to, during, and after the funeral. She'd delve into her finances and determine her worth plus the $6 million in bearer shares and bonds found in the Virgin Islands beach house, and seek advice from a financial advisor on how to convert them to municipal and government bonds.

Madge's thoughts saturated with her potential exposure and problems as she drove west on the Northern State Parkway. *The danger
passes when the officials blame Olivia,* she repeated.

*Authorities should find the Rohypnol in Olivia's handbag...if they
haven't already.*

What if they didn't?

Madge raised her defenses to red zone. She monitored her rear-view mirror at regular intervals alert to danger. Those who burglarized her home might come after her seeking whatever Austin had or stole from them, if not the money Austin had at his love nest resort. She drove with an evasive attitude. Avoiding the Meadowbrook Parkway, Madge drove the Wantagh Parkway to Old Country Road to her destination, the Roosevelt Field Mall. She wasn't followed. She'd add twenty-four-hour personal bodyguards for her, Nancy, and Pilar to the security force when they return to the house.

* * *

Mitchell lounged at home in Amagansett stretched out on the couch when Mullins called.

"I just received a call from the Virgin Islands that Rohypnol was in Austin Kiley's body. They also found Rohypnol in Olivia Greene's handbag. We're bringing her back here and charging her with murder. She insists she's innocent – that the Rohypnol was planted in her bag and wasn't hers and that she was framed. Her hysteria and violence reached a point where they had to restrain her with a straightjacket."

Mitchell refused to introduce another theory that Rodrigo killed Austin recalling Mullins saying – no more theories.

"The evidence remains strong against Olivia Greene, Moon. Anything more on Rodrigo?"

"Searching further, we found a case of Heineken on Randy Hawkins's yacht in Sag Harbor. Each can full of Ecstasy. That ties him in with the Rodrigo cabal. We already found drugs at the Graham home. We're searching for *Golden Hawk's* captain and crew. We alerted the Coast Guard with their names and data found on *Golden Hawk,* plus information acquired from them the night Randy Hawkins and Greg Morris were killed. Captain Conniver reported the murders to us. I need to know the Rodrigo cells that operate on Long Island. Rodrigo still lives until we destroy those cells. You did a great job, Mitch. Don't forget, you still owe me more evidence against Rodrigo. I'm counting on you."

"Soon, maybe sooner. Confirming Olivia's guilt changes the playing field for the 'good guy'. I'll call you right after my meeting with him. The Rohypnol makes a better case for charging Olivia Greene with Laurence Bates and Todd Hancock's murders."

"I agree. A solid case against her. It also means Stanford Crane is safe as the third attorney. You succeeded in your goal to save Stanford. Keep helping me to achieve mine to end Rodrigo. That will make me a happy man."

"There's an ancient Greek saying that goes – When you're happy, I'm happy."

* * *

Mitchell called Stanford and told him the Olivia Greene information. "Stanford, does that require a change in your trial strategy?"

"I may have to talk to Nancy and Pilar. Let's meet with them after Austin's funeral. Nancy can then focus on her problem, then her father. Olivia's guilt is dramatic placing us in a fork in the road. We'll see. Let Madge bury Austin first."

* * *

Senator Austin Kiley's funeral sparked a national media event once Olivia allegedly murdered the popular senator and his daughter's two defense attorneys. Creative television talking heads and press reports spread the scenario that Olivia Greene also tried to sabotage the Nancy Kiley trials because the Senator refused to divorce his wife for her. Reporters hounded the jilted wife for comments.

Madge refused to speak to all media.

More than four-hundred mourners and the media attended Austin's funeral in Huntington's Covington Hill Cemetery. Among them were local, state, and federal dignitaries including the President and governor of New York State.

Madge acted distressed for the media and Nancy. She couldn't bring herself to cry at the gravesite. Her dark veil covered her eyes. She dabbed her nose several times for public effect. With every pat, she prayed silently, 'Go to hell forever you miserable bastard.'

A distraught Nancy felt the impact of a daughter who loved her father.

After the funeral, Stanford scheduled a morning meeting in the solarium. He needed the day to pass before convincing Nancy. Madge, Nancy, and Pilar agreed to meet with Stanford and Mitchell. Before leaving, Stanford urged the red eyed Nancy to tell her mother the truth about Eddie and her father. Nancy hesitated.

"My father didn't want her to know to hurt her. I don't know if I should. I should respect his wish."

Stanford placed his hands on her shoulders and held for emphasis.

"Nancy, your father is gone. You need to protect yourself. Stop the charade and lies to your mother. Our meeting tomorrow is critical to you. I want her on your team knowing the truth. I know you'll shock her. She has to accept the truth. The truth will explain why you didn't confide in her. She'll understand. Your mother is a great person. It's about time you realized that." He released her.

Sad and humbled by the mournful day Nancy said, "I'll try to do that tonight."

"Better it comes from you than from a public source. If unable to, call me, and I'll tell her."

"It's important now?" she hedged.

"Yes, for the trial and your future relationship. She's here, your father isn't. She's your future. Be selfish. Think about you and your mother. Support each other."

* * *

Tomayo Suarez recognized Olivia's photo – the woman accused of murdering Senator Austin Kiley. She stole the $6 million with the Senator in Sag Harbor. They killed Randy Hawkins and Greg Morris on the yacht. They must have killed the Grahams. She killed the Senator. That money was lost to him. He still had the $4 million they found in the Senator's house to keep his operation alive. The balance of $8 million was also lost he assumed, taken by the Senator and his lover since it wasn't in the house. The $4 million sufficed as a beginning to make many more millions – all his.

The channels with Captain Conniver remained open. The original Rodrigo leaders were dead, unless silent partners existed. He was now Rodrigo, he gloated. He'd build a stronger and better organization with discipline maintained by familiar Rodrigo execution methods.

He lost a battle, not the war.

* * *

Annapolis police arrested Captain Walker Conniver for drug smuggling after he checked into the waterfront Marriott in Annapolis, Maryland. He confessed to using *Golden Hawk* as his base on Long Island. True to his word and, incredibly, he accepted the blame for running the operation. But he never killed Randy Hawkins and Greg Morris or anyone else. He signed an affidavit stating Randy Hawkins was ignorant about the drug smuggling, that it was all his idea. To plea bargain, he named the sailboats he dealt with, including *Mandalay* and their routes.

To better his deal with the prosecutors, he named Tomayo Suarez as the main cell operator and distributor on Long Island.

Suffolk police arrested Tomayo in his bodega. The $4 million was in a safe in the back, and his personal finances were subject to investigation.

With the arrest of Captain Conniver and Tomayo Suarez, the drug industry on Long Island received a severe and crippling blow. Rodrigo tumbled into a coma.

Authorities would never believe Senator Austin Kiley connected to Rodrigo, unless Nancy Kiley testified against her father.

* * *

Mullins called Mitchell in the evening to convey the good news regarding Conniver and Suarez.

"We severed the distribution channels and the main cell is eliminated. Rodrigo is on its last breath but the information you plan to provide continues as vital."

"I'll deliver as promised. In the meantime, I need to talk to you about matters regarding the Nancy Kiley case..."

* * *

Madge survived a bad night's sleep again. Now that she buried Austin, loneliness visited, and surrounded her aura. Strange, she wondered, why feel alone? She realized that the severity of Nancy's truth underscored how distant Nancy kept her. She felt the residue of rejection. Those problems and secrets vanished. Nancy confided in her with the truth about Eddie and Austin, and that mattered. She accepted that truth. Madge labeled Austin a drug dealer but acted shocked to Nancy. Madge comforted and hugged Nancy when she cried after Nancy apologized for lying to her.

Madge felt proud Nancy attempted to protect her father from himself. She accepted Nancy's act as a higher calling than divulging her father's secrets.

Madge now knew.

Her child needed her.

That was important.

Security guards protected the Kiley house when Mitchell and Stanford drove up. The new guards cleared them.

"Are the girls ready?" Stanford asked after Madge closed the door.

"They're waiting in the solarium on the couch."

"Before we go in, wait a moment. I need you in this meeting and want you to sit with them. Mitchell and I will sit opposite."

"Can you tell me what you're planning?" Madge said. "I'd like to contribute, thank you. Do you want me to say anything special, do something?"

"We have tough decisions to make this morning requiring your participation. Speak whenever you want and ask any question you wish."

"I'll do all I can."

After the men greeted the girls, Madge sat next to Pilar, who sat next to Nancy. The men reserved the Eames chairs. Madge had the broken window replaced.

Stanford said, "I need to know, Nancy if you told your mother what we discussed or shall I tell her?"

Red traces lingered in Nancy's eyes as mourning continued. "I told her everything last night." The funeral effects remained in her voice.

Stanford shifted to Madge. "Do you feel current regarding your family?"

"Yes. Incomprehensible, but assumed about Austin."

"Do you have any questions regarding her conversation?"

"No. I understand what she did and why her attitude towards me."

Stanford addressed Pilar. "This critical pretrial conference is also very important to you. You can no longer support only Nancy. You'll understand in a moment. We must all be involved in the decision making process. The decision must be unanimous before we can move forward."

"You make it sound ominous, Mr. Crane," Nancy said.

"Not ominous, Nancy. Serious. We must rethink your trial strategy. Your father's death requires a change and a new approach. Protecting him is no longer viable or realistic. The arrests of Randy Hawkins's captain and Tomayo Suarez may expose your father. They may name Rodrigo participants and your father may be among them. I know you want to protect your father. Don't. With his potential exposure hanging over us, we must consider the following.

"One, to abandon the sex assault defense...don't be alarmed," he added when the three women reacted surprised. "Two, we proceed with the truth that you killed Eddie in self-defense by accident because he beat you. Pilar, you also fought with him making you an accomplice. More important, you're an eyewitness to his assault and no longer considered an innocent." The women looked uncomfortable. "Before protesting or asking questions, allow me to finish my statement."

They assented, nodding.

"Three, Nancy and Pilar, you will accompany me to the district attorney's office to admit the sex lie, that you devised the story to protect your father. Four, Nancy, you *will* admit your father was a key figure in Rodrigo. You found out when Eddie in his drugged stupor told you. You argued, he attacked, and the accident happened. You and Pilar removed the money from his car trunk and hid it to force your father to withdraw from Rodrigo. When he left the States, you turned it over to me for safekeeping. You didn't steal the money with the intent to keep it. Five, you both *will* admit the truth without reservations.

"Six, if we go with the sexual attack, we'll be blindsided and you, Nancy, will lose your freedom. The best opportunity is the truth and a total confession. Seven, I believe I can persuade the district attorney to drop the charges against both. Eight, your courage against threats requiring security guards, and to force your father to quit the drug trade is an advantage. Safekeeping the money and damaging Rodrigo's finances is additional. I'm positive Conniver and Suarez will admit your actions damaged them. Nine, Mitchell spoke to Lieutenant Mullins of the Suffolk Homicide Squad, who will substantiate how important your actions were in Rodrigo's demise. He doesn't know your father was Rodrigo. Mitchell told him I have the money, which we'll turn over to him.

"Ten, the woman charged with murdering your father might confirm his involvement in Rodrigo and your role although she claims being innocent. She has yet to confess to anything. The threat of a prison sentence may loosen her lips. Mitchell and I believe she'll be charged with killing Todd Hancock and Laurence Bates. Rohypnol is strong evidence against her. It was in her possession. Add her to the list of Captain Conniver and Tomayo Suarez who can expose your father. The odds of you caught in the sex lie are high.

"Those are the primary reasons. The big questions – Pilar, are you willing to expose yourself as an accomplice...and Nancy, are you willing to expose your father? Don't answer me now. I want you both to leave the room to discuss your decisions. Remember, to go with the sex assault charge would be a serious mistake. Consider the current events and the future testimony of others."

Stanford's presentation pleased and thrilled Madge.

Nancy and Pilar stood and left the solarium for the library looking concerned and frightened.

"What do you think, Madge," Stanford asked.

"They'll be putting themselves in harm's way. But they did that when they hid Austin's drug money, didn't they? They made a brave decision. I'm proud of them."

"They did it for Austin. They'll have to do it for themselves."

"Mitchell," Madge said. "I'm repeating myself, but we were right about Austin, weren't we?"

"Thanks to your eavesdropping, you discovered Austin's three-year involvement with Olivia Greene. I told Lieutenant Mullins how helpful you were. I also mentioned your willingness to cooperate in their investigation of Austin's finances, if needed. Regarding Austin's involvement, Mullins will need a statement from you for Olivia Greene's indictment."

"Anything, anything at all. She killed my husband. I want to testify at her trial about their relationship. She probably forced him to join Rodrigo. Austin would never volunteer to become a criminal. She corrupted him then killed him. I hope she's sentenced to live in isolation in prison. Stanford, I agree. We must change direction and take our chances the district attorney and Lieutenant Mullins wouldn't pursue Nancy and Pilar's prosecution and that they testify as witnesses against Rodrigo."

Thought Madge – *To assure Olivia Greene's conviction.*

"It's the best choice, Madge," Stanford said. "I didn't want to insist or force them to agree. I want them to make the decision on their own. If they reject the change, we must continue to argue our position. It's important they agree."

Madge asked Mitchell, her potential threat, "What's your opinion on their decision?"

"They should heed Stanford's advice. But will Nancy condemn her father? She risked her life to save him. She also must think about Pilar as an accomplice. They stand at the crossroads to their future. Bravery is one thing – to reject common sense and good advice from their attorney, another."

"Which way will they decide?" Madge asked. "What's your opinion?"

"I never know what people are capable of under pressure and what they're willing to risk for their actions."

Madge nodded. How well she knew what she was capable of – how *well* she knew.

The solarium turned into a courtroom waiting for the jury to reach its verdict. Within a few minutes, the solemn faced jury returned. Nancy sat without making eye contact with anyone, folded knees to her chest, and buried her head in her arms.

Madge tensed. Nancy's demeanor meant a negative sign.

Pilar stood by the couch to address them looking uncomfortable. "Mr. Crane, we discussed your suggestions." She cleared her throat. "For Nancy to destroy her father and to expose my role regarding Eddie Hawkins are difficult burdens to bear and frightening. Nevertheless, we must be realistic and intelligent, and address our actions. We agree with you."

Nancy cried.

Madge edged closer to Nancy saying, "It's the right decision, Nancy. I know it's the right decision." She hugged her daughter. Nancy unraveled her body and hugged her mother for comforting.

Stanford said, "Pilar, notify your parents. Let them know of your decision and participation."

"I'll call them."

"If you wish, I'll explain your decision to them and my confidence in moving forward."

"You may have to," she replied unable to withhold tears.

Madge motioned with her hand and fingers for Pilar to come to her, to embrace her also. Pilar hurried to her.

The men let several seconds pass to allow Nancy and Pilar to settle before Mitchell asked, "Madge, may I use your phone in another room?"

"There are two in the kitchen or the library."

Mitchell and Stanford left for the kitchen. Mitchell phoned Mullins and explained excerpts of the meeting's outcome while Stanford listened on the extension.

"We can bring the Rodrigo money to your office within the next hour or two. I can tell you Nancy Kiley stole that money to force her father to withdraw from Rodrigo. He was a key player along with the Grahams, Randy Hawkins, and Greg Morris. She'll verify to you that the funds belonged to Rodrigo. This should strengthen your case against Olivia Greene's involvement with Rodrigo and her killing the two lawyers."

Mitchell slapped his desk. "Will your wonders ever cease? You told me Nancy was your source on who managed Rodrigo. She's been valuable in the demise of the drug network on Long Island. It's hard to believe the Senator associated with that scum. The county owes her a debt of gratitude. Do you still want me to go with you and Stanford to the district attorney's office? It may be advantageous if we were together. I'll do what I can for her."

"Your influence is important."

"If you want, I'll call the DA for an appointment. He'll react quicker to me."

"Hold on a second." He looked at Stanford, who nodded, pleased. "That can help, Moon."

"I'll see you soon then. I guess I owe you one, Mitch."

"You owe me more than one plus at least two dinners with the wives."

Mitchell sat with a glass of retsina wine, feta cheese with olive oil and oregano, propped his feet up on the balcony railing, and contemplated the day's events.

Thanks to Nancy and Madge for providing essential information, Rodrigo vanished from Long Island.

Mullins presented a strong case for Nancy to the district attorney, citing her contribution in ending the new drug organization on the Island. Without her actions and courage in facing death threats, Rodrigo would've expanded into an out-of-control monster. By doing so, Mullins added, "Nancy Kiley saved many lives. She deserves that consideration.She performed an outstanding public service while awaiting trial."

Stanford's reasoning also made an impact. He remained firm in Nancy and Pilar's innocence based on self-defense, plus their contribution to the Police Department in damaging Rodrigo. District Attorney Frank J. Laine promised to get back to him by tomorrow on his decision to continue the prosecution, drop the charges, or ask for a plea bargain without prison time for Nancy and Pilar. Mullins and Stanford believed the charges would drop. Mullins planned to continue to lobby for Nancy and Pilar.

Mitchell was satisfied with his own participation in this case. Those deserving punishment were under arrest or murdered. Lady Justice should be satisfied with that result with balanced scales.

Mitchell helped save Stanford's life and helped in wounding Rodrigo before it spread. He had no doubt Olivia killed Todd Hancock, Laurence Bates, and Austin. Did she kill others? She might have. Yes, his participation in the Kiley case proved productive and successful. He made important contributions in a case full of deceptions, love, and hate...and multiple deaths.

He formed a mental synopsis after a sip of wine to celebrate his successful participation – a toast to the ego with a touch of comic praise.

- Started with the first Nancy interview – where she lied.
- Provided Mullins with the Rohypnol data to investigate.
- Met with Austin in Washington.
- Made planets and moons for evaluation.
- Had second meeting – Nancy, Pilar, Madge, and Stanford.
- Jury selection in Riverhead, interrogated witnesses for trial.
- Met with Pilar and Nancy in Commack, escrowed eight million dollars belonging to Rodrigo.
- Told Mullins about Rodrigo and Mullins found the drugs in beer cans.
- Told Mullins to investigate Olivia's travels aka Noreen Gilbert and her finances.
- Met with Madge at Hilton.
- Madge eavesdropped at home on my suggestion.

- Had final meeting with Nancy, Pilar, Madge, and Stanford to change trial strategy, explained to Mullins who supported Nancy with the DA.

* * *

Mitchell remained on the balcony for an hour, lost in the world authors enter mulling the characters in their book. All involved in the Kiley case needed analysis – the Kiley's, Olivia, the victims, members of Rodrigo, Mullins, Pilar, and Stanford. He had questions – What did he know about them? What else was there? What aspects resolved? What hadn't?

He needed to research more about the main character, Olivia Greene, the core all spokes connected to; each spoke a name, a place, and an action. Her moon filled, sated, and clear. Olivia starred as the leading actor in the Nancy Kiley drama.

Mitchell had no doubt Olivia was a coldblooded killer, a femme fatale, a snake as deadly as Rodrigo. Charges against her seemed airtight.

Austin wasn't a traditional Rodrigo hit ending with a riata in blood.

During the second glass of retsina, Mitchell remembered he told Madge that he'd attend Olivia's trial to continue supporting Madge. Madge mentioned she'd attend and volunteer to testify.

He'd go and sit with Madge.

* * *

Madge had a troublesome night to add to the many more to come. She worried about tomorrow's pending decision by the district attorney and the ongoing worry for her own tomorrows as a 'fugitive'. Those concerns started rumblings of eruption deep in her stomach – a procedure that started and pursued her out of fear and distress.

She told Mitchell that Austin was in St. John. A loophole for him to have investigated if he believed, at the time, that someone other than Rodrigo killed Austin. Madge believed that the Mitchell Pappas threat to her closed with Olivia Greene's arrest. The Rohypnol in Olivia's possession was her 'smoking gun'. Madge would always feel insecure, looking over her shoulder, and checking the rearview mirror. The remaining Rodrigo remnants would blame the Senator's wife for his stealing their finances believing she and Nancy hid more somewhere, or might take their revenge on the Senator's family.

The unknown threats remained.

Would my concern continue after Olivia Greene received her sentence?

Yes, Madge concluded. Madge's guilt feelings imbedded, and tormented, and would last a lifetime and forever punished by many sleepless nights.

That one hellish act would overshadow a lifetime of decency.

It was fantasy to consider surrendering to Mullins. Surrendering would free Olivia Greene, who killed the lawyers, and stole her drug dealer husband.

Madge could live with all her worries for as long as necessary, for as long as she lived, for as long as Olivia Greene was to blame.

Madge felt guilt, not regret.

If occasional vomiting is the ultimate penalty, no problem.

* * *

At 11:00 a.m. the next day, District Attorney Frank J. Laine notified Stanford that all standing charges against Nancy Kiley would be vacated and he'd negate pursuing further charges against Nancy Kiley and Pilar Mirasol in the self-defense and accidental killing of Eddie Hawkins.

Madge popped a bottle of champagne when she heard Nancy and Pilar were free. The three women celebrated freedom.

Madge planned to celebrate alone twice more with champagne after Olivia Greene's indictment and conviction.

Mitchell started his book process after Nancy's freedom. Olivia's arrest was a fitting road to conclude a prolonged case. Mullins concentrated on other tragedies while continuing to pursue Rodrigo remnants.

Book's organization and structure required a minimum of a month with repetitive reviews of notes.

Something felt wrong, lacking in notes, and stalling progress – an open loophole that may lead to nowhere. He should investigate that loophole to complete research. Would probing the theory change history or facts? Unlikely, but it gnawed at him, clung as a leech on Humphrey Bogart in the movie classic, *The African Queen.* Questions scratched – Who knew Austin was in St. John besides Nancy and Madge? Nancy's time was accounted. Who had motive? Rodrigo and Madge had. Where was Madge – in New York City as she stated?

Mitchell noted to call Mullins to have him acquire passenger lists of flights to the Virgin Islands from New York City. Does a list include Madge's name, Margaret Kiley?

He left the computer to discuss the subject with Helene in the living room. Helene turned off the television set. He reviewed.

When he ended, Helene said, "The case is closed thanks in part to your participation and being a vital conduit of information. Let it die. Drop it. Everybody got what he or she deserved. Nancy Kiley is a hero and Madge helped by uncovering her husband's affair with Olivia Greene and learning their location. Write your book, and concentrate on what remains – Olivia's trial for your ending and be thankful you weren't killed in the process. She wanted to kill Stanford. Had she succeeded, she might have killed you also. Didn't you feel endangered, or were you oblivious to the threat?"

"No, all we had was theory and secrecy for Nancy before the Virgin Islands."

Helene yawned, rising. "It's late, come to bed. Leave Madge alone. She suffered long enough, no need to throw theoretical knives at her." Mitchell seemed lost. "Hello, Mitchell are you listening?"

Mitchell swam with his thoughts and speculation. "I'm listening. You go ahead. I'll be in soon."

"Let it go, already."

"We'll see."

Helene left for the bedroom, he for the computer.

The leech held fast.

Mitchell returned to his notes and conversations with Madge and his thoughts at the time. He found the note and read,

And if Olivia is accused of killing Austin Kiley, to no longer pursue hunches on the Kiley tragedies like the credit card checks that failed to prove Olivia visited Antigua and Liechtenstein. Mullins's words still echo – "No more hunches after this."

To let Mullins come to his own conclusions on Olivia Greene and Senator Kiley if Rohypnol was detected.

He stood, nudged the notes into a neat pile, and exited the computer. The Rodrigo, Nancy Kiley, and Olivia Greene case *was* over. Helene opposed probing the loophole and Mullins would reject another theory at this case solving stage with an obvious suspect with overwhelming evidence.

Helene came to the doorway looking stern and exasperated at his stubbornness. "Give it up. It's done. Move on. You're tripping over self-imposed obstacles. Accept that it's over. Everyone has. Find something else to do."

Mitchell nodded although reluctant, ceding to facts and logic.

"It's over, Helene. The writing remains."

"You don't sound convinced. Don't humor me or be condescending about this."

"With Olivia guilty, it's over. I can't change the outcome. Case closed."

"Good. Come to bed."

Helene returned to bed and sat up against the headboard. Mitchell entered the bedroom and started undressing.

Helene wasn't convinced he was convinced. To prevent a little theory hole from becoming a trench to nowhere she said, "Let me speculate, genius. Let's say Madge's name was on the plane's manifest. Do you believe it would change anything? Where would Madge get the illegal Rohypnol? You're thinking fantasy where she went there to try to save her marriage to plea for him to come home. That's absurd. Come back to reality. Forget speculation. The evidence screams that Olivia murdered the Senator. You would add to the Kiley suffering needlessly. Don't look distressed. So, what's the problem? Why the delay?"

Reluctant to agree, he yielded. Tomorrow, he'd immerse into the case without thoughts of loopholes to write the case history.

"I don't have a problem, Helene only an irrelevant and fictional loophole. Let's close the day."

"I don't believe you."

"Believe me, and it's your turn to make breakfast."

"Not if you need consolation tonight."

* * *

Helene slept; he couldn't for another hour. Loophole gremlins festered as advocates sitting on Mitchell's left shoulder encouraging him to continue his professional standard of investigation. He felt like a palm tree in a hurricane until evidence defeated the gremlins.

No matter the size of the loophole, nothing could change Olivia's guilt as a killer. She had the Rohypnol. She probably killed the others.

He had a scheduled meeting with Stanford at his office the next morning to benefit his research including receiving copies of the medical examiner's reports from Nassau and Suffolk counties, then dinner.

The worst was over.

So he thought.

Innocent of killing Austin, Olivia obsessed to fight for her innocence. She would persuade everyone of how much she loved him. An exceptional salesperson, she could sell her innocence. Truth was a good product. Acting calm and dressed in business attire to reflect a successful executive, Olivia pleaded not guilty at her arraignment in Suffolk County. David Kessler, a leading Nassau County criminal lawyer, whose firm was a travel program client, represented her. Kessler persuaded the judge, based on her high visibility on Long Island via her television commercials, that she wasn't a flight risk and was a responsible and successful business executive.

The judge set bail at $250,000, restricting her movements to a two-mile area of her home allowing for shopping along the Miracle Mile in Manhasset and nearest supermarket.

Olivia succeeded in remaining free – an excellent beginning on her road to freedom. She addressed media in front of the courthouse, vehement that murder was beneath her, that she never hurt anyone especially her beloved, and that the killer drugged her to kill her also but she survived – fortunate to be alive. She did not know about Rohypnol as a drug, nor did she know how to obtain that substance banned in the United States. With vehemence, Olivia claimed and reclaimed that Austin's killer planted the drug in the closet at the beach house.

She planted doubt with media.

Olivia returned distressed to her home and tormenting questions.

Who killed Austin? Why now? Who knew where we were besides his damn daughter? Who planted the Rohypnol, the damaging evidence so difficult to overcome? Why don't the authorities believe I'm a victim?

Authorities believed she ingested Rohypnol to divert suspicion away from her.

Olivia acted calm in public after her initial outbursts and when restrained in the Virgin Islands. No one listened to her, like hollering in a vacuum.

Life sank to shallow and meaningless without Austin.

At home, she cried with Austin's photographs rubbing his face, yearning, expressing her love, and loss. The photos covered the kitchen table. She often gathered photos and pressed them against her face, kissing them as she moaned in pain and with tears.

Someday, she'd exact her revenge on Nancy Kiley and her mother; months or years from today should appeals be necessary when they'd least expect it. A cold revenge would taste better. She must concentrate on her trial, to gain her freedom, and to control her future. She couldn't risk violating the judge's two-mile restriction to compound the problem. She needed to act cooperative and innocent, a victim by those who killed Austin – which she was, and who drugged her. "I am a victim!" That was her strong stand.

Olivia's long day kept her restless, tense, no appetite for dinner, snacks, or liquids. She sought the hot tub's comfort. Naked, Olivia prepared to enter the hot tub when her lawyer called. She answered the phone with an unenthusiastic hello.

"This is David."

"Hello, David. You were terrific today with the judge. You are the best."

David ignored the compliment. "Do you know a Tomayo Suarez?" he asked sounding upset.

Austin had told her Tomayo was Rodrigo's executioner.

"I never heard of him, David. Who is he? Why do you ask?"

"Suarez is the number one captain in the Rodrigo operation. I just found out that he accused you and Senator Austin Kiley of killing Randy Hawkins and Greg Morris on the yacht in Sag Harbor."

"What!" The shock bent her forward, ninety degrees to the floor. "What! What are you saying? Are you mad? Why are you doing this to me?"

"Suarez said he saw you and Senator Kiley leaving *Golden Hawk* in Sag Harbor at the approximate time of the killings. Are you sure you never met him?"

"Never, never! He's a drug dealer, dammit! His lying testimony can't be credible. When does the nightmare end? Why am I being accused of killing people? I never killed anyone." She paced erratically exclaiming, "And I didn't kill Austin! I loved him! I'm a victim here. The killer drugged me and meant to kill me, too. I'm lucky to be alive. There's a conspiracy out to get me. David, you must protect me from these lies. Believe everything I tell you. I'm innocent!"

"I will protect you and I believe you, but this witness will be trouble. Suarez also said you and the Senator stole several million dollars of Rodrigo's drug money and that you two planned to take over the Rodrigo operation with the money."

"He's insane! Insane! Oh, god David, I can't do this. I can't talk. I can't. Let's do this tomorrow." Her pacing continued as she rubbed her forehead to think. "The day has been horrendous and I'm exhausted. I can't think straight. Can you come by in the morning? I need to sleep. And I want to sue that scum. We'll talk tomorrow about Suarez and his lies. Come by tomorrow."

David Kessler accepted meeting tomorrow hoping she'd be less emotional and distraught then.

"What time is best?"

"Nine is good, David. See you then."

She ended the call without a goodbye. With a loud frustrated scream, she flung the phone at the bed. "A witness, a damn witness!"

The phone bounced and landed on a pillow after it caromed off the headboard landing face down in one piece.

Depression and Tomayo Suarez hung as a heavy overcast. Olivia's confidence of winning her trial evaporated. Her focus shifted to a life in prison, an undesirable and unlivable disaster.

She must never go to jail.

Never!

Olivia's logic and delusions blamed her lawyer for failing to protect her, considering him a part of the collusion to betray her.

She felt lost without friends or anyone to turn to, weak, and vulnerable.

Another hour passed with internal conflicts, seeking solace in any direction, and alone against the accusing world. She needed to find refuge and solutions in the hot tub where she persuaded Nancy Kiley's first two lawyers – Todd Hancock and Laurence Bates – to take the money and leave Long Island so she could kill them in Antigua and Liechtenstein.

Submerged, Olivia leaned back with her face upwards, and breathing hard with eyes closed. She soaked as the swirling waters failed to soothe her. She pretended the swirls as Austin's fingers and eased with temporary comfort with a soothing smile from her imagined massage and mental intimacy.

Her eyes flew open like a runaway window shade at the idea that forced her to sit upright and slap the water creating a mini-geyser that splashed beyond the tub.

"Yes!"

She arrived at the perfect solution to defeat her enemies, to win in her crisis, and to hell with the judge and his two-mile restriction.

I'll beat them all.

Her new direction and revelation thrust her out of the tub and dripping to her dressing room. She dried, dressed in black sneakers, a black pullover, black jeans, and ran downstairs enthused.

She felt alive again.

She didn't need anybody for this, no need for explanations to anyone.

Olivia left the house and garage with binoculars and the Lady Smith & Wesson to kill again miles beyond the two-mile restriction.

Mitchell arrived at Stanford's office after 2:00 p.m. that same day. Stanford joined him with notes, transcripts, and coroners' reports from both counties and reviewed the combined case. Stanford left two hours later to service a client out of the office and to return before 6:00.

Mitchell fulfilled his needs in the library/conference room by 6:30. Stanford ended his office legal meetings at 7:00. They left in separate vehicles for the Italian restaurant on Walt Whitman Road a mile from Stanford's office and about the same distance to the Kiley residence.

Sky dimmed expecting a thunderstorm that may bypass the area traveling northeast into New England towards Maine.

Dinner ended at 8:45. Clouds darkened as Mitchell and Stanford said goodnight by Stanford's car, near the sidewalk. Stanford reversed out of the parking area first. Mitchell felt pleased with his comprehensive notes and outcome of the case and review with Stanford. He'd begin collating tomorrow morning and submerse into his book project. He parked towards the back of the restaurant. About to reverse out of his spot, sudden thoughts of Madge and Olivia stalled the shift. He looked towards the street for Stanford to discuss the sudden thoughts with him, but Stanford left the area.

The Olivia thoughts startled Mitchell.

She was free on bail. What if Olivia blamed Nancy for causing her father to flee and confessed to the police to connect Austin to Rodrigo? What if Olivia was revenge crazed with her obsession?

Mitchell blunted the premise.

Since Olivia killed Senator Austin Kiley, why would she revenge him? That makes little sense. Wouldn't Olivia have killed Austin eventually here or elsewhere adding to her overseas murder list?

But...did the reason to kill him extend to his family?

That was possible, and troublesome.

His premise was a long shot but needed addressing and Nancy and Madge warned – an easy loophole to close. They must act cautious when leaving the house as long as Olivia remained free. Mitchell knew Madge and Nancy rehired security guards.

No longer interested in Madge's airplane loophole, he never mentioned it to Stanford that evening. Rohypnol remained conclusive evidence of Olivia's guilt. With solid evidence, timing was right to abandon the loophole merry-go-round that sometimes played on beyond common sense.

Mitchell dialed Madge's number. She answered.

"Hello, Madge. Mitchell."

Madge was pleased to hear from him, no longer concerned that he'd investigate the trip to St. Thomas.

Why would he?

Olivia is the guilty one!

"Good evening, Mitchell. Always good to hear from you. How are you? Where are you and why are you calling at night? More good news?"

"I just finished dinner with Stanford out here and about to head home. First, how are you and Nancy doing?"

"Our relationship returned to normal. The lying has ended. We both can concentrate on her future. Of course, she still has to complete her final year at the university...and put all the disasters behind us."

"Sounds good. Why I called. I worked at Stanford's office part of the day reviewing medical reports and other data with him, obtaining material for a possible book on Nancy's case. One of these days, I'll need to talk to you and Nancy for your views and perspectives. You two are essential, obviously. I'll be interested in your view as a bystander to your family's secrets, a fascinating human aspect of the case. By the time I'm through, the world will love you and how you endured and suffered."

"That sounds good to me. I look forward to you completing the book, and you know we will do all we can to help. Tell you what. Since you're in the area, let's start tonight. We're up and wide awake watching boring television. Come on by for coffee. You can start with Nancy, the more important one. She's wide awake and talkative. We haven't spoken for so long in years."

Mitchell almost said no. The trip back to Amagansett exceeded an hour. Nevertheless, that day was a 'gather information' day, and he could warn them in person about the possible danger from Olivia.

"Make the coffee, Madge. I won't stay longer than an hour tonight. We'll continue at another time, several more times to record the full story. Nancy's and your involvement are invaluable. You rehired the security guards, right?"

"Two are on duty though different from the first crew. I'll alert them you're coming. I don't trust Rodrigo's men if any are left and I don't need another break-in."

"You're doing the right thing, Madge. Good defensive thinking." He erased his speculative threat.

Mitchell stopped at the nearby Dunkin Donuts for a variety. When he left the parking area, a light rain began. Rain increased when Mitchell approached the security car. He displayed his driver license. The guard phoned the house, notified Madge that her visitor arrived, and cleared Mitchell to pass. Mitchell parked in the driveway and hastened to the front door. Lightning flashed and stutter boomed farther north. Madge opened the door and let him in.

Mitchell sensed that tension vanished from the Kiley home. She hugged him and kissed his right cheek.

"Thank you. Thank you so much for all you did for me, and Nancy. I need you to know that I appreciate your long and dedicated hard efforts."

"I'm glad I helped."

"It's our turn to help you. Nancy's excited and ready to tell all."

Nancy stood and approached Mitchell smiling. "Mr. Pappas, please accept my gratitude. I apologize if I offended you during our meetings."

"You didn't offend me, Nancy. You bravely protected your father."

"Whatever your questions, ask. You helped me. I'll help you with your needs."

She sat. Mitchell sat opposite, placed the recorder on the cocktail table, and waited for Madge. He explained his procedures in preparing a manuscript. Madge returned with a tray with donuts, a coffee pot, milk, sugar, and three cups. She poured the coffee.

The three settled; rain continued and the recorder recorded Nancy, alert and enthused to discuss her long involvement – her killing Eddie Hawkins, Pilar's loyalty and involvement, the dead lawyers, her father and Rodrigo, freedom, and the aftermath.

All felt secure with the guards outside.

Olivia and her rage raced beyond the speed limit on the Long Island Expressway to reach her destination impatient to exact her revenge. Her knuckles whitened on the steering wheel with body forward and deaf to the metronomic rhythm of windshield washers.

She exited at Exit 48, Round Swamp Road, turned left beneath the underpass, and traveled the right fork at the traffic light – Old Country Road.

She arrived at the Kiley neighborhood thirty minutes after Mitchell arrived.

Before she reached the quiet Kiley street, Olivia crept to the end of the corner house, a mini-mansion on one acre. With headlights off and behind hedges, she monitored the security car through binoculars. Light rain wasn't a hindrance. The security car faced her way, the wrong way, blunting her mission from the front of the house. She could see a guard behind the wheel. He'd see her approach. Within seconds, another guard appeared from the backyard holding a green and white golf umbrella as he hurried to the car to enter the passenger side. Security created a problem. She needed a detour.

She was vengeful, not careless.

Olivia reversed until halfway into the side street, turned on her lights, made a U-turn, and left the upscale neighborhood. Her alternate plan circumvented the Kiley's dead end street and to park by the woods behind the Kiley house and approach through the public woods, a procedure she followed several times before when her obsession to possess Austin started three years ago.

On weekends, day or night, when Austin couldn't visit her, she would often hide in those woods and observe the solarium to watch him with binoculars from afar. To her, that was better than never seeing her beloved at all that weekend. That obsessive routine happened during the first year of their affair until confident that he loved her. Then came the promises that he'd leave Madge. Olivia believed she would then own and control him.

She parked on deserted Cottontail Road and invaded the dark woods. With overcast smothering the moon, she couldn't see beyond four feet until she approached the Kiley backyard where a faint light splash allowed eight to ten feet of visibility to the woods. The absent moon served as a secure ally, an advantage. She needed to escape through those woods to her car.

She held the binoculars in front of her to protect against low and unseen branches in the limited visibility. The stainless steel Smith & Wesson revolver, in the black rain slicker's pocket, meant security and success for her mission, moon or no moon.

In the distance, the dim Kiley backyard lights shone as a beacon in the dark. Nearing the edge of the scrub oak and pine trees, she stopped and hid behind an aged two-trunk oak. She leaned against the spread trunks and raised the binoculars to view the threesome in the solarium.

Damn, a visitor.

Olivia recognized a bonus prize, Mitchell Pappas. She smiled and whispered, "You helped to kill Austin and his reputation, you dog." Hate increased a notch with the added target.Mitchell electrified her enthusiasm.

Olivia threw the binoculars away, no longer needed. Rain increased. Lightning flashed north again over The Long Island Sound and the southern Connecticut coast. She felt certain a guard wouldn't return soon in that heavy weather. She had time to finish her job, if cautious...and escape. She ignored the wetness, except for wiping it away from her eyes.

Moving as a stealth commando behind tree trunks and growth, Olivia reached a side door and tried the locked knob, and cursed. She returned to the backyard to peek into the solarium unconcerned with her soaked hair, and looking to her left for a guard as she wiped her face.

The U-shaped rear posed a problem. To shoot from that distance was risky and far for accuracy. Her revolver chambered only five rounds. She wished she owned a high-powered rifle with a scope – three quick shots then to return home unseen. If she fired the Smith & Wesson, or the wishful rifle, the guards would hear the shots unless it thundered at the time to disguise the shots. Without the thunder, she'd still have time to escape unseen by the time the guards reached the woods.

But what if I missed from this distance?

She couldn't risk the gamble.

Her covert mission couldn't risk a witness or she'd lose her freedom.

Do what you must no matter the obstacle.

Olivia advanced with stealth again to the front of the house to check on the security car, the obstacle. Her drenched hair dripped. The slicker protected the body. The hated rain functioned as her abettor, her assistant. She felt safe and daring to approach the security car's rear. The rain obscured the guards' vision through the windows and mirrors to her advantage.

She attacked.

Crouching low and running, Olivia reached the passenger side as lightning flashed. She had eight seconds. Perfect, she thought. She knocked with urgency on the window, hollering, "Open the window! Open the window!"

The startled guard lowered the window believing the distressed looking woman came from the house. She did not look familiar, but he was on duty for only a short time. Maybe he hadn't met all the family.

Before he could speak, Olivia shot him in the face below the right eye. Before the panicked second guard could react to pull his weapon to shoot, her next shot hit his head. The staccato thunder merged with and muffled the shots. She eliminated the obstacles and two potential witnesses.

Olivia ran to the front door searching the downpour for other witnesses – none. She reached the protective overhang and wiped her face. When settled, she pressed the white doorbell button, ready for the execution – *Nancy first, that unappreciative little bitch that condemned my Austin.*

Waiting, Olivia decided that if Nancy answered the door, she'd shoot her there in the face and flee through the woods to her car. Killing the two guards wasn't part of her original plan. She must improvise, to implement a field decision like a military leader. She'd kill Madge and Pappas at another time. No one would know she visited that night, a successful escape...and never violated the two-mile restrictive order.

Brilliant.

She wiped her face again and waited under the overhang, dripping, with arm extended ready to shoot Nancy when the door opened.

Nancy should answer the bell, being the youngest, and since Madge had company. The other two would run to the door when hearing the shot giving her time to escape unseen around the back.

Melodic door chimes disrupted Mitchell's meeting. He turned the recorder off. The chimes surprised and annoyed the Kileys.

"Who's that in this weather?" Nancy said, rising and curious. "Excuse me, Mr. Pappas, I'll be right back. It must be a guard to use the bathroom or something." Nancy headed for the door. "If anyone else, the guards would've called us as they did when you arrived. That's the procedure."

Madge reacted and objected.

"No, Nancy. I'll get it. You continue with the interview. Mitchell can't stay long tonight. It's best to continue your train of thought. You were doing great, very thorough so don't disrupt your momentum."

Nancy returned, agreeing. Mitchell restarted the recorder.

Madge left without hesitation to hasten her return. She'd been absorbed in Nancy's confession that cast a brighter and broader light on the collusion with her father.

Madge called out to the visitor as she approached the door, "I'll be right there. I'm coming!"

She hustled to the door to minimize the guard's exposure to the bad weather. When Madge opened the door wearing a smile, her gasp stuck in her throat as the revolver pointed at her shocked and horrified face. Her body froze – a hand on the open door.

Olivia's ugly scowl showed disappointment, unable to distinguish the muffled voice through the thick door and weather din.

Madge searched for the guards who were slumped in the front seat.

Olivia released an emphatic whisper. "The guards can't help you anymore. Don't say a word or I'll kill you now."

Madge backed away from the weapon, arms away from the body to signal surrender.

Olivia followed and closed the door. "I want to talk only to your daughter. I didn't kill Austin, she did. Don't you dare blame me." Olivia spun Madge around with her left hand, grabbed her hair, and pushed her towards the solarium. "Keep quiet or I'll shoot you."

"You're hurting me!"

The slicker wet Madge's clothes. The revolver terrified Madge, afraid to do anything but follow orders and endure the violent hair yanking pain.

Olivia had no choice.

She must kill all three.

She had three bullets left.

There could be no witnesses.

Every bullet had to hit a kill point – the heart or head.

She couldn't afford mistakes.

The plan had to change when Nancy failed to come to the door. Olivia needed to scold the little bitch before shooting her first. She attached little rage to killing Mitchell and Madge after she killed Nancy, only satisfaction.

When Madge and Olivia appeared in the solarium, a panicked Nancy stopped talking and thrust up when seeing the weapon. She ran for protection behind an Eames chair, kneeling, eyes wide in terror watching her mother's pain.

Shocked by Olivia and by his theory becoming reality, Mitchell stood and confronted Olivia to neutralize her threat. He extended his right arm and approached her.

"Don't be stupid. Put the gun down and let's talk. You'll only make matters worse for yourself." He continued walking towards her. "There's no reason to hurt these people. They did nothing to you."

"Shut the hell up, Pappas, and stay where you are. Nancy, come here or I'll shoot your mother. Now! Get up and move your ass." She pressed the revolver to Madge's head. "I said now!"

Terrified, Nancy stood wide-eyed. Her legs felt paralyzed.

Madge shook her head violently ignoring pain.

"No, Nancy!" Madge yelled. "She's crazy. She killed the guards and thinks you killed your father. She'll kill you. Run, run. She's crazy!"

With all the energy and strength that a mother can muster to protect her child, Madge summoned her willpower, spun on the next breath with a scream, and forced Olivia's gun arm down ignoring all pain.

Madge held on tight. A shot fired into a corner barely missed Mitchell, who advanced taking advantage of Madge's rebellion. The bullet shattered a tall Chinese Ming vase.

Two bullets left.

Nancy reacted and fled with her panic to the backyard door and out towards the drenched woods.

Having lost control, Olivia fought hard to dominate and maintain her balance. She overpowered Madge with defensive training and a chop to the neck then spun her around. Madge loosened her grip. Olivia shoved Madge to the couch where she tripped off balance on her back, a leg pushing the recorder to the floor, and spilling two coffee cups.

Before she overcame Madge, Mitchell charged to help subdue Olivia when Olivia recovered and pointed the revolver at him from two feet away. His arms instinctively tried to block the inevitable bullet. In that instant of distraction, Mitchell lunged and grabbed the arm that held the weapon. They wrestled on their feet, grunting as they wobbled as a warped pendulum out of control, both struggling to maintain balance.

Olivia fought stronger than Mitchell imagined. She cursed him between grunts. Her defensive training controlled Olivia, her other asset. Olivia knew the obvious that to overcome a stronger foe she must attack the vulnerable body areas – the eyes, nose to blind with tears, the throat, and groin. Lesser areas included the solar plexus, knee, or instep.

She fought to stay on her feet as Mitchell attempted to force her to the floor. Once down, she'd lose.

She stumped hard on Mitchell's instep twice.

The sharp pain eased his grip.

When they faced Madge, about to rise and run, the revolver accidently fired.

The bullet hit Madge.

Madge screamed holding her abdomen, falling on her back on the couch.

One bullet left.

Mitchell wrestled Olivia's arm, frantic to disarm her or break the arm. Pain released her grip. The revolver hurled across the room as he spun her around.

Mitchell gained advantage.

As Mitchell was about to punch her face to end the fight, she spun and kicked him in the groin. He doubled over with a howl releasing his hold to clutch the pained and sensitive area.

Defeating Mitchell, Olivia desperately searched for her revolver that had slid unseen under the brown leather reclining chair. Unable to locate her revolver, she raced out the backyard door desperate to find Nancy to snap her neck.

Through limited visibility, Olivia probed the backyard darting in several directions and the front yard for Nancy then sped into the backwoods to search. Beyond the house's light splash and in blackened woods rushing to different areas, her desperation searched the night for Nancy with arms swaying in front of her at eye level to protect against low branches.

Nancy could see Olivia enter the woods and head in her direction. She cringed lower in the deeper woods, breathing hard, and soaked with rain that provided cover with obscured visibility. Nancy covered her mouth to stifle sound, pressing her face against the soft ground, and thankful for the rain and dark.

She lay among ferns with heart racing.

Olivia approached, scanning, darting side to side, and coming nearer forty-feet away to the right. She then ran to the left closer to Nancy with an arm up to protect her face from brush and branches.

Thirty feet separated them.

Olivia probed straight ahead, head turning side to side.

Twenty-five feet.

Twenty feet.

Twelve feet.

Wet leaves stayed silent. Nancy could hear her movements by the snapping twigs and branches in the dark as Olivia approached.

She reached within eight feet to the right of Nancy, a louder snap, and a move to the left.

Nancy grew frantic, beginning to panic, and about to run like a cornered animal whose survival instincts dominated all thinking. She froze instead, praying silently with closed eyes that wept from fear of dying.

"Where are you, you little shit?" Olivia hollered and stopped.

Silence – both listened hard to hear in the tense air.

"Damn!" Olivia yelled. "Damn!"

She knew it was unsafe to search. Mitchell Pappas might come after her with the Smith & Wesson that still had one bullet. Frustrated,

Olivia retreated to her car and left the area, in chaos, her mission a dismal failure...and a disaster.

She killed two guards and exposed herself to three witnesses. Her innocent pleas to the police and the world were no longer defendable. Prison and a life in burning hell waited.

A complete disaster!

Olivia's sole consolation in failure was that she shot her Austin's miserable wife hoping she killed her.

The night wasn't a total loss.

Die you bitch!

Mitchell felt helpless from the searing pain in a sensitive area. He amassed the strength to rise. Bent over, he recovered with lessening pain and hurried to check on and help Madge writhing on the couch in agony and panic, and bleeding. Mitchell hoped Nancy had escaped. Madge was priority.

Mitchell called 911 while rendering comfort to Madge as he tried to stop the bleeding, unconcerned with Olivia returning. Olivia no longer had her weapon. He also needed to check on the guards. One or both might be alive. Nancy should be a safe distance away by now. He had no interest in locating the revolver, leaving that to the police. Mitchell talked to Madge to calm her fright, and stop the blood flow, which lessened. He blamed himself for not being alert although guards were outside.

He guided Madge's hand for her to maintain pressure on the wound.

"Madge, keep the pressure here. You'll be fine." Madge nodded and pressed. "Good, I'll be right back. Need to check on the guards."

Mitchell ran outside to verify that Olivia killed them. The open window exposed the dead bodies. Mitchell ran back to the house and Madge, wet. He maintained pressure on Madge's wound.

Nancy opened her eyes and stopped praying when she heard Olivia snapping away from her. She raised her head above the ferns.

The shot Nancy heard after she left the solarium kept her in the area. She raced to the house and saw her bloodied mother on her back.

"Mom!"

Terrorized and crying, Nancy rushed to her mother, knelt beside her, and held her hand. Madge couldn't talk. Mitchell also tried to calm Nancy assuring that her mother should be fine, although doubtful.

Mitchell wasn't optimistic.

Blood seeped although Mitchell pressed the wound as Madge weakened as he encouraged her not to speak, to save her strength. He told her that the second he reached her.

The efficient Melville Fire Department responded immediately with its medical team. Madge was in serious condition when placed in the ambulance amidst the swirl of flashing lights, including those of three police cars.

With medical help and transfusion in the racing ambulance, Madge mumbled, "I deserve this. What have I become? God, I really deserve this. I deserve this"

When the ambulance left with Madge for North Shore University Hospital in Plainview, Mitchell stood despondent in the middle of the room again feeling guilty with blame for failing to overcome Olivia, for failing to protect Madge.

Olivia's strength and agility surprised him.

He recuperated and called Mullins at home to brief him on the three new shootings and added, "We told the Suffolk police Olivia's address. The Nassau police should be responding to check if she's there."

"She'd be a fool if she went there to be trapped. If she's not there, I'll issue an APB on her. We'll get her and put that maniac away for good. I'll check in with Nassau and keep you posted. How are you do-ing? Are you hurt?"

"No, I'm okay. You have my cell number. I'm going to the hospi-tal with Nancy. I'll also call Stanford and update him. I'll keep you posted. Talk to you soon."

"Wait."

"What?"

"What did the medics say? What's your opinion about Madge?"

Mitchell stalled.

"I doubt she's going to make it, too much bleeding. The transfusion in the ambulance might help. I understand she's in good health and that should help her."

"I'll say a prayer for her."

"Amen."

* * *

Four Nassau County squad cars and a SWAT team arrived at Olivia's home without sirens or fanfare to surround the house, combat ready, and weapons drawn. A Nassau officer replaced the gate guard sealing the entrance. Lights were on inside, downstairs and upstairs.

Olivia's car parked in the driveway. An officer looked inside the empty car, including the trunk where a criminal might hide.

The police labeled her as dangerous and possibly armed. Two of-ficers approached the front door to ring the bell. To their surprise, the front door was ajar. One extended his right arm and pushed the door open.

He hollered from outside, "Police! Is anyone home? Olivia Greene, are you here?"

Absent response or any sound for thirty seconds, the officers entered with caution and alertness searching the first floor. One officer opened the rear door for two officers who entered.

Two officers edged their way up the stair, weapons at ready in extended hands, one cautious step at a time, pressing against the wall, ready to fire. Reaching the landing, they heard music, a romantic duet by Lionel Ritchie and Diana Ross emanating from an open bedroom to the left.

"*...you will always be, my endless love...*"

The hallway was clear left and right, all other doors were closed. They approached the open doorway convinced someone was inside.

Reaching there, an officer crouched by the opening, peeked into the bedroom, and saw Olivia.

53

" *...I found in you, my endless love..."*
The officer entered combat ready, primed to fire, both arms extended holding the weapon that pointed at Olivia's head. She sprawled naked in the hot tub.

"Police! Olivia Greene, you're under arrest! Raise your arms!" No response. "Let's see your hands!"

He stopped his cautious approach.

"Raise your arms!" Olivia failed to respond. She did not move. Curiosity urged him towards the naked woman until he lowered his weapon and hurried to her.

The love song repeated and mixed with gurgling water.

A hypodermic needle protruded from Olivia's arm, eyes wide in death, and a trace of a smile by her lips.

Dozens of photos of Austin Kiley swirled in the tub with several trapped by her body.

The delusional note left on the tub's edge and under the empty champagne glass read – 'This is my dying statement and the truth. No one lies before dying. I never killed Austin Kiley. I loved him. I never killed anybody. I am being framed. Now I want only to be with my love forever.'

Her official cause of suicide was Rohypnol that she drank with champagne and by succinylcholine – traces remained in the needle.

* * *

A worried Mitchell waited with Nancy in the hospital's ground floor emergency waiting room for the operation to end, and to comfort Nancy's terror as she cried and prayed for her mother to survive. Mitchell regretted not convincing Nancy to continue with the interview to divert her mind from Madge. Distress overwhelmed her. The waiting tortured them. No one else waited at that late hour, no one communicated from the staff, and both dreaded the worst.

After an agonizing two hours, a tired looking doctor entered the waiting room.

Nancy and Mitchell stood, impatient for news, tense. Mitchell placed his arm around Nancy to embrace her with comfort if the news was negative. The doctor approached. Nancy and Mitchell thought the doctor looked serious, or fatigued. Their tension deepened. Nancy's clenched fists covered her mouth, eyes wide, tensing for bad news.

Mitchell searched the doctor's face for answers.

He couldn't tell if he intended bad news.

"We moved her to the Intensive Care Unit."

Impatient Nancy urged, "How's she doing. Is she going to be alright?"

"She lost a lot of blood but we expect her to pull through." The doctor forced a tired smile. "Get some rest. We all need it. You'll see her in the morning."

Elated, they thanked the doctor. Nancy was ecstatic. Mitchell, relieved, encouraged Nancy to return to Amagansett with him and both would return tomorrow. She shouldn't be alone after the terror. The thought of being alone tonight wasn't appealing to Nancy. Nancy preferred to stay with Pilar. She called Pilar, no answer. Nancy, in her traumatic state, forgot that Pilar left for Argentina yesterday. Nancy agreed to go with Mitchell.

To distract Nancy, Mitchell asked again if she'd like to continue talking about her experience with her father all the way to Amagansett with the recorder on. Her mother was alive, energizing Nancy.

"Yes, oh yes. I have to stop worrying about my mother. Just turn it on and I'll babble. But first, stop off at my house for personals, and clothes."

They received police permission to enter the house, but upstairs only to avoid the crime scene.

Mitchell alerted Helene. By the end of the trip, Mitchell gained respect for Nancy for her courage and initiative to save her father that led to Rodrigo's demise and Mullins's victory over the beast.

* * *

The police tested the Lady Smith & Wesson Olivia left at the Kiley residence. Ballistics connected her to killing Janet and Bob Graham in their mansion, Randy Hawkins and Greg Morris on *Golden Hawk* in Sag Harbor, the two security guards, and shooting Madge Kiley. Including the two poisoned lawyers and Austin, Olivia shot, poisoned, and stabbed ten people...add herself to make eleven, plus add the pharmacist, Troy Betson, whom she had killed.

Mullins added Olivia Greene to his list of Long Island's most ruthless killers. He speculated that she shot four Rodrigo members and stabbed Senator Austin Kiley to take over the drug operation.

* * *

Madge opened champagne when she arrived home three days later lucky to be alive and celebrated alone at Olivia's death by filling a champagne glass and taking only one sip due to her surgery.

A double team of new guards protected the house against a possible attack by disgruntled Rodrigo remnants. Madge felt cheated she couldn't witness Olivia agonizing at her trial, and to relish her suffering the rest of her life in prison.

Madge reveled in Olivia's self-inflicted penalty. Adding to her joy was finding Olivia's revolver proving she killed the others in Rodrigo.

Madge was a wounded victim of Olivia's ruthless rampage.

The case against Olivia killing Austin closed tighter. The gap of Madge ever accused of killing Austin widened. Her perfect ending headed for closure.

But Madge believed that her being shot was punishment, part of a continuing guilt and burden she'd have to bear for life for killing Austin and to forever worry about looking over her shoulder to see if the unexpected gained on her.

* * *

After extensive research and interviews, Mitchell had an ending to his perspective of the case, a closing sentence – 'Two truths describe Olivia Greene; she obsessed over Senator Austin Kiley and remained a delusional deceiver up to her last breath.'

Rereading the sentence, Mitchell deleted it. An evil person should never have the final sentence in his books. He thought of Madge. She suffered through the family's series of tragedies. Madge deserved to have the final sentence to the story. He called her.

"Madge, I'm calling to see how you're feeling."

"Mitchell, I'm better, much better – more than I can say."

* * *

Memo from Gus Leodas: A Best Seller author.

Thank you for reading *The Almost Forgotten Wife*.

I loved writing my novels because I found them challenging, entertaining, and satisfying. It is my hope that they all entertain you.

Please visit my Internet bookstore page and write a brief review or blurb (e-book or print). Click on the book cover and follow the easy directions.

Also, if you enjoyed *The Almost Forgotten Wife* share the joy with friends on your social networks…and everyone likes to receive a book as a gift on holidays and special occasions.

And keep smiling…and lead a life with your glass of water always 'half full' instead of 'half empty'.

And visit my website at http://www.gusleodas.com or https://twitter.com/Gleodas for additional information on my upcoming novels. Or, say hello at Gleodas@optonline.net

ACKNOWLEDGMENT FOR *THE ALMOST FORGOTTEN WIFE*

- To the reference *Deadly Doses* by Stevens and Klarner
- To Newsday's library.
- To NewScientist.Com

SAMPLE CHAPTERS OF A MYSTERY/THRILLER
NOVEL BY GUS LEODAS

UNSAFE HARBOR (a Book of the Year Awards Finalist)

'*Unsafe Harbor* by Gus Leodas has an exciting plot that will keep readers guessing who the guilty party is throughout the novel. Just to intrigue the reader more, Leodas smartly includes riddles to give hints on the culprit's identity. The plot technique adds depth to the story. Then just when you think you've figured out whom the murderer is, Leodas throws in a twist ending. The settings are imaginative and descriptive, bringing to life the characters' day-to-day activities. A great book.'

—Writer's Digest

'Reading *Unsafe Harbor* is like going through the maze of the mythological labyrinth at Knossos, Greece that housed the man-eating Minotaur. As Mitchell Pappas proceeds through the maze of possibilities, he isn't sure which way to turn to find the Minotaur. The ultimate outcome of *Unsafe Harbor* is a shocker, and it's a testimony to Leodas' writing skills that the reader is held in suspense until the very end.'

The National Herald Book Supplement

PROLOGUE

Monday, May 6.

Pinelawn Memorial Park.

Long Island, New York.

He stood over her grave as a wilted flower.

His world was silent to the audible grief of a mother and young daughter kneeling by a new marker five graves to the left, and to the private plane overhead departing nearby Republic Airport. The mild southwest breeze, scented with gravesite floral, was unnoticed. He immersed in grief. Nothing overcame his loss.

He soothed his distress by imagining his soul reaching through the grass and earth and casket to lie beside her to savor closeness, together again sharing laughter and happy moments.

His eyes had blurred before entering the cemetery, now the tears came although restrained. He tried to stifle the anguish and sniffles. He turned away from the mourning neighbors to remain unheard, and unrecognized.

Deep breaths energized his body to return to normal, to turn and head with quickened steps to the car, a hand covering his face. He had to escape from there to go on with purpose, to dream his dreams and fantasies without his love, his murdered Renata.

Impatience had come demanding a pound of flesh for his loss.

* * *

One week later.

Arthur Dryden was frightened and had huddled in the corner of the stern's starboard side. He had felt the two powerful diesels that vibrated through the floorboards, his hands tied behind his back. Terror forced him into silence obeying the orders not to move or rise. His pleas had gone unheeded. He had been on his knees, weeping, begging to live, promising to forget tonight to his friend who 'kidnapped' him. He struggled to think above the noise, to find a way to escape, to find an argument to persuade his captor, to eliminate the death threat.

The yacht slowed, stopped, and idled on the dark The Long Island Sound. Satisfied of no boat traffic within a mile of his area – no red, green or white navigation lights on that moonless night, the captain left the wheel. He held a 6-inch strip of gray duct tape and his weapon, and approached his captive.

Arthur Dryden's eyes widened as the weapon pointed towards his face. He had no argument, only panic yelling – "You can't do this! No!" The captain came closer. "I didn't do anything!" His head shook violently to escape the tape. "You're insane!"

The tape muffled him. The captain returned to the wheel and sat in the captain's chair to watch Dryden's suffering, weapon at ready.

* * *

Saturday, May 21.

Huntington Harbor.

At 6 a.m., Luke Samuel, a broad shouldered student from Stony Brook University, guided his 12-foot outboard up Huntington Harbor's narrow serpentine shaped channel bordered by hundreds of boats on moorings: sail and motor. A swan family of seven inhabited the shallow cove north of the renowned Eastern Shore Yacht Club, gliding to create arrow shaped ripples.

Horizon clouds in the sunrise sky were pastel shades of cream and silver; a contrast to the severe thunderstorms two days ago that gusted winds to 50-knots and churned The Long Island Sound with white-caps. Luke loved being on the water at dawn when the world was less chaotic and polluted.

Luke steered to Lloyd Neck's northern edge by the red buoy where the bottom dropped to form a ledge; a favorite spot for fishing at low tide with a 3-pound magnet ordered from a direct mail nautical catalogue. The advertisement claimed the magnet could lift 180-pounds. To add variety to time on the water, Luke began using the magnet raising a knife, pliers, screwdriver, car parts, and a shattered wristwatch – worthless.

Luke found magnetic fishing more exciting and intriguing than regular fishing – concluding – One never knows what metallic treasure the water yields from sunken ships. The underwater turbulence caused by the recent thunderstorms may have dumped new booty near the ledge, a good time to go out.

Luke lowered the magnet, tied with 3/8-inch white docking line, into the water. The boat moved slowly over the bottom. The magnet glanced off rocks. The boat crept forward towards Morris Rock, a submerged hazard noted on nautical charts. Luke dragged and pulled, dragged and pulled; a procedure he termed the best method to utilize the magnet on the rock strewn floor. The pull indicated a change in weight.

This procedure continued without metallic rewards until within 100-yards off Morris Rock. When pulled, the magnet met resistance. Caught between rocks, Luke thought.

Luke tightened his hold and pulled harder. The tension held as he steered the boat in a circle hoping to free the magnet. The line remained taut needing another method.

Luke increased the throttle, gripping the line with added strength. The magnet moved several inches, stuck to something. Luke pulled and dragged for 10-yards. A heavy metallic object, he reasoned. What was it, another part from a car, from a ship? Could it be a treasure chest? The possibility evolved from tales that Captain Kidd, the famous pirate, sailed in The Sound and buried treasure in various spots. Had some fallen overboard?

Bracing and using both hands, Luke tried again to raise the magnet and its catch. Succeeding, he hoisted 4-feet before the magnet freed the captive. Luke raised the magnet and examined for damage. Finding none, the magnet lowered again, maneuvering until the magnet reattached.

He had to maneuver the object to the shallow end. If able to raise the catch over the ledge, he'd drag and pull gentler to shore. The magnet had lifted the object 4-feet, and may lift higher if he lessened strength.

Reaching the ledge's base, Luke hoisted hand-over-hand until sensing the object cleared the ledge then pulled forward and stopped. The magnet and prisoner cleared the ledge. He strained to see the bottom but visibility was limited to 5-feet. The depth was 10-feet.

Cautious, he headed for shore and shallow water dragging the line. The magnet and object moved without encountering rock. Having no desire to share his treasure, Luke searched the shore, the bluffs, and tree line to assure no one watched. This was a secret for now. Seeing no one, he smiled from greed and scolded himself.

At 6-feet depth, he saw the magnet attached to a long dark object. What was it? The object did not look like a treasure chest. Images distorted underwater. Was it a British cannon from the Revolutionary

War? A British base was in Huntington Harbor. The cannon had to be valuable to a collector. History made it treasure.

Wild with curiosity, Luke stared at the catch seeking identification as it moved towards shallow water until the depth was 3-feet.

Then Luke's eyes widened and his breath stuck.

The magnet attached to a chain wrapped around a man with his hands tied behind his back.

CHAPTER 1

Saturday.

Memorial Day Weekend.

Aboard the yacht, *Coyote.*

"A college student using a powerful magnet fished a man's body wrapped in chains out of The Sound last week. The victim was Arthur Dryden, an officer of my yacht club and a prominent attorney," said Professor Josh Trimble of New York University, owner of the 47-foot Chris Craft. *Coyote* tethered to its private mooring in Lloyd Harbor.

"Who did it?" asked his guest investigative author Mitchell Pappas as he sipped breakfast coffee on the aft deck.

"Police don't know."

Mitchell sat up amazed. "What are the odds of that student finding the body? How many people go fishing with a magnet? Was he shot, knifed?"

"He drowned. Dryden's wife reported him missing for two days. Police questioned club members and employees and have no suspects. Dryden's car had been at the club. Police assume the killer met then kidnapped or lured him from there. That's the second unsolved murder in the club this month."

Mitchell shook his head. "You're all good news this morning," came tinged with sarcasm. "What's going on?"

"My dock neighbor, Renata Tredanari was knifed and possibly raped on her yacht. The club's commodore held emergency meetings to calm the scared membership. Police patrol the club around the clock – a squad car in the parking area, a police boat in the channel.

"Detectives questioned me and Renata's neighbors on the north dock who slept on their boats that night. We're the primary suspects." Josh leaned forward. "I know who did it. I'm not telling the police."

Silence. Mitchell couldn't believe what Josh said.

"How can you not?" He was adamant. "They were fellow members, not strangers."

Unfazed, Josh rejected the retort.

"I can justify my position."

Mitchell raised a palm for Josh to wait until he poured another coffee to mull Josh's troublesome position.

"I doubt it. You'd better Professor or I'll drag you to the police and my friend Lieutenant Mullins."

Josh wore rimless glasses, was slight in built, balding and mild mannered – scholarly, non-athletic. He wore a white designer T-shirt and blue shorts; a contrast to Mitchell's colorful Hawaiian shirt and blue shorts on a 6-foot frame. His dark brown hair had some gray hair near the ears.

Longtime friends, Josh Trimble and Mitchell Pappas had worked together for several years at J. Walter Thompson, a leading advertising agency in New York City. After Mitchell left to undertake a writing career, Josh continued in the creative department for another two years writing advertising copy before teaching English and creative writing at New York University. Mitchell became a random guest lecturer to Josh's students. The students were thrilled to have a lecture by a bestseller investigative author.

Josh sipped coffee and said, "Renata was a dear friend and neighbor, a widow about forty-two, no children, wealthy, attractive, a happy, fun loving and wonderful person and I adored her. I accepted our platonic friendship and had no illusions of it going further though I wanted to."

Mitchell noticed increasing anger in Josh's face and said, "Then you owe it to her to tell Lieutenant Mullins."

"Yes, I do but I can't."

"Why not?"

"When I can't sleep, I usually take *Coyote* out for long night rides on The Sound. Other times, I'd sit on this deck and gaze over the marina area. Sometimes, I'd see Renata bringing one or two drinking buddies to her yacht after the club bar closed. They couldn't see me where I sat. They'd leave an hour or so later, or I'd get sleepy and leave before they came out. One was the man whose body was discovered with the chains, Arthur Dryden."

Mitchell's expression and interest changed. He formed a T-shape with his hands and sat up.

"Time out. This is fiction and you're testing a new book premise on me, right? Is this the start of your first novel?"

"I swear this isn't any attempt at fiction. Dryden had a terrific wife, Valerie, and two teenage daughters. Valerie probably never knew of his friendship with Renata. Maybe she did," Josh shrugged, "and decided to maintain the status quo. Some women can absorb their husband's infidelity to keep a marriage going. Valerie is a high school teacher, English and American literature. Having education in common, we talk often although I'm weak in English literature."

"What's your opinion on Dryden?" Mitchell reached for another cinnamon roll with a paper napkin.

"I also know who killed Dryden. Their murders connect."

The statement was heart stopping, leaving Mitchell openmouthed with the cinnamon roll frozen in midair.

"And you won't speak up? What's wrong with you?"

"Be patient. I need to explain in logical order. The cast of characters gets longer in this tragedy. It's not a simple whodunit case."

Mitchell remained mystified, sat back, and acted patient. "Then keep unrolling your rug and let's see if I agree."

"Another member of Renata's drinking group was the club's rear commodore, also married. Another was the commandant of the local Coast Guard station at Eaton's Neck, married. And the fourth, unmarried, is Director of the Central Intelligence Agency Edward Marlowe – area resident and club member."

Mitchell swayed his head, amazed.

"How strange and frightening does this get?"

"The night Renata was murdered, I saw Director Marlowe leave her yacht at about two in the morning. Arthur Dryden, the commandant and the club's rear commodore signed affidavits that they and Marlowe were on Marlowe's yacht playing fourhanded pinochle beginning at ten p.m. Friday to five in the morning. Those bastards lied to protect Marlowe." Josh whacked the table saying, "They lied!" Josh adjusted his jarred eyeglasses. "They're as guilty as Marlowe!"

"Calm down, Professor." Mitchell turned analytical, pensive. "What time did Marlowe visit Renata?"

"I only saw him leave. I had just come on deck; bad timing for Marlowe."

"You don't know whether he had been there five minutes, ten minutes, a half-hour or more?"

"Right." Josh breathed longer several times, taming anger. "Renata's investigation isn't going anywhere. Marlowe is connected and regarded here in Suffolk County. No one is about to implicate him or make the remotest connection without evidence. In addition, Marlowe, Dryden, and the rear commodore were partners in a law firm here in Huntington. His ex-partners were also protecting themselves and the firm."

Mitchell digested every word along with the cinnamon roll with more than storytelling interest as he leaned on the table involved and curious.

"How does the commandant fit in with the legal trio? Is the connection CIA and Coast Guard?"

"I don't know. Maybe Renata's friendship and the yacht club were what they had in common. Maybe they never had sex."

"You're convinced the police are stalling?"

"They'll satisfy public opinion and then nothing. To give a native son and Huntington's pride negative publicity because he's a murder victim's neighbor will never happen."

"Tell the media and to hell with Marlowe. Do it for Renata."

Mitchell's pleas failed to move Josh. "I'm a professor, not a guerrilla. If Marlowe abuses his power and authority, I'll be a clandestine operation chained and lost at sea, thrown in alive like Dryden with hands tied behind my back struggling to breathe and unable to prevent the inevitable. No thanks. Maybe you can solve the following riddle that may offer a clue to the killer, and no one could solve before Dryden's murder."

"A riddle?"

"The club's Board of Trustees received an anonymous note at the last monthly board meeting. I have the member distributed minutes. Excuse me." Josh left.

Mitchell remained captured and waited. Maybe Josh was right, he thought. Abusive government power was terrifying. The CIA director being a murderer was incomprehensible to Mitchell, but Director Marlowe was at the crime scene at the approximate hour of Renata's attack.

Josh returned with a manila envelope, sat, removed the minutes, and shuffled a few pages. "Here we go. 'To the Board of Trustees. It's now his turn and I say unto you – Secret guilt by silence is betrayed.' Days later, Arthur Dryden's body came to the surface. The killer was alerting and warning the board and police with this cryptic message. Sadistic, don't you think and defiant?"

"It's more like a cat and mouse game, a psychotic challenge with the killer willing to lose if outwitted. If the murders connect, you have a serial killer in your midst." Mitchell massaged the message. "Secret guilt by silence is betrayed. Arthur Dryden's killer knew Dryden kept quiet about Marlowe. I suspect one of his three card playing witnesses. Professor, does Marlowe have bodyguards? He must."

"He has two. They check around the marina and clubhouse until he leaves then go with him. When on his boat, to the right from me across the dock, they monitor the north dock ramp and club entrance."

"They must have seen Marlowe enter and leave Renata's yacht."

"They verified what the others said – Marlowe was on his boat all night. They saw no one enter the ramp after midnight, or anyone on the north dock though lacking a clear view from where they sat guarding the gate and dock approach."

"Now we have two more eyewitnesses to verify for Marlowe."

"The way everybody is protecting Marlowe, my coming forward will be discredited and put me at risk. I need your help. I know how you operate, Mitch. If anybody can find another way to expose Marlowe, you can. On the other hand, you may jeopardize yourself by investigating." He shrugged. "If that's no concern, you can write and call attention to the case for Renata's sake."

Mitchell lacked enthusiasm. "Professor Josh Trimble, I'm interested in everything you said. I'm uncertain about investigating, but I'll talk to Lieutenant Mullins. If he denies me access to this case then I'm useless to you. Mullins had been willing to work with me several times, but there's always the first time he'd say no."

CHAPTER 2

At 10 a.m., Josh dropped the mooring line and they cruised to Port Jefferson to a reserved slip at Danforth's Marina. On route, Josh pointed out the Coast Guard station and lighthouse on the bluff at Eaton's Neck, Commandant Douglas Deever's home.

Mitchell and Josh returned to the Eastern Shore Yacht Club at close to 5 p.m. Secured to the dock and fresh water, telephone, cable and electrical lines connected, Josh hosed the topsides and hull. Their schedule for the rest of the day was cocktails and snacks on the aft deck then, after a change of clothing, dinner in the club's dining room.

Renata's 46-foot Silverton, with *Champagne Lady* painted blue across the stern docked opposite Josh's *Coyote*. She rocked gentle held by six docking lines. The yellow Do Not Cross police tape kept the curious away. Her personal flag, with a blue outline of a champagne glass, fluttered in the wind. Renata flew her flag only when she was aboard. Josh decided to keep it flying in her memory.

Josh drank rum tonic, Mitchell tonic water with a lemon slice. Snacks were assorted cheese and crackers.

"From here, I don't miss much even when the plastic siding is down. I can view the dock in both directions. The yachts and boats are backed in and aft deck activity is visible," Josh said.

"Do you have a photograph of Renata?"

"Yes, from club functions in a group shot. Why?"

"To see what she looked like, to make talking about Renata personal."

Josh left and returned holding a few group shots. He pointed her out when they sat together with other couples at a social function in the dining room.

"This is Renata."

Renata Tredanari smiled raising a glass of champagne. She had long black hair, pleasant features, and a green dress with a V neckline.

"The champagne lady now has a face," Mitchell said.

"This was taken this past March at the Saint Patrick's Day gala." Josh looked bitterly across the dock and pointed to the 55-foot Chris Craft, *Legal Tender*. "That yacht next to *Champagne Lady* belongs to Marlowe the untouchable, Marlowe the butcher!"

At 7:15, they left the aft deck to shower and dress for dinner. Below deck, in the guest stateroom area, Josh opened a closet next to the twin-engine room and withdrew a Ruger M-16 semiautomatic rifle with a folding metallic stock.

"I keep this aboard for sea pirates. Thieves also steal on the sea. Boats have valuable electronics worth more than car radios or television sets. Almost all boaters have a weapon aboard. I'll keep this handy."

"You may need it if you believe Marlowe would come after you."

* * *

Mitchell liked and respected Josh, a friend and best man at his wedding. Mitchell called him Professor and referred to him as Josh. Helene, Mitchell's wife, preferred Josh. Helene held him in high regard. Josh was more than an occasional dinner companion in the city. Helene was also Josh's agent having placed two texts on creative writing with McGraw-Hill and several short stories in the *New Yorker* magazine, and articles in *Vanity Fair.* Helene urged him to write long fiction, and to use his imagination and concoct a novel length story. An excellent editor and grammarian, Josh wasn't inspired to challenge fiction – to go on the other side as novelist, to commit to such an intense and time consuming project, and to subject himself to another editor's creative opinions. Not yet, but promised he'd try to accept the challenge.

Having started a novel, Josh had difficulty continuing with consistent intensity. If nothing else to do, he'd write as much as attention span permitted. He knew that as the improper approach to finishing the story. If Josh had graded himself, he'd receive an F for failure to retain interest. If Josh couldn't get interested in his story, how could a reader? For now, long fiction had no reservation in his future. He planned to write a book on creative avenues for aspiring writers, including playwriting and screenplays, and to enhance his reputation at the university.

* * *

The weatherproof floating dock's installation began last month, supervised by Josh as marina chairperson, as soon as the cold days faded and the April wind brought the scent and memories of last year's boating season.

Mitchell and Josh headed for the clubhouse and passed the officers' reserved parking spaces, a benefit for devoting spare time to club management. They entered the modern two-story structure then veered to the left stairway leading to the dining room and to Josh's reserved table. He waved hello to several members. A host escorted to a table for two on the north side overlooking the marina, sunset, and weaving channel lined with boats. He deemed the nautical motif restaurant a perfect dining environment with great views. Two racing trophy cases were on the west-facing wall and a blue 8-foot anchor designed in the oak floor dominated the dance floor. The live piano music by the north-facing wall added to the ambiance.

"The three large round tables in front are for the three top officers. The middle one in the commodore's table," Josh said.

Those tables sat ten each and were almost full. Mitchell wasn't interested in the ambiance. He stared at *Champagne Lady,* analyzing, visualizing Renata's guests coming and going and Marlowe sneaking out heading for his yacht.

Mitchell turned to Josh. "Did you tell anyone else what you told me? Or do I have an exclusive insight on a road to nowhere?"

Josh hesitated. "I wasn't going to tell you until you agreed to help."

"I'll help if Mullins approves to give me information."

"Okay, I'll gamble that he will, counting on your friendship with him. I mentioned seeing Marlowe to Renata's cousin, Mario Colarossi, a club member. He was family to Renata. Mario also has friends and influence, a prominent businessman: restaurants, oil depots, barges plus other investments. Mario is a philanthropist, and likeable. A wing at Huntington Hospital is named after him for donating five million dollars."

"He sounds like a decent guy. When did you tell him?"

"A week before Dryden was found."

"How can Colarossi help you?"

"Mario is also the godfather of Long Island."

Mitchell's eyes widened. "As in Mafia?"

"Yep."

"Unbelievable." He slapped his knee.

"That fading label is obsolete in this area where his donations reap respect. They take his gifts and never say the label. He owns the 72-foot Broward by the channel. I needed someone who can counter Marlowe. Yes, we have two powerful persons in a locale logical for them to share. The Eastern Shore Yacht Club is the best in the region for yachts. The other major yacht clubs are sailing clubs without slip accommodations. If you own a large motor yacht, the Eastern Shore Yacht Club is the place. The Marlowe and Mario Colarossi contrast is part of the member mix."

"Professor, you've recruited Colarossi and me against Marlowe. You plan to recruit others?"

"No others. Mario knows Renata and I were friends. Mario told Renata he's loved her since she was a teenager. They'd spent time on the aft deck, an hour or so then leave, or have dinner at the club periodically. If she was sexual, Mario had been exempted as I was. Renata told me he proposed. She didn't want his world. Mario can also be a suspect as the one avenging Renata with motive. Drowning people with heavy weights is a common procedure in his world."

"If Marlowe killed Dryden, would Marlowe also kill Commandant Deever and your rear commodore? Would Colarossi? And shouldn't we warn them?"

"Then Marlowe will know I saw him. If Marlowe kills them, they deserve it for lying and defending him. Commandant Deever and Rear Commodore Alvin Dean Horatio also have to worry about Colarossi. I couldn't care less if they lived or died. My concern is Renata. I'm for what brings Marlowe to justice other than my coming forward. I shall, as a last resort."

Mitchell looked analytical again.

"Was Colarossi on his yacht the night Renata died?"

"Yes, he was asleep."

"How about those who slept on the north dock that night?"

"They were all asleep."

"You didn't see Marlowe enter so we don't know how long he visited. Maybe nothing happened. Maybe he went for a cup of sugar or something. Assume someone else visited Renata after you went below. Now, suppose that the second visitor was Colarossi."

Josh raised his brows.

"That's a frightening theory."

"We now have two high-powered candidates who may have killed Renata. Maybe Colarossi then killed Dryden assuming he was having an affair with Renata. Love does strange things. What's your prognosis now?"

"That love does strange things." Josh slapped his hands. "I knew I was right getting you involved. You have the investigative mentality for this. It could be Mario except he loved Renata. If anything, his love would kill *for* her. Do anything *for* her. I'm betting on Marlowe all around. I saw him. Since his agents lied to protect him, they could be capable of killing Dryden for him."

"I doubt government agents would kill anyone for private reasons. Colarossi also has his own protective and obedient soldiers."

"Marlowe's more than the heavy favorite."

"Colarossi and I know you're a witness. What if Colarossi is the murderer? Can he gamble you didn't see him? You can trust me, but can you trust Colarossi?"

Josh turned pensive, nodding, accepting this additional logic. His concern grew as he continued to nod over his self-destruction.

The concerned look was obvious to Mitchell and he issued a warning. "Professor, beware Marlowe and Colarossi. Include everyone who slept on their boats that night. Be careful and guarded my friend and assume nothing. You could be on somebody's hit list."

* * *

To read more or to view other novels by Gus Leodas go to:

Gus's website: http://www.gusleodas.com or purchase at your favorite Internet or local bookstore.

Made in the USA
Middletown, DE
12 June 2022